THE
LOTUS
CHILD

J.B. Vosler

The New
Atlantian Library

Manhanset House
Shelter Island Hts., New York 11965-0342

bricktower@aol.com • absolutelyamazingebooks.com

Library of Congress Cataloging-in-Publication Data
Vosler, J.B.
The Lotus Child, The Sons of Jacob Series, Book X.
p. cm.

1. FICTION / Thrillers / Psychological. 2. FICTION / Romance / Suspense.
3. FICTION / Mystery & Detective / International Mystery & Crime
Fiction, I. Title.
ISBN: 978-1-955036-93-1, Trade Paper

November 2025

THE LOTUS CHILD

Sons of Jacob

Book X

J.B. Vosler

The New Atlantian Library

Habent Sua Fata Libelli

Contents

MAP OF EUROPE

THE SONS OF JACOB Saga

BOOK I: "Shadow of the Phoenix"

This novel introduces MARTIN HENDERSON, who has survived a deadly fire only to return three-and-a-half years later as an assassin for EDWARD MORNINGSTAR, a Pentagon aide who sees himself as a Biblical Jacob. Henderson, once a brilliant entrepreneur, is now compelled to do whatever Morningstar asks – including murder – as a result of Morningstar's threat against a notable little girl, LILI PLATACIS. Henderson had sworn to protect Lili, and, when she is then taken, Henderson vows to bring down not only Morningstar, but his entire operation. In the meantime, Henderson's former lover, Senator Cynthia Madison – MADDI – has also become a Morningstar target, and it's up to Henderson to save her.

BOOK II: "The Maker's Prophecy"

The delusional Morningstar, who thinks he is Jacob, is well on his way to world domination. He has "adopted" twelve sons, who are his soldiers and will do whatever he asks. Henderson has made it his goal to stop Morningstar, and is doing what he can to undermine his efforts. Meanwhile, a deadly virus has been unleashed in Columbia, South Carolina, and Maddi's brother, ANDREW, as Medical Director of a downtown clinic, is the first to see its effects. When a more aggressive strain of the same virus shows up in Chicago, L.A., and Texas, Henderson knows Morningstar is somehow behind it. Maddi is once again threatened, and he must figure out a way to keep her safe from Morningstar's relentless pursuit.

BOOK III: "The Rise of the Avenger"

An entire village is massacred outside the town of Bariloche, Argentina, and Maddi is pulled into action at the request of one of her dearest friends, SIR ARTHUR KAUFFOLD, a former ambassador. She puts together a coalition to travel to the region. Morningstar learns of it, and sends two 'sons' to Bariloche to stop her. She succeeds not only in defending the coalition, but in averting a war with Argentina, thanks to the intervention of her former lover, HANK CLARKSON, the Deputy Director of Homeland Security. Meanwhile, Henderson has gone to Russia to undergo a revolutionary surgery designed to give him a completely new face. He then vows to seek revenge against Morningstar.

BOOK IV: "Strike of the Cobra"

A vicious assassin, COBRA, has killed a former IRA operative outside Donegal, which has thrown the Irish Republic into chaos. Cobra, also known as Dan, is one of the sons of Jacob, and has been instructed by Morningstar to carry out multiple killings in an effort to disrupt the UK and France. Maddi discovers that she is being stalked by someone from the UK, and insists on flying to London to find him. Henderson, who has undergone surgery and has changed his name to MATT, goes to D.C. to introduce himself to Maddi as Martin's cousin. He learns she has gone to the UK, and – when he learns why – follows her there. Hank does the same, and the two men are forced to work together to keep her safe.

BOOK V: "A Battle for Justice"

MARK JUSTICE, a British Private Inquiry Agent, seeks help for debilitating headaches, only to learn that he has an evil alter ego. Maddi had sought his help to find her stalker, and he has now become obsessed with her. She has left London to meet up with Henderson at his Latvian estate, their first reunion after four long, desperate years. Hank follows them, but then sees Maddi's devotion to Henderson, and decides to leave. But before he can, he learns that his CIA agent son, ROGER CLARKSON, has been taken by Cobra. He and Henderson are again forced to work together to try to not only keep Maddi safe from Morningstar, but to find Roger and save him from Cobra. It is then that Hank learns a terrible secret about Henderson.

BOOK VI: "The Morning Star"

A Nazi-era warship has been under the protection of a small group of families since its discovery in the late 1940's. Calling themselves "The Morning Star," a translation of the vessel's name, the group's mission is twofold: to understand its technology, and to keep it from falling into the wrong hands. When a powerful neo-Nazi threatens them and tries to steal the warship, the group is called into action. Led by Henderson's father, WALTER, they must do all they can to protect the vessel. Morningstar learns of the group, and assigns his son, SIMEON, to infiltrate their organization, which is about to meet in Paris. Meanwhile, Henderson and Hank arrive in Paris to save Roger from Cobra, and are led on a deadly game of cat-and-mouse. Maddi follows them, and saves Roger, but is devastated to learn that Henderson has been taken by the infamous killer.

BOOK VII: "The Vesper Bell"

Both Walter and Maddi have been lured to Lyon, expecting to meet Henderson in the town square. Instead, they are kidnapped by Cobra and taken to a remote dungeon, where they find Henderson close to death. Cobra travels to Scotland, stumbles upon an exact replica of his childhood school, and decides to bring his prisoners there. They are soon joined by Inspector Pritchard, Walter's wife Dora, his mistress Nenita, and psychiatrist James Samuels. When a fire begins to consume the old school, Cobra is prepared to leave them to die. Through the heroic efforts of Maddi's brother Andrew, and CIA agent Roger Clarkson, all seven are saved. Cobra escapes, however, and Henderson falls into a coma. As Maddi is about to go with him to the hospital, she reveals to Hank the stunning truth that Matt Henderson is actually Martin.

BOOK VIII: Part I of "The Revelation"

Maddi has spent the last five months waiting for Henderson to awaken from a coma. The time alone has forced her to revisit a past that has haunted her for twenty-two years. That past has attained new life, and will soon become a credible threat to her future. As Henderson struggles to regain consciousness, and Maddi fights her demons, Morningstar sees an opportunity to take down his two greatest adversaries in a cruel, creative fashion. He has uncovered a secret, and will use it to threaten both Maddi and Henderson, as well as the child, Lili. Meanwhile, Hank Clarkson has been assigned to bring Henderson to DC. But a sudden war in Latvia forces him to accompany the Hendersons to their castle by the Baltic Sea. As he alters his plans to accommodate the war, Maddi and Henderson slowly, painfully begin to unravel truths that will change their lives forever.

BOOK VIII: Part II of "The Revelation"

Morningstar, eager to put his Master Plan into effect, calls upon the international assassin, Cobra, to kill a troublesome adversary. Cobra's counterpart, Mark Justice, obsessed with the need to stop him, reaches out to psychiatrist James Samuels, forcing Samuels to choose between his devotion to justice and his obligation to duty. Meanwhile, as the war in Latvia rages on, a war with the past is being fought on three fronts by Maddi, Henderson, and a young Philadelphia police officer who is intricately tied to Maddi. This officer is eager to bring Maddi's old transgressions to light, but with each step he takes, he uncovers an unsettling fact about his own history. As Maddi tries to outrun her troubled past, and Henderson wrestles with a death wish, Morningstar sees a way not only to stop them from interfering in his efforts, but to end Madison's meddling for good.

BOOK IX: "The Knight Son"

A series of unexplained shootings has sparked outrage and fear, not only from Americans, but from their new President, Jerome Knight. Thrust into the role by a similar act of violence, Knight must soothe a mournful nation, while also facing the revelation that the man he has revered for twenty-four years has deceived him. This discovery will lead him on a journey to find others who may also have been misled. One such man, Martin Henderson, shattered by Maddi's death from a plane crash, is also seeking answers. He is a wanted man, however, and must stay hidden. But the more he learns about the crash, the more he knows he must venture out to learn the truth. He will soon discover that his mortal enemy, Morningstar, may have played a role. Aligning with Maddi's bodyguard, the two must not only figure out what happened, but how to prove it.

"The lotus root may be severed,
But its fibered threads are still connected"

~ Chinese Proverb ~

PROLOGUE

THREE WEEKS AGO...

Saturday, October 9th, 2004, somewhere outside Beijing

Lili was cold. Cold and weak. Her stomach growled; she grabbed it to make it stop. Though she was given food twice a day, it was hardly enough. *"And it looks like seaweed, Ching Lan."* Her teacher, who shared the cell with her, would merely frown and say, *"It is food. It does not need to look good."*

Lili and Ching Lan had been in the Chinese prison for over seven months. Lili hated the hard cot and the cold food, and she especially hated the way the guards looked at her when they walked her to the showers. They didn't watch her while she bathed; at least she didn't think so. But she got the sense that – though she wasn't even ten years old – they wanted to.

Their journey from Tibet had been a long one. Long and terrifying. They had left in the middle of the night when the air was cold, the sky dark, and the monsters – at least those that lived in Lili's imagination – were everywhere. Ching Lan had practically carried her from the dormitory to a remote set of train tracks between the base of two mountains. They had stood by the tracks for what had seemed like hours, then had jumped on a train heading east. The train had been even colder, and Lili's fingers had turned blue. They had switched trains in Xining, and again in Zhengzhou. After four long, cold days, they had finally reached Tianjin, which is where Ching Lan had said they could rest. But it wasn't to be. Within an hour of their arrival, they had been captured and brought to the prison outside Beijing.

Lili didn't know how they had been found. She also had no idea where it was that Ching Lan had been trying to take her. The wise old woman had said repeatedly, *"I cannot let them take you to America."* Lili hadn't been sure what to think about that. Uncle Mart had grown up in America; it sounded like a fascinating place. So big, so busy, so full of life. But it didn't matter. Lili was now in a prison near Beijing, China...about as far from America as anyone could be.

She had yet to cry about her situation. Lili rarely cried...about anything. She had learned how to hold back tears long before her time in China. Her father's death when she was five, followed by Uncle Mart's tragedy a few days later, and both of those heartbreaks coming only months after she was told that her mother had died; it had devastated Lili. She wasn't sure she had any tears left inside her weak, hollow body. If she did, they were well hidden...like puddles of rain that hide from the sun. Lili imagined her tears hiding in the shadows of her own dark sadness, leaving empty vessels where arteries and veins had once been.

"I can't eat this," Lili said with a frown. She no longer spoke in Chinese. Though Ching had insisted on it their first few months in the prison, she seemed to no longer care. Lili was glad; the Chinese language was hard. She had gone back and forth from her native Lettish to English, which was the language she had used with the Hendersons. She liked English the best. It made her feel less alone.

Ching looked at her and frowned. "Ni bixu, Lili. Fouze, ni hui si de." *You must eat, Lili. Otherwise, you will die.*

Though Lili had grown accustomed to Ching's frankness, the woman had never been so brutally honest. *"Otherwise, you will die."* For the first time since they had arrived at the prison, Lili sensed a loss of hope in her inspirational friend. It grieved her, but she was well aware of the truth of it. And because of it, she would eat. She didn't want to die. But she knew that that was exactly what she was doing. Dying... from hunger, loneliness, despair. Yes, she had Ching Lan, but she missed the people she loved.

Ching Lan had been Lili's sole companion since Lili had arrived in China eleven months ago. Kidnapped from Ventspils, Latvia, in the early hours of a bitter cold morning, she had been taken to Tibet and forced to live in a dark, dingy dormitory, with no one to watch over her but Ching Lan. And in that time, Ching Lan had gone from teacher to friend to protector. Lili smiled sadly as she looked up at the woman. Ching was far thinner than when they had left Tibet. Her straight black hair, normally clipped just below her ears, now hung to her shoulders in stringy clumps. Her cheeks had become gaunt, and her eyes no longer shone like they had when Lili first met the woman. *I'm not the only one who has been changed by this journey.*

She stared down at the food, a concoction of rice, beans, and some sort of lettuce. It looked barely edible. She pressed her fork against the beans. They were hard; the lettuce was shriveled. *I must eat...so I don't die.*

But if Lili was to die, at least she was ready...she wasn't afraid. She had seen enough dying to know...once it was done, there was peace. She couldn't say exactly what happened afterward; her gift – her odd intuition – hadn't let her see beyond the world of the living. But she sensed that those she had loved and lost were at peace.

Lili was surprised she wasn't already dead. Her journey had been long and hard, with the months at the prison being the worst. Not only was the food practically inedible, but the prison itself was a poor excuse for shelter. There were cracks around the doors and windows, which allowed every wind swell to find a way into their eight-by-eight cell. Luckily, the weather up to now hadn't been harsh. But winter was coming. Lili knew this because she kept track of the days on a small yellow tablet that Ching had brought with her. She had started by marking each day with a single line, drawn with dirt from the floor of the jail cell. But a few months ago, one of the guards had handed her a pencil; she didn't know why. *Perhaps it was the kindness that lingers in us all,* she thought with a sigh.

But she also knew that winter was coming because she could feel it; the chill in the air as it filtered through the cracks, the fury of the wind as it swept through the walls and ceiling as if they were made of paper. She and Ching spent much of their time huddled together on the one small cot, a single blanket to keep them warm.

Ching Lan would often sing to her; songs in ancient Chinese, her shrill voice somehow soothing. And in spite of their predicament, the teacher had done her best to give Lili structure. Though they had no books, Ching would encourage Lili to review lessons they had studied in Tibet, both of them knowing that if they didn't put some order to their days and nights, they would go crazy.

Fortunately, Lili was able to recite every lesson from every book she had ever read. It was another of her gifts. But like most gifts, it came with a price. Not only could she recall every word, but she could also remember the pain of every tragedy; her father's grief-stricken face as they told him that his wife – Lili's mother – had vanished and was surely dead, the clarity of the moon as it shone on her father's dirt-covered grave, the red-hot heat of the fire that had burned Uncle Mart so badly that the world had believed him to be dead. She revisited those events nearly every single day, the details as vivid as if she had been there. *Some gift,* she often thought.

But it was her other gift that had brought her the most hope...and the most sorrow. Lili had been blessed with the ability to see, and even talk to people who were thousands of miles away. It was how she had been able to "see" what had happened to Uncle Mart in the hotel fire. It had been as if she was standing beside him, feeling his agony, watching him as he started to die. And it had hurt her deeply.

"Transnational Telepathy," her mother Larissa had called it. Larissa had had the same gift, and had told Lili that it had been given to them so that they could help others. Her mother had used it to help the Latvian government; Lili used it to help those she loved. She would take on what she could of their burdens or fears, then do her best to try to calm them. But it was getting harder...*because I am getting weaker.*

Ching must have seen it; the weakening not only of Lili's body, but of her spirit. Because starting about two months ago, soon after the guard had given Lili the pencil, Ching had pushed her to start every day by writing a letter. *"Pick someone special and talk to them on paper."* Lili had done it, and it had helped, at least a little. She had made sure to finish each letter with a poem. Lili was good at writing poems. Through the power of a rhyme, she could somehow make sense of her feelings; it was like straightening a drawer or cleaning a closet. Once she had completed the letter and the poem, she would give it to Ching, who would seal it, address it, and hand it to the guards to mail. Lili knew they wouldn't mail it; she had watched them throw letters away more than once. But she wrote them anyway, because Ching had asked her to...and because it made her feel better.

At first, she had written to the people who were gone forever: her mother and father. It had felt odd to reach out to the dead, but it had also been comforting. Telling them goodbye on paper – something she had never gotten to do in person – gave her a sense of peace she hadn't known was missing. Once she had finished the letters to Albins and Larissa, she had written to the two people who had cared for her after their passing: Danil Latkovskis and his sister, Anna. In their letter she had written, *"Tell the cats that I miss them, and I will be home soon to feed them."* Then her eyes had begun to sting, so she had stopped and had asked Ching Lan to tell her a story.

Recently, Lili had decided to write to Uncle Mart. For the longest time she had thought he was dead – after all, she had seen him burning in a hotel fire – but had learned as she was leaving Tibet that he was, in fact, alive. He was badly scarred and full of grief, but he was alive. She had used her telepathy to reach out to him, and, though she had spoken to him many times over the last seven months, it was getting harder. Her hope was that the letters might take the place of her gift that was fading.

She hadn't known where to send the letters, however, so she had addressed them to his father, Walter, at a post box in Uzava. She knew the number of the post box, as she had gone with her father many times when he had picked up mail for the Hendersons. "PO Box 7475," she would say aloud as she wrote it on the envelope. Lili had often been the one to walk the letters to Walter's office in the back of the castle. If he wasn't there, she would leave them on his desk. But if he was there, he would smile and thank her, and then encourage her to have a piece of pie from the kitchen. Lili closed her eyes, suddenly choked up over the memory. She could practically taste the sweet goodness of an oversized piece of pumpkin pie. Uncle Mart would often join her, but he would have butterscotch, instead. Her eyes started to burn; she rubbed them.

It suddenly occurred to her that her and Uncle Mart's lives, though vastly different at the outset, had become quite a bit alike. Because of the fire and what had come after, he was deeply grieved and badly scarred. She, too, was deeply grieved and badly scarred. The only difference was that her scars didn't show.

She had written the first Uncle Mart letter six weeks ago and had given it to Ching to send. Ching had handed it to the guard, who had likely thrown it away. Lili hadn't said much in that letter; only that she missed Mart and was glad that he was alive. She hadn't told him of her prison cell, or the awful food, or the ugly stains on the walls that made her think of the Ventspils slaughterhouse. That would come later.

Lili sighed as she scraped the last of the stringy lettuce from the bowl. She set the empty bowl on the bed and pulled out a letter she had been working on for the past three days. This one was also for Uncle Mart, but it was far more honest than the first one. She had included her thoughts and feelings; things she knew Mart would be interested in. She had spoken of the tiny cell with only a cot and a rusted bucket for her and Ching to relieve themselves. She had told how the metal bars of the cell were corroded, how the walls were chipped and peeling, and how the entire prison smelled of musty grief. And, though she had also written about her loneliness, she had shared with him that they weren't alone. She could hear wails at night, and fists beating against the walls in a far-off hallway. But she had never seen anyone.

She had also told him about the guards. How they all wore the same gray uniforms and the same sour frown, and how every one of them walked with a clipped precision that spoke of discipline, not purpose. *It makes me sad, Uncle Mart. Everyone should have purpose.*

She was having a harder time seeing him...Uncle Mart. The visions she had had of him as she was leaving the dormitory had been strong; now, she could barely even sense his heartbeat. She didn't know if that was because he was fading, or because she was. She leaned back on the bed and sighed. *I miss you, Uncle Mart.*

Ching was lying next to her, a quiet snore the only proof that she was sleeping and not dead. Lili looked across the hall to a hard-to-see window. It was her only tie to the outside. If she leaned backward on the cot, she was able to see glimpses of the Juyong Pass and the Great Wall of China. But what she wanted to see was the sunlight. The only time she could see it were those few moments in early morning as it rose over the Xishan Mountains. Rays of sunlight would fill the hall outside her cell, and she would sit and wait for it as one might wait for a meteor shower or an eclipse. Her biggest disappointment? A rainy day. Today, it was raining.

She stared at the letter. It was nearly finished, just waiting for a poem. She was struggling to think of a theme; a purpose to make the poem worthwhile. She looked over at her dear friend and teacher, and sighed. The poor woman was a shell of who she had once been. Lili thought of Uncle Mart. For reasons far different than Ching Lan's, he, too, was a shell of who he had once been. Lili didn't know what he had done for the four years that the world had thought him dead. No matter how hard she tried, she had been unable to get a sense of those years. All she knew was that whatever it was had left him feeling empty and sad. The Special Lady's plane crash had only made it worse. She feared that Mart might never get past it; that he might die full of hate and anger. Though Lili had tried to reassure him, she could tell that she had failed. He was convinced that he was bad, and that the Special Lady was dead. Nothing Lili could say would change his mind. And now, she couldn't even speak to him...except in a letter.

She looked again at Ching Lan, then nodded slowly. *That is what I will write about...life and death; grief and hope...and how to find heaven through the mist.*

A sudden gust of cold air made her shiver. She laid a part of the blanket over her lap, put her pencil to the yellow paper, and with cold, weak fingers she wrote:

> *If only I could hear the song*
> > *Of angels greeting me on high*
> *For though I know it won't be long*
> > *I only hear their tired sigh*
>
> *They see the winter coming fast*
> > *And feel the cold wind chill my soul*
> *But yet they leave me here to pass*
> > *Their voices mute, their gestures dull*
>
> *But maybe I can sing so clear*
> > *To seraphs who've misplaced their missal*
> *They'll learn the songs I knew down here*
> > *And let my soul be their epistle*
>
> *We are not one – my soul and I*
> > *We share a space, but that is all*
> *My breaths do fail, my heart beats shy*
> > *But like a rose, my soul grows tall*
>
> *In spite of glares through almond eyes*
> > *Or harsh commands in Mandarin*

I find that I have a disguise
  A deeper soul that dwells within

I see the mountains of Xishan
  And as the leaves do take their fall
I see the nearby Badaling
  And the magical Great Wall

I'm soothed by their enduring heart,
  As mine grows weak in this cold jail
But I'm just here to play a part
  And wait as I will soon set sail

To parts unknown, to brave new lands
  Without a harsh determined sentry
Perhaps I won't have feet or hands
  But they are not required for entry

I'll fly so free, I'll need no song
  To guide me to my resting place
Yet will it be that when I'm gone
  You will grow weak and lose your faith?

I cannot bear to think it, Mart
  That all your pain and bitter hate
Has led you to betray your heart
  And stand outside old Satan's gate

For God won't fault a weakened man
  Undone by life's forbidding lies
He'll show you with my unbound hand
  That through you, all God's truths arise

I'll give you strength when arrows come
  To pierce you with their bitter sting
I'll be your sword, your shield, your drum
  Then you can make the angels sing.

PART I

"Coming events cast their shadows before them."

~ Chinese Proverb ~

CHAPTER 1

Somewhere north of Klaipeda, Lithuania

Martin Henderson frowned as he looked around at what he could see of the empty military base located about ten miles north of Klaipeda, Lithuania. Though he had been brought there by three American soldiers, he knew who was responsible for his imprisonment in that abandoned facility: Edward Morningstar. And he knew why. Morningstar was trying to figure out how to kill him without letting anyone know.

He had reached the old military barracks at two p.m., the hour marked by a distant tower somewhere near Klaipeda. The soldiers had unceremoniously locked him in a ten-by-ten cell in a drafty building in the middle of nowhere. From what he could tell, the base was no longer in use, evidenced by the fact that it was entirely empty of any human presence, short of him and the two soldiers who had been ordered to stay behind to keep an eye on him. The silence was profound.

The accommodations weren't terrible; he had stayed in worse. A cot with a thin mattress and a frayed wool blanket, a sink with running water, a toilet, and a narrow window that faced west, allowing him to see the fading sunlight. There was no mirror, which was just as well; he guessed that he must look terrible. Not only had he not slept in days, but Gad had punched him in the face before taking his leave.

He rubbed his jaw and sighed. The jaw was sore, but it would heal. Sleep was a different matter entirely. Even though there was literally nothing else to do, he couldn't sleep. Why? Because too much had happened. In a matter of seventy-two hours, his entire world had changed. It had started when he had learned that the tragic plane crash that had killed the love of his life hadn't been an accident, it had been intentional. Not only that; he knew who was responsible: Edward Morningstar. How was he so sure? Because one of Morningstar's soldier sons, Gad, had received a call prior to the crash, informing him that it was about to happen. Hank Clarkson had overheard that call, and because of it, had driven to the site. But Hank had vanished before anyone could talk to him, and he hadn't been heard from since. Henderson had also learned that there had been a survivor; Maddi's bodyguard, Tom Cravens. Henderson had hunted the man down, and, though the Secret Service agent had told him plenty about the minutes leading up to the crash, he had said next to nothing about why someone might want Maddi dead. But Henderson had a pretty good idea: Maddi had likely been getting too close to unraveling Morningstar's arms for cash operation that he oversaw with other well-positioned leaders from Washington's elite. With Maddi out of the way, Morningstar and his goons would be free to carry on.

The situation had been complicated even further when London Psychiatrist James Samuels had been kidnapped by Gad in an effort to lure Henderson to Lithuania, which, unlike Latvia, had an extradition treaty with the United States. It had worked. In an effort to save Samuels, Henderson had traveled to Lithuania, where American soldiers had immediately taken him into custody and had dropped him at the military base outside Klaipeda.

But none of it compared to what his father had told him just hours ago in a brief phone call as he was being driven to the prison: *Lili Platacis is alive.* Henderson had been convinced for the past ten months that Lili was dead; killed by Morningstar as a form of retaliation for Henderson leaving him about a year ago. Morningstar had gone so far as to email Henderson a photo of Lili lying lifeless in the snow, with the words, *"Meeting scheduled with Lili P. has been cancelled. Subject has been eliminated."* Henderson had come unglued. After all, it was his fault that Lili had been taken in the first place. He had barely been able to function. The only reason he had kept going had been to keep Maddi safe from men like Morningstar; men who would kill her in a heartbeat just to keep their precious money game intact. But Morningstar had managed to kill Maddi anyway...*as she was on her way to see me.*

Henderson rubbed his eyes and sighed. His heart was crying but his eyes could not. For one thing, his tear ducts had been scorched by the fire. For another, any tears he may have had for Lili or Maddi had already been shed; he had nothing left.

Which was why he had turned his focus to Morningstar. He had originally hoped to persuade Gad to turn on the man, so that the two of them could bring Morningstar to justice and topple his organization. *"You will be a hero, Gad."* But Gad hadn't even considered it. Henderson guessed that Gad had been unwilling to betray a man who, from Gad's point of view, had saved him from an empty, pointless life. That was when the gutsy Son of Jacob had punched Henderson in the face.

Again, he rubbed his jaw. He edged to the foot of the bed, shaking his head as he stared out a window across the hall. *Lili is alive.* It was overwhelming. His father's call had been brief; Henderson had been amazed that the man had been able to call him at all. The only thing he was able to tell Henderson was that Lili was alive...and in trouble. *Which means that I have to find a way out of this shithole...and soon.*

He continued to stare out the window. The clouds had drifted, leaving bright sunshine that filled the dark hallway outside his cell. A ray of sunlight was shining on a crack in the cement floor; he stared at it, trying to think of a way out of there. But he had already spent the past hour doing that same thing; it was useless. He would never get out of there, which meant that not only would he be unable to save Lili, but he would be unable to stop Morningstar and make him pay for what he had done.

He stood and walked to the door of the cell. *At least Cravens might have another shot at turning Gad.* The Secret Service agent was currently on his way to find Gad, who – according to a phone call that Dr. Samuels had overheard – was on his way to America. The goal was for Cravens to follow Gad to the U.S. and learn enough about his mission to either force him to turn on Morningstar, or at least stop him from following through with whatever Morningstar was planning. Henderson had given Cravens a key to a safe deposit box not far from DC that held video feed of Morningstar changing into the disguise he had worn in January when he had poisoned a bus full of people with the Lassa fever virus. At one time, Henderson had thought the video itself would be enough to bring down the powerful Ed Morningstar. He had been wrong. Knowing that Henderson had such a tape had likely made the man squirm for a day or two, but there was no way that Morningstar or his elite DC pals would allow a videotape to be the downfall of one of their own. Not only could Morningstar claim it was fabricated, but he had powerful ties in DC; men who either owed him or were indebted to him to keep their secrets. No, it would take more than a video to bring down Morningstar. *It will need to come from within his organization.* If Cravens was able to tie the videotape to a confession from Gad, then maybe he could get someone to take him seriously, and help him unravel Morningstar's empire.

Henderson had been looking forward to telling Morningstar that very thing; to look him in the eye and tell him that his days were numbered; that his operation was being disassembled by the very men he so affectionately referred to as sons. He had been well aware that Morningstar would strike him dead the minute he said it, but he hadn't cared. The joy of seeing Morningstar come face-to-face with his impending demise had seemed worth it.

But all that had changed once he learned that Lili was alive. If it was true – and why would Walter lie about such a thing – then Henderson suddenly had a reason to stay alive. Lili was in trouble. *And I am the one who put her there.*

'There' was China, at least according to what Walter had told him. But China was a big place. Walter didn't know exactly where in China; all he had said was that he had received letters with clues that would help them find her. What Walter didn't know was that, assuming Henderson figured out how to escape the Klaipeda jail, he would free Lili on his own. Not only had he been the one to put her there, but he had made a vow to never again allow his mistakes to put another man's life in danger. More importantly, he possessed unique skills; skills he had acquired, ironically, from the man he was trying to bring down. *The man responsible for taking Lili will inadvertently be the one to help me get her back.*

Walter had said in his call that Henderson shouldn't lose hope; that Walter would figure out how to get him out of there. Which of course meant that Walter would try to use diplomacy and his ties in Washington to convince men like Homeland's Director, Jason Hanover, that Aiden Balkus – Henderson's alias – was vital to the Latvian war effort and should therefore be released. Would it work? He shook his head and sighed. *No... Morningstar is too powerful.*

He walked to the door, put his hands on the bars, and stared at the sunlight beating down on the cracked cement. He looked at the guard down the hall. The other guard was probably trying to sleep. The soldier in the chair had an AK-15 leaning against the wall about a foot from where he was sitting. He had pushed his chair against the wall, and was leaning his head back, eyes closed, mouth open, a soft snore echoing down the hall.

Henderson looked up at the bars embedded in concrete and tried to jiggle them. They didn't budge. He forced his weight against them just to prove to himself, for likely the fiftieth time, that they couldn't be forced. The entire cell was made of concrete, and had only the bars in the front and the narrow window in back. There was no way to break out. That cell wouldn't be opened without a key, which was currently hanging from a fob on the soldier's belt buckle.

His only hope was for his father to somehow persuade American authorities to let him go. But even the respected Walter Henderson wouldn't be able to supersede Morningstar's hold over the powerbrokers of Washington, DC.

So, what do I do? he wondered, as he stared down the hall at the guard. He took a deep breath and sighed. *You find a way to convince that man to let you go.*

"Hey officer!"

He waited. The man didn't move.

He said it again. "Hey, Officer! Wake up!"

The man sputtered and nearly fell off his chair. He grabbed his rifle, shoved it under his arm, and aimed at Henderson. "What?"

"I need to make a phone call."

The soldier laughed. "Tough luck, Balkus. I've been told no phone calls."

Henderson let out an exaggerated sigh, followed by a shaking of his head. "Okay, but you're going to have quite a lot on your conscience."

The man smirked, and made an effort to ignore him. After about a minute, he looked at Henderson and said, "What d'ya mean?"

Henderson frowned. "That call I took in the car...you know the one... from the Director of Homeland Security?"

The soldier frowned. "Yeah...what about it?"

"It involved the war in Latvia. I happen to hold key information that is vital to the war effort...information that will ensure that the right people win that war."

The man narrowed his eyes. "What sort of information."

Henderson shook his head. "I was asked by the Director to not tell anyone."

The soldier rubbed his chin. "Okay, so maybe I can send someone a message."

Henderson pretended to consider it. "Nah, as I said, it's sensitive."

The soldier shrugged. "My orders are clear. No phone calls."

Henderson sighed. "Whatever you say. But like I said, buddy, World War III will be on your conscience, not mine."

The soldier let out a grunt, then closed his eyes and again leaned his head against the wall. This time, however, he kept the gun in his lap.

Henderson paced the cell, trying to come up with an escape plan. After a minute or so, he returned to the cot and laid his long lean frame on the mattress. It was useless; he had failed. The sun had begun to fade, leaving the once-bright hallway cloaked in shadow. He closed his eyes, forced to accept that he would never get out of there; not alive, anyway, which meant that he wouldn't be able to save Lili.

He heard a phone ring. He jumped up from the cot and ran to the door of the cell. The soldier was leaning forward, talking into his cellphone. Henderson put an ear to the bars to hear.

"Balkus? You're sure?"

A pause.

"The Pentagon's gonna be pissed."

Another pause.

"So, I'm supposed to pick between Homeland and the Pentagon? Great."

Another pause.

"Don't worry. I'll have him call. Text me the number."

Henderson quickly walked back and sat on the cot. He waited. He heard the click of a text, then heard the man's chair slide on the floor as the soldier stood and walked to the door of Henderson's cell. He was holding the rifle at his side. "You got your wish, Balkus. Homeland insists on talking to you." The man handed him the phone. "They want you to call the number I just entered into the phone. You just push 'send,' got it?"

Henderson nodded as he looked at the number on the screen. He recognized it. It was Walter's private cellphone. He pushed send and held the phone to his ear. While he was waiting for it to be answered, he said to the guard, "As I said earlier, it's sensitive, soldier."

The man narrowed his eyes. He shook his head. "I don't give a shit if it's sensitive. Go ahead with the call. I'm not moving."

Henderson stiffened.

The call was answered on the sixth ring. "Aiden Balkus?"

Henderson said, "Yes. What is it?"

"Be ready to go...in the next twenty-four hours."

The call ended. Henderson kept the phone to his ear. The soldier was still watching him. Henderson had told the man that he had vital information to communicate to Homeland Security. In an effort to keep up the ruse, he mumbled a few sentences, making sure to include the names of four fake soldiers, along with an old Latvian Freedom Fighter code that was no longer in use, then ended the call.

The officer held out his hand. "I'll take that."

Henderson handed him the phone.

The man said, "So...have you saved the world from big bad Putin?"

Henderson nodded. "Actually, soldier, I think I have."

The soldier smirked and turned away. As he walked back to his chair, Henderson leaned against the bars of the cell and stared out the window across the hall. The sunlight continued to fade, making the shadowed hallway even darker. There was nothing for him to do. Within the next day or so, the odds were high that his respectable, law-abiding father would defy America's government and somehow break him out of that cell.

Chapter 2

Rome, Italy

Morningstar.

Maddi bolted upright, nearly falling off the plastic chair that she had been sitting on not far from the overseas gates. She had dozed off, and that shocking word had awakened her from a surprisingly sound sleep.

She rubbed her eyes, then stared at the newspaper on her lap. Though the headline, "American President Missing Since Yesterday," had been the reason she had bought the paper, it was the article under the fold that she had chosen to read prior to closing her eyes. Discussing Putin's threat against Latvia, it had given a brief history of the Baltic country and its ill-fated ties to Russia. It had made her think of Henderson, and his family's undying pledge to that country. She had closed her eyes, certain that Henderson would be the one to fill her dreams.

And she had looked forward to it. Sleep was when she saw him...when she *felt* him best. When she was asleep, she didn't ache for him, she simply felt his presence...inside her with every beat of her heart.

Like a comfortable chair in a favorite room, he had become a fixture in her mind. Every day and night for the past two months, as she and Hank had made their vagabond journey across Europe, she had been comforted by his presence. While she had lain broken and bruised in the back of stolen cars, Henderson had laid with her. He had comforted her when she felt lonely, he had reassured her when she felt lost. He was there when she awoke, and was still there when she fell back to sleep.

So, go to him, she had told herself a thousand times, *...and not just in your dreams.* But she knew she couldn't. They had been through too much. Their love had led to heartache, and not just for them. It no longer seemed fair to make others bear the burden of their helplessly tragic love. But it hadn't stopped her from imagining it; from picturing herself phoning him from some exotic island, telling him she loved him, then asking him to join her, *"...and be ready, my love...to disappear...forever."*

But then it would occur to her that she didn't even know where to find him. Was he hiding at the Henderson castle in Latvia, or was he on the run? She had learned two months ago that he, as Matt, had been designated an accomplice in last January's bioterror attacks and was now wanted by the United States government. *And I have been designated deceased.* He was on the run; she was dead. They had too much to lose if either of them was found...or was found out. Which was why she had decided that she must let him go...forever. But the decision had nearly killed her. She had survived it by knowing that whenever she wanted him she could simply close her eyes and find him...there...in her dreams.

But just now, instead of Henderson waking her, it had been a single word: *Morningstar.* As she combed her fingers through her oddly short hair, her gut-wrenching revelations from two months ago came rushing back...and she was sickened by it.

Morningstar is behind everything. The secret commission that had put Hank's life at risk, the escalation of war around the globe, the effort to sever the tie between her and Henderson by convincing them that the only way to keep the other alive was to leave. But worst of all, had been the revelation that it was Morningstar who had been Henderson's overseer; that it was he who had trained Henderson, and, in turn, had forced him to kill good men like Al-Gharsi. She had put it all together two months ago, just seconds before her plane had been about to crash into the ground.

But clearly she had forgotten it...*until now.*

Her plan had been to reach out to President Wilcox the minute she landed in Latvia, to let him know that a top Pentagon aide was a traitor, that Ed Morningstar was hellbent on pulling the world into another world war. *So, who do I reach out to now? The old President is dead, the new President is missing, and I no longer exist.*

She frowned as she placed the folded newspaper on the chair beside her. *How do I get this information to the people who can do something about it?* Hank and her bodyguard, Tom Cravens were the only people on the entire planet who even knew she was alive. She couldn't call Hank. When she had left him in Spain, he had told her that he was going home to his ex-wife. She sighed. *So, I'll tell Cravens.* But how? Though she had memorized his number, she had thrown away her trac phone. *I'll use a payphone.* But payphone calls could be tracked. Besides, she had no way of knowing if Cravens' cellphone had even survived the plane crash. *I'll send a letter to his boss. An anonymous letter...in care of the Secret Service.*

She had bought notecards – why, she wasn't sure – and was about to pull one from her travel bag, when she was startled by an overhead announcement.

"Harriett Winthrop, si prega di presentarsi al gate 42, terminal oltremare." *Harriett Winthrop, please report to gate 42, overseas terminal.*

Harriett Winthrop...that's me! She grabbed the travel bag and ran for the gate. *I must've gotten on a flight!* she thought as she sprinted down the hall. She had been trying to book a flight to Beijing, China since nine a.m. All flights had been full. She had been forced to wait on standby for the past eight hours, and had more or less given up. Though it wasn't wise to put Harriett Winthrop's name on a flight manifest – the less exposure, the better – it couldn't be helped; she needed to get to China.

She stumbled over a random piece of luggage, but righted herself and kept running. For about the tenth time, she wondered if she should call Hank to let him know that her plans had changed. And – for about the tenth time – she decided not to. It was best he think of her tucked away in a cozy flat somewhere on the isle of Corsica. Besides, to call Hank would put so much more at risk; his job, her identity, and her need to follow through on a conversation she had had about 24 hours ago.

The conversation had taken place when Maddi had been in her cabin on the boat that was to take her to Corsica. The boat hadn't gone far; as a matter of fact, she had still been able to see the faint outline of the harbor in Valencia, Spain, where she had said goodbye to her dearest friend, Hank Clarkson. Her sense of hopelessness had never been deeper. So, when she had heard the soft voice of the little girl who had visited her in her mind several times already, she had thought that it was something that she had manufactured to soothe her lonely soul…a friend when she had none.

But her grief was more than just saying goodbye – likely forever – to her dearest friend. Maddi had essentially died. Though the plane crash hadn't killed her, it may as well have. She was grieving the loss of herself. Even worse was the thought that the crash hadn't been an accident. She didn't know who was behind it, but Hank had told her that it had been planned. That was all he would say, however, swearing that he knew nothing more. So, in an effort to keep her safe from whoever kept trying to kill her, Hank and her bodyguard, Cravens, had decided it was best that they tell the world she was dead. Which meant that she had needed to become someone else. She was now Harriett Winthrop from England, and her only tie to her old life was Hank. But even that tie was tenuous. If the world was to ever learn that Homeland Security's Deputy Director had lied about Maddi's survival, and had helped her to assume a completely different identity, his career – and likely his rekindled relationship with his ex-wife, Jenny – would be in jeopardy. Which was why, in spite of the fact that she was wallowing in despair and could use a heart-to-heart with an old friend, she had refused to call him. She had gone so far as to throw away the trac phone he had given her, ending even the possibility that he would be tied to her in any way. Hank needed to go home. *And I need to follow through on Lili's plea.*

When she had first heard the girl's sweet voice, she had ignored it. In spite of Lili's impact on Maddi's life over the last few months, Maddi had yet to reconcile the fact that Lili couldn't be seen, only heard. Maddi had never even met her; not in the flesh, anyway, and she had no explanation for how Lili had managed to show up again and again without actually being there. But even more stunning had been the fact that Lili had known things about Maddi that no one else could know. She had spoken of events that were happening in real time; inspiration when Maddi's heart was breaking, wisdom to challenge a less-than-favorable decision. But this time, Lili hadn't tried to advise Maddi, she had been frightened for her own life.

"I'm scared they are going to hurt us…maybe even kill us, Special Lady."

"Who is going to hurt you?" Maddi had asked, actually saying it aloud in the cabin of her boat.

"The soldiers."

Though Maddi still couldn't explain how Lili could talk to her without being in the room, the weak-voiced plea had been compelling enough for Maddi to feel a need to do something. She had whispered, *"Can you tell me where you are?"*

"China."

"Where in China?"

"I'm...I'm not sure. I...I can see the Great Wall. I think we're near Beijing. I heard Ching Lan say so, but only once."

"Who is Ching Lan?"

"My only friend."

That was it; that had been the end of it.

At first, Maddi had thought that she would simply look into it from afar. She could investigate Lili's claim from her Corsican apartment, then notify authorities in Beijing so they could handle whatever she was able to learn about Lili's predicament. But Lili's claim that it was soldiers that she was afraid of had forced Maddi to rethink that strategy. Soldiers implied authority. If those soldiers were operating on behalf of the Chinese government, then notifying Beijing of Lili's plight might only put her in more danger. Which had left Maddi with only one option: Lili – whoever she was – needed Maddi's help. And Maddi – whoever she was – needed to help her.

Maddi had gotten off the ship at the Corsican harbor, and had taken a cab to an address that had been etched on a scrap of paper that had been tucked inside the passport that Angelo Recito had made for her. The address had turned out to be an apartment complex on the northern side of the island. Once she had arrived, she had asked the manager to remove her name – Harriett Winthrop's name – from the tenant list. Not only did she not intend on staying there, but she didn't want anyone to know that she had ever intended on staying there...not even Hank. Why? *Because he might go to Corsica and try to find me.* Lord knows, Hank had given up enough already.

From there, she had taken a cab to a bookstore where she had bought a map of Beijing. If she was going to save Lili, she would need to know the layout of the city. But Beijing was huge. Maddi had soon come to see that she would need more details about Lili's location. *How do I ask a fantasy girl for more information?* She had left the store and had walked to a nearby park. She had hiked deep into the trees, and, in the shadows of dusk, had whispered, *"Lili, I need to know details of your location,"*

After a minute, the voice – which was now little more than a whisper – had said, *"I see mountains...near Chao...Chaoyang."*

Maddi had found a café, had ordered soup and a pot of tea, and had spent the next few hours studying the map, learning all she could about Chaoyang. She hadn't even noticed the sun vanish and the moon appear, until a tower somewhere had let out ten chimes. She had left the café and had run to the harbor. She had caught the last ferry of the day, which had taken her to Pisa. From there, she had hopped an early train to Rome, and had then taken a taxi to Rome's airport. The journey to the airport had saddened her. In the shadows of dawn, she had seen the mystical Coliseum, the ancient ruins, the narrow streets with charming cafes. What she wouldn't give to stay; to stroll among the shops, to look for the man in the alley who had sold her a pair of handmade shoes. Not that long ago, Rome had been her city of joy. A refuge from her life in DC. She and Hank had traveled there a lifetime ago – six years, to be exact – when things had been simpler. She hadn't known it at the time; she hadn't known how complicated her life was about to become...that she would meet Henderson and fall in love with him; that he would nearly burn to death in a fire and she would never get over it; that she would find him again, then force herself to leave him in order to save him; that her life would be threatened and would nearly end in a plane crash; that her love for Hank would lead her not back into his arms, but away from him and back to Rome. But now, the city that she loved was little more than a place she was passing through on her way to...where? *China...as I pretend to be Harriett Winthrop, and try to save an imaginary little girl...from what?* She didn't know; it didn't matter. Lili needed her; that was all that mattered. Maddi was best when she was needed.

She ran even faster. But as she reached the gate, she felt the weakness in her legs and the hunger in her chest, and realized just how tired she was. In the last few days, she had had little more than a few hours of sleep. Her time at the airport had been spent either studying the map of China, or shopping for much-needed supplies with money that Angelo and Hank had given her.

She had bought a travel bag, which she had filled with a dress, a raincoat, notecards, and toiletries, and had used an airport bathroom to wash up. But that, too, had been fraught with despair. In spite of every effort to avoid the mirror, she had been forced to look at herself when she had brushed her teeth. What she had seen had astounded her. Not only was her long blonde hair now short and brown, but her face itself had changed; it had become gaunt, lifeless. She looked as if she had aged a decade, not merely a few months. And she was so thin. *Maybe one of these days I'll feel like eating again.* She had existed on little more than a sandwich or a bowl of soup for the past few months. The very thought of a full meal made her stomach turn.

She reached the gate just as an agent was about to close the door. "Sbrigati, signora!" *Hurry, Madam!*

Maddi showed the agent her ticket and passport, both bearing the name Harriett Winthrop, then ran through the doorway and down the ramp to the plane. She boarded and found her seat in the second-to-the-last row. She shoved her new travel bag under the seat in front of her, then strapped in and caught her breath.

There was an older woman in the seat next to her. The woman looked at her and smiled. "Buongiorno."

Maddi gave a weak smile. "Buongiorno," she said, then quickly turned away, hoping the woman wouldn't want to talk. The less Maddi talked to people, the better. The woman took the hint, and Maddi leaned back and closed her eyes. She felt the plane move back from the gate. The flight would take nearly twelve hours; Maddi hoped to sleep the entire way. As she was about to drift off, the child's voice that she had now become so familiar with whispered, *"Please...hurry, Special Lady."*

Maddi nodded, thinking to herself, *I will, Lili...I will.*

CHAPTER 3

Warsaw, Poland

Gad – Marcus King – was pissed. He had gotten as far as Warsaw, but had been stopped before he could board the flight to DC. He had been told that his name – his fake name, Carlos DeMarco – had come up in connection with an alert that had been issued from an unnamed authority in Latvia, and that they would need to clear him before he could proceed.

That had been over two hours ago; he had been pacing ever since. They had told him that he couldn't leave the gate area unless it was to get something to eat in a nearby café, or to go to the bathroom. He had made three trips to the bathroom already, just to get away from the two men who had been assigned to watch him. But even then, one of them had insisted on going with him. Gad felt like he was about to lose it. And though Morningstar had stated loud and clear that Gad shouldn't reach out to him unless it was an emergency, Gad had put it off as long as he could. He checked the time. *Seven p.m. ...one p.m. in DC.* He walked to the far end of the gate area, pulled out his cellphone, and dialed.

"Yes?"

"Father, it's me. I'm in trouble."

He heard a sigh. "What's wrong?"

"I've been stopped in Warsaw. Something about my name – Carlos DeMarco – being flagged due to an alert from a Latvian authority."

"Shit. That asshole Walter Henderson must have done it." There was a pause. "I'll take care of it. Just stay where you are."

The call ended. Gad had wanted to say, *"It's not like I can go anywhere,"* but the man hadn't given him a chance. He slid his phone in his pocket, surprised he still had the phone. He was actually surprised he hadn't been taken into custody. Then again, what did anyone actually have on him? Only the word of a Latvian bigwig that a former employee had left under dubious circumstances. *Nothin' illegal about that.*

His flight to DC had already left. From what Gad had been able to determine, there wasn't another one until tomorrow morning at ten. Which meant that, even if Morningstar was able to square things with security, Gad wouldn't get to DC until noon on Friday at the soonest. Though it would still give him time to get to the Portland, Maine airport to meet Michael Cannon by Saturday morning, it would make the timeline a bit tighter than he preferred.

He walked back to the gate area and resumed his pacing, not taking his eyes off of the two uniformed officers who had been pulled in to watch him. What were they waiting for? *Either clear me, or take me into custody, assholes.*

He didn't have long to wait. He saw one of the men take a phone call, and, though Gad couldn't hear the conversation, it was clear the guy was getting reamed. Gad laughed. *I'll bet Jacob called that man's boss and set him straight.*

The man ended the call, then said something to his partner. The two men walked over to Gad. The soldier who had taken the call looked down at him and frowned. "You have been cleared," he said, his stilted accent almost comical.

Gad sneered at the man. "Of course, I have, asshole."

Without a word, the two men turned and walked away. Gad cursed after them, then adjusted his backpack over his shoulder. *What do I do now?* he wondered as he left the gate area for the first time in three hours. *I guess I gotta buy another ticket.*

He walked down a long hall until he came to a ticket counter. He walked up to a young woman in a blue suit and nodded. "I need to get to Washington, DC, ASAP."

She nodded in reply. "I can help with that." Her accent was far more appealing. He waited as the woman found him a seat on the ten o'clock flight the following morning. "How will you be paying for that?" she asked with a smile.

Though Gad was tempted to argue that the damn flight should be free, he decided it wasn't worth the hassle. He pulled out the credit card that he had picked up in Vilnius; the card that had been left for him by Jacob. "Just put it on here, Ma'am." He chuckled. "I'll let my boss pick it up."

She nodded, ran the card, then handed him the ticket. "Here you go, Mr. DeMarco."

He thanked her, then slid the card in his pocket. "Any good hotels nearby?"

She directed him to a hotel that adjoined the airport.

He thanked her again, then walked to the exit. He stepped outside. It was nearly eight p.m.; the sun had set. But the air was warmer than it had been in Lithuania, and the short walk to the hotel was actually pleasant. He reached the door of the hotel and walked inside. He nodded. *Not bad... not bad at all.* The lobby was clean, there was a restaurant next to it, and a bar next to that. He checked in, thinking to himself, *I'll order a thick steak and a bottle of red wine...and I'll let my boss pick it up.*

CHAPTER 4

Frankfurt, Germany

Secret Service Agent Tom Cravens ran his thick hands through his thinning hair and sighed. The trip so far had been a bust. He had been delayed getting out of Riga, mostly because of flight restrictions imposed as a result of Russia's attack on Latvia. The total embargo had been lifted, but only limited flights had been permitted to leave. But just as he had been about to board, there had been another delay, something about a need to once again lock down and secure airspace. It was then that he learned that something had happened to the President of the United States. The man had apparently gone into hiding, and no one seemed to know why. Though curious and extremely concerned, Cravens hadn't been prepared to call his boss to ask. There would have been far too much explaining to do, and he hadn't been up to it...not yet. Not until he could come up with a really good reason for his time away.

The lockdown had ended several hours later, but by the time he had finally left Riga and had landed in Frankfurt, Germany, he had missed his connection to DC. He had booked the next flight out, which wasn't scheduled to leave until midnight.

But he had just been informed that that flight had been cancelled.

"Cancelled? Who the hell cancels an international flight at the last minute?" Cravens raged as he once again stood at the ticket counter.

The man behind the counter sighed. In crisp English, but with a heavy German accent, he said, "I am sorry, sir. There is a bit of upheaval in America at the moment. Flights are limited. Would you like me to book you on the next available?"

Cravens stared at the man. The next available flight wasn't scheduled to leave for over twenty-four hours; at two a.m. Saturday. Which meant, with the time gained from traveling west, he would get to DC Saturday morning at around six. Michael Cannon's daughter was expected at Portland's airport Saturday morning at ten, which would give him only four hours to get from DC to Portland. A tight timeline, but he could make it if he lucked into a well-timed commuter flight from DC. He could even go ahead and book the commuter flight. But he had also hoped to go to Boonsboro, Maryland to pick up the flash drive that Henderson had told him about. That would now be out of the question. *I'll go there after I finish my business with Gad.*

He looked at the agent and sighed. "Fine. Book me on that flight."

The man nodded and stared at his computer screen. "You are in luck, sir. There is only one seat left." He paused. "It is the middle seat in the last row, but at least you will get to the States by Saturday morning."

"Fantastic," Cravens quipped as he grabbed the ticket. He was about to walk away, when he said, "Any good hotels nearby?"

The man nodded. "HGI or Hilton next to the airport are both quite nice, sir."

Cravens nodded, mumbled a quick "Thanks," and walked away from the counter. He bought a sandwich and a cola from a café that was about to close, stunned that it cost twenty euros just for ham and cheese, then walked the entire length of the airport to the exit that would lead to the Hilton. He checked in and walked up to his room. He downed the sandwich in a few bites, then stripped to his underwear. It was well after ten p.m. He was exhausted. He pulled back the blanket and climbed into bed. The mattress was stiff and he couldn't seem to get comfortable. After an hour or so of turning from one side to the other, he finally gave up, threw off the covers, and sat on the side of the bed. He shook his head in disgust. *Bad, over-priced food, a slab of cement to sleep on, and in about 24 hours I get to spend the next ten hours or so stuck in the back row next to the bathroom of a completely full plane. Can't wait.*

J.B. Vosler

It occurred to him that he would soon be back in the U.S. for the first time in over seven months. *I should at least see what's going on at the Secret Service.* He crawled out of bed, grabbed his duffel bag, and pulled out a laptop he had bought in the Riga airport after the first delay. He had used his credit card for both the flight and the laptop; the first time he had been willing to use the card since the plane crash. *Why not?* he had thought. *My name is on the manifest of a plane travelling to Washington, DC...my boss has probably already been alerted.*

The only cash he had had come from Henderson, who had secretly shoved 500 euros into his pocket when they were saying goodbye at the airport. It had come in handy. He had already used over a hundred euros just for food at the two airports.

He set the laptop on a side table, opened it, and waited for it to load. For the first time in over two months, he was about to log onto the Secret Service website. He didn't want to. Not only had it been so long that he would likely have a hundred messages waiting for him, but he would instantly see that the status of his protectee had changed from 'traveling overseas' to 'deceased.' And though he knew that Maddi wasn't actually dead, in a sense, she was. She was dead to him, anyway. The very thought of it made him choke up, and he quickly took a sip of soda. *Might as well get it over with.*

He logged on through the hotel's wi-fi and plugged the Secret Service address into a search engine. He reached the site and, using different links and codes that he somehow remembered, he logged into his profile. He was listed as being on a leave of absence. He scrolled down the page, stopping when he came to a photo of Maddi. Again, he choked up, and again he took a quick sip of soda. Just as he had expected, the word deceased was written beside her photo. He was about to move on, when he stopped. Next to cause of death, where it should have said 'aviation accident,' it said, 'under review.' *Why in the hell is her cause of death under review?*

He clicked on the statement, and was taken to another webpage. Listed there was a summary of the crash, followed by several amended statements. The original report had said that no one had survived. The first amendment stated that there had been one survivor: Secret Service Agent Tom Cravens. He kept reading. The next amendment referenced the location. Where originally it had indicated that the crash had occurred 'south of

32

Uzava,' the amended comment stated that the accident had taken place ten miles north of Liepaja. He kept going. Again, he saw Maddi's photo. Next to it were two more photos; the first showed her blue sweater, the second her senate ID badge. He had left those items, along with a gold locket at the scene of the crash to further support the notion that she had died. He frowned. *Where's the locket?* Next to the photos, the words 'aviation accident' had been struck through, replaced with 'under review.' But this time, something had been added. "By issue of the President of the United States, this death is being further investigated for possible wrongdoing. This is a level three, top secret notification."

Cravens stared at the statement. Again, he swallowed. Had someone learned the truth? He rubbed his eyes. More importantly, had the President – who Cravens had recently learned was hiding in some unknown location – become aware of the fact that Maddi's death hadn't been an accident, after all? Cravens frowned. *And are his disappearance and his discovery of that truth somehow connected?*

CHAPTER 5

Rome, Italy

Dr. Hank Clarkson, Deputy Director of America's Homeland Security, looked at the faces of the passengers waiting in line to check in at the counter of the Rome International Airport, and suddenly realized how tired he was. While their eyes were those of eager adventurers, his were the eyes of a beaten man. Not only had he been away from home – from Jenny – for far too long, but the last twenty-four hours had been hell. Late Wednesday night, as he had been about to board the flight in Madrid for DC, he had made the fateful decision to call Maddi. According to the boat schedule, she should have arrived in Corsica by then, and he had wanted to make sure that she had gotten to her apartment and had settled in before he left the continent. She hadn't answered the trac phone he had given her, so he had tried again a minute later. Still no answer. His flight had nearly completed boarding; he had tried a third time. Still no answer. By then, all passengers had boarded the flight but him. The agent at the counter had glared at him. *"Sir, we are going to have to close this door."* Hank had stood there staring at the agent for what had felt like an eternity. Finally, he had stuffed his ticket in his pocket, and had left the gate.

His call to Jenny hadn't gone well.

"Hank? Are you about to leave?"
Hank rubbed the back of his neck. "Jenny, something's...come up."
Silence. Then, "Hank, no. I need you to come home to me."

Hank sighed. "I know this isn't okay, Jenny, but something just happened... there's something I need to do. I promise that I'll make it up to you."

More silence. Then, quieter, "Can you at least tell me where you are?"

Hank sifted the question – and his answer – in his mind. "Jenny, I can't."

"Does this have anything to do with Maddi's...death?"

Could he do it? Could he lie to the woman he loved? "No. But it's top secret. I'm not allowed to talk about it." A half-truth...better than a full out lie.

He heard a sigh. "I see. When will you be home?"

He rubbed his eyes. "I don't know. As soon as I can."

Her silence was brutal. Finally, "Okay. Hurry home. I...I love you."

"I love you, too, Jenny."

Hank had ended the call before he was forced to tell any more lies. And now, twenty-four hours later, he was no closer to finding Maddi than he had been.

Knowing that she was supposed to be in an apartment on the island of Corsica, he had tried to book a flight to the capital city of Ajaccio, but every flight had been full. So, he had booked a flight to Rome, thinking he could then take a ferry to Corsica. Angelo Recito, the man who had pulled together Maddi's new identity, hadn't told him the exact town where she would be staying; only that it was an apartment complex in Corsica. Angelo had, however, shoved a scrap of paper into Hank's hand just as he had rushed Hank and Maddi out the back door of his house near Madrid. On the paper was an address that had been hastily scratched in pencil. Hank had guessed it was to the complex. *What else would it be?*

So, as he had waited for the flight from Madrid to Rome, he had pulled the scrap of paper from his briefcase, had used an airport computer to find the website, then had called there using his trac phone. Like the call to Jenny, that call also hadn't gone well...

A man answered, his accent a blend of Italian and French. "Appartmenti Catalina. Cumu pudariu aiuta?" Catalina Apartments. May I help you?

Hank didn't know French, so he went with Italian, which was rusty, at best. "Si, mi circa un Harriett Winthrop. Era mistu arriva a e vostre facilitador anoche." Yes, I'm looking for a Harriett Winthrop. She was expected to arrive at your facility yesterday evening.

He waited. After a minute, the man came back on the line. "Purtate, Signore. Un ci he nimu di listessu nome." I'm sorry, sir. There is no one listed with that name.

Hank rubbed the back of his neck. "Un avete mica un appartamenti chi aspetta per un Harriett Winthrop di Londra?" You don't have an apartment waiting for a Harriett Winthrop from London?

"Micca, Signore." No, sir.

That had been about twenty hours ago. Hank had landed in Rome the following morning – this morning – before dawn, and had immediately taken a train to the coast. He had then taken a ferry to Corsica to try to learn more. He had written down the address of the apartment complex, and had taken a cab to the location. Not only was Maddi – Harriett Winthrop – not there, but according to the manager, she had never been there, and there was nothing to suggest that she had ever had a lease for any of the apartments. He had had the cab driver take him around the island on the off chance that he might catch a glimpse of her, but had seen no sign of her. It wasn't until he had returned to the dock to catch the ferry back to Rome that he had gotten his first bit of helpful information.

As he had waited for the five o'clock ferry, he had asked a couple of dockhands if either of them recalled seeing a thin woman with short brown hair, glasses, and distinct blue eyes. *"She's likely wearing a ruffled dress and a brimmed hat."* Neither one had seen her, but a dock worker standing behind them had said in broken English, *"I see her, standing there—"* the man pointed to the other end of the dock, *"—with hat low on forehead. She talking to young boy. Maybe her son? She point at dolphins."* He had added that, though she had been waiting for the last ferry of the night – which would take her to Pisa – he had overheard her asking how to get to Rome's airport.

Hank had headed back to the airport in Rome, and had arrived there just after seven p.m. It was now eleven p.m., and he had spent the last four hours asking every staffer he ran into if they had seen a woman fitting Maddi's – Harriett Winthrop's – description. So far, he had had no success. He was now sipping coffee at a café, picking at bacon and eggs with no idea what to do next. He took a bite of eggs and pushed the plate away. He sat back and sighed. *Maybe it's time I go home.*

But he couldn't go home. Maddi was alone in the world and clearly something had gone wrong. Had someone identified her and turned her in? Or maybe kidnapped her? Or, worse, killed her? He laid his napkin on the table and shook his head. *Don't be ridiculous, Hank. No one would have recognized her...she doesn't look one bit like Maddi.* But he couldn't shake the notion that something was wrong...terribly wrong.

But what could he do about it? Though he hated the idea of giving up, he had nowhere to look; no place to even begin to search for her. Rome's Airport connected to cities all over the world. *She could be anywhere,* he thought as he stood and threw ten euros on the table. *It's time for me to go home.*

He walked to the nearest ticket counter and approached an agent. "I need a flight to America."

The woman smiled. "Certainly, sir. I'll see what I can find."

Her English was flawless; no accent. *American?* "Are you from the States?"

She nodded. "Michigan," she said, adding, "The Blue and the Maize."

Hank laughed. "I'm from Ohio...the Scarlet and Gray."

She chuckled. "Oh no! Is that where you're heading?"

Hank frowned. "No, I need to go to DC."

She began typing. "You don't seem too excited."

"I'm not. I came here to find someone, and I've failed."

Hank handed her his Homeland Security ID.

She looked at the ID and frowned. "Homeland Security? Maybe I can help."

His eyes widened. He hadn't even thought to use his role as Homeland Security's Deputy Director to find Maddi. He had spent so much time trying to hide who he was – who *she* was – that he had failed to appreciate the value of his credentials. "Harriett Winthrop. I'm guessing that she flew out of here sometime in the last twenty-four hours or so."

The agent typed, scrolled, and typed some more. "Ah, here she is." She looked up from her computer and frowned. "Though I can tell you that she did, in fact, fly out of here, I would need a compelling reason to tell you anything more than that."

Hank sighed with relief. At least he knew that Maddi was alive. He was about to protest the agent's refusal to give him more information, but she was right. Though Hank's credentials were beyond reproach, the woman was simply doing her job. He would need to give her a good reason to tell him anything. He tugged at his collar as he prepared to once again lie to a person who had every reason to trust him. He had gotten fairly good at it over the past two months. "She's wanted...for tax evasion."

The woman narrowed her eyes. "Homeland Security is in Italy trying to find someone wanted for tax evasion?" She frowned. "Interesting... especially since it says here that she's a citizen of Great Britain."

Think Hank. "Yes, but she spent time in the U.S. promoting an... invention. She made quite a bit of money, then left the country without paying any taxes."

The woman crossed her arms. "So, they sent the *Deputy Director of the Department of Homeland Security* to find her?"

"Uh...yeah. It was a lot of money...and we have reason to believe that she has recently been in contact with a group of...Middle Eastern extremists."

The woman shook her head as she handed Hank his Homeland ID. "Though I don't believe a word of what you just told me, your credentials are sound. So, in spite of your Ohio State ties," she leaned in and lowered her voice, "I will tell you that your Ms. Winthrop left for Beijing about six hours ago."

Hank stared at her. "Beijing?"

"Yes sir. Is there anything more I can do for you?"

Hank thought about Jenny. He thought of how long it had been since he had seen her or held her or looked in her eyes. Then he thought of Maddi...alone in the world. No friends, no contacts. He sighed. "Yes, would you please book me on the next flight to Beijing?"

CHAPTER 6

On the road to Klaipeda

Seventy-two-year-old Walter Henderson said nothing as his head of security, Dimitri Kauss, drove the black BMW down highway A11 toward Lithuania. They had been on the road for about forty minutes, and, in that time, Walter had done his best to nap. But it was no use...not with the mission he was about to carry out.

Never had Walter been more thankful for his relationship with the Director of Homeland Security, Jason Hanover. Brought about by the tragedy of the hotel fire that had changed his son forever, the tie between the two men had given Walter a much-needed voice within America's government. Twice now, the Director had allowed Walter to talk to a prisoner who was off-limits to nearly every other person on earth. What the Director didn't know was that the prisoner was his son. Known as Aiden Balkus to Hanover, as well as to the soldiers watching over him, he was wanted by the Pentagon for what had been referred to as *"...treasonous actions that must remain top secret."* In spite of it, Hanover had taken Walter at his word that the U.S. Army's latest overseas prisoner was vital to the Latvian war effort.

Hanover had unwittingly helped him in another way. During their phone call, he had said offhandedly, *"Why on earth they chose to put him in the old military base outside Klaipeda, I'll never know."* Walter frowned. He knew why. *Because whoever is behind this wants to kill my son...in secret.* He flinched. *And Martin knew that.*

But Martin had chosen to go in spite of it. He had claimed that not only did he need to save the psychiatrist, Dr. James Samuels, who had been kidnapped by a man named Gad, but he had a score to settle, as well. Walter wasn't sure with whom, but he had good reason to think that it was Edward Morningstar. Before Martin's attempt to kill himself, he had left a note that had implicated Morningstar in a number of illegal schemes. When Walter had later confronted Martin with the note, his son had told him that he had written it in error; that he had overreacted, and Walter should just 'let it go.' *Fat chance,* Walter thought, convinced that Morningstar was the Pentagon advisor who had put the 'do not touch' warning on his son.

If Morningstar was, in fact, behind his son's imprisonment, or if the man had played a role in even one of the events that Martin had laid out in his letter, then he needed to be brought before a military tribunal, exposed for his crimes, and thrown in jail, or maybe even shot, depending on the severity of what he had done. Walter narrowed his eyes. *I'll deal with Morningstar once I have Martin safely away from that Klaipeda military base.*

But saving Martin's life wasn't the only reason that Walter felt compelled to free him. Walter had learned just twenty-four hours ago that Lili Platacis, the sweet girl who had practically become a member of the Henderson family, was alive. She had been kidnapped in January and, after months of searching by both the Hendersons and a close friend, Danil Latkovskis, it was presumed that she was dead. Martin had told Walter that he felt responsible; that it had been his actions that had led to her death. He had also told Walter that, because of it, his own life held little meaning. *"I've done enough damage, Dad...just let me go."*

But now Walter knew that Lili was alive. That fact had been confirmed by two letters he had received yesterday afternoon. Though the dates on the letters suggested that they had been written weeks apart, they had arrived together, somehow salvaged from a garbage bin outside Beijing's Great Hall. An American double agent had been the one to find them, and he had given them to a Latvian soldier who was in China monitoring the Henderson's affairs. The unlikely chain of events had seemed farfetched, and, at first, Walter had wondered if the letters had been some sort of disinformation campaign. But once he had read them, there had been no doubt not only that they had come from Lili, but that she had written them with the utmost sincerity. It was clear that she wasn't doing well; she was frightened, weak, and lonely. But she had said that she wasn't alone, that she had a friend with her, an older woman, who Walter would try to save, as well. *They'll be extracted as a team,* he thought, as he stared again at the setting sun...*and Martin must help me do it.*

Why Martin? For one reason, to alleviate his son's unrelenting guilt over what had happened to Lili. For another, Martin's skills – acquired over the last four years – would be undeniably helpful for the task at hand. If Lili's letters were accurate, then they were about to go up against a ruthless Chinese military machine. Walter's conventional methods would be of little use in such a fight. As a matter of fact, it might be best if Martin carried out the operation alone. Not only did Walter have his own war to fight in Latvia, but he was old...*too old to be mixing it up with a nation like China.*

But freeing Martin wasn't the only thing on Walter's mind. Just hours before Martin had left for Lithuania, Secret Service Agent Tom Cravens had given Walter a briefcase he had found in a town square in Lyon, France. The briefcase belonged to Walter, but he had been forced to leave it behind when Cobra had kidnapped him and Senator Madison back in March. Cravens, who had been assigned to find the senator, had recognized a unique emblem on the briefcase and had elected to hold onto it rather than turn it over to French authorities. His goal had been to figure out who it belonged to, then return it to the owner. But the case had no identifying marks other than the initials JH, and had been secured with a fingerprint and a numerical code. Cravens had known that he couldn't get past the security measures, so, in a fit of desperation, had asked a former criminal by the name of Shaw to open the case to learn who it belonged to. He had then instructed Shaw to forget that he had ever seen the briefcase or Cravens. Why Shaw? Because according to Cravens, the man was a reformed safecracker who now worked for MI6. *"I can break into about anything, Tommy,"* he had told Cravens once he had heard what Cravens wanted him to do. He had succeeded, which was how Cravens had known the briefcase belonged to Walter.

The problem was that the contents of the briefcase, which Shaw had clearly seen, was top secret, intended only for the eyes of a small group of men who formed an elite organization known as the Morning Star. Their name was based on the words *"Der Morgenstern,"* which were written on the side of a unique airship that had been discovered soon after World War II. The Nazi war vessel possessed technology far beyond anything anyone had ever dreamed of, and the men of the Morning Star felt it their duty to ensure that the ship never fell into the wrong hands. The contents of the briefcase – 22 drawings of constellations as seen from around the world – would, according to Walter's father, someday be vital to protecting the ship. Walter's fear was that by pulling in Shaw, the drawings were now compromised. Though Cravens had vouched for Shaw based on some naïve notion that '...*my gut has never led me astray,*' Walter felt a pressing need to find Shaw and at least debrief him regarding the drawings. Because Shaw had claimed to work for MI6, Walter had reached out to England's former ambassador, Arthur Kauffold, a fellow member of the Morning Star who just happened to be good friends with the top man at MI6. Kauffold had agreed to look into the matter and call him back. That had been about thirty-six hours ago.

In the meantime, the psychiatrist, Dr. Samuels, had arrived at the Henderson castle yesterday afternoon, after being freed from the kidnapper, Gad. Which meant that Martin's efforts to free the man had been successful. But the poor doctor had been with Gad for a full day-and-a-half, and had been forced to spend nearly all of that time strapped to a rigid wooden chair. *"Except for a car ride to some military base in the middle of nowhere,"* he had shared. Samuels had likely been referring to the abandoned base in Klaipeda, but had been blindfolded for most of the car ride, and was unable to provide clues as to where it was or what it looked like. Thankfully, Hanover had given Walter the information with his offhand comment about Klaipeda.

Samuels had clearly been exhausted both physically and mentally, so Dora had immediately stepped in to comfort him, leaving little time for the two men to talk. Samuels did manage to reiterate the claim that he had made months ago, however, that Cobra was somehow involved in the war in Latvia. He hadn't elaborated, only to say – again – that he had gotten the information from Cobra's alter ego, Mark Justice.

Which was another concern that was keeping Walter on edge. Probably the best kept secret on the planet was that the killer known around the world as Cobra was actually Mark Villamor, Walter's biological son with his mistress, Nenita. She had informed Walter as she lay dying in Dalgety

Bay that their son had two distinct personalities; a killer who the world knew as Cobra, and a respected investigator, Mark Justice. She had begged Walter to save the better of the two.

The entire concept had seemed unfathomable, but the psychiatrist, Samuels, had told him that it was true, and that he had witnessed the transformation between the two egos himself. *"It's referred to as Dissociative Identity Disorder, Walter, and I assure you, it is very real."* According to the psychiatrist, Mark was actually a conglomeration of three separate personalities. The first, Walter's son Mark, seemed to be stuck at the age of eleven or twelve, while the second, Cobra, was a killer, and the third was the respected private inquiry agent, Mark Justice, who lived and worked in London. It was that man who Nenita had wanted Walter to somehow save.

In an effort to meet Justice without Cobra being aware, Walter had invited Justice to a coin show in Aberdeen, Scotland. The reason he had chosen the coin show was because Dr. Samuels had told him that Justice shared his interest in old coins. The psychiatrist felt certain that Cobra would detest anything to do with coins, as he would consider them to be a tie between Walter and the boy, Mark; a tie that he would surely resent. *"I think if you want a good shot at getting Justice to go somewhere that Cobra wouldn't go, then a coin show would be a good choice."*

The goal was for Walter to lure Justice to the show, and somehow empower the Justice ego to triumph over the other two, thereby banishing the boy, Mark, and the killer Cobra forever. But Walter had no illusions. Even if he was to somehow compel Justice to become the dominant personality, the man – in his role as Cobra – had committed terrible atrocities. He would need to be held accountable. Walter's hope was that the authorities might at least spare Cobra's life once they saw that he did, in fact, possess another personality with far more reputable qualities. Though Justice would be imprisoned for the rest of his days, at least he would be alive.

Walter flinched. *And Cobra will be dead and gone...as will any evidence that he and I are related...or that I have hidden that fact for all of his adult life.* He ran his hands through his hair and sighed. *So, get on with it, Walter.*

Assuming he was able to free Martin tonight, his hope was to meet with Justice tomorrow at the coin show, compel him to become the dominant ego, then return to Latvia in time to either join Martin on his journey to China, or at least see him off before he left.

But the timing couldn't be worse. The meeting with Justice had been set up months ago, before the war in Latvia, or Martin's capture by U.S. soldiers, or the discovery that Lili was alive but struggling in a Chinese prison. And though Walter was tempted to forgo the coin show and meet Justice at a different time and place, he couldn't bring himself to do it. He felt an urgency to replace Cobra with Justice. *The sooner that Cobra is no longer a part of this world – or my life – the better.*

Walter looked over at his head of security, Dimitri Kauss. Though Dimitri had barely slept in the last forty-eight hours, he didn't show it. He seemed fresh and ready to go. The same couldn't be said for Walter. He hadn't slept well in weeks, and it was definitely starting to show. He saw it whenever he looked in the mirror. Again, he looked at Dimitri. Thirty years younger than Walter, the man had fewer wrinkles, brighter eyes, and a vigilance that defied fatigue. *Oh, the joys of youth,* Walter thought as he closed his eyes and leaned his head against the seat.

But again, it was no use. There was no way he was going to get a single wink of sleep in that car. Especially in light of the fact that he – the respected patriarch of the Hendersons of Boston – was about to break his son out of a jail cell that had been commandeered by the U.S. Government. He had asked Hanover to try to get 'Aiden Balkus' released under Walter's protection, but Hanover had had no success. *"Somebody at the Pentagon has put a 'do not touch' order on the guy, Walter. Whoever this Balkus guy is, they want him pretty bad."*

There was a day when Walter could have simply called the President – his good friend, Jim Wilcox – and asked him to pull a few strings, but those days were gone. Wilcox had been assassinated just over two months ago, and the new President was pretty much a stranger to Walter. As a matter of fact, President Knight was a stranger to most in DC. *How that man rose so fast to be President is beyond me.*

The news that the U.S. President had gone into hiding had shocked the world. In the nearly 230 years of America's republic, such a thing had never occurred. The acting President, Vice-President Harrington, had implied that the President's life had been threatened. Walter had found that to be a woefully inadequate explanation for the man's disappearance. A President's life was always being threatened, wasn't it?

Walter shook his head and sighed. It was no use. He sat up, rubbing his eyes as if that would somehow erase the need for sleep. The sun was setting over the Baltic Sea to the west, casting heavy shadows on the highway. He was glad for the sunset. Breaking a man out of prison would surely be easier in the dark.

He looked over his shoulder at a black, oversized suitcase, which had been filled with everything they would need. Two semi-automatic rifles, a supply of grenades, and several flares to serve as a distraction. There was also a coat and scarf for Martin, along with two hooded sweatshirts, two black ski caps that covered all but the eyes and mouth, and two bullet-proof vests. He checked his watch. Seven p.m. His goal was to have Martin out of that jail and back at the castle by midnight.

"Shall I turn here, Mr. Henderson?"

Walter leaned forward and looked for landmarks. He spotted a familiar lake by the side of the road that was about a kilometer from the Lithuanian border. "No, go ahead and cross, Dimitri. We'll wait until we reach route A13 in Lithuania before we start heading west."

Dimitri nodded and drove on toward the border. He reached it a few minutes later, and showed both of their passports at the checkpoint. They were waved through. It wasn't long before they came to A13. Dimitri made the turn and headed west.

As Dimitri drove, Walter looked again at the sun, which had become little more than a hazy red ball over the horizon. It was breathtaking as it reflected on the Baltic Sea. *We're getting close,* he thought, which was confirmed when he spotted a sign that said, "Klaipeda 50 kilometers." He turned to Dimitri. "Are you sure you want to go through with this? You don't have to, you know."

Dimitri looked at him and frowned. "Sir, I will do whatever it takes to get your nephew out of that prison."

Walter smiled. Men like Dimitri were rare. Walter had been fortunate to have several men like Dimitri in his life...loyal, reliable, capable. "Thank you," he said with a nod. He then spent the next few minutes going over the precise details for how they were going to break Martin out of the military prison. As he finished, he looked at Dimitri and frowned. "Well, what do you think?"

Dimitri nodded. "It is a solid plan, sir. I'm sure it will go off without a hitch."

Walter nodded, but as they grew ever closer to the turnoff for Klaipeda, he doubted very much that it would go off without a hitch. All he could pray was that by the time the sun came up tomorrow, his son would once again be at his side.

CHAPTER 7

London, England

Cobra opened his eyes slowly and rubbed his temples. His head was killing him. As his eyes adjusted to the dim light from a lantern sitting on a nearby table, he sat up and looked around. *What the hell happened?* He was in his lair; that much he could tell. But he had no idea how long he had been in the small London flat. The last thing he remembered was getting on the train in Barcelona, Spain, Wednesday night. He checked a clock by his bed and frowned. *Seven p.m. ...but is it Thursday? Friday? Dear god, I hope it's not Saturday. I'm supposed to be on my way to America.*

He looked for his watch, which would have the date. He found it lying on the floor. As he strapped it on his wrist, he nodded with relief. Friday, October 29th. He wasn't to leave town until Saturday the 30th. But he had lost a full two days.

He ran his fingers through his long black hair and sighed. It wasn't the first time that he had lost time. It had happened many times over the course of the last few years, and always it was the same. He would wake up, usually in a hostel or a strange hotel, and would have no idea what had transpired during the time that he had lost.

At least this time he had wound up in his own home. The cozy lair that sat beneath the banks of the River Thames had been his home for years. And though it was small, it was big enough to hold all that mattered. A few disguises, a narrow bed, and a trunk full of clothes. He stood and was about to walk outside to relieve himself, when he caught sight of a two-foot-square corkboard hanging on the wall behind his bed. He smiled. He had had the board for years. He used it to hold souvenirs; mementos from the tasks he had completed. Photos, pieces of clothing, locks of hair...fond reminders of the good work he had done over the years. He let out a deep sigh as he felt his shoulders relax. Those treasures soothed him.

He walked over to the board. The first item that caught his eye was a nylon ribbon that had marked the page of the Bible verse that he had read to Lida Mae McLeod as he had bled her dry in her cottage in Donegal. He chuckled as he recalled the woman's defiance, followed by her submission as she came to terms with her fate. Next to the ribbon was a pair of stockings that he had taken from the beautiful French model, Adrienne Bergeron. They were charred and a bit torn, as they had been tucked in his pocket at Dalgety Bay, but they could still serve as an inspiration.

He continued his inspection, taken aback as his eyes fell upon a photo of a British aristocrat's daughter. It was hanging with several others across the top of the board. Though he couldn't recall when he had hung it there, he remembered well the day he had taken it. It had been in the middle of June at the Inverness train station. He had spotted the lovely girl with several other alluring young ladies, likely traveling to the northern islands of Scotland for holiday. Having his own fondness for the islands, Cobra had been tempted to accompany her, but, as he had been about to get a ticket for her train, he had realized that CIA Agent Roger Clarkson was hot on his heels. Though he would have enjoyed getting to know the noble lady, he had been forced to make do with a photo.

But when did I put her picture on my wall? Out of nowhere, he was stunned by an awareness that, just maybe, Tonna and that same CIA agent were more than friends. Not only did he remember them dancing together at the Queen's Ball, but now, suddenly, somewhere in his psyche, he was seeing them, not at the Queen's Ball, but huddled closely together on a bench in back of a castle somewhere outside Chesham. Where was the memory coming from? *Justice?* he wondered with a turn of his lip. "Who cares," he hissed as he brushed over the photo with his fingers. *This photo has just become a very powerful card that I will play when the time is right.* For now, he would focus on the CIA agent who had followed him across Europe for the past eight months, and had managed to put a bullet in him more than once. He flinched and rubbed his thigh where one of those bullets had nearly killed him. He sneered. "Not only are your days numbered, my dear Roger, but you will soon learn that your lover's days are numbered, as well." He laughed. "So put that in your pipe and smoke it."

He walked to the door. He stepped outside to air that was cool and damp. He breathed in, smiling as he relieved himself off to the side. He looked up at the stars and pondered the task ahead. He would soon complete his final mission for the man who called himself Jacob. Once it was done, he would be given the castle that was his birthright; the Henderson castle that sat tall, majestic, and veiled in the trees along the coast of the Baltic Sea. He had imagined a hundred times how his life would change once he took charge of that castle. *So many wrongs will be made right.*

He zipped his pants, wincing as his hand brushed his thigh where the CIA agent had put a bullet in him. Roger would be his first target of revenge. Cobra hadn't laid eyes on Roger since Dalgety Bay. But there was no doubt the agent was still after him; he had felt his presence chasing him on the moors, stalking him over Scotland's highland rises and beyond. As a matter of fact, he could feel his presence now. He scanned the area around the wharf. *Are you out there, Roger, just waiting for me?* He laughed. *That poor boy won't stop hunting me until one of us is dead.*

Which was just one more reason why Cobra's takeover of the castle was so important. It would give him a bit of credibility as he battled the likes of Roger. Yes, Cobra had spent much of his life as a killer, but he would soon be the respectable owner of a castle on the coast. From his bulwark by the sea, he would set the record straight. He would start by having Walter Henderson tell the world all that Walter had done to Mark Villamor to make his life a living hell...*beginning with that damn boarding school.* How good it would feel to avenge the boy who had lived a life of deprivation, while his half-brother Martin had been given the life of a prince.

But I can't do any of it until I kill a Chinese military leader's son, along with a United States senator, he thought as he walked back inside. Though he would enjoy killing the Chinese leader's son, he would find it especially gratifying to kill the American. Cobra hated Americans. They seemed so confident, so self-assured...*and so goddamned optimistic.* He bristled. *Good to bring 'em down a peg, I say.*

It was the mission in China that had compelled him to come home after his failed attempt to kill Hank Clarkson. Cobra had no idea why Morningstar had wanted Hank dead, or why he had suddenly changed his mind just as Cobra had been about to kill the man; he didn't care. All that mattered now was to get the castle.

He walked to his bed and was all at once overcome with weakness; a sudden heaviness that seemed to take over his entire body. His knees buckled and he fell onto the bed. He hadn't felt well since leaving Spain. He couldn't recall ever having been sick; it made him nervous. He had lost strength, stamina...even his wit. *I must've caught a bug,* he thought. Which was what he had been telling himself ever since he had left Barcelona some sixty-odd hours ago.

He laid there with his eyes closed. After another minute or two, he felt his strength returning. *Probably just a lack of sleep,* he thought as he stood up slowly. He put his hand against the wall to steady himself, and took several deep breaths.

Once he felt like himself again, he reached under the bed for his suitcase. As he laid it on the bed, he tried to think how long it had been since he had been to America. *Twelve years.* His father's mansion in Boston had been his last stop in the overrated country, and he had vowed to never go back. *Why couldn't the senator meet me in London?* he wondered. He frowned. He knew the answer. If he was to be taken seriously as the senator's bodyguard, he would need to start the journey with the man.

Whatever, he thought as he reviewed the details of his assignment. It would be no easy feat. He was to kill Tai Chu, the son of a Chinese military leader. Protection for the boy – who was actually a 32-year-old man – would surely be impressive. Cobra hoped to gain access to the young man by using the authority of the senator that Cobra had been assigned to escort to China, Charles Sturgill. Then it would be a simple matter of poisoning Tai Chu's tea. *Snake venom, perhaps?*

He laughed. As he did so, his hand brushed over his pocket. There was something in it. He reached in and pulled out a handwritten note. He read it through. He was baffled. Though he had no recollection of doing so, he must have gone to the safe deposit box that Morningstar had told him about, where he was to find details of his assignment. The note was a justification for Tai Chu's murder. It stated that Senator Sturgill – on behalf of the U.S. Government – had killed the man in retaliation for *"...unfair* trade practices, human rights abuses, and the persecution of millions of Uyghurs. The murder of Tai Chu represents our first strike in an effort to stifle your imperialism." Cobra laughed. That oughta stir things up.

Jacob had told him that once Tai Chu was dead, Cobra was to kill Sturgill, as well, in order to ensure his silence. "Make it look like a murder-suicide sort of thing." Cobra grinned. He wouldn't need to kill Sturgill; the guards would do it the second they concluded that it was he who had poisoned the boy's tea. The tea would kill Chu, the guards would kill Sturgill, then Cobra would kill the guards. He laughed aloud. Not only was he about to kill again, but the actions he would take over the next several days would likely start a world war. I'll be even more famous than I am now.

He returned the note to his pocket, then checked the other pockets to see what else he might have picked up during his time 'away.' He found a passport and a credit card. He took a quick look at the passport. "Agent Daniel Frisk," he read aloud. He looked at the photo. Cropped blonde hair, blue eyes, dark-framed glasses. He nodded. He already had the blue contacts and the dark-framed glasses. The only thing he would need to buy would be the blond hair dye, which he could pick up on his way to the train station.

He stared at the passport. Except for his olive skin, Daniel Frisk was almost an exact replica of his half-brother, Martin. Why, we could be taken as twins, he thought with a chuckle. But unless things had changed, Martin's hair was now dark, and his jaw had been altered; first by a fire, then by a clever surgeon. Regardless, Cobra, who was, after all, a Henderson, shared many of the family traits: the broad forehead, the keen eyes, the quick smile. He flinched. The only feature I lack is the prestige.

He returned the passport to his pocket and packed a pair of shoes in his bag. As he was about to throw in a change of clothes, he saw something lying next to the suitcase. He picked up a three-by-five pamphlet from the bed. "The Aberdeen Coin Show, Saturday, October 30th." He opened it. Inside was a list of times and events. Someone had written 'noon' next to an entry, "Coins from around the world." Cobra stared at it a minute longer, then tossed it on the bed. I must've picked it up while I was wandering the earth outside myself.

Though he had tried to convince himself that the loss of time didn't bother him, the truth was, it bothered him quite a bit. To know that hours, sometimes even days had passed, yet have no recall of what he had done or where he had been was unnerving. He took another look at the pamphlet. It would appear that this time, for whatever reason, he had gone to Aberdeen, Scotland...to the site of an upcoming coin show of all things.

Cobra hated coins; especially the sort that would be showcased at a coin show. Mark's father, the revered Walter Henderson, was fond of coins, and had foisted them on the young Mark Villamor to the point of annoyance... at least as far as Cobra was concerned. Not only did Cobra feel it was a tiresome pursuit, but he also believed it to be insincere; just a way for his father to try to buy his son's love. *A son's love doesn't come that cheaply,* he thought as he wadded up the pamphlet and threw it to the floor.

Big Ben rang out eight chimes. *Time to go.* But as he finished packing and zipped his suitcase, he found himself curious about what might be happening at noon tomorrow in Aberdeen, Scotland. He was tempted to go to the coin show and find out, but he couldn't; by tomorrow noon, he would be well on his way to America.

He took the toe of his boot and dug it into the crumpled pamphlet, tearing it. *I don't give a damn what's happening in Aberdeen. For soon, in spite of Clarkson's tireless pursuit, I'll fly to China, kill a military leader's son, and start a world war.*

He grabbed a pair of clippers and quickly cut his hair. He slid in the blue contacts, put on the dark-framed glasses, and tucked his shorter hair under a hat. He blew out the lantern and left the flat. As he locked the door and headed for the train station, he laughed. "Put that in your pipe and smoke it, Roger."

CHAPTER 8

Outside Klaipeda, Lithuania

A sliver of moonlight had just appeared in the window across the hall when Henderson heard the first blast. He had been lying on his cot, unable to close his eyes, knowing that at any minute he might need to run. His father had told him to be ready within the next twenty-four hours; that had been yesterday afternoon. The darkness outside was a clear indication that over twenty-four hours had passed, leaving Henderson to wonder if maybe Walter had failed in his efforts. But the minute he heard the blast, he knew...Walter hadn't failed. Walter never failed.

He sprang up from the cot and stood at the door. He waited. So far, there had been only the one blast. It had sounded like a grenade. He looked down the hall. There was no sign of the guard. *He's likely looking for the source of the blast.*

He continued to wait at the door. Suddenly, he heard what sounded like a scuffle, followed by the thud of someone falling to the floor. He waited, stunned when he saw a man wearing a ski mask run up to his cell. The mask covered the man's entire face, except for his eyes and mouth. Henderson backed away from the door. The man pulled off the mask. Henderson was stunned to see the castle's head of security, Dimitri Kauss. He was armed with a high-caliber rifle, and was wearing a bulletproof vest. He was holding a fob with a single key dangling from the end. He slid the key into the lock and turned. The door opened; Henderson ran out of the cell. "Where's Walter?" he asked as he looked in both directions down the hall.

"Follow me." Dimitri handed Henderson a jacket and scarf. "Put these on. It's cold out there. Cover your face with the scarf." He then handed him a pistol.

Henderson shoved the pistol in his pants, put on the coat, and wrapped the scarf over the lower half of his face. He followed Dimitri down the hall. It was dark; he was having a hard time seeing. Putting his hand on the back of Dimitri's bullet-proof vest, he stayed with him as he walked past the chair where the guard had been sitting. Henderson nearly tripped over the guard, who was lying motionless on the floor. They came to a door and stopped. Dimitri held his finger to his lips, then raised his rifle and put his ear to the door. After about thirty seconds, he kicked open the door and stepped into the night. Henderson followed him and they sprinted toward a black sedan parked at the far end of a parking lot. The car was running, and Henderson could see the silhouette of a man behind the wheel. They had nearly reached it, when they heard a gunshot. They knelt low and ran for shelter behind a row of dumpsters. Another shot was directed toward the car. The driver spun the car around and was about to drive to where they were hiding, when a third shot hit the back tire. The driver stopped, threw open the door, and jumped out of the car. He used the open door for cover, as gunshots were exchanged between him and the mystery shooter. Dimitri began firing in the direction of the shooter, giving the driver cover as he ran to the dumpsters where Henderson and Dimitri were hiding. As he drew closer, Henderson was able to see that it was his father.

"Jesus, Dad, what the hell are you doing?"

"Getting you out of jail. Now, come on."

The shooting had stopped, which meant that the shooter – probably the second guard – was moving closer. Walter led the way as the three men ran zigzagged from the dumpsters to a thick row of trees that bordered the parking lot. They had nearly reached the trees, when more shots filled the silence. Dimitri fell to the ground. Henderson ran back, grabbed him under his arms, and carried him into the trees.

"Where were you hit?" Henderson asked, as he laid the man on the ground.

"My...my leg...just below my knee."

Henderson looked at the leg. Blood was spurting from the man's calf. Henderson pulled off his scarf and tied it like a tourniquet just above the wound. "Let's go."

He helped Dimitri stand and, with Dimitri's arm over his shoulder and his arm around the man's waist, they ran deeper into the forest, far more comfortable among the trees than they were on open ground. In spite of

Dimitri's injury, they made good time as they followed a barely visible path through the trees. The sun had set hours ago, but the half-moon was bright, giving them enough light to avoid the roots and rocks that littered the ground.

After about fifteen minutes, they came to a break in the trees, and Henderson was able to see the ocean less than twenty feet away. A motorboat was moored to a large rock. With Walter in the lead, the three men ran for the boat. Walter dislodged the rope, while Henderson helped Dimitri onto a seat at the back. Walter shoved the boat deeper into the water, then jumped aboard and turned on the engine. They glided in the darkness, the halfmoon their only light as they headed northwest away from the coast. Henderson grabbed Dimitri's rifle and held it ready as he looked back, guessing that the second soldier had followed them to the coast.

That fact was soon confirmed with a sudden volley of gunshots. One hit the rim of the boat. Walter yelled, "Hold on!" then zigzagged the boat as he sped north toward the open sea. Henderson fired into the trees, and the back-and-forth continued for another minute or two. Suddenly, the shooting stopped. Had Henderson hit the soldier? Maybe killed him? Another good man who had to die so he could live? Or had they simply gotten far enough away that the man's bullets no longer reached?

Henderson continued to hold the gun steady as he watched the Baltic coastline fade in the darkness. He looked back at Dimitri, who had his leg propped on the side of the boat. Though the air was cold, Henderson could see the sheen of sweat on the man's brow. He was glad it wasn't far to the Henderson compound by sea; less than an hour if the water wasn't too rough.

He walked back and knelt next to Dimitri. "Well, that was easy enough."

Dimitri forced a chuckle, as Walter looked up from the tiller of the boat and shook his head. "That's one way to look at it." He frowned. "You okay, Dimitri?"

Dimitri nodded. "I am fine, sir. Nothing but a flesh wound."

Henderson knew that it was more than a flesh wound. Again, he was glad they were close to home. He turned to Walter. "Won't that soldier be able to identify the Henderson car?"

Walter nodded. "Yes, if we had used a Henderson car. Which is why we swapped cars in Klaipeda. We parked the Henderson car at one of the nicer hotels in town. No one would think twice about a BMW in the lot of that hotel."

"But how did you know this boat would be here?"

Dimitri puffed out his chest. "That was my idea. I had one of the guards bring it down about an hour ago. I told him to dock it about twelve miles north of Klaipeda, which was about two miles from the military base. Earlier in the day, another guard had, um, 'borrowed' an unregistered Buick from a used car lot outside Uzava. I had him drive it to the docked boat, where he picked up the first guard, then drove the Buick to the hotel, where we swapped it with the BMW."

Walter added, "The Buick was what we drove to the military base."

Henderson nodded. "Not bad. But what do we do now?"

Walter looked at him and frowned. "What do you mean?"

"I'm clearly a fugitive of the United States Government."

Walter shrugged. "You've been a fugitive for the past four years, son."

Henderson looked at his father, wondering if he realized he had just referred to Henderson as his son, and also wondering if Dimitri had picked up on it.

As if in confirmation, Dimitri, who had been staring at the blood-soaked scarf on his leg, looked up, his eyes wide. He looked first at Henderson, then at Walter.

Walter nodded. "I need you to keep it to yourself, Dimitri, but at this point it's probably best that you know the truth."

Even in the darkness, Henderson could see Dimitri's eyes fill with tears. He turned to Henderson, staring in disbelief as he whispered, "Are you... Martin?"

Henderson nodded. "I am."

"How did you—"

"It's a long story, Dimitri. I'll fill you in once we get back to the compound."

Dimitri said, "Forgive me, sir, but—" Suddenly, in spite of his wounded leg, he stood awkwardly, and reached over and hugged Henderson.

The boat bobbled with the movement, and Henderson grabbed the sides to stabilize it. He gave Dimitri a quick hug, then eased him back onto the seat. "You're gonna overturn the damn boat, Dimitri," he said with a grin. "Now sit down and keep your leg up...I don't want to have to clean your grimy blood off of this boat."

Dimitri laughed as he resumed his position on the seat with his leg propped on the side. Henderson knelt beside him, and the three men rode the rest of the way in silence. As the familiar landscape that blanketed the hidden estate came into view, Henderson said, "What about Dr. Samuels, Dad? Did he make it to the compound?"

Walter nodded. "He did." He turned the boat toward the shoreline and killed the engine. As they eased into the dock, he added, "And he's got quite a story to tell."

Henderson frowned. "About his kidnapping?"

Walter jumped out and Henderson tossed him the tie rope. He wrapped it around a hitch, then knotted it several times. He and Henderson helped Dimitri out of the boat, carrying him between them as they crossed the rocky beach to a path that was marked with a tall boulder. The path itself was well-hidden by a thick grove of trees, and, going one at a time, they slid around the boulder and onto the path. With Dimitri once again between them, they started down the path that led to the barracks behind the castle. When they had gotten within a hundred yards, Walter looked at Henderson and frowned. "Not only about the kidnapping, son, but about the ties between this war that we're fighting," he grimaced, "...and a killer named Cobra."

CHAPTER 9

London, England

Finally, I'm getting close to that bastard. CIA Agent Roger Clarkson sprinted through an alley as he tried to recall exactly what he had been told. *"I saw a man – 'e mighta' been Cobra – runnin' toward the River Thames about two hours ago, I did."* The witness, a clerk from a local haberdashery, had reached out to the police after he had spotted a man who looked like Cobra running past the front of the shop earlier that afternoon. The police had called Scotland Yard, and Chief Inspector Pritchard had immediately called Roger. The two men had become close as a result of their quest to bring down the killer, along with their shared rage at the number of innocent lives he had taken. It had been good to hear from Pritchard. He had been on leave ever since Dalgety Bay, and had only just gotten back to work. To think that he was able to give Roger a clue to find Cobra had been gratifying...likely for both of them.

Though the Yard could have sent a team of officers to follow up on the clue, Pritchard had told Roger that he had come to appreciate the CIA's approach of having one man, laser-focused, pursuing the killer. For one thing, a single agent would be harder for Cobra to spot; for another, Roger's sole purpose was to bring in Cobra, preferably alive.

Fortunately, Roger had already been in London, having received a tip the day before from a fellow CIA agent stating that he had seen a man who resembled Cobra stepping off a train on London's south side. The location was also near the River Thames, which meant that Cobra had been spotted twice in the same area. Was his home somewhere nearby? If so, it might be a chance for Roger to get a glimpse inside the man's most personal space.

He had immediately reached out to the shop owner, and was able to narrow the location to a one-mile sector at the south end of the river. With his collar zipped to his chin and a stocking cap over his hair and forehead, he ran through parks and down alleyways, making sure to keep to the shadows. He came to a road that ran alongside the Thames and followed it south, uneasy the further he got from downtown. The area was rough and remote, with homes and businesses located far apart from one another. He kept on, nearly missing an unmarked door wedged beneath the bank. Cobra's lair? It seemed an odd place for it; then again, what better place for a snake to hide than under a riverbank.

He positioned himself behind two thick oak trees and stared at the door. He was cold and tired, but most of all, he was frustrated. He hadn't had an actual sighting for months; not since he had confronted Cobra in the Dalgety Bay schoolhouse back in March. Cobra had been straddling Matt Henderson with a knife in his hand ready to strike. Roger had shot him in the shoulder just as he had been about to land the fatal blow. Cobra had fled, running out of the school and up a hill into the trees. Once Roger had carried Henderson away from the burning schoolhouse, he had run up the hill after Cobra. The only way he had been able to track him was by the trail of death that Cobra had left behind. The first poor victim had been at a house not far from Dalgety Bay. Cobra had killed an old woman and had left her hanging from a tree. Roger had nearly run past her, but his eyes had been drawn to the woman when droplets of blood had fallen onto his forehead. Luckily, she had been the only one home, otherwise there would have been more bodies hanging from that tree. Cobra had then headed northwest, evidenced by three more murders along the way.

But then, the trail had gone cold. Roger hadn't heard or read of a Cobra-like kill for months. There had been two murders in Finland at the end of August that could have belonged to Cobra, but Roger had let them go. Not only would Finland be far from Cobra's normal hunting grounds, but the murders had taken place long enough ago that, even if they were Cobra kills, he doubted they would be of much help. Even so, he had asked the Finland authorities to keep him informed.

They had surprised him with a call two nights ago, saying that they had evidence not only linking Cobra to the murders, but possibly revealing what he had done and where he had gone afterward. Roger had been halfway across the North Sea to Finland when he had received the alert from the CIA agent that Cobra had been spotted getting off a train in the southern part of London. Roger had turned the boat around, had hopped a train, and had arrived in London late last night.

He shivered as he stood behind the two oak trees. He wrapped a scarf over the lower half of his face, and, grabbing his binoculars, scanned the area surrounding the wharf. It was an unsavory part of London, and, as he took it all in, it was a struggle to overlook the crimes taking place right before his eyes: trysts with prostitutes, drug buys, the endless shakedowns outside a nearby pub. He shook it off. He wasn't there to bust penny-ante crime...he was there to capture Cobra.

He pulled off his cap and ran his fingers through his hair. It had gotten so long. He did his best to pat down the curls he had hated all his life. He had gotten those curls from his father, Hank. He typically kept his hair short to hide them. But he had vowed after Dalgety Bay that he wouldn't cut it until he had captured Cobra. *At this rate, I'll soon be braiding it...like Ragnar.* He grinned as he thought of Ragnar Lothbrok Sigurdsson, the Viking farmer who killed evil King Froh in the late 700's. *That's me... Ragnar Clarkson.*

A truck drove by, disrupting his dreams of Viking glory, and he raised his binoculars and stared at the door across the road. He put on his hat and pulled on a pair of gloves. He took his gun from his pocket and stole across the street. Night had descended on the wharf, and the smells of the river were thick...diesel, brine, and the unmistakable odor of dead fish. There were few lampposts in that part of London, and a heavy mist was coming in off the river, making it even harder to see. He tripped over a rail tie, righting himself as he reached the door. He could feel the hair rising on the back of his neck. He took a quick look around. He knocked. No answer. He took a bump key from his pocket and slid it into the lock. He jiggled it, felt it come loose, then lifted the lock from the door. He opened the door, then stepped back and waited. Nothing. With his gun raised, he stepped inside. The place was pitch black. He was struck by the smell. *Mold.* He pulled out a flashlight and turned it on, holding it under the hand with the gun. With his back against the wall, he scanned the flat. It was little more than a hole in the wall. A single room with a sink on one side, a bed on the other, a chest under the bed. He walked to the bed, knelt down, and saw a pair of black boots next to the chest. He dragged the chest to the middle of the floor. He tried the lid; it was locked. He was about to pry it open, when he stopped. Cobra may have rigged it to either explode or release a toxin if forced open. He slid it back under the bed. *I'll leave it to the bomb specialists from the Yard.*

He heard the crackle of paper; he looked down. He had stepped on a wadded up piece of paper. He picked it up and unfolded it. It was a pamphlet. He frowned as he saw 'noon' penciled in off to the side. The date on the pamphlet said Saturday, October 30th. *Tomorrow.* Did it represent Cobra's next destination? He stiffened when he read that the Queen was coming. *I'll notify the Yard the minute I leave here.*

He memorized the information, then dropped the pamphlet where he had found it. He shone his light around the flat, flinching when he spotted a corkboard hanging on the back wall. He walked over to it and, as he got closer, he could feel his stomach start to turn. It was a wall of fame...Cobra's exploits hanging on a two-by-two corkboard. Photos, a pair of charred nylons, a ribbon from some sort of book. Would Roger recognize the items? Would he know who each one belonged to? It was likely. Even before he had begun to hunt Cobra, he had dedicated the better part of a year knowing everything about the killer. Not just his methods, but his prior murders, as well. But was Roger ready to see it hanging before him, especially the more recent ones...reminders of the number of times he had failed to stop the killer?

He held his breath. *You need to look, Roger.*

He raised the flashlight to the ribbon. Beside it was written, *"Lida Mae."* He remembered Lida Mae. Her murder was his first encounter with the killer. The old Irish woman, a former member of the IRA, had lain sprawled on the ground, her eyes wide in unmistakable terror. That ribbon had most likely belonged to the Bible that had been sitting not far from where she lay. Roger rubbed the back of his neck, then moved on to the next item. It was a pair of women's stockings. *Adrienne Bergeron?* he wondered, as he felt a lump in his throat. Roger had been kidnapped and locked in a cave by the time the French model had been murdered. He looked at the next item, a newspaper article decrying the tragic demise of

America's Secretary of State, Jane Harper. *"Killed with a simple blow dart, the respected diplomat had no idea what hit her."* Roger closed his eyes, recalling all too well the calamity at the Queen's Ball.

But then, in spite of all he had just seen, for a brief moment he lightened. He couldn't think of the Ball without thinking of Tonna Kauffold, the woman he had escorted to that same event to give him cover as he kept an eye out for Cobra. The mere thought of her made him smile. What was she doing on a Friday night in Oxford? *Likely having a drink with friends.* He sighed. He hadn't seen her in months. His pursuit of Cobra put anyone close to him in danger. Because of it, they had resorted to using carrier pigeons raised by a former spy who lived in London's East End. They had used the birds to exchange messages since March. Roger shook his head. He had had no time to even visit Hobbs to see if Tonna had sent him a reply. His last message had been sent over a month ago. *Roger, you need to go see Hobbs.*

He took a last glance at the board and decided he had seen enough. He was about to turn to leave, when his eyes fell on a row of photographs hanging across the top. He took another deep breath, then forced himself to look at them. They appeared to be mostly older crimes. A priest lying prostrate on the steps of the Vatican; a Saudi princess, clearly violated, her burqa pulled to her thighs as she lay at the foot of a mosque. All Cobra's exploits, hanging like prizes that one might display on a bedroom wall or in a high school yearbook. *Trophies for the hunter.*

Then he saw it. A photo he hadn't expected. It hung randomly at the right upper corner of the board. Roger stared at it, unable to look away as he moved closer, shone his light on it, then fell against the wall. It was a picture of a woman he knew well. Auburn hair, keen blue eyes. The photo had clearly been taken in a train station. *When?* he wondered as he felt his entire body start to shake. As he continued to lean against the wall, he rested his fingers gently on the photo, his heart breaking at the truth that was now staring him in the face. Tonna – his beautiful Tonna – was hanging on Cobra's wall.

CHAPTER 10

Warsaw, Poland

For probably about the twentieth time, Gad checked the time. It was almost ten p.m. *I have been at this damn airport for over twelve hours!* Gad had spent the night at the airport hotel, thinking he would leave Warsaw on a ten a.m. flight Friday morning for DC. But for whatever reason, the flight had been cancelled. He was told that it was because of *"...the situation in America."* It was then that he learned that the U.S. President had gone into hiding. Never had he heard of such a thing. *"What has that got to do with me flying to America?"* he had asked. The agent at the counter had merely shrugged, and had booked him on the next available flight, which wasn't scheduled to leave until midnight. It would get him to Washington, DC, by Saturday morning at four. He was to meet Michael Cannon at ten a.m. in Portland, Maine. It would be cutting it close, but it was his only option. From what he had been told, flights around the world had either been cancelled or rescheduled due to the disruption caused by the President's disappearance.

Gad had spent the day at the airport, eating, drinking, and thumbing through bullshit magazines. He skimmed through an issue of "Men's Health," irritated not only at how overpriced the magazine had been, but how utterly ridiculous the articles were. Finally, he reached the end and tossed the magazine onto a nearby table.

He stood and rubbed his eyes. He was tired. Though he had gotten a decent night's sleep, sitting in an airport all day was exhausting. And it had given him far too much time to think. The task in Maine was weighing on him. In spite of the fact that he had done plenty of terrible things in his time – he had actually gunned down an entire village in Argentina – never had he been asked to kidnap someone. *That shit's face to face,* he thought as he walked aimlessly through the airport. The fact that he was using a man's child as bait was even more of a challenge. In the jungle in Argentina, he was far enough away from those villagers that he couldn't really see them, except through the lens of his rifle scope. But with this assignment, he would be using a young girl to lure her father into a trap. Gad stiffened as he felt a pang of guilt. *Then what?* He sighed. *Then I do whatever it takes to get the man to cooperate.*

He shook his head. He knew what it felt like to not have a dad around. It left a child feeling incomplete. And though he had no intention of killing Michael Cannon, he knew, more likely than not, that was what it would come down to.

Tough shit, he thought, as he tried to think about something else. *Life's hard all around.* He stopped outside a book store and sighed. *Henderson... I'll think about how I captured Matt Henderson.* Gad had completed the task well; brilliantly, as a matter of fact. Using the psychiatrist, Samuels, to lure the guy to Lithuania had been a stroke of genius. He chuckled as he thought of the hapless Henderson suffering in a jail cell. He wondered how long it would be before Jacob would kill the man. He sighed. *Probably before I can get my ass on a plane out of here.*

He continued his walk down the hall. He was about to walk into a café to get another cup of coffee, when his phone vibrated. He walked to an alcove, opened the phone, and checked caller ID. He didn't recognize the number. He answered with a cautious "Hello?"

"It's me. Owen Collins...one of the soldiers who took custody of your prisoner in Vilnius."

Gad sneered. *Why am I still dealing with this shit?* "Why are you calling me?"

"Well...the mission was...um...pretty hush-hush, which means that you're my only contact."

Gad let out a sigh. *Great.* "Okay, so what's up, Owen?"

"Well...um, the prisoner...he just escaped."

CHAPTER 11

Rome, Italy

Hank rubbed his eyes; he was exhausted. Not only that; he was worried. He had been at Rome's airport for well over twenty-four hours, and over the course of the last twelve, he had tried to call Jenny's cellphone six times. Every time it had gone straight to voicemail. It had taken all he had had to even make the calls; he knew she would be upset with him when he told her – once again – that he wasn't coming home. But he had decided that it wasn't fair to simply leave her in the dark.

After the sixth attempt to reach her on her cell, he had tried the phone at his DC townhouse, knowing that she had planned on moving to the townhouse two months ago. There had been no answer there, either. He had even tried her home in Ohio, thinking maybe she had had a change of heart after he had ditched his plan to come home two nights ago. That phone line had been disconnected. He had left messages on the first two phone lines, but had yet to hear back from her. Though his last conversation with her Wednesday night hadn't gone well, he couldn't imagine that she was mad enough to not even answer his phone calls. She had, after all, been putting up with his change of plans for the past two months. *Actually,* he thought with a sigh, *she has been putting up with my change of plans for the last twenty years.*

He stretched his arms and leaned back in the stiff chair by his gate. He and Jenny had been through quite a lot over the last two decades. First, had been his decision to go into medicine soon after the birth of their child, which had left Jenny to keep things going with their home and family. Then, had been his decision to fall in love with another woman. Actually, that hadn't been a decision at all; it had simply been his fate. His love for Maddi hadn't been expected, nor had he wanted it. It had completely destroyed his marriage and wrecked his home.

But over the course of the last several months, triggered by Roger's near-death experience in Paris, he and Jenny had rekindled their relationship. And he loved her more now than he ever had before. *Now, if I can just get her to answer the phone!*

He rubbed the back of his neck and sighed. His flight to Beijing was scheduled to leave at midnight; they would begin boarding soon. He looked around the gate area. There were couples chatting, a mother reading to her child, a few people sleeping as they waited for the flight. *Which is probably what I should be doing.* But he couldn't sleep; not without knowing that Jenny was okay. He needed to call someone to at least check on her, but he had yet to speak to anyone – except her – since going AWOL over two months ago. Who could he call that wouldn't ask a million questions; questions he wasn't prepared to answer. He sighed. *There's no one.*

He ran his hands through his hair. Though he had cut it twice during the long journey through Europe, it was still longer than normal. *I need a haircut,* he thought as he stared at the mother with her child. *It'll be the first thing I do when I get home.*

He hadn't left the airport since last night, when he had decided to fly to China. The next two flights to Beijing had been completely full, leaving him with this flight. But waiting had given him plenty of time to worry, not only about why Maddi had gone to China, but where Jenny might have gone...*and why she won't take my calls.*

Yes, it was possible that she was just mad at him for changing his mind about coming home, but he found it hard to believe that she would simply ignore him; it wasn't in her nature. If nothing else, she would worry about the number of times he had tried to call. Even after the divorce, they had stayed in touch. In spite of all Hank had put her through, there had never been a time when Jenny hadn't taken his calls.

He rubbed his temples. *Something's wrong...I can feel it.*

He sat up as they announced the first call for boarding. He gathered his things, what little there were. He had been a vagabond for the last two-and-a-half months, leaving the Henderson compound with nothing more than the clothes on his back and his wallet. Along the way, he had bought a backpack, three pairs of underwear, two pairs of pants, and a few shirts; that was it. And that ensemble had taken him across six countries – now seven – and had seen him through three youth hostels and about ten hotels. He threw the pack over his shoulder and walked to the line of passengers preparing to board the plane. He opened his trac phone and tried Jenny one more time, squeezing the phone when he heard the call go to voicemail. He shoved the phone in his pocket and inched closer to the counter.

He reached the agent, who smiled warmly. "Have a good flight, sir," she said in Italian. Hank gave her a weak smile and nodded. But as he walked down the jet bridge to the plane, he took a deep breath and sighed. He wasn't going to have a good flight; he wasn't going to have a good anything...*until I know that both Maddi and Jenny are safe.*

CHAPTER 12

Washington, DC

"Tell him to call me the minute he gets out of his meeting. I represent the Chairman of the Joint Chiefs of Staff, and it is urgent that I speak with the acting President at once!"

Edward Morningstar slammed down the receiver. He had been trying to reach Vice-President Harrington – the acting President – for the past six hours, but the man had refused to take his calls. Though it was plausible that Harrington was legitimately distracted by all that had gone on in the last forty-eight hours, it was no excuse to ignore the top aide to the top general of the United States Military.

He paced his small office as he waited to hear back. A lot had happened in the forty-eight hours since his soldier son, Judah – President Jerome Knight – had decided to go AWOL. Not only had the country essentially gone into lockdown, but the efforts that had been underway to confiscate the peoples' guns had come to a halt. It had baffled him. If anything, the need to keep the people from rising up was greater now than it had been before Knight had left the White House. But the cabinet secretary overseeing the task had insisted. *"We can't occupy ourselves with an unpopular confiscation when there's a threat to the President that is so grave that he felt compelled to go into hiding."* Though Morningstar had been tempted to tell the secretary to go to hell, he had refrained, knowing that as an aide, he was in no position to challenge the authority of a cabinet secretary.

But Judah's antics weren't the only thing occupying his mind. His soldier son, Gad, had somehow managed to get Joseph – Martin Henderson – secretly jailed in an abandoned base outside Klaipeda, Lithuania. Morningstar needed to find a way to get to him and kill him once and for all. He had it all planned. A quick trip to Lithuania to question the prisoner, followed by the discovery that the man was unfortunately already dead. *"He must have died from a heart attack, General."*

But finding the time to make that trip was proving difficult. Not only did Morningstar have Knight's disappearance to deal with, but Dr. Hank Clarkson had once again gone missing. Two nights ago, Clarkson – Homeland's Deputy Director – had had a one-way ticket to DC on a ten-p.m. flight out of Madrid, Spain. For whatever reason, he had changed his mind. *Why? Why would a man who's been away for over two months, suddenly bail on his plan to fly home?*

Morningstar had arranged for one of his sons to meet Hank at the DC airport with orders to then get rid of the man. Though Cobra had been about to kill Hank that same morning, Morningstar had pulled him from the task. Why? For one reason, Cobra had indicated that the kill would be messy, which meant that it would draw a lot of attention, which would ultimately entail an investigation. That was the last thing Morningstar needed. The second reason was that Cobra's unique skill set was needed to carry out a far more important mission in China, and the timetable was tight. So, Morningstar had told Cobra to stand down, and had counted on Hank's return to the U.S. as a way to finally get rid of the irksome Homeland Security agent.

Hank had been a thorn in Morningstar's side for over a year. He had been on a committee that Morningstar had pulled together in February of 2003. The events of 9-11 were still fresh in everyone's minds, and Morningstar had portrayed the committee as a way to unite factions of the U.S. Government in an effort to prevent another attack. But the true purpose had been for Morningstar to obtain information that he otherwise wouldn't have access to. But as he had acted on the intelligence that he had received from each of the members, he had begun to see that it would soon be obvious to at least a few of them that something nefarious was going on within the committee. His solution: to systematically kill off each member, making their murder look like either an accident or a suicide.

Hank was the only one left of the eight-member committee, other than Morningstar. The minute Hank realized that, Morningstar's entire operation would be in jeopardy. *Which is why the man must die.*

But when Hank didn't show at the airport, Morningstar had been forced to reach out to another one of his sons, Reuben, more commonly referred to as Pocks. Pocks was still in London, where he had sabotaged Cynthia Madison's plane before her fateful flight to Latvia. Though the poor boy was still struggling with his guilt over the tragedy, he had agreed to help find Hank. *"Start in Spain, Pocks...in Madrid. It's his last known location. Call me when you find him. I'll take it from there."* Morningstar would then give Simeon the task of actually killing Hank.

But it had occurred to Morningstar that, in spite of their agreement, Pocks might balk on the mission. He had proven to be a weak man with an even weaker constitution. Morningstar had decided, at the very least, he would need a backup plan.

Which was when, in a flash of genius, he had called on his newest son, Issachar, a former Philadelphia police officer, to address the matter from an entirely different angle. That plan was currently underway, and Morningstar expected to hear from Issachar anytime now. He chuckled. *That should make things interesting.*

Either way, whether it was Pocks who found Hank and Simeon who killed him, or whether Issachar's plan was ultimately successful, soon Hank Clarkson would either be very preoccupied, or he would be dead.

Morningstar chuckled as he stopped at the window of his Pentagon office and looked out at the fading sunlight. *Bye bye, Hank.* But suddenly the chuckle turned to a scowl. It had been a full two days since Judah had pulled his disappearing stunt. "Whoever heard of such a thing?" Morningstar hissed as he stared at the deepening shadows. Fortunately, he had come up with a way to at least get Knight's attention. But he couldn't do that until Harrington – the patsy who was filling in for Knight – called him back. *Once I gain control of this country, I'm going to send that man to—*

His office phone rang. He walked to the desk and lifted the receiver. "Morningstar here."

"Yes, Mr. Morningstar. It's President Harrington. You wanted to talk to me?"

Acting President, you dumbass. "Yes, thank you for getting back to me." He paused. "It is my job to monitor the pulse of this great nation, sir, and I will have to say that the pulse of the country can only be described as erratic."

"What do you mean, Morningstar?"

"What I mean, sir, is that in light of President Knight's departure, we have become a very unstable country."

"I beg to differ, Morningstar." A pause. "I have taken great pains over the last forty-odd hours to ensure that all military personnel are ready to battle whatever unrest might crop up due to President Knight's unprecedented departure."

"Perhaps, but I think it would be wise to tie those efforts to the gun confiscation that had been started before President Knight left the White House."

"That's not my call, Morningstar. You'll have to take it up with the cabinet secretary." Harrington cleared his throat. "But I don't think it will be necessary." A pause. "As I said, I've taken steps to keep this country safe."

Morningstar bristled. *Weak-kneed son-of-a-bitch.* "Fine. But have you thought about where that might leave us overseas?"

Another pause. "It won't affect our ability to fight a war in Latvia, if that's what you're trying to imply."

Morningstar cleared his throat. "That is exactly what I'm trying to imply. Putin is no fool. He sees the upheaval we're in, and you can bet your ass, Harrington, that he will do whatever he can to take advantage of it."

This time, the pause was longer. Morningstar wondered if Harrington had hung up. "Sir, are you there?"

Harrington cleared his throat. "I agree, Mr. Morningstar, that Putin will likely see this as an opportunity, but I daresay that the tyrant will be wrong."

Morningstar laughed. "With all due respect, Mr. Vice-President, he will not be wrong. And he will be emboldened." He paused. "Have you seen the latest reconnaissance showing a buildup along Latvia's eastern coast?"

"Of course I have."

"Well, if I were a betting man, I'd wager that within the next twenty-four hours, Putin will move his troops beyond Latvia's border to one of the other two Baltic States." He paused for effect. "Unless you can find a way to remind him of what's at stake."

A pause. "What are you getting at, Morningstar?"

Morningstar grinned. *Time to reel him in.* "What I'm saying, Harrington, is that you might want to either directly or indirectly threaten the man." Another pause. "And I'm not talking about useless sanctions."

"Then what *are* you talking about?"

"Nukes."

"Nukes? Are you out of your mind, Morningstar? That would be suicide, not only for America, but for the entire planet!"

Morningstar chuckled silently. "I'm not saying to use them, Harrington. I'm simply suggesting that you put the threat out there. It will make him think twice before he embarks on some crazy scheme to take over all of Eastern Europe. It was bad enough that he felt comfortable going after a NATO country in the first place. Once he takes Estonia and Lithuania, what is to stop him from going after Poland or Germany or France?"

More silence. Finally, "I think you're overestimating what Putin can do."

Morningstar laughed out loud. "How many times do we need to *underestimate* Putin before we realize that the man is crazy? That he would rather die than lose?"

Harrington let out a sigh. "I'll take your recommendation under advisement, Morningstar, but I do think that you're wrong...very wrong."

Again, Morningstar chuckled silently. "Fine, sir. Let's hope that I am."

Morningstar ended the call. *That oughta do it.* He pulled out his private cellphone and dialed.

"Yes sir...um...Father."

"Levi, it's time to take the Baltic assault to the next level."

He ended the call. Levi would know what to do. It had been prearranged. He would plant a seed that would imply to the surveillance agent in Uzbekistan that Putin wasn't merely issuing threats to expand his operation; he was actually about to do it. The wording would leave the undeniable impression that within the next twenty-four hours, Putin would make a move not just for Latvia, but for all three of the Baltic States. Johannson would dutifully relay that information to Morningstar, after which he would share it with his supervisor, who would most assuredly alert the acting President. *Who will realize not only that I'm right, but that the threat of a nuclear war is his only play.*

Then what would happen? If Morningstar had gauged the self-doubting Vice-President accurately, Harrington – too nervous to act on Morningstar's recommendation on his own – would reach out to Knight. He would tell him that Ed Morningstar from the Pentagon was urging him to threaten Putin with nuclear war. Morningstar laughed. "Then Judah will know exactly who is calling the shots."

He was about to lay his cellphone on the desk, when it rang. He hissed, "Yes!"

"Father, it's me, Gad...and just so you know, I'm still in Warsaw. My ten a.m. flight was cancelled. Somethin' about the horseshit goin' on in America. I won't be able to leave this hellhole until midnight."

Morningstar laughed in spite of himself. "Don't worry, Gad. A midnight flight from Poland gets you to DC by three a.m.; four at the latest. You'll still have plenty of time to get to Maine and follow through on what we discussed."

He was about to end the call, when Gad said, "Um...yes Father, but there is actually another reason for this call."

"Get to it, Gad...I've got a lot going on."

"Um...well, sir...I was just notified by one of the soldiers who took our... uh...prisoner to the base outside Klaipeda that he has...um...escaped."

Morningstar nearly dropped the phone. "What did you say?"

"Our prisoner has escaped. I don't have details. I'll let you know when I—"

Morningstar threw the phone on the desk. "Shit, shit, shit, shit, shit!" He paced the office, gripping his hands so tightly that his nails carved grooves in his palms. Henderson had escaped. How had he done it? *There is no way he could've escaped...not on his own anyway.* So, who had helped him? Morningstar bristled as he smashed his hand against the wall. *His goddamned daddy, that's who.* It was just like in Edinburgh. Hank Clarkson had been ready to bring Henderson back to the States, when his powerful father had intervened and had insisted that the ailing man was needed in Latvia to help with the war effort. He stiffened. Walter Henderson had undermined Morningstar's efforts in Edinburgh, he had forced Gad's detention at an airport in Warsaw, and now he had somehow freed a prisoner from an American-held base in Lithuania. Morningstar felt certain that Walter had been behind all of it.

I have had enough of that man's meddling! He continued to pace. What should he do? He needed to find Henderson, but just as important, he needed to come up with a way to punish the powerful and well-heeled Walter. *I'll send in a battalion to find Henderson, and I'll have them start by tearing up that goddamned castle!*

He gripped his fists tighter. He couldn't do that; Gad's capture of Martin Henderson Thursday morning hadn't gone through the proper channels. It was one thing to pull in a few soldiers from a foreign base without clearing it; it was quite another to call up a full battalion.

He stopped at the window and stared out at the dusk-ridden sky. Suddenly, he smiled. *Morningstar...if you want something done right, then do it yourself.*

He walked back to the desk and picked up the landline. He cleared his throat, then pushed the button. "Priscilla, put me through to General Daniels."

"He's in a meeting, sir."

Morningstar squeezed the receiver so hard it nearly broke. He took another deep breath. "Fine. Just give him this message. Edward Morningstar will be out of the office indefinitely. In an effort to show support for our soldiers as they assist NATO in their effort to hold off Putin's army, Morningstar will travel to Latvia...at once."

"Yes sir. Would you like me to make arrangements for you, sir?"

Morningstar sneered. "Yes, Priscilla. How about finding me a nice bed-and-breakfast where I and two of my men can set up shop."

"A bed and breakfast, sir. Near Riga?"

Morningstar chuckled to himself. "No, Priscilla, why don't you make it along the coast...near Uzava, if possible."

CHAPTER 13

The Henderson compound, outside Uzava, Latvia

Henderson woke with a start. Though it was still early morning and the sun had yet to rise, the moonlight shining through the window gave off enough light for him to see that he was back in his childhood bedroom. The pitted concrete of the jail cell had been replaced by the rough stone of the castle's south wall. Though the castle had been remodeled several times over the years, his mother Dora had elected to keep the south wall as it had been for centuries; coarsely aged rock, mortared with the blood of the knights who had once stood guard over the majestic castle.

That bedroom had become a metaphor; the place he had landed after whatever disaster had befallen him. It had started with the battle nearly five years ago when Albins Platacis was killed. Henderson had come to that room to recover, and to prepare to look after Albins' daughter, Lili. Then, after a four-year journey as the assassin, Phoenix, he had come back to that room, not as Martin but as Matt, again for the purpose of recovery. And, after a five-month coma that had nearly killed him, he had come back there to regain his strength. Then, after his failed suicide attempt from that very window, he had awakened in that same bed to finally confront his demons. And now, after his imprisonment by U.S. soldiers in an abandoned military prison outside Klaipeda, Lithuania, he had awakened in that room, safe – for now – from the man who was eternally trying to destroy him. And always, for a few brief seconds after he opened his eyes, he would be okay;

everything would be as it should be. Albins would still be alive, Lili would never have been taken, Henderson wouldn't have become a world-class assassin, and Maddi wouldn't be gone forever.

But then it would hit him. Albins was dead, Lili was in trouble in a far off land, Henderson had done terrible things as Morningstar's personal assassin, and – worst of all – Maddi was dead, murdered by Henderson's arch enemy.

This morning was no different, and, as he came to terms – again – with all that he had done and all that had happened because of it, he simply closed his eyes and sighed. He got out of bed slowly, his legs aching from the number of times he had either been shot at or beaten, his head pounding from the amount of deception he had been forced to accept as he tried to make sense of his life. *There is no sense to my life,* he thought as he hobbled slowly to the window.

He, his father, and Dimitri had arrived at the castle just before midnight. Henderson had pretty much carried Dimitri to the barracks on the opposite side of the courtyard, where a medic had gone to work on his gunshot wound. Though it had torn a considerable amount of tissue in Dimitri's calf, the bullet had gone on through, missing his shin bones entirely. How had the medic put it? *"Damn lucky you are, 'Mitri...that bullet coulda' crippled ya' for life."* Henderson stared out the window and sighed. *Damn lucky, indeed.*

He had been surprised that he had been able to sleep. After all, he had just been freed by his law-abiding father and his head of security from a military base under U.S. control. What would come of it? Would the guards know who had been behind the escape? Had Walter left evidence of his involvement without realizing it? Henderson prayed that the answer to both of those questions was no, otherwise his father would be in a whole lot of trouble, and Henderson would have to come to grips with the fact that he was once again responsible for the downfall of a good man.

Fortunately, there was nothing to tie Walter to the prisoner, Aiden Balkus. No one besides Jason Hanover was even aware that Walter had spoken to the man. As for the two soldiers charged with watching Balkus, they would be in no hurry to admit that they had allowed a highly-valued target to escape. Which meant that, other than Morningstar, no one would likely even know that it had happened.

Let's hope so, Henderson thought, as he leaned against the window sill and awaited the promise of daybreak. He brushed his hands over the rough stone, reassured by all that that wall had endured. As he watched the moon fade with the dawn, he thought again of the soldiers who had once stood at that spot, planning for the castle's defense. What he wouldn't give to channel their nobility. To erase all the evil he had done...to have lived nobly enough to deserve to stand in their shadow. But he hadn't lived nobly; for the last four-and-a-half years, all he had done was kill and maim and put people in danger...often people he loved.

There's nothing I can do about it now, he thought, as he turned and walked to the bathroom. Walter and Dimitri had freed him for a purpose. Lili was alive, she was in China, and she was in trouble. That much he had been able to determine from the two letters that had been sent to his father. Walter had shown them to him once they had been assured that Dimitri would be okay. The first letter had revealed very little, other than that Lili was alive. The second letter had revealed quite a bit more.

He brushed his teeth and combed his hair; the blonde hair of Aiden Balkus. He pulled on a pair of sweats and a sweater and walked to his desk. Though he had wanted to leave for China last night, it would have been reckless. First of all, he had barely slept. He would need at least a solid four hours of sleep to sustain him if he was to make the long journey. Second of all, he would need a plan. China was, after all, a very big place. He and Walter had agreed that he would take the morning to dig through Lili's words and pinpoint her location. Then he would fly to China.

Walter had said that he wanted to join Henderson on the journey, but that he had an obligation in Scotland at noon. *"The meeting will likely be a short one, son. If you haven't left by the time I get back, I'd like to go with you."*

Henderson sighed as he slid into a pair of loafers. He didn't want his father to go with him. For one thing, the man was needed in Latvia to manage the war with Russia. For another, Henderson had learned over the course of the last four years that he worked best alone. He was nimbler; he could change course quickly if he had no one else to worry about. He could also be more ruthless, not having to see in his father's eyes the shock of watching his son be so capable of inflicting pain on others. He flinched and walked out of the room. *I'll be sure to be gone before he gets back.*

He hurried downstairs for coffee, said no to breakfast, then ran back up to his bedroom. With coffee in hand, he sat at his desk and reached for Lili's second letter. He laid it in front of him and, cupping the coffee with both hands, he read it through for about the tenth time. He set the coffee on the desk and pulled a pen and paper from a drawer. He jotted down what he was able to determine. Lili was in China, somewhere near the Xishan Mountains outside Beijing. She had a view of Badaling and the Great Wall. She wasn't alone; a woman was with her who she had referred to as a friend. There were soldiers standing guard.

He smiled as he read her words about the soldiers' lack of purpose. Lili was remarkably wise; so much wiser than her years. He sat back and sighed. It would be an unbearable tragedy if she were to die in that prison.

He leaned forward and stared at his notes, more determined than ever to find her. Why had she been in China in the first place? Why hadn't Morningstar killed her when he said he had; what was he saving her for? Why was she being kept in a prison where she was practically being starved to death? Who was the woman with her? Lili had said that her name was Ching Lan. How had she found Lili? *Or, did Lili find her?* Had Morningstar meant for Lili to stay in China, or did he plan on one day bringing her to the United States? If so, why? Was he aware of her remarkable abilities? Did he hope to somehow use them in his wicked game? Why had the Chinese been the ones to take her? Were they working with Morningstar? *They must be,* he thought with a sigh. It was the only thing that made sense.

He ran his hands through his hair. So many questions that he knew wouldn't be answered until he pulled Lili out of that prison.

He looked again at the penciled letter in front of him. He couldn't help but smile as he reread Lili's poem. She wasn't just incredibly wise, she was also a remarkably good lyricist, especially considering that she wasn't even ten.

> *"I see the mountains of Xishan*
> *And as the leaves do take their fall*
> *I see the nearby Badaling*
> *And the magical Great Wall..."*

That single stanza had given him his most useful information, and he grabbed his map of China from the floor near the desk. He shoved aside Lili's letters and laid the map on his desk. He had already circled the Xishan Mountains. He located the part of the Great Wall known as Badaling and drew a circle around it, as well. Together, they provided an area with a ten-mile radius. He wrote down the coordinates.

Lili had gone into detail describing the prison. The bars of her jail cell were rusted metal, the walls were chipped and peeling, and the entire prison smelled – how had she put it – *"...of musty grief."* She had spoken of wails at night and fists beating against the walls in far-off hallways. She had never actually seen any other prisoners, which meant the prison itself was quite large. He jotted on his sheet of paper, "Very large, very old prison." He pulled out his cellphone and dialed the Henderson security office. He was stunned when he heard the familiar voice of Dimitri.

"Hello?"

"Geez, Dimitri, don't you think you should maybe take the day off?"

The soldier laughed. "No sir. Not until I have gotten you on your way."

Though neither Walter nor Henderson had given Dimitri details of Lili's plight, or even that she was alive, Dimitri had been made aware that both of the jets would be needed that morning, and that Henderson would be traveling to the Far East.

Henderson smiled. "Well, I appreciate it. I wonder if you could get me a schematic of a region of China...a ten-mile area outside Beijing."

"Certainly, sir. Do you have the coordinates?"

Henderson relayed the information.

"I'll get something to you within the next fifteen minutes, sir."

"Thank you, Dimitri. I'm upstairs."

"Yes sir."

The call ended. Henderson looked again at Lili's letters. The fact that the Hendersons had received them at all was nothing short of a miracle. It was one of the first things he had asked his father after the man had shown him the letters...

"How did you get these, Dad?"

Walter leaned back and sighed. "As you know, Martin, we have a presence in Beijing, where we operate an investment company in the heart of the city. Because of the volatility of the region, we hired four Americans – former military – to oversee the safety of our staff there, as well as the security of the material that goes in and out of our facility. One of the soldiers was handed both letters three days ago as he was leaving the office. He saw that they were addressed to me, so he had them overnighted through one of our couriers. I got them soon after you left for Vilnius."

"Who was the man that handed him the letters?"

Walter cleared his throat. "He's what some might refer to as a double agent."

Henderson's eyes widened. "A spy?"

Walter nodded. "You might say that." He sighed. "It has long been suspected that China has imprisoned at least a few American diplomats...two that they claimed were killed in a plane crash thirteen years ago, along with two more who were taken in January while on a fact-finding mission regarding China's treatment of the Uyghur refugees." He cleared his throat. "The spy was sent in six months ago to infiltrate the prison system. He works as a janitor in the Great Hall of the People. He doesn't have access to the prisoners, but is able to pick up discussions from time to time among the prison soldiers who report weekly to the Great Hall. He has yet to hear specifics about how many Americans are being held or where they're kept, but there's no doubt about it: there are American prisoners somewhere near Beijing. The agent spotted the first of the letters when he was emptying the trash."

"Why would a letter – from a remote prison – be in the garbage at the Beijing Hall of the People?"

"I'm guessing that a prison guard threw it away rather than mail it. I've been told that all garbage from the prisons is brought to the Great Hall to be inspected." He paused. "When the double agent saw my name as the addressee, he shoved it in his pocket. He held onto it, and then, when he spotted a second letter two weeks later, he felt compelled to deliver both letters to the security team at the investment house."

"Any idea why the letters weren't destroyed? They contain a lot of clues, especially the second letter."

Walter shook his head. "One of two things. Either the agent grabbed them before they reached the inspectors, or the inspectors read them through and failed to appreciate the messages they contained."

Henderson frowned. "In the first letter, Lili mentions that I'm alive. Did the spy read it? Does he now know that Martin Henderson is alive?"

"I'm afraid so. I had him detained briefly. He has been sworn to secrecy."

"Can you trust him?"

Walter shrugged. "Let's hope so."

Henderson looked again at the second letter. It was dated October 9th, 2004, which confirmed that – at least three weeks ago – Lili was alive.

There was a knock. He walked to the door and opened it. Dimitri was standing in the doorway, leaning on a single crutch, holding a map in his hand.

"That was quick," Henderson said as he took the map.

"Yes sir. We've actually created maps from every region of China due to the unreliability of the maps they provide. This map is a composite of the area that you requested, with every known landmark, as well as any military presence in the area."

Henderson nodded. "Thank you, Dimitri. Is the jet ready?"

Dimitri nodded. "Yes sir. Do you need a pilot?"

Henderson considered it, then shook his head. "No, I'll go alone."

Dimitri nodded, then turned to go. As he walked to the stairs, Henderson said after him, "Dimitri...thank you...for everything."

Dimitri stopped and turned around. Looking to make sure they were alone, he whispered, "I know that now isn't the time, Mart, but I look forward to your return so you can tell me of your adventures...for the past four-and-a-half years."

Henderson took a deep breath, then nodded slowly. "Agreed."

Dimitri smiled, then turned and limped down the hall. Henderson watched him as he reached the stairs and struggled with the first few steps. Henderson shook his head, filled with guilt that another good man had been injured because of him. He cleared his throat and tightened his jaw, then turned and walked back to his room.

He went to his desk and laid Dimitri's map over top of the other map. He studied it, looking for a prison, or even a warehouse. There was neither. Which meant one of two things. Either he was wrong about the location, or the Chinese had gone to great lengths to hide the facility. He doubted he was wrong about the location; Lili's clues were rather precise. Which meant that the Chinese were hiding the existence of the building. Why? He flinched. *Because they want to make sure that the world never finds out that such a place exists, or learns of what they might be doing there.*

He heard a knock. He walked to the door and opened it, surprised to see Walter holding a plate of eggs in one hand, a briefcase and a paper bag in the other.

Henderson smiled. "I'm not really hung—"

"You need to eat, son." Walter handed him the plate, then walked into the room and looked around. He spotted the map on the desk and walked over to it. He studied it briefly, then turned to Henderson. "Do you think you know where she is?"

Henderson nodded as he set the plate of food on the bed. "Based on her landmarks, she's somewhere near Chaoyang...just outside Beijing."

Walter nodded, then he sighed. "This meeting I'm about to go to in Scotland is important; otherwise I'd cancel and go with you. But if you're still here when I—"

"I'm leaving within the hour, Dad. It's okay. I work best alone."

His father nodded. "I don't doubt it." He sighed, then reached out and hugged his son. He handed him the briefcase. It was the same briefcase that Cravens had returned just three days earlier.

"Dad, I don't think—"

"Take it. It has accompanied the members of this family on vital missions throughout the last sixty years, son. It will bring you luck."

Henderson took the briefcase and ran his fingers over the initials "JH." They were the initials of Jeremy Henderson, his grandfather, Walter's father.

Walter said, "I've removed the drawings and locked them in my safe. I also disengaged the fingerprint ID. Here's the code to get in." He handed Henderson a scrap of paper with eight numbers. Henderson shoved it in his pocket. Walter added, "There's a sat phone in there, pre-programmed with numbers that might be useful."

"Such as?"

"Mine, Dimitri's, Jason Hanover's, Sam Allen's."

"You've included Homeland's Director and the head of the Secret Service?"

Walter nodded. "I think I mentioned to you that Hanover and I had become friends after the DC fire. As I'm sure you picked up, he was helpful with your prison break, though he had no idea what I was up to." He paused. "I'll call him later and reassure him that I have no idea what happened to prisoner Aiden Balkus, who I insisted on talking to, not once, but twice. Then I'll brief him on your trip to China."

Henderson frowned. "I don't think you should say a word about my trip." He paused. "You do recall that Homeland Security has the entire world looking for me?"

"No, they're looking for Matt Henderson. You are now Conrad Gibbons."

He handed Henderson the brown paper bag, along with a badge that had his photo embedded on the front. The badge indicated that he was a representative for Henderson Commodities. His hair in the photo was brown and cut just below his ears; his eyes were green. He had no mustache, but was sporting a well-trimmed beard.

"So, I need to cut my hair?"

Walter nodded. "Yes, and dye it brown."

Henderson sighed. It would be his sixth identity, and that was if no one counted the countless identities he had assumed as the Phoenix. He nodded. "Thanks, Dad...for everything."

Walter nodded. "There is a letter of introduction in the briefcase, which identifies you as a representative for Henderson Commodities. We do quite a bit of business in China, and this letter should give you cover if anyone questions your presence there." He paused. "I've also put a gun in the briefcase, Martin. You'll need to hide it, of course, once you get to China, but I felt like it might come in handy."

Henderson nodded but said nothing.

Walter added, "I was going to suggest that maybe you hit the firing range before you go, but something tells me that your skills with a weapon have been tested many times since your days as a Freedom Fighter."

He looked at his father and said evenly, "I'm pretty good with a gun, Dad."

Walter sighed. "Yes...well, I need to prepare for my trip to Scotland. Call me if you need anything. I'll see you...and Lili...when I get back."

Henderson hesitated, then reached out and hugged his father. "I'll see you soon, Dad."

Walter hugged him back, then turned to walk away. As he was about to leave, he said over his shoulder, "Make sure to say goodbye to your mother, son."

"Does she know what I'm about to do?"

Walter shook his head. "I didn't tell her about Lili, just in case—" He let the rest of the sentence go. "She thinks you're going to China on business. It seemed best that I tell her at least that much, in case someone calls here to verify your story."

Henderson nodded. "Did you tell her that I was wearing a disguise? That I'm now Conrad Gibbons? Won't she find that odd?"

Walter shook his head. "No, she's used to it. We often use aliases when we travel abroad...especially to China. It makes it less likely that we'll be taken."

Henderson nodded. "Okay. I'll be sure to see her before I go."

Walter left the room. Henderson went to the door and watched him walk down the stairs. For the first time in Henderson's life, his father seemed old. He shook his head. *I did that...I made that poor man grow old.*

He turned and walked back to his desk. He laid the briefcase and the brown paper bag on top of the maps of China. Using the code that Walter had given him, he opened the briefcase and pulled out a business card, a passport, and the cover letter. All three identified him as Conrad Gibbons, cousin of the Hendersons, an emissary for Henderson Commodities, Inc. Again, he looked at the photo. Short brown hair and green eyes. No mustache, but a neatly trimmed beard. He opened the paper bag and looked inside. There was hair dye, contact lenses, and a fake beard. He shook his head and frowned. *Maybe someday I'll get to be who I really am.* He grabbed the sat phone and, without thinking, dialed the number of a man he had called many times in his search for Lili: Dain Rozenblats. Henderson had hired the man soon after Lili had gone missing, but he hadn't spoken to Dain since Morningstar told him that Lili had been 'eliminated.' What would Dain think when Henderson told him that she was alive? Could he maybe help Henderson save her? He shook his head. No, what Henderson had told his father was true...he worked best alone. The call went unanswered. He didn't leave a message. Actually, as he thought of it now, Dain hadn't answered his calls for many months now. He let out a deep sigh, then returned the phone to the briefcase.

He pulled out the gun. It was a Luger. He held it up and looked through the sight. He checked the chamber; it was loaded. There were two extra clips in the briefcase. He laid the gun on the desk. If it was to go with him to China, he would need to find a way to hide it, otherwise, it would be a red flag. *An innocent businessman doesn't carry a luger.*

He left the briefcase on the desk and walked to his closet. He picked out a nondescript gray suit and laid it on his dresser. He reached behind a pile of sweaters and pulled out a gun holster that would allow him to hide the gun under his suit. The gun would do him no good if it was locked in a briefcase. The holster would keep it hidden as long as no one did an actual pat down.

He laid the holster by the suit, then walked to the bathroom. It was time to once again immerse himself in a disguise. He laid the bottle of hair dye by the sink and searched for a pair of scissors. He thought again of the pistol. His father had told him that he had given it to him *"...in case you need it, son."* As he reached for the scissors, he frowned. *There's no doubt in my mind that I'll need it.*

CHAPTER 14

The Henderson Compound

Walter left Henderson's room and walked downstairs without a word to the guard who was standing at the front door. His mind was occupied, not only with what his son was about to do, but with what he himself was about to do. He marched down the hall, turned right at the den, and walked past the kitchen. He passed the entrance to the garage, then turned right down a hallway near the back door of the castle. As he walked toward his office, he couldn't shake the feeling that he should be going with Martin. After all, if Lili was in trouble, then Martin could soon be in trouble, as well. Though he had known that Martin would insist on going alone, the fact that Walter *couldn't* go with him had left him feeling guilty; guiltier than he had felt in a long time. *And that's saying something,* he thought as he walked into his office.

He looked out the back window at the courtyard and sighed. The sun had begun to rise, and he could see its reflection on the Baltic Sea that sat about a hundred yards beyond the courtyard. Martin didn't want him to go...the man had made it clear that he worked best alone. *And – in this instance – so do I.*

Just as he had done with his son, all Walter had told Dora was that he had a meeting in Scotland. And though Dora was used to him flying off to meetings around the world, she had asked him not to go. The conflict with Russia had deepened over the last twenty-four hours, and she felt certain that he would soon be called upon to send in one of the Henderson battalions. *"Can't the meeting wait, Walter?"*

"I'm sorry, Dora, but it can't." He had quickly walked away, unwilling to deceive her anymore.

He had originally intended to bring Samuels with him, and had said as much when he had called Justice's office with the invitation back in August. But the poor doctor had been through quite an ordeal, so Walter had left it to him to decide. Samuels had begged off, likely feeling it best that Walter confront Justice alone. *"I can't go with you, I'd only be a burden."* He had added, *"Just keep in mind, Walter, that that man is your son."*

Walter checked the time. Seven a.m. His meeting in Aberdeen was scheduled for noon. The flight itself would take about three hours, which meant that he needed to get moving. He opened his safe and took out a pistol; an unregistered .35. He flinched as he shoved it in his pocket. It was possible that Justice might not be the one to show up. If it turned out to be Cobra, Walter needed to be ready.

He walked over to a glass case and unlocked the metal-encased door. Inside was a series of coins from ancient Latvia. He would use the coins to try to cement his tie with Justice...a promise of sorts that he valued their relationship and wanted it to last. But as he slid two of the priceless coins in his pocket, he shook his head. *Will this work?* He turned and walked to the door. *Probably not, but I at least have to try.*

Chapter 15

Washington, DC

Tall, rugged Jake Donovan folded a pair of pants and laid them in his suitcase. Though the trip he was about to take hadn't been planned, he was ready. He had been trained to be ready. *"Always have a bag ready to go...you never know when you'll need to leave quickly."* It was only three a.m. in Washington, DC, but he didn't care; he had always enjoyed those early hours before dawn. *It's when the crazies are out.*

He also didn't care that he had gotten in late the night before and had had only a few hours of sleep. It came with the territory. *"The need for sleep is a state of mind."* Something else he had been trained to accept.

The last thirty-six hours had been challenging. On Wednesday night, he had been sent to the DC airport to meet a late plane, with an understanding that one of the passengers was a highly valued target; a high ranking administrator within the federal government. *"He will need protection,"* had been the command. Donovan had done as instructed, and, using credentials given to him by his boss, he had waited at the gate until the last passenger had gotten off the plane. When his target wasn't among them, he had put in a call to his boss, who had clearly been angry. In response, Donovan had been sent to secure another target, which he had been instructed to deliver to an offshore location. It had taken him a full forty-eight hours, and he had returned to DC about four hours ago, just before midnight. Then, at about two in the morning, just as he had been about to fall asleep, he had been roused by a rather heated call from his boss, who had told him to pack and get to the airport for a new assignment. *"I want you on a plane by seven a.m. ...got it?"*

Donovan chuckled. *Got it, boss.* He zipped the suitcase and carried it to the front door. He grabbed a heavy coat from the closet. He knew enough about his destination to know that it would be cold there at the end of October. He was about to grab his briefcase, which was sitting on a desk, when he stopped to look at himself in a mirror. He nodded. *Polished and professional.* He had trimmed down a bit over the past several months, still muscular, but leaner, and the high-quality suit fit him well. Using both hands, he brushed back a few strands of light brown hair. He had been growing his hair for months; his goal: a ponytail like Johnny Depp had worn in the movie *Chocolat*. He smiled as he rubbed his chin; the five-o'clock shadow was now a constant; he liked that as well. *Also, Johnny Depp.* But the eyes were the biggest change; they surprised him every time. Deep green, they reminded him of a cat.

He put on the overcoat and draped the strap of the briefcase over his shoulder. He grabbed his suitcase, walked out of the hotel room, and went down the hall to a flight of stairs. He took the stairs to the lobby, nodding at a concierge who was sitting behind a tall marble counter. He walked out to the street. It was still dark. He walked to the nearest corner and stood next to a lamppost to wait for a taxi. After about five minutes, a Yellow Cab drove by and Donovan waved it down. He climbed in back. "Dulles," he said, as he tossed his bags on the seat beside him.

The driver said nothing and pulled away from the curb.

Donovan sat back, gawking like a tourist as they drove past the many shrines and monuments in downtown DC. He shook his head. Here he was, a smalltown boy in the epicenter of the world. He could only imagine what might be going on in those half-lit government buildings, or behind a few of those awe-inspiring statues. *A perfect place for criminals to gather... or for undercover cops to lay in wait.*

They arrived at the airport in thirty minutes. Donovan said nothing as he paid the fare, then grabbed his bags and stepped out of the cab. Still no sign of sunrise as he hurried to the terminal. Though he had had little sleep, he felt rested and ready to go.

He walked into the terminal, sighing at the fact that he had been at that same airport less than five hours ago. He walked up to a ticket counter and smiled at an attractive brunette. He read the nametag on her chest and nodded. "Hello, Darlene. Nice crisp day ahead, eh?"

She smiled. "Yes sir. May I help you?"

He winked. "You already have."

She blushed.

"I need a ticket."

"Where to, sir?"

He hiked his briefcase onto the counter. "Indianapolis."

"Not a problem, sir. I can have you there by nine a.m. Is that soon enough?"

He grinned as he pulled out his ID. "Darlene, my dear, that will work out perfectly."

CHAPTER 16

Washington, DC

Senator Charles Sturgill couldn't sleep, and it had little to do with the fact that the house phone was ringing for the hundredth time it seemed, or that the President of the United States had decided to go into hiding. Sturgill had had his fill of phone calls, and he had certainly had his fill of the current DC crisis. *A President wouldn't go into hiding...unless he had to.* Wherever he was, Knight was far safer away from Washington than he was sitting in that fishbowl known as the White House. Why didn't the nervous nellies in DC get that? It wasn't that Charles didn't share their concerns; he did. He just wasn't all that worked up about it.

My job was just to raise the man. He had kept his end of the bargain; he had nurtured Knight under his own roof for the last twenty-four years. Though he had grown fond of Knight, he had avoided forming any deep attachment. He was certain that the minute he did, it would put the nail in the coffin of his true son, Jamey.

He checked his cellphone. Few calls came in on that line; it was for his private use only. But he knew, if Morningstar was trying to reach him, he would use the cell. So, he had ignored the landline as it had rung almost nonstop, leaving Beatrice to handle the calls. *"Say whatever you have to, Bea...I don't want to talk to them."*

Knight's disappearance had resulted in what could only be described as chaos in DC. Emergency congressional meetings had gone well into the night, along with even more security than usual throughout the Beltway;

all things Charles could have done without, especially since he was preparing to leave the country. But the phone calls had been the worst of all. They had started soon after the VP, Bob Harrington, had shared the news Wednesday night, and they hadn't stopped. At first, Charles had taken the calls, and always it was the same: *"You raised him as your own, Senator, don't you have any idea where he might have gone?"* Charles had wanted to scream, *"No, dammit, and I don't care! The boy – who is now a powerful man, I might add – will come home when he's damn good and ready."* Instead he had politely told those who called that he, like the rest of the country, had no idea where the President had run off to. After an hour or two of that, he had had Beatrice tell whoever called that he wasn't available. *"I don't care if it's Jerome, himself, I'm not talking to anybody!"*

She had wanted to disconnect the phone; he had forbidden it. After all, one never knew when a person of importance might call. He couldn't deny that years of waiting for someone to phone and say they had found Jamey had made it impossible for him to allow her to unplug the phone. Which meant that Bea had spent most of the last forty-eight hours either answering the blasted thing, or hanging it up.

He glanced at a clock by the bed. *Four a.m.* He felt wide awake. *I may as well just get up.* He was to leave for China later that morning; there was no sense trying to sleep. He had told his wife that he was making the trip on behalf of the Senate. She didn't care. She did her thing; he did his. That had been their life for the past twenty-seven years; it would likely be their life for the next twenty-seven.

If I get that many.

He sighed as he ran his fingers through his thinning gray hair. Though he was about to turn sixty, he felt much older. His parents had both lived well into their nineties. Would he do the same? *Doubtful,* he thought, *I am, after all, married to Bea.* He chuckled as he dragged his large frame from the bed. *With that woman in my life, I'll be lucky to make it to sixty-one.*

It wasn't that he didn't love Bea; he did. Just not the way he had when they had gotten married. Lord knows, she didn't love him the same. The years had taken their toll on Charles and Beatrice Sturgill; the years...and the loss of their son, Jamey.

They had been married just six years when Jamey was kidnapped. Not nearly enough time to have the moorings necessary to weather such a thing. Jamey had been only five at the time. The family had been on a mission trip in China, and had chosen a region where Beatrice's ancestors had once lived. They had located only one distant relative still living in the region, however, and he had been quite old, which meant that they had essentially been on their own, not only with the mission trip, but to find their son after he went missing. Though Charles had moved heaven and earth to try to find the boy, the fact that he hadn't was just one more thing Bea held against him.

Which was why the meeting with Morningstar twenty-four years ago had been so significant. Prior to that meeting, Charles had been left with nothing...no son, no wife to speak of, no faith. Morningstar had at least offered him a shot at vengeance. *"Vengeance is mine, sayeth the Lord."* Charles smirked. *Yeah...whatever.*

There was no question that the Mephistophelian bargain that the two men had struck at the time had been corrupt. Charles didn't care. Devil or no devil, their arrangement had been the only thing that had kept him from blowing his brains out. Charles' part of the bargain had been to raise Jerome Knight into the sort of man who might be President someday. *"I'll take care of the rest,"* Morningstar had told him. Charles had performed his task well. Jerome had grown into a remarkable man, with keen political instincts and a good head of hair. Charles laughed. *You can't be bald in this business...at least not until you're well into your seventies.* After law school, Jerome had moved to Florida to take advantage of the changing political winds that had begun to blow over the state. Three years later, after gauging partisan leanings, he had aligned himself with the party that he had predicted would soon rise to power. He had run for a seat in the State House, and, though he had been a long shot to win, a strong message combined with even stronger charisma had pulled him over the top. Four years later, just before his 33rd birthday, he had made a run for a U.S. Senate seat, and had somehow won against an eighteen-year incumbent. It was a stunning upset which had left the pundits mystified. He had held that seat for five years, when, out of the blue, he was tapped to fill the vacancy left by Vice-President Conner, who, for whatever reason, had decided to quit just months before the President's reelection campaign. The untimely assassination of President Wilcox had thrown Jerome into the Presidency in an ascendency that had been unlike anything ever witnessed in the history of the United States. And as each step of it had played out, Morningstar had called and said, *"So, Sturgill…I'll bet you're glad you backed the right horse."*

But Jerome wasn't the only one who had had a miraculous rise in status. Morningstar had risen, as well. His boss, General Daniels, was now the Chairman of the Joint Chiefs, and was arguably the most powerful military man in the country. Morningstar's role as the man's top aide had given him access to key players in America's upper echelon. And it had worked out well. Everything Morningstar was involved in seemed to flourish under his steady hand. Even Charles himself had managed to win re-election over and over again…twice when no one thought he had a snowball's chance in hell. He didn't know if Morningstar had played a role; he assumed so, especially when, soon after each election, he would get a call. *"By now I hope it's clear, Sturgill, that I've got your back. Please send my regards to Jerome."*

Truth be told, both men had profited handily from the relationship. Morningstar had managed to get his 'boy' into the presidency, and Charles had managed to hold onto a position of power within the United States Senate. *And now, finally, Morningstar will make good on his promise of revenge.*

But that revenge had taken a strange turn. Not only because Knight had run off, which might cause Morningstar to balk on his promise, but because Charles had just learned that the son of China's top military leader was a thirty-two-year-old white man. China rarely, if ever, granted power to anyone other than a man of Chinese lineage, which could mean only one thing: the boy, Tau Chu, somehow *carried that lineage,* and had been 'taken in' by a Chinese leader. Which also meant, at least as far as Charles was concerned, the boy had to be his kidnapped son Jamey. Nothing else made sense. Not only did the timeline fit, but because of Bea's Chinese ancestry, Jamey possessed the proper lineage. *So now, regardless of what Morningstar says, I must bring that boy home.*

Charles walked to the window and looked out at the darkness. Their home in Washington wasn't nearly as nice as their place in Maine, but Charles had made sure that his bedroom in the small townhouse had a view of the Potomac. He and Jamey had always enjoyed the water. They had spent many happy hours fishing in the depths of the Atlantic. *Do you still love the ocean, Jamey?* Charles stared at the mist over the water and grinned. *The first thing we'll do is take out the boat.*

He couldn't imagine what his son's life had been like. The boy, taken from his parents when he was just a child, had been raised by a man who would become one of the most powerful military leaders in China. In spite of how awful it had been for all of them, Charles couldn't help but smile at the fact that Jamey had become a warrior, a member of the ruling elite. *Of course, he did...he was destined for greatness.*

Charles continued to stare at the black Potomac. The mist had dissipated. In its place was the reflection of a gold half-moon on the dark water. The stars were shining as brightly as they ever had. It was a good sign. The house phone rang; he ignored it. *Whoever wants to talk to me can wait until I get back...with my son.*

He turned away from the window and walked to his dresser. He took a Cuban cigar from a gilded box; a box that had been given to him by his 'adopted' son, Jerome, just before he was to leave for Florida. A Groucho Marx saying was engraved on the cover. *"Given the choice between a woman and a cigar, I will always choose the cigar."* Charles chuckled. "I couldn't have said it better, Groucho."

He walked back to the window and opened it just a crack. He clipped the cigar, then struck a match and lit it, puffing several times until the flame took hold. Sleep was out of the question. He would spend the rest of those early morning hours staring out at the water, making plans. *You'll be home soon, Jamey. And the first thing we'll do is take out the boat.*

CHAPTER 17

Ventspils to Uzava, Latvia

Morningstar squinted against the sun as he stepped off the plane at the small Ventspils airport along Latvia's west coast. Though the flight from DC had been a long one, he had been able to secure a government plane with plenty of room, and he felt surprisingly rested after the nine-hour flight. He was excited for what he was about to do, but he was also irritated. About four hours before he landed – which would have been around two a.m. in America – he had received a call from Levi, stating not only that he had failed to find the tape recorder that had been left at the scene of Jeannie Madison's murder, but that Andrew Madison had gone missing.

"Missing? How the hell can he be missing, Levi?"

"We had him in our sights, Jacob, and we were ready to grab him, but he escaped. I think he's in Evansville."

"Indiana? What makes you think he's there?"

"I hacked all plane, Amtrak, and bus services, and just learned that Andrew Madison bought a bus ticket to Evansville, Indiana on Wednesday afternoon."

"Wednesday! He's been gone since Wednesday, and I'm just hearing of it?"

"Um...yes sir. Like I said, I just found out. And there's been a lot going on."

Morningstar had been furious. But he couldn't deny that there had, indeed, been a lot going on. Levi alone had been responsible for about four different tasks. But the time lag had given Andrew Madison a full two-day head start. Morningstar had smacked the arm of his chair. *That bastard could be anywhere by now.* He had been about to accept Levi's assurances – again – that he would find both Andrew and the recorder, when he had come up with a different plan. *"Forget it, Levi. Just stay focused on Russia."* Morningstar had then immediately reached out to another son. *"There's something I need you to do,"* he had said as he had relayed his plan. The young man had been enthusiastic. *"Yes sir! Don't worry, sir, I'm ready; you have taught me well. I'll take care of it."*

Morningstar chuckled as he walked down a set of stairs to the tarmac. *I'm sure you will, son...I'm sure you will.*

He took a deep breath and felt the cold air sting his lungs. *Cold...but crystal clear,* he thought as he looked up at a stunningly blue sky. A black sedan pulled up to the plane, and one of the two soldiers who had accompanied Morningstar quickly dismissed the driver and slid behind the wheel. The other soldier grabbed Morningstar's suitcases, threw them in the trunk, then opened the door for Morningstar to slide into the back seat.

Morningstar grinned. *Such well-trained young men.*

Priscilla had assured Morningstar that the drive to the bed and breakfast wasn't far. *"Just fifty minutes or so from Ventspils to your location, sir."* About an hour later, just before two p.m., the car pulled up to a small, nondescript cottage in the middle of nowhere. At least a foot of snow was piled on each side of the drive.

Morningstar's door was opened and he stepped out. He looked around. There wasn't another house in sight. *This'll be perfect,* he thought as he walked toward the house. The driver, Steve, gave a quick knock on the front door. Without waiting for an answer, Steve opened the door and walked inside. He made a quick sweep of the cottage, then motioned to Morningstar that it was safe. Morningstar walked in, while the other soldier, Scott, carried his bags into the foyer and set them on a marble floor.

A fire was burning in a massive hearth and Morningstar smiled at the welcoming flames. He walked over to a large window that looked out on what he guessed was a pond. The recent snow had covered it to the point that all he could see was a vague outline. The blue sky was quickly becoming gray as dark clouds moved in. He nodded. *More snow on the way.* He spotted a shoveled walkway that led from a back door through a tree-filled garden toward the pond. He ran his fingers through his short black hair and grinned. *A perfect setting for what I am about to do.*

He took off his overcoat, walked it to a hook by the door, then went back to the window. He found himself captivated, not only by the snow, but by the solitude. After a minute or two, he turned and leaned his back against the sill. He took in the spacious living room, admiring the open layout of the home. Though he could see several doors coming off a long hallway, the house appeared to be empty. He nodded. That had been the plan. He looked at Steve. "Put my things in the largest bedroom. Then see if you can find the owners so I can inform them of my expectations."

Steve nodded and left the room.

Morningstar turned to the second officer. "Go with him, Scott, so I can have a moment to myself."

Scott followed Steve down the hall.

Morningstar walked over to the stone fireplace and put out his hands to warm them. He grinned. *Priscilla has outdone herself.*

"Here they are, sir."

Morningstar turned to see an older man and woman standing in an arched doorway between what was clearly a kitchen, and the room where he was warming himself by the fire. They were both wearing heavy coats that were covered in snow.

"Mr. and Mrs. Klosky, I presume?"

The couple nodded as if their heads were glued together. In surprisingly clear English, the man said, "Yes sir. Welcome. I was told that there are three of you?"

Morningstar nodded. "Yes." He narrowed his eyes. "And, as I'm sure my secretary made clear, I expect no one else to check in while we're here. Is that clear?"

The man hesitated. "It...it is not customary, sir." He swallowed. "We... have four other rooms in our establishment. Our income relies on those rooms being full."

Evenly, Morningstar said, "I don't give a shit how many rooms you have, Klosky, or what your financial needs might be. I get the whole place, as requested by General Alexander Daniels, Chairman of the Joint Chiefs of Staff of the United States Army, or I report you to the International Tribunal on NATO Warfare."

The fact that there was no such tribunal didn't matter; the Klosky's would never know.

Mr. Klosky quickly agreed. "Cer—certainly, sir. Make yourselves at home."

Morningstar chuckled. "I will. And I'll need both of you to stay out of my way, except to change my sheets, fix my meals, and keep the fire going."

The couple nodded, again in unison, clearly frightened by the prospect of facing the Tribunal.

Morningstar added, "Speaking of which, I don't suppose your wife could whip us up some lunch."

The man shifted awkwardly, then looked over at his wife. She gave a subtle nod. He looked at Morningstar. "Will soup and sandwiches be acceptable, sir?"

Morningstar sighed. "I suppose so. We'll discuss meal plans later."

He turned back to the fire, leaving the man and his wife standing in the doorway. He looked over his shoulder and said, "Well, get on with it; we're starving."

The couple scurried into the kitchen. Morningstar hid a laugh. *Servants do best when put in their place from the start.*

He stepped back from the fire and looked around for a liquor cabinet. There was an armoire on the other side of the room. He walked over and opened the door, pleased to see a row of bottles labeled "Riga Black Balsam." Though he had never tasted it, he guessed it was of high quality. *Those Latvians love their liqueurs,* he thought, and helped himself to a glass.

"Your room is ready, sir." The comment had come from Steve.

Morningstar nodded and gulped the drink. He grimaced; sweet, but not altogether unpleasant. "Steve, you and Scott go to your rooms until I call for you."

The man bowed his head slightly and left the room. Morningstar couldn't help but chuckle. *It's like a giant game of chess,* he thought, as he poured another glass of the liqueur. *I simply put the pieces where they need to go.*

He was about to carry the drink to an oversized chair sitting near the fire, when he noticed a shelf filled with what looked like board games. He walked over and pulled a box from the shelf. He carried it and his glass of balsam to the chair. "Speaking of which," he said to no one as he set the box on his lap. He opened it and pulled out a square chess board, which he laid on a nearby table. He reached in the box for sixteen white chess pieces and set them on the board in their proper positions. He stared at the black chess pieces and nodded. *These will represent me and my sons.* He reached first for the castles. There were two: one would denote the White House – *his* White House once his renegade son returned to the fold – and the other would signify the Henderson castle that would soon be his. He set the pieces at each end of the board. He pulled out the knights; there were two of them, as well. Though he only had one true Knight – Jerome Knight, his Judah who just happened to be the current U.S. President – the other knight would represent another son, Joseph, who had been a knight among his peers. The irony was that both had left their posts. Judah had gone into hiding – *whoever heard of a President going into hiding* – and Joseph, Martin Henderson, had vanished, as well, somehow escaping a Lithuanian jail cell. He bristled as he set the two knights on the board. *I'll get them back...then I'll kill them.*

He pulled out the two bishops and set them on the board. *Asher and Gad...one dead, one alive...both exceptional.* He grabbed the queen, held her up, and smiled affectionately. He placed her between the two bishops. *My lovely Janet, who will stand near me...but always in my shadow.* With the box still on his lap, he pulled out the first of eight pawns and held it up. *Reuben – Pocks – who, in spite of a weak constitution, managed to kill Cynthia Madison by sabotaging her plane.* He laughed and set the pawn on the board. He pulled out another and held it high. *Levi – Josh Adams – my technology wizard who, from the basement of the Pentagon, has created truths from lies with the magic of a computer.* He set that pawn on the board and grabbed the next one. *Dan – Cobra – a notorious serial killer. Just one more murder, in China, and he will have fulfilled his destiny.* He set that pawn on the board, then pulled out two more. "Naphtali and Simeon," he said aloud as he placed the pawns on the board. The two men were in France trying to find the lost warship, *Der Morgenstern,* the Morning Star. He grabbed the next pawn and held it high. *Issachar, a former Philadelphia police officer, who, having inspired a series of well-timed shootings, is now carrying out another vital mission.* Morningstar set that pawn on the board, then took out the last two pawns. He held up the first one and smiled. *Zebulun, the remarkable Russian who has cemented his place among the sons by assassinating an American President.* He set it on the board. He held up the last of the pawns and said aloud, "Last but not least is Benjamin, who will be born soon and will prove to be the greatest of them all." He placed that pawn on the board, then pulled out the only remaining piece, the king, and held it up triumphantly. In a bold voice, he said, "And now, with the placement of this king, I declare today as the beginning; the start of the Reign of Morningstar." He laughed heartily as he set it on the board.

He tossed the empty box on the floor and arranged the board squarely on the table, the black pieces closest to him. He sipped his liqueur and admired his kingdom. Sixteen soldiers on a ten-by-ten board: twelve sons, two castles, a queen and a king.

He stared at the board a minute longer, then stood and returned to the window. The snow had once again begun to fall, and he watched as it covered the pond, the garden, and the path that led to both. He grinned. Everything was in place. Except for a hiccup here and there, things were going well. The biggest coup of all would take place in a matter of days. A U.S. senator, accompanied by his 'bodyguard' – Cobra – would fly to Beijing. Then, on November 4th, Cobra would kill Tai Chu, the son of a Chinese military leader. After that, Cobra would kill the senator. The Chinese soldiers would then surely kill Cobra, removing any evidence of Morningstar's involvement.

He chuckled as he said aloud, "November 4th, a day that will live on in infamy." The assassination of Tai Chu would alter U.S./China policy for the next thirty years, and could quite possibly bring about a third world war. Morningstar had given Cobra a note to leave at the scene that would make it look as if Sturgill had killed the young man on behalf of the American government. China would be in an uproar, and the rest of the world – already in chaos – would demand a response. Longtime U.S. allies would be forced to renounce their ties as China declared war on the West. With one simple murder, Morningstar will have disrupted the entire geopolitical map for decades to come. "Which is when I, the Great Morningstar, will step in as the voice of reason, the man who will avert World War III." He laughed. "I'll be seen around the globe as the Savior of the World."

Through well-timed murders and maneuverings, Morningstar hadn't only spurred the conflicts that were taking place in so many different countries, but had also positioned himself to take charge of the army of each of those countries, thereby ending all opposition. He would unite those armies, and then, using the greatest militia ever assembled, would silence nonbelievers with a wave of his hand. He would affirm his reign over all things: Good and Evil, War and Peace, Life and Death. Once he had reached that final pinnacle and had led his sons to the mountaintop, then and only then would he relinquish his hold over them. *They will thank me for their very lives, which will inspire others to believe in me.*

He opened the window, letting in a burst of blowing snow. He ignored it as he said, "No force will be needed. My sons and all mankind will bow to me of their own volition, recognizing that I, Edward Morningstar, am the rightful king of the world."

He shivered and quickly closed the window. "But there are loose ends," he whispered softly. He would need to tie them up if he hoped to have any chance of success. Three men were missing: Hank Clarkson, Martin Henderson, and Jerome Knight. It was vital not only that he find them, but that he kill them.

Clarkson would either be found by Pocks and killed by Simeon, or Morningstar's brilliant backup plan would distract him to the point where he would become ineffective. *Then it will be easy for any one of my sons to kill the bastard.*

And Knight would surely come home soon, likely on his own. Why? *Either to save Emma's husband and daughter, or to save the country after Harrington tells him that I dared to utter the words 'nuclear war.' He will then know that I mean business.*

As for Henderson, Morningstar would use the same tactic on him that he had used in the past...vowing harm to someone Henderson loved if he didn't come back to him. It had worked well with Lili Platacis; Morningstar had gotten nearly four years of killing out of Henderson just by threatening a little girl. *But this time, I'll threaten the man that he worships more than any other.*

Morningstar pulled out his cellphone. He dialed as he looked at his watch. *Oh dear, only seven-thirty in the morning in DC...and on a Saturday, no less. Oops.*

A sleepy voice said, "Hello?"

"Priscilla, it's Morningstar."

"It's Saturday, sir...I'm not at work. And it's rather early here, sir."

"I know it's Saturday and I know it's early, dammit!" He took a breath, then, much calmer he said, "Could you please put me through to General Daniels?"

"I'll have to try him at home, sir; I doubt he's in the office...so early on a Saturday."

He rolled his eyes. *Cry me a river.* "Certainly, Priscilla. I'll wait."

Within minutes, he heard the raspy voice of his boss. "Dammit, Morningstar, don't you ever sleep?"

Morningstar forced a laugh. "Not when the fate of the world is at hand, sir."

"So, how's it going over there, Morningstar?"

"Good, sir. I just got here. The owners have been most accommodating."

"Glad to hear it. So tell me...why are you there...exactly. What is your plan? Your message said it had something to do with NATO, but I've known you long enough to know that you're up to something."

Morningstar chuckled to himself. *If only you knew, General.* "Actually sir, it's exactly as I said. My goal is to firm up America's ties to Latvia's military leaders." He paused. "As you know, sir, in the last twenty-four hours, Putin has increased his presence along Latvia's eastern border." Another pause, "What you may not know, sir, is that he appears to be planning a sea invasion, as well." He paused. "Because of this, I feel a need to move quickly. I thought I might start with Walter Henderson, who controls an impressive militia here in Latvia, including a sizeable flotilla of ships. Which would be especially helpful if Putin decides to attack from the Baltic Sea." He cleared his throat. "If possible, I would like to have dinner with Walter and his wife at their home." He hesitated. "My concern, sir, is that they are very private. I believe that their estate isn't even visible on any of our standard charts."

"That's true, Morningstar. But we have maps that outline it in explicit detail."

Morningstar chuckled to himself. *As if I didn't already know.* "I guessed as much, sir." Again, he cleared his throat. "I was wondering if you could call Walter on my behalf, sir, and arrange the dinner for say...seven-thirty this evening?"

"Tonight? That's rather short notice, don't you think?"

"Yes sir, but like I said, I believe we need to move quickly."

There was a pause. "Yes, I think you're right, Morningstar. Let me get some coffee, and then I'll give Walter a call. I'll have to hunt down his private cellphone number."

"I believe Jason Hanover has it, sir."

"Excellent. I'll have Priscilla call Hanover once I hang up here." There was a pause. "And I'll have her send you the Henderson compound coordinates and the maps that outline their estate. I'll also have her send you a phone number to the Henderson security team so that you can coordinate your visit."

"Thank you, sir." Morningstar ended the call. He laughed aloud as he looked out the window at the snow-covered pond. *Nothing like having the Chairman of the Joint Chiefs paving my way...and giving me cover.*

CHAPTER 18

Chengdu, China

Hank stretched his arms as he stood in the aisle and waited to leave the plane. The flight from Rome to Chengdu, China, had been a long one, and, though he had tried to sleep, he had had a hard time. He was worried about Jenny. He had finally lulled himself to sleep, only by convincing himself that when he landed in Chengdu he would try her again and this time she would answer. It would be early Saturday morning in America. It wasn't like she would be out and about at that hour.

He was eager to get off of the plane. He reached the door, surprised to see that there was no jetway. He was met with bitter cold air as he walked down the stairs. *Why couldn't Maddi have decided to fly somewhere like Tahiti?* He zipped his jacket and followed the other passengers across the tarmac into the terminal. Thirty minutes later, he was through customs and made a quick stop at a bathroom. He relieved himself, then washed his hands and rinsed his face. He left the bathroom and found a quiet place to make the call. But as he heard it go to voicemail, his worst fears were realized. Jenny wasn't answering. No doubt about it; something was wrong.

So, who do I call to find her, he wondered as he stood outside what he guessed was a coffee shop. There was no one he could call. After all, there were only three people who had any idea what he had been through: Jenny, Maddi, and Maddi's bodyguard Cravens. Two of those three were missing. *I guess that leaves Cravens.* But he and Cravens had said their goodbyes at the plane crash. They had left it that they wouldn't speak to one another any time soon, or maybe ever. They couldn't even hint that they were anything more than acquaintances. The fact that between the two of them they had manufactured one of the biggest lies of the century was something no one could ever know. *But Jenny is missing...and I have no one else to turn to.*

He stared at his trac phone. He didn't know Cravens' number. Then he remembered; just as he had been about to drive Maddi away from the crash site, Cravens had handed him a scrap of paper with Angelo Recito's number. It had been torn from some sort of work memo, and on the other side, it included part of Cravens' name, along with his Secret Service email address and a cellphone number.

Hank pulled out his wallet and took the scrap of paper from a hidden compartment. He stared down at the number. Had Cravens' phone survived the plane crash? What if he had gotten a new phone? *Just try it, Hank.*

He dialed the number and waited. *One, two, three, four...*he was about to hang up, when the call was answered with a gruff, "Yeah?"

Hank hesitated. Just hearing Cravens' voice made him ache for how things used to be a mere two or three months ago...when Maddi was still Maddi, Hank was with Jenny, and the world wasn't hovering on the precipice of war.

Cravens barked, "Who is this?"

"It's me."

There was a pause. Then, quieter, "Hank? Geez, buddy. What's up? My flight's just pulling away here in DC. We probably shouldn't be talking unless—"

"I need your help," Hank swallowed, "...something has happened to Jenny."

CHAPTER 19

Aberdeen, Scotland

Walter paced the courtyard in front of the Hazlehead Park gate as he once again checked his watch. It was 12:58; only three minutes later than the last time he had checked. He shook his head and stared at the stragglers walking into the park. He was looking for one man in particular; Mark Justice. Tall, well-dressed, blond hair to his shoulders; that was how the psychiatrist, Samuels, had described the man. *"You can't miss him, Walter. A very distinguished young man."* To think that that same man was also the Cobra was almost incomprehensible.

Walter had arrived in Aberdeen just after 11:00 a.m. and had immediately taxied to the park. The coin jubilee – his lure for getting Justice to meet him without his alter ego in tow – was an annual event that took place in October. Walter had asked Justice to meet him at the gate at noon...*nearly a full hour ago.* The Queen Herself was expected at two p.m. to celebrate the latest royal coin. Though Walter had hoped that he and Justice might share in the festivities, it would appear that for whatever reason, Justice had chosen not to come.

Thank God I didn't call in the police, he thought as he made another circle outside the gate. He was fully aware that he should call them if there was even a chance that Cobra's location might be known. He had decided against it, however, telling himself that there was no need to involve them if the invitation had fallen on deaf ears. The truth was that he wanted to meet Justice face-to-face to see if what Nenita had told him was true. *There's a good version of our son out there, Walter.*

But as Walter noted the large number of police at the park – likely due to the impending arrival of the Queen – it occurred to him that maybe their presence had spooked Justice. He shook his head. Not likely. From what Samuels had told him, Justice not only saw himself as a law-abiding citizen, but had actually worked *with* the police on many occasions.

Walter turned and was about to complete another lap, when his cellphone vibrated. He pulled it from his pocket and answered with a quick, "Hello."

"Is this Walter Henderson?"

Walter's eyes brightened. *Justice?* He cleared his throat. "Who's speaking?"

"Alexander Daniels."

Walter frowned. *Why is the Chairman of the Joint Chiefs calling me on a Saturday afternoon? That's not good.* "Hello, General. What can I do for you?"

"I'm calling to request an audience on behalf of an aide of mine."

"An audience?"

"Yes. The aide has just arrived in Latvia, and has asked that I introduce him to you by way of this phone call."

"Has he come to support our efforts against Putin?"

"Yes. And he's brought with him another battalion of U.S. soldiers, which will be stationed not far from Latvia's western border."

Walter narrowed his eyes. "With all due respect, General, that seems like a strange place to station your soldiers. The battle is coming from the east."

"Yes...until it isn't." A pause. "My aide has informed me that a possible sea attack has been identified. And though I know that the Latvian army, as well as your own personal army, are quite capable of battling such an attack, the U.S. wanted to reinforce to the world that we stand beside you."

"Thank you, General. That is deeply appreciated. When might I expect a visit from this aide?"

"Tonight, if it's not too presumptuous of me to ask." There was a pause. "He feels the need to move on this quickly, considering the fact that, over the last twenty-four hours, Putin has begun a buildup of troops on Latvia's eastern border."

Walter checked his watch. It was now exactly 1:00. He would need to leave soon if he was to be home and ready for a visit from a U.S. military aide. He looked at the people coming to the park. The foot traffic had picked up as it was getting nearer to the Queen's arrival. He shook his head. There was no sense waiting any longer. Clearly, Justice wasn't coming. *And I have no desire to deal with the chaos of the Queen's arrival.* He sighed. "Certainly, General. When might we expect him?"

"I believe he requested seven-thirty. Again, if it's not too presumptuous, he was hoping to meet with you over dinner...you and your lovely wife, Dora."

"It will be our pleasure, sir. His name?" Walter turned to walk to the exit.

"Edward Morningstar."

Walter stopped. He had certainly heard that name before. Morningstar was the name that Martin had written on the scrap of paper before he had tried to hang himself. In Martin's suicide note, he hadn't bothered with 'I love you's' or 'I'm sorry's,' but had used what he had expected to be his final words to say that Morningstar was an awful man who had done awful things. Dinner with that same man seemed like a bad idea. He frowned. *Then again, what better chance to gauge the measure of the man.* He nodded. "Seven-thirty it is. I'll make the arrangements."

"Thank you, Mr. Henderson. And please don't hesitate to call if you need anything from the U.S. military. I can vouch for the man that you're about to spend the evening with. He has been with me for over twenty-five years. There's not a more loyal or patriotic American."

"I'll look forward to meeting him, General."

"Good. Again, thank you."

The call ended. Walter dialed his wife. "Dora, I'm sorry for the late notice, but we've been asked by the Chairman of the Joint Chiefs to host his top aide for dinner tonight at seven-thirty." He paused. "I believe he'll be coming alone. Ed Morningstar is his name. I'll leave the details to you, and I promise to get home as soon as I can."

Thankfully, Dora didn't ask questions. She had never read Martin's suicide note, and as such wasn't aware of his concerns regarding Morningstar. Walter was surprised that Daniels had given Morningstar such an enthusiastic endorsement. Maybe he wasn't so bad after all. Martin had told Walter that he had overreacted when he had written that note. Perhaps Walter should give the man a chance.

He took one final look at the incoming visitors and sighed. Justice wasn't coming. He walked to the courtyard exit to wait for a taxi. After a minute or so, a black cab pulled up. Just as Walter was about to slide into the back, he heard someone calling his name. He looked toward the voice, hoping to see the tall, distinguished Mark Justice. Instead he saw an older man; short, stocky, and dressed like a seventeenth century court jester, running toward him. Walter said to the driver, "Please, give me a minute," then stepped from the cab.

The jester ran up to him. In a very strong Scottish accent, the man said, "Are ye Walter 'enderson?"

"Who's asking?"

The jester took a minute to catch his breath. "I...I was asked to give Mr. 'enderson a message, but I need to know if yer 'im."

Walter considered it, then nodded. "I am...I'm Walter Henderson."

The jester cleared his throat. "Could ye maybe show me some ID?"

Walter hesitated, then pulled out his wallet and showed the man his U.S. driver's license.

The jester looked from the license to Walter, then back at the license. He nodded and reached in his pocket. He pulled out a notecard-sized envelope, and handed it to Walter.

Walter took the card and frowned. "When did you get this?"

"Yesterday, sir. Around four p.m. I was 'ere gettin' things ready fer today."

"Can you tell me a bit about the man who gave it to you?"

The jester nodded. "Yessir. 'e was quite respectable, 'e was. 'e 'ad blond 'air to 'ere," the man pointed to his shoulders, "...and 'e wore a snappy, bone-colored suit, 'e did. But it were 'is eyes that struck me."

"Struck you? How?"

The man moved closer and stared at Walter, his eyes narrowed to slits. "As a matter of fact, they looked a lot like yer eyes, sir. A remarkable blue, they were." He paused. "Actually, 'e looked quite a bit like you, 'e did."

Walter shifted uncomfortably, then nodded slowly. "Did he say anything?"

"Only that I was to give this 'ere note to a tall, distinguished-looking man with dark hair, who would likely be lingerin' at the gate at noon."

Walter frowned. "It's after one p.m. Why did you wait?"

The man nodded. "Because 'e told me that I needed to make sure it was you, and that the best way to know would be to watch ya fer a bit. 'e said if it was really you, that ye would stay at that gate; that ye wouldn't walk inside, but ye wouldn't leave." The man paused. "I gave it an hour, I did... and ye fit the bill."

Walter nodded. "Why did you do this? It seems like quite a lot to ask of you."

The jester shifted awkwardly. "Honestly, sir, I'm not quite sure. The man did pay me, but there was another reason I decided to honor 'is request."

"And what is that?"

The man paused. "'e seemed so...sincere. So eager to get ye this message." Another pause. "'e told me 'e was sposed to meet ya, but that 'e wouldn't be 'ere tomorrow, which is today, but 'e wanted ya to know that 'e had wanted to meet ya."

"Did he say why he couldn't come here today?"

The jester frowned. "I asked 'im the same thing. His answer was quite odd." The man paused. "'e said it was likely that, by then, 'e would no longer be himself."

Walter nodded. "I see." He reached in his wallet and took out a twenty-euro bill. He was about to hand it to the man, when the jester waved him off. "As I said, sir, Mr. Justice paid me – 'andsomely, I might add – to give ye this note. I certainly don't expect money from you."

Walter smiled. "Thank you."

The jester gave a quick bow, then turned and ran back to the gate. Walter watched him go, then looked down at the notecard. High-quality and gold-embossed, it had "Walter" written across the front in bold, flowing letters. He unsealed the envelope and pulled out a card. He opened it and saw the same flowing letters.

"Good afternoon, Walter.

"I had so looked forward to meeting you, and to sharing your interest in coins; particularly the Queen's coin that was to be presented tomorrow – which, if you're reading this, is today.

"Unfortunately, I have only a limited time when I am confident of who I am. I know that that sounds quite odd, but trust me when I say...you don't want to see that other side of me.

"Regardless, I couldn't let the opportunity pass without at least finding a way to make contact with you. Not only to make your acquaintance, but to impart vital information regarding the impending war with Russia. Unfortunately, it is not suitable for me to include it here. As such, I would like to arrange a meeting, perhaps at a place where I am more likely to be myself. My offices are in downtown London, at Belgrade Square. I would be honored if you would meet me there in three weeks, at noon, Saturday, November 20th.

"I look forward to finally having the opportunity to meet you, Walter, as I have read so much about you. I must say that I feel like I know you. We share a common acquaintance with Dr. James Samuels. Perhaps he could join us, as well. Such a fine man.

"Yours respectfully,
"Mark Justice"

Walter stared at the note. Out of nowhere, he felt a sudden urge to cry. He cleared his throat, then slid into the back seat of the taxi and said quickly, "Aberdeen airport."

The cabby nodded and drove away. As they left the park, Walter looked over his shoulder at the gate. Though he had missed an opportunity to meet what was clearly a more desirable version of his son, he now knew two things that he hadn't known before. The first was that Nenita had been correct about their son; he had a side to him that was decent...even respectable. The second was that the man, Justice, did, in fact, have vital information regarding the war with Russia.

He thought back to what Samuels had told him months ago. The psychiatrist had called and had relayed a rhyme that he had received from Justice that had implied that Lithuania might not be a reliable ally should the war expand to the entire Baltic region. Walter had asked Samuels to look into it, but due to the man having been kidnapped in Lithuania and all that had happened since, Walter hadn't had a chance to discuss with Samuels what he had learned. But now, Walter felt a sense of urgency to learn whatever he could from the psychiatrist. He nodded. *I'll talk to him the minute I get back to the castle.*

He shook his head. He couldn't talk to Samuels when he got back; he and Dora were to have dinner with Edward Morningstar from the Pentagon. Walter would barely get to the castle in time, as it was. His discussion with the psychiatrist would have to wait until the dinner had ended and Morningstar had left the castle.

Or...perhaps I could include Samuels in the dinner. He chuckled. It would be intriguing to hear the doctor's impressions of their guest. But the more Walter thought about it, the more he decided it would be a bad idea. His meeting with Morningstar had to occur as planned with just the three of them. Otherwise, Morningstar might put up his guard...*especially when it's a psychiatrist sitting at the other end of the table.*

He rubbed his eyes as he thought again about the letter from Justice. It was revealing on many fronts. Not the least of which was that Walter was about to once again know Cobra's exact location. Mark Justice – Cobra – would be in downtown London on the 20th of November. He shifted awkwardly. *I should notify the police.*

He took a deep breath and sighed. Yes, he should notify them, but he wouldn't; he knew that now. *Not until I have a chance to know my son.* He would meet Justice on November 20th and do whatever it took to restore, and then keep Justice as the dominant personality.

Then what? he wondered as the cab turned onto the drive that led to the small Aberdeen airport. *What will you do then, Walter?* He had vowed to either turn in the man himself, or compel Justice to turn himself in. Could he do it? He took a deep breath and sighed. *I'll have to. It's the only way I can live with the choices I've made.*

CHAPTER 20

Portland, Maine

Gad had finally left Warsaw on a 747 that pulled out of the gate at exactly twelve a.m. Saturday. He had arrived at Dulles Airport in Washington, DC, nine hours later, at three a.m. Saturday, EST. He had been lucky to find a commuter flight from DC to Portland that left at five, getting him to a small Portland, Maine airport by seven in the morning. Between the two flights, he had managed to string together about five hours of sleep. It wasn't much, but it would have to do. As his Father had impressed upon him time and time again, *"The need for sleep is a state of mind."*

The plane pulled to the gate of the commuter airport and stopped. Gad zipped his hoodie and grabbed his backpack from under the seat. He stood and threw it over his shoulder, then put on sunglasses and followed the passengers off the plane. He walked down a set of stairs to the terminal, making sure to keep his head down. He couldn't risk being stopped for any reason; there wasn't time. Galina Cannon was due to arrive at Portland's International Airport in less than three hours; he had a lot to do.

He walked through the terminal and out the door to the taxi queue. "The nearest library," he mumbled as he climbed in the first available cab. He was driven downtown to the main branch of the Portland Library and let out at the door. He paid the fare, but was forced to wait outside until

8:00, a full twenty-five minutes, for the library to open. He had only the hoodie, and was freezing by the time they unlocked the door. He ran past the clerk to the back of the library in search of a computer.

There was a row of them along one wall, and he took a seat behind the one furthest from the door. He logged on, hopeful that Morningstar had sent details about Michael Canon and his daughter, Galina. If Gad was to kidnap Michael, he would need to know what the man looked like.

He typed in the address to a secure website known only by a few. He clicked on links buried in three different sites, and was soon taken to a top secret location. He clicked on an email with the heading: M. Cannon. His eyes widened when he got to the part about Emma Melnikov, Cannon's wife. She was the daughter of Russian expatriates, and had dated the U.S. President, Jerome Knight, sixteen years ago while they were in college. Suddenly he stopped. He reread the line he had just read.

"Jerome Knight, aka Judah, has disappeared."

Gad hadn't been aware that Judah was also President of the United States. He laughed. *Holy shit, Morningstar, you managed to get one of us into the White House?*

He kept reading. Apparently, just a few days ago, Knight and Emma had rekindled their romance, and, for whatever reason, Morningstar wasn't having it. As Gad read through what was expected of him, he chuckled. *This should be fun.*

It was eight-thirty by the time he left the library. He had printed a photo of Michael Cannon, and had memorized the man's features. White, six feet tall, light eyes, lighter hair. With his cap pulled low over his forehead and still wearing his sunglasses, Gad walked several blocks to an American Legion on the corner of Apple and Fifth. Yesterday, while he was stuck in Warsaw's airport, he had sent a text to a contact he knew from his days in DC. The man had promised to hook him up with a gun runner from Maine, who went by the name Augusta. Augusta had texted him while he was in the library, and had told him to be at the corner of Apple and Fifth at nine. They had agreed upon a coded exchange involving Stephen King and Maine's extremely cold weather. Gad reached the corner at 8:55, praying that the man would get there on time. *Let's go, Augusta...I ain't got all day, and it's cold as hell out here.*

He paced the sidewalk as the seconds ticked by. He checked his watch again; it was 8:58...he was starting to get nervous. He couldn't do what he needed to do without a weapon. He waited another five minutes, then walked toward the American Legion to get warm. He was about to walk in, when out of nowhere, a heavyset man walked up to him wearing a loose-fitting overcoat. The man was wearing sunglasses, a hat, and a scarf that covered most of his face. He was about five-ten, had leathered skin, and looked to be in his late sixties or early seventies.

The man shivered and said, "Damn, it's cold out here."

Gad narrowed his eyes. "It's always cold in Maine...somethin' to do with the squalls comin' in off the sea." He paused. "At least that's what Stephen King says."

The man lowered his voice. "What d'ya need?"

"A .32 should do it."

"It'll be eight hundred."

"For a lousy .32?"

"Take it or leave it."

Gad hissed as he paid the man in cash. The gun runner pulled a pistol from an inside pocket of his overcoat. Hiding it in his oversized palm, he slid it to Gad by way of a handshake. Gad gripped it tight to gauge the fit, checked to be sure it was loaded, then shoved it in his pocket.

The man turned and walked away. Though Gad was tempted to go into the American Legion to get warm, he didn't have time. He jogged three blocks to a row of stores, and found a costume shop across from a department store. He walked into the costume shop and quickly found what he needed: a black beard. He bought it, then walked to the store across the street, where he bought a heavy coat. He put it on, walked to an alley, and pasted on the beard. Now all he needed was a new ID; a simple driver's license would do. A bookie friend in DC had given him the name of a guy on the south end of town who could hook him up. He checked his watch. *Shit!* It was already nine-thirty. He had to get to the airport. He would arrange for the ID after he was done. Glad for the warmer coat, he ran to the nearest corner, relieved to see a cab come by in less than a minute. He waved it down and slid in back. "Portland International...and hurry."

* * *

Secret Service Agent Tom Cravens ran his fingers through his wispy gray hair as he walked off the commuter plane in Portland, Maine. The last thirty-six hours had been tough. He was already sleep-deprived, and the delays in Riga and Germany, combined with the rigors of overseas travel, had given him little chance to make up for it. He had never been good at sleeping siting up.

He had landed in DC at six in the morning. The first thing he had done was contact his boss. If he was to confront a seasoned killer, he would need a gun. Though he would have preferred to not call Allen until the situation with Gad was taken care of, the only way he could get a gun legally was if his boss somehow okayed it.

As expected, the call to Allen hadn't gone well. For one thing, Cravens had wakened him from a sound sleep. On top of that, Cravens had been forced to side-step questions about what he had been doing for the past two months, or when he was coming back to work. *"With all due respect, sir, I can't tell you. But I wanted you to know that I am back in America, and that I'll report as soon as I can."* Allen had insisted that he come in right then; Cravens had told him that that was impossible.

He had been tempted to tell Allen about the situation with Hank's wife, so that Allen could assign an agent to try to find her. He had concluded that he couldn't risk it. To tell Allen about Jenny would require that he explain how he knew the woman, and why Hank would call him in the first place. Hank had been on a leave of absence for over two months. As far as Cravens had been able to determine, Hank hadn't told a single soul where he was or where he had been. Which made sense. He was, after all, trying to hide a U.S. senator who had lived through a crash that the world thought had killed her. Allen would logically ask questions...about Hank, his location, his state of mind after Maddi's death...questions that Cravens wasn't prepared to answer.

His boss had filled him in on the President's disappearance. Apparently, three nights ago, with the help of a Secret Service agent, Knight had left the White House and had gone into hiding. According to the VP – who was now the acting President – Knight had told no one where he was going or why; only that he was in danger.

Cravens had been floored. *"Presidents don't just 'go into hiding, sir. What would make him do such a thing?"*

"All the VP said was that Knight had become aware of a threat." Allen had paused. *"I heard a rumor about a Russian spy, but I've heard nothing more about it."*

"So, who was the agent who helped him escape?"

Another pause. *"You won't believe it, Cravens, but it was Jerry Foster."*

Cravens had been shocked. Foster was one of the most respected men on the force. Just as the call had been about to end, Cravens had asked Allen for a gun.

"Why do you need a gun, Cravens?"

"Because I'm a Secret Service agent who will quite possibly have a need for a weapon in the near future, sir. Can we leave it at that?"

"No, we can't, dammit! Now, tell me what is going on, Cravens."

Cravens had hesitated. *"Will it suffice for me to tell you, sir, that I have been asked by a well-respected patriot to handle a sensitive matter?"*

The response had been fierce. *"No, it will not suffice! You work for the United States of America, and you report to me!"*

Cravens had been forced to pull in the grief card. *"Sir, I recently lost my protectee and my partner. I nearly died myself. I need a bit more time, sir."*

After a long pause, Allen had given in. *"Okay, fine. But why the gun?"*

"All I can say, sir, is that I feel naked without my weapon."

Apparently, that had been enough, as, after a bit more back and forth, it was agreed that Allen would have a gun waiting for Cravens at Portland's downtown police station by nine a.m. *"Be prepared to show ID."*

Cravens had thanked the man and had ended the call. An hour later, he had boarded the commuter flight to Portland, which had just landed at a small municipal airport. It was nine a.m. He had one hour to pick up his gun and get to the airport.

But it was the call from Hank that had hit him the hardest. The poor man was clearly distraught. The call had come through just as the flight to Portland had been about to take off. *"I need your help...something has happened to Jenny,"* Hank had said, the panic evident in his voice. He hadn't shared his location, nor had he said a word about Maddi. They had both known instinctively that if Hank was going to risk calling Cravens, the last thing either one of them should do was talk about Maddi.

But the timing couldn't have been worse. Not only had Cravens already boarded the flight for Portland, but he was pressed for time. Nonetheless, he had promised Hank that he would do whatever he could to find Jenny. Why? *Because Hank and I have been through way too much for me to not help him now.*

But first, Cravens had to pick up his gun at the police station, then confront Gad at Portland's International Airport, all in less than an hour. Fortunately, he had used the delay in Germany to do research on the man Gad was to meet up with. Using the laptop he had bought in Riga, he had learned quite a bit about Michael Cannon; where he worked, what he looked like, who he was married to. He had printed out his photo, and, by the time he had boarded the overseas flight, he had acquired a working knowledge of the man – and the family – that the fake DeMarco had come to torment.

And now it's time to use what I learned. Cravens walked out the door of the small airport and approached a waiting cab. He climbed in back and asked the cabby to take him to the downtown police precinct. They reached it in ten minutes; he asked the driver to wait as he ran inside. After a show of his ID and a verification call from the police chief to Allen, he was given his gun. He ran back to the cab and had the driver take him to Portland's International Airport. He checked his watch. 9:35. With any luck, he would get there before Gad had a chance to kidnap Michael Cannon.

* * *

Gad reached Portland's International Airport at 9:52. On the way, he had made a quick phone call to a number he had pulled from his research on Michael, and was ending the call just as the cab pulled up to the drop-off point. He paid the fare and slid out of the cab. He ran inside, checked to make sure Galina's plane was on time, then walked to the area outside the security checkpoint to look for Michael. Referring to the photo he had printed at the library, he scanned the faces of those standing outside the checkpoint. No Michael. He found a bench where he could see anyone who walked in or out of the area. At 9:57, he saw a man who looked to be in his late thirties, about six foot, running to the checkpoint. Average weight, average height...average in about every way. Gad double-checked the photo. It was him.

The man stopped about four feet from where Gad was standing. He stood outside the secure area, facing the hallway where the passengers would walk through.

Gad walked up to him and smiled. "Michael Cannon?"

The man looked at him and narrowed his eyes. There was no doubt about it; he was Michael Cannon. Gad could see the strain that the past forty-eight hours had had on him. Worry combined with a lack of sleep was visible in every line on the man's face. "Yes...can I help you?"

"You can." Gad lowered his voice. "I know where your wife is."

Michael stared at Gad. He stepped away from the crowd, and was about to say something, when Gad added, "If you come with me, I'll take you to her."

"Why would I do that?"

"Because if you don't," he whispered, "I'll tell the men who are holding her to kill her."

"The men who are...holding her?"

Gad nodded. "Yeah...so let's go."

Michael had begun to shake. "What...what about Galina?"

"I've made arrangements for your mamma to pick her up."

"You what?"

"I called your mother in Falmouth about fifteen minutes ago." He grinned. "Arlene, isn't it? Charming gal. Glad to help, considering all you're going through."

Michael's jaw was set, but Gad could see that his hands were shaking. Gad turned and walked toward the door. "Follow me." He reached the door, opened it, and walked outside. He waved down a taxi and opened the back door. He motioned for Michael to get in, then slid in after him. He said to the driver, "Front and Norman."

* * *

Cravens had arrived at the Portland International Airport at 9:54. He had forced himself to walk calmly into the terminal, then had looked for a vantage point from where he could spot either Michael Cannon or Gad without being seen. He had picked a row of chairs near the entrance, and had sat next to an oversized planter. He had spent the next few minutes looking back and forth between those heading to Security and those heading for the exit. He had guessed that Gad wouldn't risk crossing Security, and had hoped to stop him before he could get to Michael.

He was watching the exit, when he spotted a black man about the same size as Gad walking toward the door. The man looked nothing like the man he had seen at the site of the plane crash, however, so, at first, he dismissed him. But then the man took off his sunglasses to rub his eyes, and Cravens caught a glimpse of the unique glass eye. In spite of a stocking cap and a beard, there was no mistaking it: *it's him.*

There was a man walking behind him, but on his other side. Cravens was unable to get a good look at him. He guessed from the man's build, and from the fact that he was walking so close to Gad, that it was Michael Cannon.

Cravens stood, and, well aware that Gad would likely recognize him from the plane crash, he stayed back and did his best to hide among the many people who had begun to filter in and out of the area. He crossed to the other side of the walkway. From that vantage point he was able to see the face of the man walking behind Gad. Except for an unmistakable expression of panic, he looked exactly like his photo.

Gad and Cannon walked out of the terminal. Cravens stayed with them. Gad directed Cannon to the taxi queue. Cravens was forced to practically jog to keep up with them. He needed to stop them before they got into a taxi. Just as he was about to yell "Stop!" he saw Gad shove Michael into the back of a cab.

"Dammit!" he muttered as he hailed the next taxi. He flashed his ID and said, "Follow that cab."

CHAPTER 21

Portland, Maine

Neither Gad nor Michael said a word during the twenty-minute cab ride. The whole time, Gad made sure that Michael could see the bulge of his gun in his pocket.

When they reached their destination, Gad paid the fare and stepped out of the car. Michael didn't move. Gad glared at him. "Get out."

Michael hesitated, but then did as he was told. Gad waited for the taxi to leave, then led Michael up a set of stone steps to the door of an old Episcopal Church on the corner of Front and Norman. Gad pointed to the door. "In there."

Michael planted his feet. "No, not until I know—"

"Shut up, Michael. I'm in charge."

Reluctantly, Michael walked to the door. He tried to open it; it wouldn't budge. He looked at Gad. "What now?"

Gad walked to the door and, using the grip of his gun, he smashed the lock and opened the door. He motioned for Michael to hurry into the church. He followed Michael inside and closed the door behind him. He checked his watch. Ten-thirty. He had read about the church online, and knew that it was no longer used for regular services. All that took place there now was choir practice and the occasional wedding. He also knew that it would be empty, because Saturday was cleaning day, and the cleaning was typically done between nine and ten a.m. According to the article he had read, the local Bishop stopped by around one to bless a few of the parishioners who had refused to leave the church of their childhood. Gad's hope was that the church would remain empty from the time the cleaning people left around ten, until the Bishop arrived at one o'clock.

So far, so good, he thought as he deadbolted the front door. He pulled out his gun and walked around the vestibule, listening for footsteps or the sound of voices. There were neither; he and Michael were alone. Motioning for Michael to walk ahead of him, he steered him to the altar at the back of the church. Standing face to face on the raised platform, Gad held his gun to Michael's head. "Gimme your cellphone."

"I don't have—"

"Bullshit! Everyone's got a cellphone. Give it to me!"

Michael stiffened, then reached in his coat pocket. He pulled out a phone and handed it to Gad.

Still holding the gun to Michael's head, Gad opened the phone. He saw a photo on the screensaver and whistled under his breath. "I don't know which one's better lookin;' your wife or your daughter." He chuckled as he scrolled through the contacts until he came to the name Emma. He pushed send, but it went straight to voicemail. "Shit," he said, then handed the phone back to Michael, who managed to shove it in his pocket in spite of his shaking hands. Gad pulled out his own phone, scrolled to a number that Morningstar had given him the day before, and dialed.

"Who...who are you calling?" Michael managed to say.

Gad grinned as he shoved the pistol into Michael's temple. "Since your wife didn't answer, I'm calling her boyfriend. I'm calling your traitor wife's boyfriend."

* * *

Luckily, Cravens' cab driver knew the city of Portland well, so it wasn't hard for him to stay with Gad's taxi. Twenty minutes later, Cravens watched from the back seat as Gad's taxi stopped in front of an old Episcopal Church.

"Stop here," Cravens said, about half a block from the church. The cabby pulled over. Cravens handed him two twenty-dollar bills. He scanned the area. Other than Michael and Gad, there was no one around. Cravens watched as Gad led Michael up a set of stairs. The minute he saw Gad break the lock with his pistol and force Michael inside, he jumped out of the cab.

"Should I call the police?" the driver asked.

"No...I am the police! Just go!" Cravens yelled as he sprinted toward the church. He heard the cab drive away.

He reached the church and pulled out his gun. He climbed the stairs, stopping just outside the front door. He put his ear to the door. He heard nothing. He gave the door a quiet tug; it was locked from the inside.

He ran down the stairs, all the while scanning the area to make sure no one was in danger of getting hurt. He crouched behind a row of thick bushes on the south side of the church. Staying low behind the bushes, he crept toward the back. He was looking for a way in. He came to a window and stopped. He raised his head just enough that he could see inside. It was dark in the church and it took a minute for his eyes to adjust, but the minute they did, he was shocked. There before him was Gad, standing at the altar, holding a pistol to the temple of a very frightened Michael Cannon.

CHAPTER 22

Great Kills Harbor, New York

President Jerome Knight and his entourage had reached Great Kills Harbor in the early hours of Saturday morning. Their boat captain, Colt, had kept them at sea for a full 48 hours, as the entire country had gone into lockdown, and the surrounding waterways had been filled with boats of every size and shape. Though it had been expected, the increased security had extended further out than had been anticipated. At one point, Colt had expressed to Secret Service Agent Foster his concern regarding the amplified scrutiny of the ports. *"Don't know how we'll get through,"* he had said as they had finally started their journey to shore. Foster, who had been sick as a dog on the sea's rocky waves, had merely nodded and said, *"I have faith in you, Colt."*

In the dark hours before dawn, Knight had heard Colt kill the engine, and had seen the single light at the front of the boat go off, as well. Using only the moonlight, Colt had rowed the small fishing boat toward a barely-visible harbor, and had docked at a pier that was hidden among a thick grove of overgrown brush. He had tied the boat without a word, had told the passengers below to stay silent, then had proceeded to take a nap in the cabin. His goal had been to seem like nothing more than a man who spent his days and nights on the sea. It had worked; so far, anyway. A patrol boat had come by just as the sun had started to rise. Though Knight had been able to hear only bits and pieces from his hideaway in the hull's storage closet, he had heard enough. Colt had convinced the agent that a storm on the open sea had forced him to dock there for the night. *"I'll be on my way as soon as it calms down out there."* Colt had done a bit of fishing while they were at sea, for just such an occasion, and was able to show the agent his catch. He had invited the man onto the boat, at which point Knight had crept out to the galley, had awakened Foster, and had silently motioned him into the storage closet. Foster had immediately instructed Knight and Emma to lay flat on the floor. He had laid next to them and had pulled a tarp over the three of them. They had waited, barely breathing, as the exchange with the agent had gone on. After what had felt like hours, the agent must have bought Colt's story, as Knight had heard laughter, followed by the sound of footsteps, then a boat's engine departing the bay. They had all breathed a sigh of relief. Knight hadn't wanted to think about what would have happened if any one of them had been discovered in the hull of that boat.

And now, hours later, as Knight stared at the ceiling of the eight-by-eight storage closet, he tried to guess what time it was. He absently looked at his wrist where his watch would normally be. It wasn't there. He had left it at the White House, worried that Morningstar might have somehow tagged it to track his every move. But he did still have his phone.

He looked over at Emma. She was asleep. As he felt her quiet breaths against his cheek, he marveled at the fact that, though he had slept in some of the finest hotels in the world, he had never slept better than he had on the floor of that boat with her lying next to him.

He sat up, careful not to wake her, and crept out to the galley, where Foster had returned once the agent had left the pier. He was asleep. He looked terrible. He had done little more than sleep or vomit the entire trip. Knight crept past him to the front of the hull and looked up past the stairs. He could see slivers of sunlight.

He fumbled in his pocket for the phone he had kept; the phone that couldn't be traced, tracked, or destroyed...the one Morningstar had given him on that first day when he had taken the oath of office. *"Keep this with you at all times, my son. It will allow us to maintain our relationship...in secret."* Knight stared at the phone. He had turned it off after telling Morningstar that he would kill Emma. That had been three days ago; it hadn't been turned on since.

Reluctantly, he turned it on. 'Saturday 10:45 a.m.' flashed on the screen. He did the math. They had been in the hull of that boat for a full sixty-five hours. As he stared at the phone, he wondered if maybe it was the phone and not his watch that had allowed Morningstar to track him so effectively. He quickly dismissed the notion. Morningstar had told him when he had given him the phone that he had disabled its tracking capabilities in case the two men ever needed to meet. Knight had tested the theory more than once, and was convinced it was true; Morningstar was more afraid of exposing their relationship than he was of losing track of his 'son.' *But why would I even risk keeping it?* he wondered as he continued to stare at the phone. He nodded. *Because it is far better for me – and the country – if I have a way to reach that son-of-a-bitch.*

And now that Knight had successfully left his post, it was time to play the first card of his complicated hand. He would leave the phone on and wait for the call that he knew would come. He sighed. *And when Morningstar does call me, I'll tell him in no uncertain terms that his powerful son has just become his powerful enemy.*

He shoved the phone in his pocket and crept back to the storage closet. He knelt down and, without making a sound, slid next to Emma, who was still asleep. He laid there in perfect peace for a full seven minutes. Suddenly, the phone vibrated. It felt like an earthquake inside the quiet room. *That was quick,* he thought as he slid from under the blanket and crept to the back wall of the closet. Though he didn't recognize the number, Morningstar was the only one who knew how to reach him. Gripping the phone tightly, he answered with a hushed, "Don't try to find me."

It wasn't the voice he expected. It was lower, and the man spoke not with the authority of a Pentagon official, but with a tone more characteristic of a mobster. "Lemme talk to your bitch."

"Who is this?"

"I need to talk to Emma. Emma Melnikov."

The way he said 'Melnikov' made Knight's stomach turn. "Forget it. I'm hanging up. Don't call again."

"I have Emma's husband."

Knight flinched. "Who are you?"

"I'm Gad, Judah. I'm your brother."

The man laughed and Knight wanted to crawl through the phone and strangle him. He whispered "You will never talk to Emma. You can talk to me instead."

"Whatever you say, brother. Like I said, I have her husband. I just picked him up at the airport. He was about to pick up *Galina.*"

Knight stiffened. "Do you think you can use Emma to get to me?" He forced a laugh. "To hell with you," he said as he did his best to keep his voice low and even.

"I can and will use that bitch. Cut her loose, Judah. Forget this trip you're on and get your ass back to the White House. Jacob says that all will be forgiven."

There was a pause, then a different, far more panicked male voice said, "Emma? Is that you? Are you okay?"

Knight tightened his jaw; he didn't know what to say.

Gad was back on the phone. "In case you're wondering, that was Michael."

Emma stirred, her eyes fluttering as she woke and looked over at him. He held the phone closer to his ear. She whispered "Who is it?"

He shook his head. "No one" he mouthed. Into the phone he said, "Touch one hair on that man's head and I'll kill you myself, Gad." He paused. "As for your threat, you can take it and stick it up your ass. We won't be blackmailed. Go tell that to our *father.*" He ended the call, his hand shaking as he shoved the phone in his pocket.

Emma sat up, strands of black hair falling over her face. She brushed them aside. "What is it? What's happened?"

He looked at her, his heart aching. "Is there some reason that your... husband, Michael...would be picking up Galina at the airport?"

Emma stared at him, her eyes wide. "What...what time is it?"

"Almost eleven...in the morning."

"Saturday?"

"Yes."

She began to shake. "She...she flew in from overseas...about an hour ago."

CHAPTER 23

Portland, Maine

Cravens had tried to see more clearly what was happening in the church, but it was dark inside, so he had raised the window about a half-inch to hear what was going on. He had been stunned when he had heard the back and forth between Gad and whoever was on the other end of the phone. *"Let me talk to your bitch."*

He had recognized the voice. He had heard it before, at the site of the plane crash. The man had added, *"I need to talk to Emma. Emma Melnikov."* There had been a pause, followed by, *"I'm Gad, Judah. I'm your brother."*

Cravens had been about to call for backup, when the next sentence had forced his heart into his throat. *"Cut her loose, Judah. Forget this trip you're on and get your ass back to the White House. Jacob says that all will be forgiven."*

Gad had then held the phone to the ear of a very panicked Michael. The poor man had stammered, *"Emma? Is that you? Are you okay?"*

Gad had taken back the phone. *"In case you're wondering, that was Michael."* There had been another pause. The man, Gad, had then cursed and had thrown the phone on the floor.

Cravens could feel his legs shaking as he knelt at the window. There was no time to call for backup. *I have to do something...now.*

With his gun in his right hand, he used his left to raise the window the rest of the way. Firmly he said, "Drop your weapon, DeMarco...or should I say, Gad. This church is surrounded. One move and I'll put a bullet through your head."

Gad turned to face him. He was still wearing his sunglasses. He hissed, and in one motion grabbed his prisoner by the arm, pulled him in front of him, and shoved his gun harder into the man's temple.

Keeping his pistol aimed at Gad's forehead, Cravens climbed through the window, heaving his thick frame over the sill and into the church with surprising agility. "Step away from him!"

The man shoved the gun even harder into Cannon's temple, causing him to wince in pain.

Cravens said evenly, "I said, step away from him."

The man grinned and tightened his grip on his prisoner's arm.

Cravens yelled, "Down!" praying that Cannon would understand.

Cannon dropped to his knees. Cravens pulled the trigger, aiming for Gad's shoulder, needing him alive so he could honor Henderson's request to try to turn the man against his boss. But Gad moved at the last second, and the bullet hit him square in the forehead. He fell against one of the pews, then to the floor, his body eerily still as blood ran down his cheek and onto his shirt.

Cravens ran over, kicked Gad's gun away, then knelt beside Cannon, who was still on his knees. "You okay?"

Cannon said nothing, simply staring at the lifeless body. A vase near the altar had fallen to the floor, and pieces were scattered over Cannon's bent knees. Cravens brushed the pieces away.

He looked down at Gad. The man's sunglasses had come off, allowing Cravens to see the glass eye that he remembered so well. He put two fingers to Gad's neck. No pulse. *Shit. I can't turn the bastard against his boss when he's dead.*

Without thinking, he closed the man's eyes, then looked over at Cannon. "Who was he talking to?"

Cannon had begun to shake. "A man...a man who is apparently with my...my wife...Emma. Emma Cannon."

Cravens pulled out his phone and dialed his boss.

A stern voice said, "Cravens, are you ready to tell me what the hell is going on?"

"I need you to find out why someone might want to kidnap Emma Cannon."

There was silence.

"Sam, did you hear me?"

"Cravens, you need to tell me this very minute how it is that you know that name."

Cravens frowned. "Why? What's up?"

A pause. "I was told just days ago that Emma Melnikov Cannon could very well be the Russian spy that is responsible for President Knight's disappearance."

CHAPTER 24

Great Kills Harbor, New York

Secret Service Agent Jerry Foster rubbed his arms and legs, doing his best to stay warm. Never had a man been more eager to get off a boat. He, along with the U.S. President and his lover, had been on that boat for far too long. And Foster had spent most of that time throwing up. Though he was still queasy, he had nothing left. Knight had forced him to take sips of water throughout the long journey, while Emma had kept his forehead cool with damp paper towels. Between the two of them, he had survived, but he would feel a whole lot better once he could get off that boat.

They had finally docked in the early morning hours, and were supposed to have been picked up at eleven a.m. Colt was to let Foster know the minute the driver, a trusted friend of Colt's, had texted him. He checked his watch. *Eleven-thirty. Where the hell is he?* He sighed. Had something happened? Had they somehow been betrayed? Regardless, they couldn't stay on that boat. Not only was Foster terribly seasick, but he was fully aware that there would be heightened security at every port, even the smaller ones. It was only a matter of time before another coast guard vessel came by, and the next group of agents might not be so agreeable. He, Knight, and Emma were taking a huge risk with every second they spent in the hull of that boat.

I need to talk to Colt. But he couldn't just climb out of the hold. For one thing, he wasn't sure his legs would hold him. For another, the danger of him being spotted was a risk he couldn't take. If a missing Secret Service agent – who had been a part of the President's normal detail – was seen on a fishing vessel docked at an obscure port, all bets would be off.

He pulled out his phone and stared at it. Up to that point, he had kept it off, knowing that if someone wanted to find him, they could do so by tracking his phone. He continued to stare. *I'll make it quick.* He turned it on and dialed. It rang several times before being answered with a gruff, "Yeah."

"Colt, it's me. Is your guy coming?"

"Yeah. Says he got delayed in Boston. Be here in about ten minutes."

Ten more minutes on this damn boat? "Well tell him to hurry up!"

Foster ended the call just as Emma and Knight walked out of the storage closet. Knight looked at him and frowned. "We have a problem."

"What's wrong?"

"Someone is trying to use Emma's family to blackmail her."

"Jesus!" Foster tried to sit up, but fell back onto the cot. Emma ran to his side and grabbed a damp cloth from a table beside the cot. She held it to his forehead as she and Knight helped him sit up, then leaned him against the side of the hull. He closed his eyes as he said, "Blackmail her? What does he want from her?"

Knight frowned. "He wants her to leave me. To go home to her family and force me to go back to the White House."

Foster swallowed and shook his head. "How is he using her family?"

Knight flinched. "He has apparently kidnapped her...husband...and is threatening him and their daughter, Galina."

Foster's eyes shot open. "Dear God!"

Knight nodded. "Yes."

Foster took several deep breaths, then leaned forward and pulled himself to the edge of the cot. "What would you like to do, sir?"

Knight looked at Emma, then back at Foster. "Well, we can't have this man threatening Emma's family. I think we should probably do what he says."

"Wait." It was Emma. "Jerome, do you know this man...this kidnapper?"

Knight sighed. "I know...of him."

Emma frowned. "Will he stop if I go back home? Will that be the end of it?"

Knight sighed. "I doubt it. My guess is that he – or his boss – will eventually come for you, Emma. He'll most certainly come for me." He frowned. "But I don't think we can risk your family's safety. We should do what he says, at least for now."

She was about to speak, when Foster's phone vibrated. "Hello?"

"He's here." It was Colt. "He's parked behind the pines."

"The pines" referred to a row of thick white pines about half-a-mile from the pier. Foster said, "Got it" and ended the call. He looked at Knight. "Time to go, sir."

He tried to stand, holding the wall to support himself. His knees buckled. Knight stood and grabbed his right arm, while Emma grabbed his left. Together, the three of them crept up the flight of stairs. They stopped just below the deck floor. Foster craned his neck, and was able to see Colt sitting by the steering panel, his feet propped on a cooler, a can of beer in his hand.

"Colt!" he whispered as loud as he dared. "Is it safe for us to leave?"

Colt quickly scanned the bay. He stood and walked closer. He said casually, "It's all good, mate, but I'd hurry if I was you." He took another sip of beer.

Foster looked at Knight and Emma. "Are you ready?"

They nodded.

He turned to Knight. "Could you hand me my backpack?"

Knight looked at Emma; she nodded. "I have him."

Knight ran down, grabbed the backpack, and handed it to Foster. He draped it over his shoulder, then grabbed the stair railings for support. "I'm good. Both of you, go get your gear. And don't forget to pull up your hoods and put on your sunglasses."

Knight and Emma ran down the steps and into the storage closet. They came out seconds later wearing their hoodies and sunglasses, and carrying their backpacks. They climbed the stairs and stopped just behind Foster. Colt gave Foster a nod. Foster pulled up his hood and put on his own pair of sunglasses, then led the three of them onto the deck. Actually, it was more like they led him. They had to help him from the deck to the shore, and they had to practically carry him to a nearby grove of trees. He fell to the ground, and it took a full five minutes for him to banish his sea legs and regain his equilibrium. Once he felt up to it, he walked them the half-mile to the agreed-upon meeting spot for the truck. They could hear sirens in the distance and helicopters overhead. Foster frowned. "Get lower," he whispered as he led them to a thick row of maples. He spotted an old pickup truck parked about ten feet away. A man who Foster guessed was their driver had unloaded bales of hay and was standing next to the bed. Foster stopped and scanned the area. The sirens were getting louder. They needed to hurry. When he felt certain that no one else was there, he looked at Knight. "When I give the word, sir, you and Emma will run to the bed of that truck."

Knight nodded and took Emma by the hand. Foster took another look around, then turned to Knight and nodded. "Now."

The three of them ran to the truck. Foster looked at the bed of the truck and frowned. Though it had been lined with a two-inch mat, he doubted it would offer much comfort once the truck was on the move. *It'll have to do,* he thought as he motioned for them to get in. Knight helped Emma onto the mat, then climbed in next to her. He pulled her into his arms and Foster grinned. *Something tells me they'll be just fine.* The driver covered them with blankets, then handed Knight a flashlight. He inserted a fake metal bed over them, leaving just enough room that they wouldn't be crushed. He piled the hay bales on top, then laid a tarp over the bales.

He motioned for Foster to get into the truck, then walked to the driver's seat and slid behind the wheel. Foster got into the passenger seat and looked at the driver. He was average height, with a heavy build, dark eyes, and gray, spindly hair. A crusty man, similar to Colt, who was probably enjoying the prospect of sticking it to the U.S. Government in whatever form that took. "Can I ask your name?" Foster said.

"Call me Ralph."

Foster nodded. "Do you know where we're going, Ralph?"

"To Maine...then to the mountains."

"That's right," Foster said as he settled into the seat.

Ralph turned on the engine and eased onto a dirt road.

Foster said, "Maybe take it slow, Ralph, I'm sure it's bumpy back there."

Ralph nodded, and kept the speed of the truck at 35 mph. They had driven only a few miles, when Foster was startled by the vibration of his cellphone. *Shit!* He wanted to kick himself. He had forgotten to turn it off after calling Colt. *Should I answer?* He didn't recognize the number, but the caller had already connected with his phone, which meant that the caller was already able to track Foster's general location. *I should probably find out who's about to know where I am.* "Hello."

"Foster! Thank god I finally got a hold of you. It's Johnson, Scott Johnson, Secret Service. Remember me?"

Foster frowned, trying to remember. "Oh yeah...the Conner detail, right?"

"Yes, and I've been trying to reach you for the past three days."

Foster frowned. "As you might guess, Johnson, I'm in a bit of a situation."

"I'm sure you are, Foster. That's why I'm calling. We need to meet."

"I can't meet, Johnson. Like I said, I'm in the middle of something."

"You'll want to meet with me." He paused. "I have information that will impact the future of this country."

Foster frowned. He had to shut off his phone now if he hoped to have any chance of keeping the details of his location secret. "Cut to the chase, Johnson."

"What if I was to tell you that a high-ranking Pentagon aide by the name of Ed Morningstar has embarked on a plan to bring down this country?"

Foster frowned. "Have you been drinking?"

"I'm serious."

"Let's assume that what you're saying is true. Why call me?"

There was a pause. "Because I think he's using your President to do it."

CHAPTER 25

En route to Maine

Knight, Emma, and Foster had had no time to finish their discussion regarding the call from Gad. The truck had arrived soon after, and Knight and Emma had needed to focus on helping Foster from the boat to the truck. But now, as Knight laid with Emma beneath the metal overlay, he could feel her shaking, and he doubted it was because she was cold. He turned on the flashlight, pointing it away from them so it would reflect from the underside of the fake bed. He was able to see the worried look on her face and he shook his head. "Are you okay, Emma?"

She turned to him and whispered, "No...no, I'm not. We have to stop that kidnapper. We can't let him hurt Michael."

Knight flinched. There was nothing he could do. Gad could have taken Michael anywhere. Knight was in no position to put out an APB, and even if he was, it wouldn't matter. It was Morningstar who had put Gad up to it, and Morningstar was always one step ahead of everyone else. "I...I don't think I *can* stop him, Emma."

She frowned. "What do you mean? You said that you knew him...or at least knew his boss. Can't you do something to stop him?"

Knight sighed. "The man calling the shots is quite powerful, Emma."

She put her hands on his cheeks. "You're quite powerful, Romer." She looked away and said softly, "but if you can't stop him, then we'll need to do what he says." She shook her head. "I'm not willing to let others die just so we can be together."

Knight forced her to look at him. "I've had time to think about it, Emma. If you want to leave to protect your...husband, I'll understand. Foster can have you home before dark." He sighed. "But like I told you on the boat, the kidnapper and the man he works for won't stop. If you do what he asks, then you don't only jeopardize our future, but you open yourself to all kinds of blackmail. He'll come after you, your husband, even your daughter. He won't stop until you – and your family – are destroyed."

Her shaking intensified and he took her in his arms.

She whispered, "Who...who is he?"

Knight hesitated. He didn't want to involve Emma in any way with Morningstar. Even saying the man's name felt like it would poison her. But she was already involved...far deeper than he had ever intended. "He's a very powerful man," Knight whispered, "...who wants to tear down this country." He rolled onto his back and stared at the metal overlay. Quietly, he said, "And I used to be a part of it."

Emma said nothing. She, too, turned onto her back. The two of them just laid there, saying nothing, staring up at the metal ceiling only inches from their faces.

Knight could feel the rumble of the truck beneath him. Without looking at her, he said, "You need to know, Emma, that no matter what you decide, I can't go back. If you choose to leave, I'll understand. But I can't go back until I bring that man down."

He felt her hand reach for his. He looked over at her. She was crying, silent tears that said so much. He turned onto his side and hugged her to him. All at once, the quiet moment was shattered by the vibration of his cellphone. *That son-of-a-bitch Gad is calling back.* He pulled it blindly from his pocket and answered. "What!"

"Who am I speaking to?"

Knight frowned. It was a different voice. "Who is this?"

"Uh...Agent Tom Cravens. I'm with the U.S. Secret Service."

What the hell? "How did you get this number?"

"Um...about an hour ago, I overheard the conversation of the man who called you on this phone." There was a pause. "I...I know you're somehow connected to the White House. I also know that you have a tie to Emma Cannon, who I just learned is a spy." Knight heard him clear his throat. "It...it was obvious that the guy who called you was threatening you...

maybe even threatening the President." There was a pause. "Look, I get it if you don't want to tell me who you are, but I need to know if our Commander-in-Chief is in any sort of danger."

Good god! What the hell is happening? Why do they think Emma is a spy? He squeezed the phone so tightly it nearly broke in half. *Morningstar! The son-of-a-bitch has told all of DC that Emma is a traitor.* Knight needed more information, but first he had to verify that the man on the phone was truly who he said he was. "Who are you charged with protecting, Agent Cravens?"

There was a pause. "I—I was the agent assigned to Cynthia Madison."

Knight closed his eyes. *Cravens...of course!* Tom Cravens had been the lone survivor of the plane crash that had killed Cynthia Madison. Of all the strange coincidences. But Knight still needed proof; he couldn't just take the man's word. He knew that, as her agent, the man would have a code word for her. The only ones who had access to that code were the director of the agency, the agents themselves, and the President of the United States. Though there were hundreds of code names, Knight knew Madison's; he knew it because he had made a point of knowing everything about her after the plane crash. "What was her code name, Agent?"

There was a pause. "I...I don't know who I'm talking to, so I can't say."

Knight frowned. It made sense. But he still needed a way to trust the man on the phone. "She's dead, Agent. Just tell me the first half of the name."

There was a longer pause, followed by a whispered, "Blue."

Knight closed his eyes. Her code name had been Blue Angel. Was it enough for him to trust the man? *It'll have to be...he already knows too much.* He cleared his throat. "There's a lot we need to talk about, Agent, but now isn't the time. Can you tell me if the man who was being held by the caller is safe?"

"Yes, he's standing right here."

Knight sighed, relieved. "Good. And what about the guy who made the call?"

Another clearing of the throat. "I'd prefer not to say. Just know...he's no longer a threat."

Cravens killed Gad! "Good work, Agent. I'll need to know everything about him...his identity, who he's working for...anything you can pull together, Agent."

"I'm working on it. Who might I be obtaining the information for?"

Should he tell him? Should he let the agent know that he was talking to the President of the United States...*who has gone missing and is hiding in the back of a pickup truck?* Cravens had overheard the conversation with Gad. He would be curious. If Knight froze him out, the agent might look elsewhere for answers. *Like the Pentagon.* After all, he had been told that Emma was a spy. And now that he had Michael, he would hold him as an enemy combatant if Knight didn't set the record straight. But how would he do that? And why should Cravens believe a word he said?

He cleared his throat. "Cravens, listen closely." He took a deep breath. "You are talking to...Jerome Knight...the...uh...President. You need to keep this call a secret. Keep the whole thing a secret, if you can."

There was a long pause. Finally, "Um...yes sir. Certainly, sir." Another pause. "Could you give me your code name, sir? Just as a precaution?"

It was a reasonable request, but Knight didn't know if he could bring himself to say the word. "My code name is...Judah."

"And your identifier?"

Knight frowned. An identifier was to be used if there was suspicion that the President was in trouble. He sighed. "5648 Concord."

"Thank you, sir. Is there anything that you need, sir?"

"Your total silence, Cravens. I give you my word that Emma Cannon is in no way a threat to either me or the country. That is a lie being spread by a vile but powerful enemy. She is with me, and I am safe. Do you understand, Agent?"

"Um...yes sir. Certainly, sir."

"Good. Take Michael to his daughter. Then post an agent that you trust to keep them safe. He has to be a man who will accept the assignment without asking questions. Do you understand what I'm saying?"

Another pause. "Yes sir. I'll find someone, sir."

"Good. And don't talk to anyone but me. I'll be in touch."

He ended the call. Gad was dead and Michael was safe...*for now.* He whispered to Emma, "Michael's okay. The man who was threatening him is...dead."

Emma looked at him, her eyes wide. Her shaking had intensified.

They were jostled as the truck came to a sudden stop. A door slammed and Knight put a finger to his lips. He turned off the flashlight. He heard footsteps and held his breath. There was a knock on the back of the truck. A quiet voice said, "Sir, I need to ask you a question." It was Foster.

"Go ahead."

"Are you acquainted with a man named Morningstar...from the Pentagon?"

Knight tensed. "The aide to General Daniels?"

"Yes sir."

"I am. Why?"

"I've just received word that he is...trying to bring down this country, sir."

Knight kicked at the back door of the truck, breaking the latch. He edged from under the false bed and stood behind the truck. He felt as if his head might explode. Keeping his voice low, he said, "Where did you hear that?"

"From a Secret Service agent, Scott Johnson. He said he was speaking on behalf of the former Vice-President, Jim Conner."

Knight began to pace a small circle behind the truck. *How do they know about Morningstar?* "Do you believe him? Agent Johnson, I mean?"

"I do, sir. I don't think Johnson would lie about such a thing." He paused. "He says that he intercepted an email from a guy named Levi."

Knight stopped. "Did you say Levi?"

"Yes sir. He said the email had something to do with planting evidence."

"Did he give you any details?"

"No sir. He said that you were somehow involved...unwittingly, he guessed. He asked if we could meet so that he could show me his evidence."

Evidence; it was what Knight would need if he was to go after Morningstar. Hopefully, Cravens would get evidence from the dead Gad, and now it was possible that Johnson could bring him evidence, as well. Had Johnson found dossiers that outlined Morningstar's plans? Notebooks where the maniac had written the steps he would take to overthrow the U.S. government? *I need to know what he has.* "Tell Johnson that you'll meet him soon. Say...Monday night, somewhere near DC. You pick the spot." He paused. "We can at least see what the man has."

Foster nodded. "Yes sir."

Knight crawled back in the truck. As he felt the vibration from Foster slamming the back door and reinforcing it with a metal chain, he sighed. Evidence. There was actual evidence. *A way to go after – and hopefully bring down – the man who has been my guide, my inspiration for the past twenty-four years.*

CHAPTER 26

Portland, Maine

"I'm Gad, Judah. I'm your brother." The words had played in Cravens' mind over and over like a recording. Knight's Secret Service code name was Judah. A coincidence? Cravens didn't believe in coincidences.

But he didn't have time to dwell on it; he needed to take care of the scene in the church. First he had to calm down the husband of the missing Emma. The man had just witnessed and overheard far more than he should have about things that no one – not even top-level brass in DC – knew. Michael Cannon had suddenly become a significant liability...for someone. *But who?*

Michael hadn't moved since the shooting. He was still kneeling by the dead body, and, just by looking at him, Cravens could see that the poor man was shaken to his core. Slowly, Cravens helped him stand and led him to a pew. "Sit down, sir." The man eyed him cautiously, but sat in the pew as instructed. Cravens stood in front of him, his hand on the arm of the pew, bending just enough that he was looking in the man's eyes. "Mr. Cannon, I'm doing my best to make this as easy on you as I can."

The man simply stared at him.

Cravens sighed. "First of all, is Emma Cannon your wife?"

The man nodded.

"Second, do you happen to know where she is or who she's with?"

Never had Cravens seen a more dejected man. He bowed his head. "No."

Cravens ran his hand through his hair and sighed. "Okay. Sit tight while I take care of this mess."

He turned away from Michael and looked down at Gad lying dead on the floor of the church. *What the hell do I do now?* Learning that it was the President on the other end of that phone had tested his loyalties. Was his duty to his country, and he should therefore report to his boss that Knight was with the spy, Emma Cannon? Or was his duty to the man who held the office, President Knight, who, if he was telling the truth, clearly needed Cravens' help. He didn't know, and he hadn't answered the question by the time he had cleaned up the church...nor had he answered it by the time he had snuck the dead man outside.

He would need to work quickly; someone could walk into that church at any minute. But there was a lot to do. *Michael will have to help me.* Again, he walked over and stood in front of him. "Michael, I need you to pick up every piece of that broken vase and throw it in a trashcan. Then we'll toss it outside into a dumpster."

Michael looked at the floor in front of the altar where the vase had broken into pieces. He nodded, then stood and silently got to work.

Cravens walked back to a small kitchen and found two washrags. He dampened one of them in a sink, then walked out to the vestibule and used the dampened cloth to wipe Gad's blood from where it had spattered the altar. As he did so, he searched for the slug from his gun; he couldn't find it. He saw Michael pick up the last piece of the broken vase and throw it in a trashcan he had taken from behind the altar. Cravens looked at him and said, "Leave the trashcan by the back door; I'll take it out in a minute." He paused. "Would you see if you can find the pistol slug?"

The man nodded obediently.

Cravens walked over to the dead body. He took the second rag, the dry one, and wiped the inside of the dead man's mouth. He now had saliva, which would give him DNA. He walked back to the kitchen, rummaged through cupboards until he found a pencil, a notepad, and a pack of baggies. He took out a handful of baggies and slid the rag with Gad's saliva into one of them. The man claiming to be the President had told Cravens to try to learn Gad's identity. Cravens was curious, as well. Gad had pretended to be Carlos DeMarco, but who was he really? Though Henderson had admitted that he knew the man, he had shared little about him. Cravens shoved the baggy in his pocket. *This should tell me something...assuming the guy is in the system.* He nodded. Something told him that Gad was in the system.

He walked back to the sanctuary. Michael was busy searching the floor near the altar. Cravens knelt by Gad. He took the pencil and rubbed it over the top sheet of the notepad. He then rubbed Gad's fingertips one at a time on the charcoaled page. The tips were scarred, suggesting that they had likely been burned in an effort to hide his identity. Nonetheless, Cravens patted each fingertip onto a sheet of the notepad, then ripped off the page and slid it into a baggy. He shoved the baggy in his pocket.

He stood and walked to the back door. He propped it open and looked outside. There was a small courtyard in back. He scanned the area. No one was around. Though it was almost noon, a thick row of clouds was hiding the sun, leaving the courtyard covered in shade. There was a dumpster on the other side of the courtyard, and a row of bushes about ten feet from the dumpster. He looked for a camera. He didn't see one. He grabbed the trashcan, carried it to the dumpster and emptied it. He walked back inside and handed it to Michael. "Put it back where you got it."

Michael nodded and carried the trashcan to the back of the altar.

Cravens said, "Any luck finding the slug?"

The man shook his head.

Cravens walked over to the dead Gad. He looked down at him and sighed. Though Gad had been a small man, he was now literally dead weight. Cravens' back had already been through too much. He looked at Michael. As much as he hated to do it, he would need the man's help. "Michael, I'm gonna need you to help me here."

Michael simply stared at him.

Cravens shifted awkwardly. He was asking a lot of this poor man. He took a deep breath and sighed. "I don't think I can—"

Without a word, Michael walked over and grabbed the dead man by the ankles. Cravens grabbed him under the arms, and together they dragged the dead Gad through the church to the opened back door. They set him down by the doorway, and Cravens pointed to the bushes he had spotted earlier. "Over there," he said.

Michael nodded, and again picked up the dead man by his ankles. Cravens grabbed him under his arms and they half-carried, half-dragged him down a set of stairs and across the courtyard to the bushes. Cravens said, "On three." He counted down, and, in unison, they tossed the body into the bushes. It landed with a thud. Cravens flinched. "You can go back inside, Michael."

Michael said nothing and walked slowly back to the church.

Cravens reached over and pushed the dead Gad deeper into the bushes. He picked up a pile of leaves and threw them over the body. He tossed on more leaves until Gad's body was completely covered. He found a good-sized tree limb and laid it on top of the leaves. He then threw more leaves on top of the limb. He stepped back and looked at his handiwork. He nodded. *Good enough.* The man was invisible, at least to any casual observer. The smell would eventually draw attention, but not until Cravens and Cannon were long gone.

Cravens walked back into the church. Michael was standing by a pew holding something in his hand. "I think I found it," he said flatly as he held up a pistol slug.

Cravens walked over and took the slug. "Where was it?" he asked as he pulled out a third baggy, dropped in the slug, then slid the baggy in his pocket.

"There," Michael said, and pointed to a railing on one side of the altar. "It was lodged partway in the wood."

Cravens walked over and looked at the railing. He did his best to smooth over the edges surrounding the bullet hole, then turned to Michael and nodded. "Thanks."

He pulled out the first rag that he had used to clean the blood from the altar, and, using the opposite end, he wiped the floor where Gad had fallen, along with everything he himself had touched. He finished by wiping down the railing where the slug had been. He slid that rag into a fourth baggy, walked it over to his duffel bag, and dropped it in. He would throw it away someplace far from the church.

He used another baggy to hold Gad's pistol so it could be tested for prints, and to see if it was registered. He doubted it was. He put it in the duffel bag, along with the three baggies from his pocket, then took a final look around. Satisfied, he ushered Michael to the back door. "We're done here. It's time to go."

Cravens removed the wedge that was holding the door, but held it open as he motioned for Michael to go down the stairs. Michael went down the first step and stopped. He looked back at Cravens. He was visibly shaking. "Where is...my wife?"

Cravens sighed. "I don't know, but I'll find her." He paused. "I do know she's safe." He put his hand on Michael's shoulder. "Go home. Go home to your daughter."

Michael shoved the hand away. "Take me with you."

Cravens sighed. "I can't, Mr. Cannon."

"I'm not leaving here unless you do."

Cravens sighed. *I guess I'll have to pull out the credentials.* He took his wallet from his back pocket, opened it, and showed Michael his badge. "Mr. Cannon, I'm a Secret Service agent for the United States of America, and I insist that you go home and keep your mouth shut." He paused. "Otherwise, I'll arrest you as a traitor."

Michael frowned. "A traitor? That's preposterous!"

"Yeah, well, there's a whole lot here that's preposterous."

Michael narrowed his eyes. "Fine. But you need to promise me that you'll call me the minute you can tell me something about my wife."

Cravens nodded. "I promise. But I can't stress enough, Mr. Cannon, that you mustn't tell a soul about what you saw and heard here today." He paused, unsure if he should say the next line. Finally, he cleared his throat and said, "Your wife's very survival is dependent on your complete and total silence. Do you understand?"

Michael stared at him, then nodded solemnly. "I do."

"Good." Cravens handed him the pencil and the pad of paper. "Now, write down your number so I can call you."

Michael wrote down his cellphone number and handed it to Cravens. He went the rest of the way down the steps and walked to the corner to wait for a cab. Cravens watched him, not taking his eyes off the man. Michael was now a material witness in what could only be described as a horrific crime with national – and international – implications. Though Cravens would have preferred to lock the man in a safehouse somewhere, he didn't have the time or the resources to do so. All he could count on was that Michael was scared enough about what he had seen in the church, as well as the safety of his wife, that he would honor Cravens' request, at least in the short term.

After about five minutes, a cab drove by. Michael waved it down and the taxi pulled to the curb. Michael ran to it and slid in back. He closed the door and stared out the window. Cravens gave him a quick wave. Michael just continued to stare.

So, what now? Cravens thought as he watched the cab pull away. Though he had believed his boss, Sam Allen, when the man had told him that Emma Cannon was a spy, Knight – America's President – had explicitly told him that she wasn't. While Allen had likely gotten the information on good authority, Knight had apparently been sitting right next to the woman. Were Knight and Emma family? Old friends? Cravens needed to know more. *"If you want to know something, Tommy, just ask."* He grinned as he thought of his ex-wife's words of wisdom. *You're right, Betty.*

He walked inside and pulled out the phone he had taken from the dead man. He dialed the same number he had called earlier. The voice sounded tired. "Yes?"

"Um, sir, it's Agent Cravens again."

"Yes Agent?"

He paused. Why on earth had he thought this was a good idea? "Um, sir. I didn't know who else to call."

"Go on."

"I'm doing my best to ignore what my boss said about the woman, Emma. I guess what I'm wondering is this: she's not holding you against your will, is she?"

He waited; there was only silence. *Shit! What a stupid thing to say.* Then he heard a chuckle. "Trust me when I tell you, Agent...Emma is not a spy. Has she lured me away? Yes. But it's because I've been in love with her for the past sixteen years."

Cravens grinned in spite of himself. "I...I see. What should I do now, sir?"

"Have you learned the identity of the man who was holding Michael?"

"Not yet, sir. I know that he refers to himself as Gad, and that about two months ago he pretended to be a driver for the estate of Walter Henderson in Latvia. The actual driver is missing; I'm guessing Gad killed him, sir." He paused. "I made sure to get fingerprints and DNA from the guy, but I'm not quite sure where to take the samples." He waited for a comment; there was none. He went on. "Also, my boss has insisted that I explain how I know of Emma. I don't know what to tell him, sir."

"If you could refrain from telling him anything, I would appreciate it, Agent."

Cravens sighed. "Certainly, sir." He hesitated. "Um, sir, if I may...are you the Judah referred to in the phone call?"

Again, there was silence. Finally, "Can we leave it alone for now?"

"Um, yeah, sure."

"Agent Cravens?"

"Yes sir."

"A lot is being asked of you. If it's too much, I'll understand. I will never ask you to betray your commitment to your country."

But that's exactly what I'm being asked to do, Cravens thought with a sigh. "Thank you, sir. I'll need help to uncover the identity of our dead guy, sir."

"Whatever you need, Agent."

"I'm almost certain that this Gad character wasn't working alone. He said something about Jacob."

Another pause. "I'm certain he wasn't working alone. Bring me all that you've collected, Cravens. I'm on my way to a secret location where I will have a team of investigators that can analyze the samples you've collected and give us answers without anyone else knowing."

"Where are you going, sir?"

A pause. "I'll send someone to pick you up. I'm guessing that you're in Portland, since Michael had been on his way to pick up his daughter at the airport. Is that right?"

"Yes sir."

"Can you get to Bangor?"

"Yes, not a problem, sir."

"Good. I'll have someone meet you sometime after midnight...at the downtown post office. Hang on to that phone." He paused. "And Cravens, trust me when I say...this reaches about as high as you could imagine."

"Yes sir." Cravens ended the call and stared at the phone. *No shit, sir.* Here he was, a lowly Secret Service agent, talking to his Commander-in-Chief on a confiscated phone, through veiled messages, with a code name that somehow connected the President to a dead man who was likely a killer. No, there was no doubt in Craven's mind that whatever he had stumbled onto, it reached pretty damn high.

CHAPTER 27

Uzava, Latvia

Morningstar straightened his tie as he looked in the mirror. He was wearing a black tailored suit and a red tie. He pinned a U.S. flag emblem to his lapel and straightened his collar, then ran his fingers through his styled black hair. He smiled. The dimples appeared instantly, reminding him of his charm...not only with the ladies, but with the men, as well. Actually, it wasn't charm the men saw...it was power. Though Morningstar was a mere five-eight, he had cowered men far taller. He was like Putin... powerful, virile, bigger than life. *But Putin has far less vision.*

Morningstar's purpose for the evening was two-fold. First, he would try to get a sense of whether or not the Hendersons were hiding their dear son, Martin, somewhere in that drafty castle. He felt certain that he would be able to tell, simply by their mannerisms.

He also hoped to send a message to that same dear son: *"Morningstar has entered your private lair."* He laughed as he smoothed down his suitcoat. *He'll shit a brick when he learns that I've been welcomed to dinner at his precious castle.*

He took out his phone and dialed. "Steve, I need you to drive me to the Henderson estate. I'll be right out."

He ended the call without waiting for a reply. He walked to a table by the bed and picked up a pair of cufflinks. Given to him by General Daniels, they bore the symbol of the U.S. Marine Corp, along with the words "Semper fi." As he latched them in his cuffs, he grinned. *That's me...always faithful.*

He grabbed his overcoat from where he had left it hanging by the door and put it on. He walked outside, pleased to see Steve in his military uniform, waiting by the same black sedan that he had driven from the airport.

Morningstar walked down a flight of steps to the car. A harsh wind was blowing in off the Baltic Sea, and he shivered as Steve opened the back door for him. He climbed in back and said crisply, "Do you know where we're going, Steve?"

"I do, sir."

Morningstar had briefed both Steve and the other soldier, Scott, on the location of the Hendersons' secret compound, but not until Priscilla had sent over the coordinates. Though Morningstar was already well aware of those coordinates, it was important that his trip to Latvia appear to be aboveboard in every way.

Steve drove down the long drive from the bed and breakfast to the road. He took several back roads to the main intersection, then followed it to a roundabout where he headed south on route P111. Morningstar looked out the window at the passing scenery. Though the sun had set, the moon was bright and he was able to see what amounted to flatlands and trees. He tried to imagine what it would be like to live in such a desolate place. He chuckled to himself. *I guess I'll find out soon enough.*

After about twenty minutes, Steve slowed the car, and Morningstar pulled out his phone. He dialed the number that General Daniels had texted him earlier.

The call was answered with a brisk, "Henderson Residence. May I help you?"

Morningstar smiled. "Yes. I believe that you were contacted by the U.S. Pentagon earlier today?"

"Yes sir. Are you Mr. Morningstar?"

"I am."

"The Hendersons are expecting you. Have your driver ease into the graveled berm just after the big curve in the road and cut his lights. Have him pull forward in the brush until he sees an open gate. Once he is past the gate, he can turn on his lights and follow the drive to the front door."

Morningstar relayed the information to Steve, who drove another half-mile until he came to the curve the man had described. He pulled off the road onto a patch of gravel and turned off his lights. Using the light of the moon, he inched the car forward through thick underbrush until they were able to see the edges of an open wrought-iron gate. He drove through the gate, turned on his lights, then followed a paved drive that meandered through lush trees and a neatly manicured lawn. Morningstar nodded. *Impressive.* As they rounded the last bend, the mansion appeared before them, and Morningstar had to catch his breath. The manor – a true castle – was like something out of the Middle Ages. Tall gray battlements with broad crenels and beautifully etched merlons; battle-stained turrets, evenly spaced, which had surely stood as lookout posts from the days when marauding armies attacked without warning. A massive drawbridge was lowering toward the southeast corner of the castle, with a black BMW waiting to drive in, while to the north, a timeless iron gate opened to a bridge and a gravel walkway. At the end of the walkway was a metal sign that said "The Hendersons." The walkway eased into a set of stairs that led to an ornate front door. As the car pulled to the gate, Morningstar could see a rampart at the back of the castle. It towered over many of the trees, but was well-hidden with sprigs of ivy and thick vines. He imagined that if one stood at the top of that rampart, they would have an unparalleled view, not only of invaders, but of the Baltic Sea. He found himself trembling with excitement. *Welcome to your new home, Morningstar.*

Steve stopped the car, stepped out, and walked around to open the door.

Morningstar slid from the back seat. "Find a place to park, and wait for me."

Steve bowed slightly, waited for Morningstar to reach the stone path, then got behind the wheel and pulled away.

Morningstar walked along the walkway to a bridge that crossed what was clearly a moat. He passed the Henderson sign, then walked a few more feet and climbed five cement steps to the front door.

He was about to knock, when the door was opened by a man dressed completely in black. The man bowed from the shoulders. "Good evening, Mr. Morningstar."

Morningstar gave a quick nod and walked into the foyer. An elegant woman was standing at the foot of a large staircase, while a harried but impressive man was rushing from the back of the castle to join her. Morningstar recognized Walter and Dora Henderson from a magazine article he had read in *The New Yorker*. They were even more striking in person. He noticed immediately that they were both tall, and that Walter had styled black hair with well-placed hints of gray. Morningstar stood a bit taller and smoothed down his own black hair as he walked over to meet them.

Walter held out his hand. "Good evening, Mr. Morningstar. My wife and I are delighted that you could come."

Morningstar had to fight a grin. *I'll bet you are,* he thought, as he shook the hand and gave a subtle bow – actually more of a nod – first to Walter, then to Dora. In spite of her age, Dora Henderson was stunning. Her hair was a fashionable shade of blonde, her eyes a distinct blue. They were intelligent and alive, and he had to fight not to stare as he shook her outstretched hand. "I'm honored to be here," he said, adding, "I've been asked by General Daniels to extend his warmest greetings."

Walter nodded. "Yes, he called me earlier today. He spoke quite highly of you, Mr. Morningstar."

Of course, he did...the man couldn't wipe his ass without me. "Please, call me Edward."

Walter nodded. "Certainly, Edward. Shall we go to the sitting room for a drink before dinner?"

Morningstar nodded and offered his arm to Dora. "That would be delightful."

She looped her arm through his. He was forced to ignore the fact that she was a few inches taller as they followed Walter down a wide hallway with tall, curtained windows. As they walked, Morningstar did his best not to gape at the tall ceilings and the elegant surroundings. *I'll follow you, Walter...as you and your lady show off your castle...the castle that will soon be mine.*

CHAPTER 28

The Henderson Compound

Walter did his best to watch Morningstar without staring. He had expected him to be taller. He had also expected him to be far less personable. Nonetheless, Walter had no illusions about Edward Morningstar. Though Martin had wavered in his disgust for the man, Walter had every reason to be wary. Was he the monster that Martin had described in his suicide note? Or was he the loyal, patriotic man that the general had gushed about so enthusiastically? It was hard to say. Regardless, he was now a guest in Walter's home. But the general's hearty endorsement of him did confirm one thing: Morningstar had powerful friends. Was that why Martin had pulled back from his criticism of the man who *"...carries burdens of sin that would shame the devil himself."* Walter frowned as he continued to watch him. *It wouldn't surprise me.*

Walter had been delayed by a weather front on his flight out of Scotland, and had gotten back to the castle only minutes ago. He had quickly changed into his black suit, grateful to have something to take his mind off the letter from Justice. That letter had confirmed what Walter's dying mistress had told him: that their son wasn't just a cold-blooded killer...that there was a version of the man who wasn't merely respectable, but, from the tenor of the note, seemed worth knowing. All Walter could hope was that the meeting in three weeks in Justice's London offices would go well, and that he could somehow entice the Justice ego to stay.

But there had been more in that note from Justice. He had said that he had vital information regarding Latvia's war with Russia. *What could Justice know about this war?* he wondered as he led the way to the sitting room. He had yet to discuss it with Dr. Samuels. The man had been sleeping when he had returned to the castle, and Walter hadn't had the heart to wake him. Besides, he had had only minutes before Morningstar was to arrive. *We'll talk after I get through this interminable dinner.*

He smoothed down the lapels of his suitcoat as he and Dora led Morningstar into a sitting room at the northwest end of the castle. Though it had a stunning view of a well-lit, landscaped garden with the rich forest beyond, the room was rarely used, and Walter had been glad to give Dora an excuse to prepare it for company. He had told her nothing of Martin's remarks about their dinner guest. For one thing, he didn't want to alarm her; for another, he was looking forward to her unbiased impression of the man. Dora had keen instincts when it came to the unspoken motivations of others.

He offered Morningstar a seat in a long leather divan, and he and Dora sat in Queen Anne chairs across from him. The oversized furniture, along with a massive hearth with a roaring fire at one end of the room, gave it the feel of a cozy den.

A servant walked in. Walter said, "Bring us the Glenfiddich 1942, Claude."

The man nodded. "Certainly, sir." He turned to Dora. "And for you, Madam?"

She smiled. "I'll have the Chateau Montelena Chardonnay."

The servant left the room.

Walter reached for a box of cigars sitting on a table beside him. He held out the box to Morningstar. "Please, have one. They're pre embargo."

Morningstar's eyes widened as he reached for a cigar. A guillotine was sitting on a table next to him; he looked at Walter and smiled. "May I?"

"Certainly."

Morningstar clipped the end of the cigar. Then, using a table lighter, he lit it and puffed several times to get it started. He leaned back and took a slow, deep drag. He exhaled a plume of smoke that formed a perfect white ring in front of him.

Walter watched him. Other than the hint of a limp as they had walked into the sitting room, Morningstar's actions were crisp and disciplined, suggesting a military upbringing. His black hair was short, but not too short, and professionally styled. He wore a tailored suit, along with Italian Moreschi shoes that had clearly been designed to make him at least an inch taller than the five-seven or eight that Walter guessed him to be. He was formal and reserved, but seemed comfortable in their home. He was confident, maybe even cocky, unable to hide a smirk, especially when he was deep in thought.

Walter leaned forward in his chair. "So, tell me Edward, is this your first time to Latvia?"

Morningstar took a drag on the cigar, blew another smoke ring, and nodded. "Yes, Mr. Henderson, it is."

Walter smiled. "Please, call me Walter." He paused. "So, do you like what you've seen of our country?"

The smirk appeared, then disappeared in a flash. "Yes, most certainly. Such a wide expanse. I'm sure you favor it to your busy Boston."

Walter nodded. "Yes, very much so. But our tie to Latvia is far greater than an appreciation for the great outdoors."

The bottle of wine and the Glenfiddich were brought into the room. Walter nodded at the man. "We'll take it from here, Claude."

The man nodded and left the room. Walter uncorked the wine and poured Dora a glass. He then opened the whiskey and filled two small glasses half-full. He offered one to Morningstar. "Shall we?"

The three of them raised their glasses, then sipped their drinks. Morningstar allowed the whiskey to sit in his mouth before swallowing, after which he closed his eyes and nodded. "Excellent, Walter."

Walter leaned back and crossed his legs. "The Henderson legacy in Latvia started in the nineteenth century."

Again, the quick smirk. Morningstar smiled. "I see. Please, tell me more."

Walter summarized the history of his grandfather and the battles of the late 1800's, including the gifting of the castle as a gesture of thanks. "The only request was that the Henderson family devote themselves to the preservation and protection of Latvia." He paused. "Which is what we've been trying to do ever since."

Morningstar listened with narrowed eyes. He leaned back and took another sip of whiskey. "So that is why you've taken such an interest in this Russian invasion."

Walter nodded. "It is our duty," he paused, "...a duty we don't take lightly."

Morningstar flashed a smile. "I see." Another sip of whiskey. "I'm curious about your relationship with our Director of Homeland Security, Jason Hanover. I've been told that the two of you have become good friends."

Walter stiffened. He sensed Dora stiffen as well. How had Morningstar learned of their friendship? How much did he know about Hanover's role in giving Walter access to Henderson at the base outside Klaipeda? He cleared his throat. "Yes, the man was quite helpful during the aftermath of the fire that killed my son."

Morningstar nodded, seemingly hiding another smirk. "Such a tragedy. But as my dear preacher friend has always said, 'The dead do finally know true peace.'"

Dora stiffened even more; Walter said, "Perhaps. I would like to think so."

"As would I," Morningstar offered quickly. "For if he were still alive, I'm sure he would soon encounter dangers unlike anything we could ever imagine."

Walter's eyes narrowed. "What are you referring to, Edward?"

Morningstar frowned. "This war with Latvia is unavoidable, I'm afraid. Your son was a heroic freedom fighter, if I'm not mistaken."

Walter nodded. "He was."

"Well, all I'm saying is that he would likely be called upon to fight." Morningstar paused. "And we all know that Putin is a ruthless opponent." Another pause. "Your son is now freed from that worry...wherever he is."

Walter said nothing. Had Morningstar just issued a threat? A bit veiled, perhaps, but a threat nonetheless. He could feel the coldness from Dora; she had sensed it too, he was sure. He took a breath and sighed. "Yes, that is true." He cleared his throat. "So, tell me, Edward, what has brought you to our home?"

Morningstar smiled. "Hopefully, General Daniels explained to you that I've come to offer the support of the U.S. military on Latvia's behalf. As NATO allies, we're here to serve you in any capacity that you see fit."

Walter forced a smile. "That is greatly appreciated."

Dora cleared her throat. Evenly, she said, "So, tell me, Edward, is there a Mrs. Morningstar waiting back in the States?"

Morningstar smiled; Walter sensed it was the first genuine smile since he had walked into their home. "There is no Mrs. Morningstar, but there is a woman I'm quite fond of who is biding her time back home."

Dora nodded. "I see. Such a shame that she couldn't join you." She paused. "Do you expect to stay long?"

The smirk had returned. He finished his whiskey and grinned. "Only as long as I'm needed, Ma'am."

CHAPTER 29

Evansville, Indiana

Andrew Madison stood in his hotel room and stared down at the alley, watching as a scraggly tomcat climbed onto a rusted trashcan in search of a snack. There were several cans to choose from, each one overflowing with the filth of the downtrodden. It was just after noon, and the sun was shining directly on the alley, spotlighting the misery of that melancholy place. As he watched the cat, he thought about all that had happened to land him there...in that rundown hotel on the south side of Evansville, Indiana.

Three days ago, he had gone to the Evansville Prosecutor, and had played a tape for him that had more or less proved that it wasn't his sister, Maddi, who had killed police officer Evan Jackson 22 years ago...it was his mother who had killed the man. But Andrew hadn't stayed long, convinced that the Pentagon agents who had been harassing him for the past several days had followed him to Evansville. As he had been about to leave, Maddi's former therapist, Claire Porter, who had come there to tell the prosecutor that Maddi had, in fact, admitted to killing Evan Jackson, had suggested that Andrew join her for dinner at her hotel. *"It looks like I'll be stuck here for the weekend anyway, Andrew."* She had told him where she was staying, and, after promising to call her at her hotel, he had excused himself.

After he had left, he had jogged down back alleys to a downtown bank and had locked the recorder in a safe deposit box. Though the Prosecutor had insisted that Andrew give him the tape, Andrew had refused, telling

159

the man that, unless he had a warrant for the device, Andrew would hang onto it. *"You aren't the only one who wants it,"* he had said as he had slid it in his pocket and had run out a side door.

As for Claire, he had called her...the very next day, as a matter of fact. He wasn't sure why he had agreed to meet her for dinner; the woman had, after all, been willing to tell the world that Maddi had killed Evan Jackson. But he had gotten the sense that her revelation to the Prosecutor had been the last thing she had wanted to do; that she had done it out of an obligation to duty. Though it still irritated him, he did admire duty.

But there was more to it than that. Even from their short exchange in the Prosecutor's office, he had seen that Claire had an especially kind demeanor. Behind those round eyes and welcoming smile, he had sensed wisdom and a deep sense of compassion. Not only that; he looked forward to spending time with someone who had gotten to know Maddi well. He was eager to see Maddi through Claire's eyes.

It was Andrew who had suggested that they have dinner in Claire's hotel room instead of the dining room, certain the Pentagon agents were looking for him. He had snuck up to her hotel room and, sitting across from her at a table brought in by room service, Andrew had shared his tragic story over a bottle of wine and a not-bad steak dinner. It had felt good to talk about it, and Claire had been remarkably easy to talk to. He had told her much of what had happened since he had found his mother Jeannie dead on the floor in her own home, including the letter she had left on a table, and the tape recorder that he had found next to her dead body. He had also told her about the Pentagon agent's overbearing presence, both at his mother's house, and the many times since.

He hadn't gone into detail about the tape; there was plenty on there that no one needed to ever hear or think about. But he did share that he had heard a man that Jeannie had referred to as Todd – who Andrew felt certain was Todd Jackson, son of police officer Evan Jackson – strangle Jeannie to death. He had then told Claire about Todd's offhand remark, which had been caught on the recorder as he was leaving Jeannie's house. *"It doesn't matter if I never find Cynthia, because a man named Jacob will soon use the power of the Pentagon to end your daughter forever."*

Coming on the heels of Maddi's plane crash, Andrew's suspicions had been raised, and he had decided that the only way to learn the truth was to find Todd Jackson. He had concluded that the best way to begin would be to find Todd's mother, which was how he had come to be in Evansville, Indiana, at the same time that Claire was meeting with the Prosecutor. He had walked in just as she was telling the Prosecutor that fifteen-year-old Maddi had killed Evan Jackson. Andrew had been able to play the last minute or so of the recording, where his mother had claimed that it was she, Jeannie, who had killed Evan Jackson twenty-two years ago.

"And now you're up to date, Claire," he had said as he had finished the summary. Claire had nodded, and had offered a soothing, sympathetic smile. They had then talked about Maddi; Claire's thoughts about her, *"I have never met such a genuine and uplifting spirit,"* and Andrew's anguish over losing her and his mother within hours of one another. *"Thank God for Amanda and Adam or I'm pretty sure I wouldn't have made it."* They had ended dinner at nine, and he had gone back to his hotel. They had agreed to meet for a late lunch two days later, Saturday, which was today.

The following morning, Friday, he had snuck out and, wearing a stocking cap that he had bought at a convenience store, along with a pair of cheap sunglasses, he had gone back to the courthouse. His goal: to see if he could learn the name and current address of Todd Jackson's mother. Because of Andrew's own experience with losing a police officer father to violence, he was aware of a file that was kept on all policemen killed in duty, and, after thirty minutes of rifling through old records, had learned that the woman's name was Mona. He had written down her phone number and address and had taken a cab to her house, but had been disappointed to find that she wasn't there. There were three or four newspapers piled on the porch, suggesting that she had been gone for at least a few days.

He had vowed to go back, but then, as he had been sneaking away, it had occurred to him that the Pentagon agent could very well be surveilling the woman's house. After all, if the agent was aware of Todd Jackson's role in Jeannie's death – and that Andrew might at least suspect it – he would have every reason to think that Andrew might try to speak to the mother of that man. So, instead of going back to Mona's house, Andrew had decided to call her, which he had done several times over the past 24 hours. She hadn't answered; he had been unwilling to leave a message.

There had been many times over the course of the last three days when he had had to fight the urge to call Amanda. He couldn't involve her in this mess. Two people were dead – his mother and his sister – and it was possible that both of those deaths had something to do with a man named Jacob. The further Andrew could keep Jacob from his family, the better.

One thing was certain; the claim that Jeannie was involved with terrorists had been a red herring. Those agents had come to her house for one reason and one reason only: to get that tape. Why? Because Todd had allowed himself to be recorded admitting that a man, Jacob, was about to go after Cynthia Madison. The arrival of the agents implied that Jacob, whoever he was, had considerable clout. The question was, how far would he go to get the tape. *Pretty damn far,* Andrew had concluded.

Which was why he was hesitant to leave the dreary hotel outside Evansville. Though he was desperate to go home, he couldn't; not yet. Not only did he need to protect his family from the mysterious Jacob, but he needed to find Todd Jackson and confront him about Jeannie's murder. He also needed to learn the truth about Maddi's plane crash. How was it determined that the crash had been an accident? Had Jacob played a role in the crash? If so, how? Why did he want Maddi dead? And why did Todd feel the need to kill Jeannie? What had made him think that Maddi had killed his father? How was Todd tied to Jacob? Last but not least...*who the hell is Jacob?*

He had already tried to answer the last question. Before he had left Jenny Clarkson's house in Strongsville, he had looked up every Jacob at the Pentagon. He had gotten nowhere. It had occurred to him that Maddi's secretary, Phil Jenkins, might know who he is. After all, if Jacob had wanted to kill Maddi, wasn't it possible that they had known one another? Even if it was just casually through a shared effort on a senate subcommittee, or an investigation that both Jacob and Maddi had been a part of, it seemed reasonable that Phil might recognize the name.

Andrew had no number for Phil other than Maddi's senate office, so he had dialed it, and had been disappointed – and grieved – when someone else had answered on behalf of Maddi's replacement. The woman had been unable to tell Andrew anything about Phil. Frustrated, he had looked online; there were dozens of Phil Jenkins in DC. He had finally decided that he would fly to DC and try to track down Phil himself. The only problem; the Pentagon was looking for Andrew. The agents had likely alerted airports, train stations, and harbors. If he was going to travel, it couldn't be as Andrew Madison. He would need a disguise and a new ID. He had no idea how to get either one. Left with no resources other than the cash he had with him, and fully aware that his life might be at risk, he had called the person who had helped him before: Jenny Clarkson. Again, she had been willing to help. *Let me see what I can do, Andrew.* That had been two days ago. He had yet to hear from her.

He closed the curtain and walked to the bed. He had just over an hour before he would need to leave to meet Claire. He sat on top of the comforter and turned on his laptop. He clicked to the website that he had looked at so many times of late; Maddi's old Senate webpage. He had hoped to run across a reference to Jacob; he had found nothing. As he stared at the picture of his sister on the page – the bright eyes and the infectious smile – he was suddenly overcome. He and Maddi had gone through more than most, and they had done it together...the murder of their father, the alcoholism of their mother, the lechery of a cop named Evan Jackson. He tightened his jaw as he slammed shut the laptop. *I'll be damned if I'm going to let Jackson's son get away with killing my mother, while some asshole, Jacob, gets away with killing my sister!*

His trac phone rang and he jumped. He answered with a whispered, "Jenny?"

There was a pause. A deep male voice said, "Is this Dr. Andrew Madison?"

Andrew tensed. "Who's asking?"

"I'm calling on behalf of Jenny Clarkson. She didn't give me details, but she said that you might be in a bit of a jam." A pause. "Can I be of help, doctor?"

Andrew's hands were shaking. *A trap?* "How...how do you know Jenny?"

"I work with her ex-husband, Hank. I'm an agent in his department."

Andrew's eyes widened. "You work for Homeland Security?"

"Yes. I've known the Clarksons for quite some time." There was a pause. "The best way I can put it is this: a friend of Jenny's is a friend of mine."

Andrew narrowed his eyes. Could he trust this man...this stranger? "Who are you and why should I believe you?"

"Donovan's the name. Jake Donovan...and I've come to keep you safe."

Chapter 30

En route to China

Henderson had been flying for nearly twelve hours; the last four had been in darkness. Fortunately, he was a seasoned pilot, his father having taken him flying as young as the age of seven. *"It's good to acquire confidence at an early age, son."* Other than a quick stop in India to refuel, the flight thus far had been unremarkable. Ironically, the flight restrictions out of Latvia had actually helped him...that, and being a Henderson. Walter had spoken with the administrator overseeing flights out of the Riga airport, and had requested an emergency flight plan for his representative, who had important work to conduct in China. Though Walter had implied that the work was related to diplomacy and the threat of war with Russia, he had never actually said so, allowing him to avoid a lie. The administrator had cautioned that it wasn't safe, and it most definitely wasn't safe for his representative to fly anywhere near Russia. They had agreed that he would fly south toward India, then east over Tibet, which would add about six hours to the trip. The flight plan would take him as far as Tianjin; he would be on his own from there.

His cellphone rang and he jumped. Only Walter had the number. Henderson answered with a quick, "Hey Dad."

"It's me." In spite of her whisper, he recognized his mother Dora's voice.

"What's up, Mom?"

There was a pause. "Son, I need your help."

Henderson frowned. "Why? What's going on?"

"We have a visitor...here at the mansion. He has come for dinner." There was a pause "He says he's with the military, but I don't have a good feeling about him." She hesitated. "It's his mannerisms. I've dealt with military leaders for many years, son, and the man at our dinner table is different. He lacks something."

"What do you mean?"

"I don't know...he doesn't possess the humility of a seasoned soldier." A pause. "He says he's from the Pentagon, and that he's here on behalf of the Joint Chiefs to offer support in our battle against Putin. But son...he has this...smirk."

Dear god, it can't be. Henderson's hands had begun to shake; he gripped the yoke tighter. "What's his name?"

"Morningstar. Edward Morningstar."

Henderson stiffened, sickened by the thought of that man in his parents' home. *How much do I tell her?* He cleared his throat. "I know him, Mom. And you're right about him: he's no good. He is, however, incredibly powerful." Henderson rubbed the back of his neck. "What does Dad have to say about it?"

"We haven't had a chance to talk. He's with the man now. I excused myself to check on dinner. You were the only person I could think of to call."

Henderson swallowed. "Dad knows a little bit about him, Mom, but not much. He knows that he might not be who he seems."

A pause. "Then why would he welcome him into our home so graciously?"

Good question. "I'm guessing that someone called ahead."

"Now that you mention it, I believe that is exactly what happened. Walter spoke with someone...one of the generals, I think."

"Dad would be hard-pressed to ignore such a request." Henderson sighed. "I'm guessing Dad will use the opportunity to gain some measure of the man."

Still whispering, Dora said, "I can give him whatever measure he's looking for. This Morningstar is not a good man...and he's up to something."

Henderson again rubbed the back of his neck. Truer words had never been spoken. "I'm guessing that's why Dad didn't tell you his impression of the man. He's wanting your unbiased thoughts about him." He paused. "Here's the thing, Mom. As I said, the guy's powerful. Not only is he Alexander Daniels' right-hand man, but he's also got a private group of soldiers who will do whatever he says." He winced. *And I used to be one of them.* "You need to figure out what he's up to, Mom, but play it cool. As I said before, this man is powerful and he's ruthless." He squeezed the yoke tighter. "Tell you what. When Morningstar leaves, let Dad know your concerns. And tell him that you called me. There are now three of us that know who – and what – Morningstar is." He sighed. "I just hope it's enough."

"Enough? Enough for what?"

Henderson narrowed his eyes. "To stop him."

CHAPTER 31

Bangor, Maine

Cravens clutched the wheel as he steered the rental car along the back roads of Maine. The sun had come out, making it easier for him to maneuver on the unfamiliar roads. He had just turned onto US-201 north, and was looking for the Bridge Street exit that would take him into Bangor, where he was to rendezvous with President Knight's team at midnight. It was only two p.m., but he was concerned that he might not find the place in the dark. And, though he had promised Hank that he would try to find Jenny, he couldn't very well ignore a request by his Commander-in-Chief.

But Hank's worries weren't sitting well with him...not at all. Cravens was well aware of what it had taken for Hank to call. A lot was on the line if what they had done to protect Maddi ever came to light. Not only had they faked the death of a prominent U.S. Senator, but they had hidden evidence that a plane crash – which had been listed as an accident – had actually been intentional. *Obstruction of justice, treason...take your pick.* Cravens sighed. Yes, it had taken a lot for Hank to call.

And now that the matter with Gad had been taken care of, Cravens wanted nothing more than to help his friend. Cravens had met Hank's ex-wife Jenny only once, back in August, when she had flown to London to find Hank. She had called Maddi, swallowing her pride as she had asked for help from the same woman who years before had stolen Hank away from her. And Maddi, being the gracious woman that she was, had offered it. By the end of their time together, the two women had become friends, which meant that Cravens now felt an even greater obligation to do whatever he could to find Jenny. And because of the secret that he and Hank shared, he felt tied to Hank almost like a brother. *Jenny is important to two people who mean the world to me.* There was no way around it; he had to try to find her.

But the timing couldn't have been worse. Not only was he deeply involved in an effort to cover up what had gone on at a church in Portland, but he was also supposed to bring whatever evidence he had found to the drop-off point in Bangor. He had also been instructed to assign an agent to look after Michael Cannon and his daughter. On top of that, he had been asked by Martin Henderson – who might be dead now, for all he knew – to retrieve a flash drive from a safe deposit box at a Savings and Loan in Boonsboro, Maryland. According to Henderson, that flash drive could help to bring down the powerful man who was seemingly behind everything; the plane crash, the kidnapping of Dr. Samuels...even to some extent the Latvian war.

He looked over at his duffel bag, which was sitting next to his sooty overcoat on the passenger seat. In that duffel bag were five baggies that held the evidence that would hopefully reveal the identity of the shadowy Gad. He was to bring the evidence to someone in Bangor, who would then take it to wherever the President was hiding so it could be processed. Cravens wasn't sure if he would be asked to go along, or if he would be free to go on his way. He frowned. It was quite possible that once he met his contact in Bangor, he would be in no position to complete any of the other tasks.

Hank had said that Jenny's last known location was Hank's townhouse in Georgetown, which was an upscale part of DC. Hank had estimated at the time that she had been missing for at least thirty-six hours. *"Maybe even longer, Cravens...I was boarding a plane when I last spoke to her."* Hank's call to Cravens was eight hours ago...which meant that Jenny Clarkson had been missing for nearly two days.

Cravens guessed that Jenny's disappearance would turn out to be something simple, like she had made weekend plans with a group of girlfriends and had left her phone behind. Cravens had, after all, been married once. But he had heard the alarm in Hank's voice and he knew not to take it lightly. Hank wasn't prone to hysteria. If anything, Hank had proven to be one of the more resolute and resilient men that he had ever met. *So, how do I go about finding her?*

He thought again about asking his boss to assign an agent to the task. But, for the same reasons as before, he let it go. He couldn't say that Hank had called him and was worried about his ex-wife; Hank hadn't been heard from in months. The request itself would raise too many red flags. He frowned. *I could say that I was the one who noticed her missing.* He ran his hands through his sparse gray hair and sighed. He couldn't say that, either. Why would Cravens be in a position to notice anything about Jenny Clarkson? He and Hank were supposed to be acquaintances, at best. He sighed. *There's no way around it...I'll have to go to DC and look for her myself.*

But could he get there and back in time? He checked the dashboard. Two p.m. He was to meet with Knight's agent at midnight...*which gives me ten hours.* He guessed that the flying time from Bangor to DC was around two hours. Fortunately, there were lots of flights to DC. If he could get on a flight in the next two hours, he could be in DC by six. He could take a cab to the townhouse, look for Jenny, and take a cab back to the airport, where he could catch a flight back to Bangor in time to meet with whoever was coming for the evidence from the Gad/DeMarco shooting. As long as he left DC by nine or nine-thirty, he could make it to Bangor in time.

He turned onto Bridge Street, drove to the site of the midnight rendezvous, and pulled to the side of the road. He etched the location in his mind, then reached for his cellphone to call an old friend, a retired Secret Service agent, to watch over Michael Cannon and his daughter, Galina. As he did so, he felt the key in his pocket. It was the key to the safe deposit box that held the flash drive that Henderson had asked him to pick up in Boonsboro, Maryland. *Maybe while I'm in DC, I'll have time to take a cab to the Savings and Loan in Boonsboro.* If things went as planned, he just might be able to make it all work.

He opened his phone and called the retired agent, a man he would trust with his life. He asked him to look after the Cannons, gave him their address, then made sure that he understood that he must tell no one what he was up to. *"I'll take care of it, Cravens,"* the agent had replied. He didn't ask a single question.

169

Once Cravens had completed the call, he plugged in the address for the Bangor airport. A rudimentary map popped up on the screen. He turned on the engine and eased into the flow of traffic. His priorities had just changed. Yes, he would do his best to honor his commitment to his Commander-in-Chief, but more importantly, he would do his best to find Jenny. He had to. He knew – better than most – that Hank had no one else to turn to.

CHAPTER 32

Evansville, Indiana

Andrew zipped his coat to his chin as he crept slowly along the side of an old, two-story building in downtown Evansville. He had a good view of the diner across the street. He guessed that Claire Porter would already be there. But he couldn't just walk in to meet her. He was almost certain that the agents from the Pentagon were looking for him. But they would expect him to be alone. Which was why he was waiting for a group to walk into the diner; a group he could casually become a part of.

He pulled his hood lower on his forehead and adjusted his sunglasses. He stuck his hand in his pocket, absently feeling for the recorder. But it wasn't there. He had hidden it in a safe-deposit box in a bank in downtown Evansville.

He continued to watch the diner as he thought about the call from Jake Donovan. It couldn't have been better timed. Other than Claire, Andrew had felt pretty much alone in the world...under siege by a powerful Pentagon, and overwhelmed by the truths he had uncovered. The offer to help had been a godsend. The fact that the agent was friends with the Clarksons made it even better. Nonetheless, he would proceed with caution. He wouldn't put it past the Pentagon agents to use a decoy to try to get to that tape.

He had agreed to meet Donovan at four p.m. at the diner he was staring at; the same diner where he was to meet Claire at three. He checked his watch. *Two-fifty-eight.* There were no groups of people walking toward the diner. Andrew might have to risk going in alone. *I'll give it another minute or two.*

Andrew was looking forward to seeing Claire again. She had a comforting way about her. He imagined that she was excellent at her job. Fortunately – for Andrew anyway – the Evansville Prosecutor had insisted that Claire stay in town until he could make inquiries into the twenty-two-year-old murder of Evan Jackson. Though he had said it was unlikely he would pursue the case, he had at least wanted to verify a few facts. He had promised Claire that he would have something by Monday. *"Then, if I need to impanel a Grand Jury, I'll get your testimony and let you go home."* He had arranged for Claire to stay – at the county's expense – at the downtown hotel to await the outcome of his investigation.

He looked up and down the street, relieved when he spotted three young women walking toward the diner. Would they go inside? He continued to watch. Yes, they were definitely going into the diner. He slid from his hiding place, jogged to a statue across the street, then fell in behind them. He bumped one of the women's elbows and laughed apologetically. He was heartened when she laughed in reply. "I am so sorry," he said, as he opened the door for the trio and followed them inside. He saw Claire sitting in a corner booth near the back. Short, plump, with strawberry-blonde hair, she was hard to miss. He walked to where she was sitting and took a seat across from her. He took off the sunglasses, but kept up the hood of the sweatshirt.

She looked at him and frowned. "Sunglasses and a hooded sweatshirt? Are you seriously in that much danger?"

He nodded. "As I told you the other night, that recording I played for the Prosecutor has lots of secrets on it, Claire. And because of it, I'm almost certain that I'm being followed."

She shook her head. "By the agents from the Pentagon?"

"Yes, and they are desperate to get a hold of that tape."

Claire shook her head. "Dear lord. Isn't there someone you can confide in? Could you maybe ask the Prosecutor to help you, or go to the local authorities?"

Andrew sighed. "Think about it, Claire. It's 'the authorities' who're after me."

She shook her head. "So, what are you going to do with it...the tape, I mean."

A waiter came, set two waters on the table, and pulled out his pad. Andrew ordered coffee and a piece of pie. Claire looked at Andrew and frowned. "I shouldn't," she said with a sigh. "Then again, these are stressful circumstances." She looked at the waiter and said determinedly, "I'll have the same."

The waiter walked away and Andrew frowned. "I don't know what I'm going to do with it, Claire...I truly don't know."

* * *

Jake Donovan had driven to the diner where he was to meet Andrew, hoping to scope out the place, and get comfortable with the area before the four o'clock meeting. He had pulled into the parking lot at three p.m., surprised to see Andrew walking into the diner with a group of young women. *Who are they?* Pulling out a pair of binoculars given to him by his boss – high grade with the ability to take pictures – he had watched Andrew leave the women and walk to the back, where he then sat down across from a stout woman with reddish-blond hair. Donovan had immediately snapped the woman's picture, then had plugged the binoculars into his laptop. He had run the photo through facial recognition software. The report had come back within minutes: Claire Porter, DC therapist. *How does Andrew know her, and why is she in Evansville?*

He reached into the back seat of the rental car he had picked up in Indianapolis and grabbed his briefcase. *There's only one way to find out.* He opened the case, and shuffled through files and notepads until he found what looked like a simple paper napkin. He slid it in his pocket, and, popping his collar and pulling his cap low on his forehead, he stepped out of the car. He walked into the diner. With his back to Claire and Andrew, he waited at the counter for the order he guessed would go to their table. Looking at a mirror mounted in the corner, he could see everyone in the diner. Other than Andrew and Claire, there were the three young women, four teenagers, and an older man. Donovan spotted a tray that had coffee and pie for two. *That's gotta be them.* In one fluid motion, he pulled out the napkin and set it on the tray. He pretended to get a phone call, and, with the phone to his ear, walked back out to his car.

The napkin, a highly sensitive listening device, would hopefully let him hear what was being said between Andrew and the therapist. He frowned. *That is, if I picked the right table.*

He opened his car door and slid behind the wheel. He pulled a speaker the size of a matchbox from his briefcase and held it to his ear, adjusting the frequency until the static disappeared. He could hear two voices; a man and a woman. He heard the woman address the man as Andrew. He nodded. *It's the right table.*

* * *

Their pie came and they dug in. Andrew had had little to eat over the course of the last three days, and the pie tasted good. In-between bites, he said, "So, tell me what Maddi told you," he lowered his voice, "...about Evan Jackson."

Claire took a sip of coffee. "I hate to say too much." She paused. "Even though she's...gone...I still feel a need to protect her privacy." She leaned closer. "What do you know about that time in her life, Andrew?"

Andrew wiped his mouth with his napkin. "Not much, I'm afraid. I was away at school for most of it." He frowned. "I know she was very troubled by it, however."

Claire narrowed her eyes. "Are you aware, Andrew, what it was that was troubling her?"

Andrew took another bite of his pie. "Yeah...an asshole cop took advantage of her. She had a thing for him, and he pretty much hung her out to dry." He stopped eating and looked at Claire. With narrowed eyes, he said, "Is there more to it?"

Claire looked around as if to make sure no one was listening, then leaned in closer. "Andrew, Maddi was pregnant."

Andrew felt like he had been kicked. Suddenly, everything made sense. Her over-the-top distress over a bad relationship, the weight gain which he had attributed to despair, the sudden trip to Darlington, England, to spend time with their grandparents. He shoved his plate away. Keeping his voice low, he said, "My god, Claire. Do we know what happened to the... the baby?"

Claire narrowed her eyes. "All I know is that Maddi's grandparents – your grandparents – arranged for the child to be adopted by people they could vouch for."

Andrew's mind was going a mile a minute. Though his grandparents had come to Indiana at least twice a year, he didn't really know them. He certainly didn't know who they were close to in Darlington. The only acquaintance of theirs that he did know was the former Ambassador to the United States, Sir Arthur Kauffold. He had met Kauffold after being summoned in March to a meeting of a secret organization known as The Morning Star. Present at the meeting had been four men: Kauffold, Walter Henderson, a man they had referred to as the Caretaker, and an expatriated Brit, Johnny Canterbury. Though Andrew hadn't established any sort of deep connection with any of the men, he did feel like he could at least call Kauffold and ask him what he knew about the people in his grandparents' world. It would help that Kauffold had been close to Maddi. *I'll call him once Claire leaves.*

He sat back and sighed. "Tell me more...about Maddi's baby."

Claire shook her head. "I don't know much. I think it made Maddi sad to talk about it." Claire hesitated. "I know she hated to give the baby up for adoption...but then again, what choice did she have?"

Andrew shook his head. "Why had Maddi come to see you in the first place?"

Claire sighed. "As I said earlier, I hate to say too much," she hesitated, "...but I can tell you this much. A friend of hers had been murdered while she had been sitting directly beside him. A Middle Eastern man."

Andrew nodded. "Abdulkarim Al Gharsi."

"Yes. It had taken a toll on Maddi. She had felt that Al-Gharsi was a good man making a real difference in the Middle East." She paused. "Anyway, it brought up other traumatic losses...her father, a friend from DC, and Martin Henderson. She had needed a way to process it, especially since so much of it had involved violence. That was how the Evan Jackson thing came up." Claire leaned in even further. "I'm not sure what to think regarding who it was that actually killed that terrible man, but I will tell you this, Andrew...Maddi *believed* that she had done it."

175

Andrew frowned. *Why would Maddi think she had killed him if she hadn't?*

Claire quickly added, "But I'll say this about that girl...nothing could take her down, not for long, anyway. She had a strength of spirit the likes of which I've never seen. Even amid all her grief, there was this underlying joy...like it was her steady state, no matter what happened."

Andrew swallowed, then cleared his throat. It was true. He nodded, but said nothing. There was nothing to say.

He checked his watch. Nearly four p.m. ...almost nine p.m. in the UK. He wanted to talk to Kauffold before Donovan arrived at the diner. He looked at Claire and smiled. "I'm meeting someone at four, Claire, but talking to you has been so good for me. Since you're here until Monday, perhaps we can meet again tomorrow?"

She patted her mouth with her napkin. "I'd like that. What time tomorrow?"

"I'm not sure. I can give you a call. Should I call the hotel again?"

She stood, put on her coat, and reached in her purse. She pulled out a business card and handed it to Andrew. "Call me on my cell. The number's on the back."

He shoved the card in his pocket, standing as she turned to leave.

She hesitated. "Is there a way that I can get a hold of you if I need to?"

He frowned. *The fewer people who have this number the better.* "I'll call you soon, Claire."

She nodded and walked away. Suddenly, she stopped and looked over her shoulder. "Andrew, take care of yourself."

He gave a weak smile as he sat back down. "I will, Claire."

She continued to the door; he watched her leave. He pulled out his phone. *Now...how to get in touch with Kauffold.* The man's number – a landline because Kauffold didn't want the hassle of a cellphone – was in Andrew's cellphone that was back in South Carolina. He had left the phone at the office, knowing that it was a way for the Pentagon to track him. It was four p.m.; Amanda would still be at work. *I have no other choice,* he thought as he opened his trac phone and dialed.

Amanda answered with a hushed, "Andrew?"

Andrew closed his eyes. God, how he missed her. "Amanda, there's something I need you to do."

"Is everything okay?"

"Do you happen to have my cellphone nearby?"

"I do. I locked it in the top drawer of your office. Give me a minute." There was a pause, followed by the sound of a drawer opening. "Okay, I have it."

"Good. Open it and find the number for Arthur Kauffold."

After a few seconds, she said, "Here it is." She read off the number.

Andrew wrote it on his placemat. "Thanks, Amanda."

"Wait. Don't go. Are you coming home soon?"

Andrew flinched. He wanted to; he wanted to go home so badly. He missed her. He missed Adam. "As soon as I can...I promise. I love you, Amanda." He ended the call before she had time to say anything more.

He noticed that his hands were shaking. His heart ached as he thought of his wife and son. They were the only family he had left. Suddenly his eyes widened. No, that wasn't actually true. *Maddi had a child.* He choked as he dialed Kauffold's number. *Which means that a part of my family – a part of Maddi – is out there somewhere.*

Donovan sat back against the seat. He was stunned. He had endured Andrew and Claire's boring conversation, not caring in the least if *Maddi,* as they called her, had been joyful as she had fought her despair. But his ears had definitely perked up when he had heard the therapist say that Maddi *believed* she had killed officer Evan Jackson. That shock had been preceded by the revelation that she had been pregnant by the man and had had the nerve to have his baby. He imagined the headlines. *"Recently deceased senator killed a man, then gave birth to his illegitimate child."*

As he had held the listening device with one hand, the binoculars with the other, he had seen Claire walk out of the diner. He had listened as Andrew had pulled out his phone and dialed. From what Andrew was saying, it was clear that he was speaking to his wife. Donovan grinned. *Amanda.* He continued to watch Andrew as he wrote something on a placemat...likely a phone number. Was Andrew – and therefore Donovan – about to learn the who, where, and how of Madison's child? Donovan checked his watch. *Four o'clock.* He was supposed to be meeting Andrew inside the diner, but he didn't want to distract Andrew from his phone call. *I mustn't get in the way of him learning the truth about 'Maddi's' baby.*

CHAPTER 33

Chesham, England

Sir Arthur Kauffold, former ambassador to the United States, sat his old, tired frame in his favorite chair. Unlike most favorite chairs, which were over-stuffed and situated in a dark den or a high-ceilinged study, his roomy Chesterfield sat in the dining room in front of French double doors. From there he could see everything important to him, starting with the garden and its year-round colors, and ending with the photo of his wife, Annabelle, vigilant as it stood watch on the sideboard by the door. She had been with him for forty years, the two of them a team as they had faced life head-on, raising up the beautiful Tonna, whom they had watched from that dining room table so many times as she had run among the flowers. And it was Tonna he was watching now. Though it was nighttime and the air had grown colder, she had stayed in the garden, and was now sitting among rows of pruned roses. The light of the moon was her only companion as she huddled in a blanket and stared out at the endless countryside. The garden – her playground as a child – had become her refuge. It was where she went to walk, to think, to mourn.

Neither she nor Arthur had fully recovered from the death of Cynthia Madison. Arthur had expected it to be hard on them. He had, after all, served as Maddi's unofficial mentor, and Tonna had learned just last spring that Maddi was her biological mother. He shook his head and sighed. *It's never easy to lose one's mother.*

Arthur had learned of the biological tie between the two women only two months ago, as Maddi had been about to board a plane for America. She had shared the stunning truth with Kauffold in anticipation of her return to the States, where she expected to be arrested for her involvement in the death of Tonna's father.

She never boarded that plane, however. Had she done so, she would likely be alive today. For whatever reason, a day later she boarded an RAF jet instead, and was killed when it crashed during its descent into Latvia. Though he would have given anything for her to have gone home to America, at least she hadn't been forced to face the shackles and the jackals that would surely have been waiting for her once that information came to light. As far as he was concerned, the secret died with her. *Fate is a cruel mistress,* he thought as he watched Tonna shiver in the cold.

He took a deep breath and sighed. *Perhaps Tonna will feel better when – if – Roger comes to visit.* Roger Clarkson, the CIA agent who had accompanied Tonna to the Queen's Ball in March had clearly charmed the girl. But because of his work with the CIA, they had been forced to hide their relationship from the world. The only thing he had shared with Tonna regarding the task he had been assigned – which she had then shared with Arthur – was that the nature of it was such that Tonna could be in danger were his target to learn of her and Roger's relationship.

Though Arthur was quite fond of Roger, it had angered him to think that the relationship had put his daughter in danger. *"It isn't like we planned to fall in love,"* Tonna had said as she had tried to soften that anger.

Arthur nodded sadly as he thought of the words of the lovelorn Pip from the Dickens classic, "Great Expectations," *"I loved her against reason, against promise, against hope, against happiness, against all discouragement that could be."* He fought back tears as he again turned his eye to the photo of Annabelle.

Tonna hadn't seen Roger but once since his near-death experience in Paris, which had taken place soon after the Queen's Ball. He had stopped by the Kauffold residence, and Arthur was certain that the visit had been at grave risk...to both Roger and Tonna. It had been only days after Maddi's death, however, and they had needed one another. Maddi had meant a lot to both of them. Roger had known her mostly as the woman that his father Hank had loved for years, and Tonna had known her as her mother. Was Roger aware that Maddi was Tonna's mother? Arthur had no idea.

Nonetheless, Roger's twenty-four-hour vigil had given them time to mourn together, and it had seemed to help them both. But now, with Roger back in the underworld, Tonna spent her days and nights alone, most of that time spent in the garden. She had come home from university immediately upon learning of Maddi's death, and had yet to return. Though Arthur felt it would do her good to get back to school and be among friends, she had simply been unable to face the challenges of school, and had taken great comfort in being home...in being in the garden. And, if he was honest with himself, he didn't want her to go. He, too, was grieving, and having her there with him had been a balm to his soul.

He leaned back and sighed as he watched Tonna stare up at the sky from her bench in the garden. Now that he knew the truth about Maddi being her mother, he was surprised that he hadn't seen it before...the way Tonna laughed, the things she said, even the questions she asked; she was Maddi through and through. Maddi had been only fifteen when she had come to England to visit her grandparents in Darlington. And Kauffold had spotted it immediately; her charm, her natural grace, her keen wit. With a little coaxing, and Kauffold's connections throughout the UK, he had made it possible for her to attend the prestigious Oxford University. She had earned her Magister Juris degree in only four years, applying herself unlike anyone he had ever seen. And it had changed her. She had gone from an awkward teenager, to a cultured, well-educated dynamo. Kauffold couldn't help but congratulate himself for the role he had played. But it was Maddi who had done all the work; to call her remarkable would be an understatement. She had been a genuinely good woman, with a smile that would warm the room and comfort those around her. He choked and put a hand to his heart. Even now, over two months later, it could still bring him to tears.

He looked up to the heavens and, with his voice shaking, he said, "I'm losing my patience with You, God. You continue to take the good ones, and leave the rest of us here to suffer." He waited, thinking just once, God would reply. Maybe not with words, but with some sort of assurance that there truly was a Grand Design; a purpose for all of the pain. But he got nothing.

He shook his head and looked again at Tonna in the garden. He ran his fingers through his thinning white hair, and tugged at his mustache...his pride and joy, he used to tell Annabelle. He sighed. He had become an old man. As he looked from Tonna to the picture of his lovely Annabelle, he smiled sadly. He had had a good life; a good seventy-four years, probably the best a man could hope for. He had traveled the world, had served his country and his Queen, and had been blessed to know three very remarkable, very beautiful women: Annabelle, Maddi, and Tonna. Again, he choked back a sob. *But only one of them is still alive.*

He watched as Tonna shifted on a bench that looked over the estate. Though she had wrapped herself in a blanket, she continued to shiver. He stood and was about to take her another blanket, when the phone rang. He checked the time. *Nine o'clock...a bit late for a call.* His butler, Alfred, had gone to London for the evening, so Kauffold shuffled to the den, moving far slower than he had when he used to cross the sea and mix it up with the Americans. "Hold on...I'm coming."

His hope was that it was his friend from MI6 returning his call. Walter Henderson had called Arthur two nights ago, inquiring about a man who allegedly worked undercover for the elite British organization; a man named Shaw. *"First name or last?"* Kauffold had asked. Walter had replied, *"I don't actually know."*

Kauffold got to the phone on the sixth ring. He picked it up and, a bit short of breath, huffed, "The Kauffold residence."

There was a pause, followed by, "Is this Arthur Kauffold?"

"Yes, it is. May I ask who's calling?"

"Arthur, it's me...Andrew Madison." Another pause. "I know we're supposed to...um...keep our distance, but I need information...about Maddi."

Again, Arthur put a hand to his chest. Just hearing Maddi's name – spoken by the only member left of her tragic clan – shot a pain through his heart. "Andrew, it is so good to hear from you." He hesitated. "I am so sorry for your loss...your losses."

There was a pause. "Thank you, sir. That's part of the reason I'm calling."

"What can I do for you, son?"

Kauffold heard a sigh. "Are you sitting down?"

Kauffold frowned. "Why, no. Should I be?"

Another pause. "Kauffold, I have just learned that Maddi – back when she went to visit my grandparents at the age of fifteen – had been... pregnant."

Kauffold chuckled to himself. "Yes, I recently learned that myself."

"Apparently, my grandparents encouraged her to give up the child for adoption." A pause. "I'm told that she did, and that the child was given to a couple that my grandparents knew and trusted. I'm trying to figure out who they were."

Kauffold smiled as he nodded knowingly. "Yes, Andrew. That is correct."

Andrew added, "What I'm saying Arthur...is I'd like to find Maddi's child."

Kauffold sighed. How much should he share? Was it fair for him to be the one to tell Andrew that Tonna was Maddi's child?

"Arthur, are you still there?"

He frowned. "Yes...yes, I'm here, Andrew. How much do you know?"

"Only that it was a closed adoption. I don't know if it was a boy or a girl...I actually know very little."

The door to the study opened. Tonna walked in, her red face a testament to how much colder it had gotten. He looked at her and mouthed 'Andrew Madison.' She shook her head sadly. He said into the phone, "A closed adoption, you say?"

Tonna's eyes widened.

Kauffold looked at her. Was she willing to reveal such a secret? To let someone else know that Maddi was her biological mother? It was up to her to decide such a thing. "Let me look into it, Andrew. I'll ring you back shortly."

He laid the phone in its cradle and turned to Tonna. "Apparently, Andrew has just learned that Maddi had a child." He grinned. "Would you like me to tell him about you, Tonna?"

Suddenly, a rush of tears poured from eyes that looked so much like Maddi's it made his heart hurt. She rushed to hug him. The tears ran down her cheeks and she buried her head in his shoulder. He held her close, letting her cry as he thought back over the last twenty years. How incredible to think that the woman he had encouraged to stay in London and attend college, who had then blossomed into one of the most amazing women to ever set foot in the U.S. Senate, had actually been the mother to his darling Tonna. *A part of Maddi, right here...in my arms.*

Tonna looked up at him. "What do you think I should do, Father?"

He sighed. "You and Andrew are all that are left of Maddi's family. I think it would be exceptionally kind of you to tell Andrew – your uncle – the truth."

Tonna nodded.

Kauffold said, "He will want to see you...maybe even be a part of your life."

Tonna smiled. "I would like that. Yes, Father, please let him know the truth."

CHAPTER 34

Evansville, Indiana

Andrew drummed his fingers on the table as he waited for the callback from Kauffold. He checked his watch. *Two minutes after four...Donovan will be here any minute.* He didn't want to talk about his dead sister in front of a stranger, let alone her secret child. His hope was that Arthur would call back before Donovan arrived.

The waiter came by and asked if he wanted anything more. "Just coffee. I'm waiting for someone to join me." The man nodded, filled his cup, and walked away.

Andrew sipped the coffee, trying to imagine who Arthur might be calling. *Likely the parents of Maddi's child,* he thought as he took a sip of the coffee. But the adoption had clearly been a well-kept secret. *So why was Kauffold let in on it?*

The phone rang and he answered with a quick "Yes."

"Andrew, it's Kauffold. I believe I have an answer for you."

Andrew tensed. "You do?"

"Yes. Now, I need you to understand that I only learned of it a couple of months ago. I was quite overcome by it, actually."

"Why? Do you know the couple?"

He heard a chuckle. "I do...quite well, as a matter of fact."

"Who is it? Who adopted Maddi's baby?"

There was a pause. It almost sounded like Kauffold was crying. "Maddi had a daughter, as it turns out."

"A little girl?"

"Well, she's not so little anymore. As a matter of fact, she is sitting right across from me, and has grown into a beautiful young woman."

Andrew's thoughts were racing. *How could Kauffold be looking at Maddi's daughter?* Then he remembered; Kauffold had told him during their first meeting that he had a daughter. *What was her name?* "Tonna?"

Definitely tears. "Yes. The lovely daughter of our dear Maddi is my beautiful girl, Tonna...Tonna Kauffold."

Andrew's jaw dropped. "Maddi's daughter...is your daughter."

"Yes, Andrew...yes, she is."

* * *

Donovan flinched as he held the speaker closer to his ear. Had he heard Andrew correctly? Cynthia Madison had had a child – a girl – and the UK's former ambassador to America had adopted her? He stared out the front of the rental car window, too stunned to even move. What were the odds?

He checked his watch. Four minutes after four. He needed to go. He pulled the speaker from his ear, turned it off, and shoved it and the binoculars into his briefcase. He shook his head, still stunned by the revelation. He smoothed down his jacket and sighed. *I'll deal with it later. Now I need to save Andrew Madison from the Pentagon.*

CHAPTER 35

Chesham, England

Roger barely noticed that his legs were cramping as he knelt high in a tree, half-a-mile beyond the gardens of the Kauffold estate. He lowered the binoculars, having watched Tonna finally leave the bench and walk inside. *You had to have been freezing to death, Tonna,* he thought, as he continued to stare at the bench. Though the temperature had dropped considerably, he didn't feel it; he didn't feel anything.

Roger had become numb.

He hadn't expected to actually see Tonna. When they had last spoken, she had had every intention of going back to school. She had come home after hearing of Maddi's death. He had come to her then, and they had shared their grief for a few short hours. Those hours would be the last he would ever spend with Tonna.

He understood that now.

But watching her had hurt him...in a place he didn't even know existed. It had been all he could do to not jump from the tree, run through the garden, and go to her. To hold her one more time and tell her that he loved her.

But he couldn't. It was too dangerous. Especially now that he had seen her photo on Cobra's wall. *Tonna is a target...because of me.*

That truth had nearly done him in. It had all but paralyzed him. How could he keep her safe? No one knew better than Roger that if Cobra wanted someone, he tended to get them. *Then again, he wants me, but he doesn't have me.* Except for four days in the Paris catacombs when Cobra had nearly killed Roger, the maniac had done little more than taunt him. Ironically, the same could be said of Roger. He had gotten close to Cobra; he had even shot him a time or two, but he had yet to capture the man who had become his sole objective.

My sole objective. He hadn't understood that phrase until twelve hours ago, when he had seen Tonna's picture on Cobra's wall. It was as if a switch had been flipped. His entire worldview had changed. Not just his worldview...everything about him. His breathing, his heart rate...his very sense of self. All of it had slowed and grown darker...*like nightfall,* he thought, as he felt the world outside disappear. The moon had vanished; the stars had lost their glow. He was living completely and wholly inside his head.

And it had started the minute he had seen the photo on Cobra's wall. Instead of calling Inspector Pritchard to let him know that he had found Cobra's lair, or to alert him to Cobra's possible attendance at the Aberdeen coin show, he had chosen instead to keep the information to himself. Cobra was no longer a target for the world; he belonged to Roger. *I and I alone will be the one to kill that bastard.*

The pamphlet in Cobra's flat had implied that he would be at the coin show at noon on Saturday, which was today. Roger had arrived at Hazlehead Park in Aberdeen, Scotland, at ten in the morning wearing a stocking cap, dark glasses, and a fake beard. He had worn the disguise not to hide from Cobra, but because he knew that the minute he saw him, he would shoot him on sight. Such an act wouldn't just be a stain on his soul; it would be a stain on the agency. He didn't care about his soul, but he did care about the agency.

He had given it until well after one p.m. Cobra hadn't showed.

That was when Roger had decided to make one last trip to Chesham. He had boarded a train in Aberdeen and had arrived in Chesham two hours ago, still wearing his disguise. During the trip, his boss had tried to call; he hadn't answered. Pritchard had tried to call as he was arriving in Chesham; he hadn't taken that call either. He didn't want to talk to his boss, he didn't want to talk to Pritchard. He didn't want to talk to anyone. He no longer answered to anyone. His master had become the hatred in his heart. He hadn't eaten, he hadn't slept. All he could think of was killing Cobra.

He untangled himself from the branches of the tree, dropped to the ground, and took a final look at the Kauffold estate. Inside that stately manor was a woman he loved...a woman he would love until the day he died. But it wasn't love that he felt; it was hate...a deep, unabated hatred that had no place in Tonna's world. And that hate had taken over...like a virus that was eating him alive. And it would end him...that much he knew for sure.

Goodbye, Tonna.

He turned and sprinted through the trees until he came to a river where he had left a canoe lodged under a pile of brush. He pulled it free, then climbed in and rowed away. Would he ever see Tonna again? It didn't matter. Roger had changed. In twelve short hours he had gone from a man of reason to a madman with one sole objective: to kill Cobra. Until he did that, nothing else mattered. And once he did that, dead or alive, he would be gone.

CHAPTER 36

Evansville, Indiana

Andrew hadn't expected the Jake Donovan who had waltzed into the Evansville diner at 4:05 Saturday afternoon. He wasn't sure what he had expected, but the impeccably dressed, erudite man who was sitting across from him wasn't it. His light brown hair, which was down to his shoulders, had clearly been professionally styled, and the unique green of his eyes had been hard to ignore. He was handsome, sophisticated, and clearly well-connected. *So, what is he doing here?*

He had asked Donovan that very question. His reply: *"As I said on the phone, I'm here to help, Andrew. I'll do whatever you need…as a favor to the Clarkson's."*

Andrew was surprised that Jenny had called in someone from Homeland Security. After all, he had more or less begged her to not tell anyone what he was up to. Not because he didn't want the help, but because he knew that if the Pentagon was involved, it was possible that other agencies were involved, as well.

Andrew had challenged Donovan about his relationship with the Clarkson's. The man had grinned and, in a manner that was undeniably comforting, he had assured Andrew that he was one of the good guys. *"Jenny and I have been friends for years. I've known her and Hank since the mid-nineties. I'm guessing that she called me because she saw me as an ally… someone that she – and you – could trust."* He had added, *"Call her, please. She'll vouch for me."*

189

So, Andrew had made the call...with Donovan sitting right in front of him. Jenny hadn't answered. He had left a message; she had yet to call back.

But Andrew didn't have time to wait. He was in trouble and needed help. He had to trust someone. The most powerful military agency in the world was after him...and now he understood why. He had in his possession proof that whoever Jacob was, he had definitely played a role in the murder of a civilian – Andrew's mother – and he might very well have played a role in the murder of a high-ranking senator – Andrew's sister. Jacob obviously held a position of power, which meant that Andrew would need someone well-versed in the ways of Washington, DC to help him fight such a man. As he stared across the table at Donovan, he was hopeful that that was what Jenny Clarkson had sent him.

Donovan was going over his credentials, but Andrew found himself distracted, still reeling from the fact that Maddi had had a child – a daughter – and that she had turned out to be the ambassador's adopted daughter, Tonna. Urgently wanting to end the call before Donovan showed up at the diner, Andrew had pressed Kauffold to tell him all that he could about Tonna *"...in less than a minute."* He had asked Kauffold if Maddi had known that Tonna was her daughter, and had been surprised to learn that it was Tonna who had figured it out...by cyberstalking Maddi from across the sea. Andrew had laughed. *"She got her tenacity from her mother."* Kauffold had laughed, as well. *"That is so true, Andrew."* Apparently, Tonna had told Maddi of their connection back in March, but they had shared it with no one. *"Why do you think that is, Arthur?"* Andrew had asked. The old man had merely sighed. *"They wanted the timing to be right, I suppose."*

Although Andrew was thrilled to think that a part of Maddi was still alive, he was surprised – and hurt – that Maddi hadn't told him about Tonna. Then again, Maddi hadn't been back to America since leaving in March. The discovery had been sometime after that, and it had likely stunned her. It was also a bit delicate. After all, Tonna hadn't just come from Maddi, she had come from Evan Jackson, too. Andrew guessed that Maddi had decided to wait until she could tell Andrew face-to-face.

According to Arthur, Tonna had spent much of the summer with Maddi in Edinburgh, as Maddi had sat at Matt Henderson's bedside. Which meant that Tonna was one of the last people to talk to Maddi...to see her alive. *I wonder if she knows anything about the mysterious Jacob.*

They had ended the call by Arthur inviting Andrew to visit them in the next week or two. Andrew had thanked him but had begged off, certain he wouldn't be in a position to make such a trip any time soon. But as he half-listened to Donovan go through his history with Homeland Security, suddenly, Andrew wanted – no, he *needed* – to meet the cultured, clever, quick-witted woman who was the daughter of his sister.

So…why can't I go to the UK and meet my niece? It was actually a perfect time for such a journey. Andrew was being hunted by the Pentagon. Wouldn't a trip to the UK give him a bit of breathing room? But it wasn't like he could just get on a plane and fly overseas; not as Andrew Madison anyway. He would be lucky to get as far as DC.

He stared at Jake Donovan…a well-connected Homeland Security agent who appeared to be eager to help him. Could Donovan get him out of the country? Perhaps with a disguise…or a well-placed word at Customs? *Maybe both?*

Donovan looked at him and smiled. "So, to finish, Andrew, I'm here and well positioned to do pretty much whatever you need."

Andrew narrowed his eyes. "That sounds great, Donovan. But I'm still not sure why you're so willing to help me."

Donovan leaned closer. "As I said earlier, a friend of the Clarksons is a friend of mine."

Andrew looked hard at the man across the table. Though the last few days had taught him to trust no one, he was painfully aware that if he was going to accomplish anything with regard to finding Todd Jackson or Jacob, he would need to trust somebody.

He cleared his throat. "Okay, here goes. To start with, there's a man out there who…killed…my mother and is currently walking free." He frowned. "I…I need to find him."

Donovan narrowed his eyes. "I can do that. Do you know his name?"

Andrew nearly choked on the words. "Todd. Todd Jackson."

Donovan pulled out a notepad and wrote down the name. "Anything else?"

"Yes, there's another man – Jacob – who works for the Pentagon. He wants something that I have." Andrew wiped his forehead with a napkin. "And I'm almost certain that he's willing to kill me to get it."

Donovan widened his eyes. "Does this Jacob have a last name?"

Andrew frowned. "I don't know."

"You don't know?"

Andrew shook his head. "I don't know if Jacob is his first name or his last. All I know is that he was referred to as Jacob."

Donovan rubbed his chin. "Okay. Do you know anything about him?"

"No. Todd Jackson made a reference to him on a tape recording."

Donovan shifted in his seat. "A recording?"

"Yes."

"Can I listen to it?"

Andrew frowned. "I don't have it with me." He paused. "It's hidden."

Donovan nodded as he wrote down the name Jacob. "What did Jackson say about him...about Jacob, I mean?"

Andrew flinched. "That he was after my sister, Cynthia Madison."

Donovan whistled under his breath. "That's quite a statement... especially considering what happened to her."

Andrew looked down at his coffee and sighed. "Yeah."

Donovan sat back and ran a hand through his hair. "I'll see what I can find on..." he checked his notes, "...Todd Jackson and Jacob from the Pentagon. Anything else?"

Andrew took a deep breath, then said with a nod, "I need to travel... overseas."

Donovan frowned. "Overseas?"

"Yes, to Chesham, England."

"What's in Chesham?"

Andrew hesitated. He had already said more than he had intended. "Family."

Donovan cleared his throat. "Well, you can't travel under your own name."

"I know."

Donovan frowned. After a few seconds of staring at his notepad, he nodded. "I can get you out of here, Andrew. A different name, a private plane...piece of cake. When do you want to leave?"

Andrew thought about it. *What is holding me here?* The tape recorder was in a secure location...in a safe deposit box in an Evansville bank. As for the location of Todd Jackson and the identity of the mysterious Jacob, Donovan had agreed to use his resources to look into them...*and he certainly has more resources than I do.*

So, what was stopping Andrew from leaving? He sighed. *My family.* Then again, as long as Jackson and Jacob and the hostile Pentagon agent were out there, his family wasn't safe, regardless of where he was. As a matter of fact, they were probably safer if Andrew was nowhere near them.

He looked at Donovan and frowned. "Can we leave in the next hour or two?"

CHAPTER 37

Uzava, Latvia

Morningstar raised his eyes to the night sky as he looked out the window of the bed and breakfast near Uzava. It was nearly midnight in Latvia, and, though he should try to get some sleep, he wasn't ready to turn in...not yet. There was too much going on; too much excitement about what he had achieved, and what was to come.

The dinner with the Hendersons had gone well. He could tell that they had been enamored by his intellect and charmed by his wit, and, though he had found them to be rather dull, he had pretended to enjoy their senseless banter. *I can't wait to see their faces when I take over that castle.*

Though he had learned nothing about the location of their son, Martin, he felt certain that the man wasn't at the castle. *There's no way they would have let me, an agent of the U.S. government, anywhere near that place if he was...and they certainly wouldn't have been so gracious.* That was what he had been telling himself anyway since he had gotten back to the bed and breakfast.

He bristled as he thought of Walter's smugness whenever Morningstar brought up the man's son...who everyone was pretending was his nephew. Morningstar had been tempted to challenge him and make him confess that Matt was Martin and that the charade needed to come to an end. But then it occurred to him that it would be harder to kill Henderson as Martin – the Phoenix – than as Matt, the assassin's accomplice. Multiple agencies had waited for months to get their hands on the Phoenix, including the

CIA, which meant that Morningstar might not even be able to get close to him. But Matt, the 'cousin accomplice,' would be easy to hide away in some remote military prison, and eventually kill with no one being the wiser.

So, Morningstar had played along and had expressed concern for the nephew, Matt. *"I hope he's safe, Walter,"* he had said with all the sincerity he could muster, after reminding Walter that the man was still wanted by America's Government.

Walter had seemed unmoved as he had shaken his head and said, *"I am fully aware, Edward, but I truly have no idea where he's gone."*

Bullshit! Morningstar thought as he stared out the window. He had steered away from acknowledging that Matt – as Aiden Balkus – had been taken prisoner in Lithuania. Morningstar had gone to great lengths to keep from being implicated in that deed. Walter had seemed to steer away from it, as well. It was certainly possible that he didn't know about it; that he truly had no idea that 'Matt' had been taken to a Klaipeda jail cell under orders from the United States Government. But something told him that Walter did know, and that he was the man responsible for helping Henderson escape. But all Walter had said about 'Matt' was that he had left the castle several days ago because he had needed time alone. Morningstar sneered. *I'll give him time alone...in an isolation cell at Leavenworth,* he chuckled, *...before I kill him.*

Morningstar had let it go, and had gone through the evening with his usual charm and grace. *Dora was clearly taken with me,* he thought with a grin. The poor woman, surely overcome, had blushed several times throughout the evening. At one point, she had even walked away, claiming to need to check on the kitchen. But he knew better. *She had needed to collect herself as she fought her attraction toward me.* He smiled. The more he thought about it, the better he felt. The dinner had gone well.

"But will it be enough?" he said, as he continued to stare out the window. It was one thing to infiltrate the Henderson's home base, but he needed to do more. *I need to undermine them.* He chuckled and looked up at the night sky. *What do those highbrows value more than anything else?* He sneered. "Their goddamn honor, that's what." He frowned. *So, how do I attack their honor?* Suddenly, his eyes lit up and he laughed. *I know just the thing.* He pulled his cellphone from his pocket and dialed.

It was answered quickly. "Yes, Father." Though it was midnight in Eastern Europe, there was no trace of sleepiness in his son's voice.

"When did you get in, Zebulun?"

"Two nights ago, sir."

"Any problems getting through security?"

"No sir. My disguise has held up well."

"Good. Where are you?"

"Estonia, just north of the border. I'm preparing to carry out your plan, sir."

"Excellent. There is something that I need you to do first, son."

"Certainly, Father...anything."

Morningstar smiled. *Such a good boy.* "I want you to sneak into Latvia, and, acting on your Russian heritage, I want you to arrange a meeting with whoever is in charge of Latvia's insurgent forces; the armies that are helping Putin take Latvia."

"Yes Father. Then what, sir?"

"I want you to tell them that the Hendersons from western Latvia are interested in working with them – secretly, of course – to assist in Putin's efforts."

There was a pause. "With all due respect, sir, the insurgent leader will find that hard to believe. What will I use as a reason for such a drastic change of heart?"

Morningstar flinched. "Tell him that Walter has expressed an interest in becoming a Russian oligarch."

Another pause. "Again, Father, it will be a challenge to sell such a story."

Morningstar bristled. Zebulun's insolence was intolerable, but he wasn't in the mood to fight with his son. He took a deep breath. Evenly, he said, "It doesn't matter if they believe it or not, Zebulun...all that matters is that you plant a seed of doubt."

A sigh. "Yes sir. I will leave right away, sir."

"Good." Morningstar ended the call. He dialed again.

"Yes sir?"

"Levi, I need you to plant an email in a Latvian government official's inbox."

There was a pause. "An email?"

"Yes. I want it to seem as if it was picked up on a surveillance sweep, or some such thing." He paused. "It needs to be from someone representing Walter Henderson, and I want it addressed to a known Russian oligarch. It should imply that the overseer of the castle, Walter Henderson, is reaching out to him with an appeal."

Another pause, this one longer. "An appeal? What sort of an appeal?"

"An intimation that he is interested in becoming one of them."

He heard a laugh. "No one will ever buy that, sir."

Why do these boys continue to challenge me? "Dammit, Levi...just do it!"

"Um, yes sir...yes, Father. Right away, sir."

Morningstar slid his phone in his pocket. *That should get things moving.*

He turned from the window and walked back to his chair. He sat and stared at the fire. *Now...if I can just convince Judah to get back to the White House.* He cocked his head. *Then again...what's my hurry?* As he thought about it now, Knight's sudden departure from Washington had had a silver lining. *Never underestimate the value of chaos.* With all eyes on the missing President, Morningstar had been free to carry out his plans with far less scrutiny. But it didn't change the fact that he would need Judah in the White House if he was to complete the final part of his strategy. And though he had already assigned Levi the task of tracking every satellite feed around the globe to find the missing President, he had called Levi just before he had left for the Hendersons, and had instructed him to find a way to bug the Oval Office. *"I want to know the minute that boob, Harrington, reaches out to Knight."*

Levi had balked. *"Almost impossible, sir. They sweep the room nonstop."*

To which Morningstar had replied, *"Yes, my son, so you'll need to come up with a clever way to keep your device from being found, now, won't you."*

Morningstar felt certain that once Harrington told Knight of Morningstar's comments regarding nuclear war, Knight would grasp the implications and return to the White House at once.

But that still left Hank Clarkson and Martin Henderson unaccounted for. He frowned, then let out a sigh. Between Pocks and Issachar, he should be able to dispense with Clarkson soon enough.

As for Joseph, that might be a bit trickier. But Morningstar had a plan for that, as well. Though he no longer suspected that Martin was hiding out at the Henderson castle, Morningstar having dinner there – at

Henderson's boyhood home – might be just the thing to get the man's attention. He laughed as he turned away from the window. "Time to let that boy know where he stands."

He walked over to a small but elegant writing desk that faced the fire. He sat and pulled his laptop from his briefcase, which he had left locked by the desk. He opened the laptop and logged in. As he waited for it to load, he tried to imagine where his wayward son might have run off to. France? Germany? The UK? He laughed. *It doesn't matter. What I'm about to do will bring that pitiable man running back to me.*

He typed in an email address that had belonged to Henderson when he had worked for Morningstar as the Phoenix. Though it was doubtful that Henderson still checked that email, Morningstar's hope was that it would trigger his laptop with an audible alert, much as it had before he had gone astray. Under subject, he typed, "Walter and Dora." Then he wrote: "I had such a nice dinner tonight with your parents, my son. They're vital to Latvia's war effort...I certainly hope they stay safe." He signed it, "Lovingly, Jacob," then added, "P.S. Call me." He grabbed a glass of champagne and drank it down, laughing as he thought, *that oughta get his attention.*

But was it enough? After all, it was possible that Henderson wouldn't get the message; that he no longer even owned a laptop. *What else can I do to make sure that I get that man's attention?* He began to chuckle. *I know what will do it.* He pulled out his private cellphone and dialed. Before the caller could say a word, he said, "Levi, I want you to put an article in every major newspaper around the world."

"Um...okay. What should it say, sir—Father?"

"The headline should read something like this: 'In an effort to show support for our NATO ally, the top aide to America's top general has spent the evening with the respected Hendersons of Boston, who are leading a resistance effort within Latvia.'" Morningstar paused. "Include a statement that says that Edward Morningstar – on behalf of General Alexander Daniels – spent a delightful evening with Walter and Dora Henderson at their castle in Latvia. Then just throw in a bit more fluff...you get the message." Another pause. "Have you got that, Levi?"

"Um...yes...yes sir."

"Good. Get it out as soon as you can." He was about to hang up, when he added, "Oh, and Levi, make sure to include that the Hendersons have expressed their willingness to include Mr. Morningstar in every strategic decision from this point forward, for the duration of the war."

He ended the call and slid the phone in his pocket. He closed his laptop, locked it in his briefcase, then stood and walked to the fireplace. As he leaned against the mantle and stared at the flames, he tried to imagine what it would do to Henderson to learn that his arch enemy had infiltrated the very heart of his world. He burst out laughing. "It will destroy him."

CHAPTER 38

The Henderson Compound

Walter was keyed up, which wasn't surprising after all that had happened in the last forty-eight hours. The dinner with Morningstar had been instructive on several fronts, not the least of which was the visceral disdain Walter felt toward the man. Morningstar had certainly been agreeable enough, but there was something deeper that had managed to show itself regardless of how politely the Pentagon aide had behaved.

Dora had sensed it too. After Morningstar had left, she and Walter had gone to the sitting room for a nightcap. She had stunned Walter by sharing that, just before dinner had been served, when she had excused herself to check on the kitchen, she had actually called Martin to let him know that an unsavory government agent had joined them for dinner.

Walter had chuckled. *"Unsavory is a good word for him."* Then he had frowned. *"But why call Martin?"*

"Well, other than you, I could think of no one better to analyze such a man."

Walter hadn't shared with her the uncanny truth of her words. He had begun to sense that Martin knew Morningstar better than most...far better than he wanted to.

Dora had gone on to say that Martin had shared his concerns about the man, and had told her that she and Walter should be on their guard. Walter had reassured her that he had gotten that same impression; he would most definitely be on his guard.

They had spent another hour or so discussing their dinner guest, and, at around midnight, she had finally begged off. He had walked her as far as the bedroom, but had stopped outside the door. *"Aren't you coming to bed, Walter?"* she had asked as he had kissed her goodnight.

He had nodded. *"Soon, I just have some correspondence to take care of regarding my meeting earlier today."*

It wasn't a complete lie. Though it wasn't correspondence he needed to take care of, there were definitely details from his meeting with Justice that needed to be processed and reviewed with someone. *And who better than the psychiatrist who knows the man best,* he thought as he walked upstairs to the guest bedroom.

He knocked lightly on the door, heartened when he heard a soft, "Come in."

He walked in, surprised to find Samuels sitting in front of the fire, dressed in silk pajamas and smoking a pipe. He grinned as he was immediately reminded of Sherlock Holmes. *A somewhat older version, perhaps, but the imagery holds true.*

"You have a truly lovely home here, Walter," Samuels said.

Walter was about to thank him, when Samuels added, "No, it's more than lovely...it's inspiring. I find myself more clear-headed than I've been in months."

Walter, still wearing his suitcoat from dinner, took it off and walked it to the chair next to Samuels. He hung it over the back, loosening his tie as he sat in the chair and kicked his feet up on an ottoman. "Thank you, Doctor. I'm glad you're finding your time here comfortable." He paused. "I have something I need to talk over with you, if you're not too tired."

Samuels smiled. It was a rare smile; welcoming and forgiving, all at the same time. "I am quite well-rested, Walter, and would enjoy an absorbing conversation."

"Good." Walter hesitated. "As you know, Doctor, earlier today I went to meet Justice."

Samuels nodded. "I guessed that that was what you wanted to discuss. However, I am also aware that he didn't show."

Walter's eyes widened. "How did you know?"

Samuels grinned. "Your countenance. Had you seen him, you would be conducting this conversation from an entirely different perspective." He put up a hand. "But I mustn't distract you. Please, go on."

Walter reached behind him and pulled from his jacket pocket the letter he had been given by the jester. He handed it to Samuels, who read it, read it again, then handed it back to Walter. Massaging his beard with one hand, gripping his pipe with the other, Samuels nodded and said, "So, tell me, Walter, what are your thoughts?"

Walter folded the letter and slid it back in his coat pocket. He looked at Samuels and sighed. "I have two thoughts, actually. The first is that Justice is, just as you said, a charming and respectable man." He paused. "The second is that he knows something important about this war that he has yet to share with either you or I."

Samuels nodded. "Yes, I agree."

"So, why doesn't he just tell us?"

Samuels sighed. "As I told you several months ago, I feel that he is purposely being cryptic." He paused. "And I think I know why."

Walter's eyes widened. "I'm all ears."

"I told you before that Justice thinks that Cobra can – for lack of a better way to put it – 'hear' him. So he is being careful to not say too much."

Walter frowned. "But if it's Cobra who is participating in whatever war game we're talking about, what does it matter if he 'hears' Justice say it aloud?"

Samuels leaned forward, and with a slow but steady hand, took the pipe from his mouth and tapped it in a tray on a table by his chair. He adjusted his robe, then turned to Walter and sighed. "That is what I've been thinking about for these last two months," he paused, "...and it's what I've spent the night considering in this meditative chamber." He nodded. "And now, after eliminating every other possibility, I feel that there is only one option that remains."

"And what is that, Doctor?"

Samuels narrowed his eyes. "I believe that, just maybe, Justice isn't merely worried about what Cobra might be planning, but that he is also concerned for him, for his wellbeing." He paused. "The truth of the matter, Walter, is that I think that there might be something wrong with Cobra; that perhaps he is ill." He paused. "If that is the case, then Justice knows it, and feels that if he isn't careful with his words, he might provoke Cobra in a way that he had never intended."

Walter shook his head. "That doesn't make sense, Doctor. First of all, if Cobra is ill, then wouldn't Justice be ill, as well?"

Samuels sighed. "You would think so, but I don't believe it works that way."

Walter frowned. "Okay...then what about the fact that Cobra is a crazed and unstable killer. What could Justice say or do that would make him any more so."

Samuels smoothed down his beard, and stared over his glasses at Walter. "Have you ever seen a wild animal when it's wounded, Walter?"

Walter nodded. "Yes, but—"

"I'm just guessing, mind you, but I think Justice is worried that whatever it is that Cobra is planning to do, if Justice was to harbor a wrong thought or utter an insensitive comment, it might throw Cobra over the edge. Then, whatever damage he had been set on doing could be compounded."

Walter frowned. "Compounded?"

Samuels nodded. "Yes." He paused. "What if the war that Justice has been alluding to isn't confined to Latvia and Russia, what if he's referring to a bigger war."

"A bigger war?"

Samuels sighed. "Think about it." He shook his head. "I don't know how much you know about Cobra's actions over the past nine months, but as I scrutinize them through the prism of intent, they seem almost strategic."

Walter considered it. He knew quite a bit about Cobra's actions over the past nine months...actually, over the past nine years. But Samuels was on to something. As Walter thought of it now, Cobra's actions of late did seem almost...sequential. "You're talking about the murder of the IRA woman in Ireland?"

Samuels nodded. "Yes, followed by the Scottish Nationalist on the Isle of Skye, then the terrible tragedy of America's Secretary of State in the UK, and finally, the French prefect's wife, Adrienne Bergeron."

Walter frowned. He was beginning to see what Samuels was trying to say.

Samuels went on. "Ireland, Scotland, the United Kingdom, America, and France. Each one of those murders led to a response by the victim's respective government – an international response with international ramifications." He sighed. "It was as if each step was leading to more and more chaos around the globe."

Walter frowned. "But you still haven't explained what that has to do with Justice, or with the fact that Cobra could be ill."

"I think that Justice might see an opportunity here."

"An opportunity?"

Samuels nodded. "Yes. A way to possibly stop Cobra."

Walter's eyes widened. "That would be fantastic."

"Yes, it would. But it brings to light two unique problems." He sighed. "The first is that stopping Cobra might also stop Justice." He looked at Walter. "Then where would we be?"

Walter frowned. "As much as I hate to say it, we would be in a good place. I mean, to stop either one of them would be to stop the escalation of war...right?"

Samuels shook his head. "Wrong. I don't get the sense that Cobra gives a damn about world peace or world war." He leaned forward and stared at Walter. "Which means that he is carrying out these murders at the direction of someone else."

Walter sat back. The thought was horrifying...two madmen that had aligned for the purpose of what...destroying the world?

Samuels nodded. "I see that you understand what I'm trying to say." He sat back and sighed. "As for the second problem," he took a deep breath, "...this is where things get a bit tricky." He took another deep breath, then cleared his throat. "There have been times over the course of the last eight months or so when I have...uh...erred greatly in my judgement regarding Justice, and thereby Cobra." He hesitated. "In my...eagerness to bring Justice to the fore, I have on occasion," he shifted awkwardly, "...allowed Cobra to escape those who are trying to bring him to justice." He frowned. "And forgive me for my impropriety, Walter, but I think that perhaps you, too, have been subjected to a similar error in judgment."

Walter adjusted the collar of his shirt, but said nothing.

"I quite understand it, Walter. The boy is, after all, your own flesh and blood." He paused. "And I'm guessing that you – like me – have beaten yourself up over this lapse in judgement." He leaned forward and reached for his pipe. He puffed it, seeming to weigh his next words with the utmost care. "Though we both know that the correct path here is to include either the Yard or Interpol in our efforts as we gain greater access to Justice, the situation has changed."

"What do you mean?"

Samuels took a deep pull on his pipe. "What I mean is this: More than ever, Walter, it is vital that we keep our conversations with Justice to ourselves. We cannot let anyone know what he's up to or where he might be found. He mustn't be stopped until he has succeeded with whatever he is trying to do to stop Cobra...and to stop whoever is behind these murders...and this war." He looked Walter in the eye. "In other words, my friend, if we are to save the world, we must protect Justice. Which means that, no matter what, we must protect Cobra."

CHAPTER 39

Washington, DC

The plane set down at Dulles International just before six p.m. Tom Cravens waited for the other passengers to leave the small commuter jet, then stood and threw his duffel bag – which contained the evidence from the Gad crime scene – over his shoulder. He grabbed his coat from the overhead compartment, the smell of soot unmistakable as he draped the tattered coat over his arm.

He hurried off the plane and practically ran through the terminal and out the door. He pulled on his coat and fell in line at a taxi queue, impatient as he waited for a cab. He climbed in back of the first available, and mumbled, "Century Townhouses." He pulled out a scrap of paper, adding, "Rockefeller and 21st Street."

The cabby nodded and pulled away. Cravens rubbed the back of his neck. He was tired. He felt like he hadn't slept in months. He was startled as the car next to them blared its horn, suddenly realizing how much he had missed the chaos of Washington, DC. It had been seven months since he had left for Lyon to find the missing Senator Madison after the tragedy at Place Bellecour. Since that time, he had gone from France to Latvia, back to France, on to Scotland, and finally back to Latvia. In the meantime, several men had been killed, and his protectee, whom the world now thought was dead, had gone into hiding. *No wonder I'm tired,* he thought, as he closed his eyes and leaned against the seat.

Twenty minutes later, the cab pulled up to a row of attractive two-story homes. A sign out front read, "Century Townhouses." Cravens had exchanged his euros at the airport, and he handed the driver a twenty-dollar bill. "Can you wait for me?" The cabby nodded.

Cravens grabbed his duffel bag and stepped out of the cab. He checked his watch; six-thirty. The sun had already set. It was dark and it was cold; he buttoned his coat as he walked to the door of townhouse number four. "Clarkson" was written in bold letters on a mailbox to the right of the door. There were only two items in the box, both postmarked two days ago. Cravens frowned. *Hank has been gone for months. If he had requested a mail stop, there would be nothing in here. Which means that someone – Jenny? – has been taking in the mail...likely as recently as yesterday or the day before.*

He pulled out his pistol and released the safety. He tapped on the door and waited. After a few seconds, he tapped again, this time a bit harder. The door opened a few inches, and the hair on the back of his neck stood up. He could hear seventies music coming from somewhere inside. He set his duffel bag outside the door, and pulled a flashlight from the pocket of his overcoat. Holding the gun in one hand, he placed it overtop the hand holding the flashlight. He kicked the door wide and took a step into the townhouse. He scanned what he could see of the first floor. Whoever had been there had left in a hurry. An upstairs light was on, and several pieces of mail had been dropped by the door. Holding his gun and flashlight steady, he scanned the entire front room, then walked into the kitchen and, using his elbow, he clicked on a light switch. A salad bowl was on the counter, with a head of lettuce sitting beside it. Half of the lettuce was in the bowl. A wine glass – half full – was sitting next to the bowl. Cravens felt his throat tighten. He breathed in deep, relieved when he didn't pick up the unmistakable odor of decaying flesh. He walked through the kitchen to the bedrooms. The door to the first bedroom was open about an inch. Holding the flashlight steady, he led with his gun as he kicked it open the rest of the way. The bed was made, but the covers were wrinkled. The drawers were open; clothes were scattered on the bed. *Someone packed in a hurry.* He walked further into the room and looked behind the bed. Nothing. He let out a sigh as he rounded a corner and came to a bathroom. The door was open. Gripping his gun firmly, he walked in and switched on the light. There was a towel hanging on the rack, but there were no toiletries by the sink.

He shut off the light, then examined the rest of the townhouse, including two upstairs bedrooms, a living room, an office, and a laundry room. Other than two open drawers in one of the upstairs bedrooms, there was nothing. No dead bodies, no blood. He slid his pistol into its holster and took another walk around. No sign of Jenny, but clear evidence that whoever had been there had left in a hurry.

He checked his watch. *Almost seven.* He was scheduled on a flight out of Dulles at nine-fifteen, which meant that he would need to be at the airport no later than seven-forty-five. If the flight was on time, he would be back in Bangor by eleven-thirty. But he didn't want to leave the townhouse. It was clear that something had compelled someone – most likely Jenny – to leave in a hurry. Hank had entrusted Cravens to find her. But Cravens also had an obligation to his Commander-in-Chief.

Maybe I can do both.

He took one last look around. He was tempted to turn off the music, but decided that it was best to leave everything as it was. He shut off the light in the kitchen, then left the townhouse. He grabbed his duffel bag and jogged to the curb, glad to see that the cab was still waiting. As he was about to slide in back, he pulled out his phone and dialed a number that had been etched in his memory since his early days as a Secret Service Agent.

"DC Metro Police."

Cravens cleared his throat. "Um...yeah, I'd like to report a missing person. Jenny Clarkson, ex-wife of Homeland Security's Deputy Director, Hank Clarkson. She was last seen three days ago in townhouse unit number four at Century Townhouses, on the corner of Rockefeller and Twenty-first."

He hung up before they could ask his name. He would wait to contact Hank; maybe give Metro Police a chance to find her first. *They'll probably find her safe and sound and have it all wrapped up by Monday.* But as he climbed into the back of the cab, something told him that it wouldn't be wrapped up by Monday...not even close.

CHAPTER 40

Somewhere in the Katahdin Mountains in Maine

It took Knight and the others over three hours to reach the Katahdin Mountain Range, and from there it was another three to get to the base of the mountain. All the while, he and Emma were tucked underneath the fake bed, packed tightly together with little room to move. It was okay with Knight; he felt like he could never get close enough to Emma.

As for whatever lay ahead, Knight had no choice but to trust Foster and his friends: the boat captain Colt, the truck driver Ralph, and four other 'off-the-grid' friends who were preparing a place from which Knight could govern the country in secret. Knight was an American President on the run, with evidence of a plot to dismantle the United States of America... he needed to trust someone. The fact that he couldn't trust those who had been given that task spoke volumes about the sphere of influence held by one Edward Morningstar.

He would also have to trust Secret Service Agent Tom Cravens. The man certainly seemed trustworthy, though Knight had sensed caution in the man's voice. Who could blame him? Hopefully, the evidence he would bring to Bangor, combined with whatever Foster would acquire from the former VP's Secret Service agent, would be enough to prove that Edward Morningstar was planning to destroy the very fabric of the United States of America. He flinched. *And I was about to help him.*

Learning that there were others suspicious of Morningstar had been a welcome turn of events. And not just anybody: the former Vice President of the United States. But Knight would need to rein in the former VP, if for no other reason than to keep the man from acting on whatever he had learned. No one could tip their hand until Knight had built an impenetrable case against Morningstar. Otherwise, Morningstar would have time to prepare a counteroffensive. Morningstar was a lifelong chess player; the counterattack was his specialty.

But Knight knew that the former VP, Jim Conner, wasn't a man to be held back. So, he had encouraged Foster to take Conner's Secret Service agent, Scott Johnson, into his confidence. The men had agreed to meet Monday night at a diner in downtown DC. Johnson had promised to say nothing to anyone until then, and to get his former protectee to do the same. That gave Knight 48 hours to build his case.

As the truck barreled over rough terrain, Knight pulled Emma closer. She had been through quite a lot. It had helped her to learn that Michael and Galina were safe...*but for how long,* he wondered. She had said very little since the ordeal with Michael. He didn't blame her; what was there to say?

He kissed her forehead and sighed. To feel her next to him, to hear her heart beat, was more than he could have ever hoped for. And to think that the man he had placed his faith in for the past twenty-four years had tried to have her killed made him sick inside. Yes, there had been times when he had questioned Morningstar's means, but never had he questioned the man's motives. Morningstar wanted and believed in a better, stronger America. Knight did too. But as he thought about it now, he realized how many times he had turned a blind eye to the actions of the man he revered.

The truck came to a stop. Knight checked his phone: *Seven-thirty p.m., Saturday.* They had been either tucked in the hull of a boat or shoved underneath the fake bed of a truck for three full days. *The world would be shocked if they were to see me now.* He pulled Emma closer and whispered, "I think we're here."

The truck door opened and they crawled out into the starlit black of a bitter cold night. There were trees everywhere, the darkness broken only by single rays of moonlight that found their way through thick evergreen branches. In spite of their predicament, it was beautiful and undeniably remote. *Morningstar will never find us here.* The deep forest of the Katahdin Mountain Range in Northern Maine was as isolated as anywhere in America. *We might as well be on the moon.*

Knight breathed in the fresh mountain air. The smell of pine mixed with the cold, and filled his lungs with memories of the past; good memories of a simpler time. He looked at Emma. She felt it, too...those same scents amid those same trees. They had been there so many times.

Foster was checking the area as if Knight was simply at a campaign stop in a small Midwestern town. Knight watched him go through his paces, thinking again of all that Foster had sacrificed. He could be hanged for his part in Knight's escape. Knight shivered and zipped his coat to his chin. *I will die before I let that happen.*

The driver had taken three sets of gear from the backseat of the truck and had set it all on a nearby rock. Foster gave the man a quick wave, then walked up to Knight. "A short climb and we'll be there, sir."

The truck pulled away leaving just the three of them. Three people standing alone amid timbered mountains on a cold night in Maine. *Perfect,* Knight thought as he watched the taillights fade into the night. It was as if the world he had been a part of was fading with them; as if the last sixteen years had never happened. Were it not for Foster standing beside him, he would think the Presidency had been a dream.

"We should go, Mr. President," Foster said, as he gathered up the gear.

It was no dream.

Knight was stiff and he flexed his knees to try to get his legs working.

Foster grinned. "With all due respect, sir, you look terrible."

Knight laughed. Emma shook her head and frowned. "I'm sure we both look awful. I'll be glad to get a shower and a nap on a real bed."

Foster nodded. "We're close, Ma'am. Once we reach the site, there'll be all that and more." He handed Knight and Emma the appropriate gear to climb the ridge.

Knight frowned as he tucked the gear under his arm. It had been years since he had climbed a mountain; hopefully he remembered what to do.

"It's like riding a bike," Emma said, as if reading his mind. Her mood had seemed to lighten just from being in the mountains. She grabbed her gear and started up the trail, adding, "...and...if I recall...bike-riding was something I always did better than you." She chuckled, and sprinted ahead. Knight and Foster ran after her.

It took about an hour to reach the mountain; they quickly took the first ledge. With the moon lighting their way, they used picks and ropes to scale one ridge, then another. They made sure to keep close to the tree line along the side of the mountain. Those evergreens would offer at least a semblance of cover should any stray satellite pick up a presence there. Knight and Foster both knew that the NSA would have satellites scanning every inch of America – and beyond – for the missing President.

In spite of the many risks they all faced, Knight felt invigorated. It had been so long since he had used his legs and arms for anything other than campaign stops, parades, or quick walks through the halls of the White House. He looked at Emma ten feet away and, though he could barely see her, her eyes reflected the moonlight, and he gave a quick wave. She waved back and he fought a surprising urge to cry. He knew in that instant, if he were to die, he would die in profound and perfect peace.

They continued up the mountain, following only those paths that were covered by trees. After about thirty minutes, they reached a protected shelf near the top. They slipped behind a half-circle of evergreens to catch their breath.

Emma was about to trek to the next rise when Foster whispered, "Wait, Ms. Cann—Emma. We're here."

He motioned to a thick pile of brush. "Hide your gear there." They placed their climbing gear underneath the brush, then watched as Foster walked a few steps and shoved aside a row of branches with a single sweep of his hand. The branches had more or less made a screen that hid a row of ten-foot boulders. The boulders were piled next to one another with no space in-between, serving as a blockade to whatever was behind them. Foster pushed aside more tall branches until he reached the far side of the boulders. He motioned for Knight and Emma to slip through a narrow opening to the side of the last boulder, then he quickly replaced the branches behind him as he followed them through the opening. They found themselves in a six-by-six covered area, which had the feel of an enclosed courtyard. The boulders served as the back wall, while thick branches from the surrounding evergreens created a ceiling. Across from the boulders was another barrier of thick pine branches lined in a row. Foster pushed a few of those branches aside, revealing a door with a three-by-three metal plated cover. He lifted the cover, which gave him access to a numbered keypad. He punched in a series of numbers, then placed his thumb over an area beneath the keypad. The door opened and light filled the makeshift courtyard.

Foster hurried them inside. "We must be quick, sir."

They had to stoop to fit through the opening. Once inside, Foster did his best to pull the limbs over the door as he pulled it closed. It locked automatically.

Knight breathed in, trying to identify the scent. *Pine,* he thought, ... *mixed with cinnamon.* He waited for his eyes to adjust. Once they did, he was stunned. They were standing in a massive room with tall ceilings, tiled floors, and curtains covering windows that were likely nonexistent. Overhead light from an invisible light source adjusted for the time of day, and the light reflected from walls made of rock and shale. The walls looked as if they had been designed that way, the rough texture almost trendy. There was an overstuffed couch in one corner of the room, a table and chairs in another, with flowering plants scattered throughout. In front of the couch was a coffee table with a couple of magazines, adding a touch of normalcy to a situation that was anything but. Knight could see only partway down a hallway, but was able to catch a glimpse of heavy wooden doors along the corridor.

Foster grinned. "Well sir, what do you think?"

Knight held Emma close as he shook his head and sighed. "It's... remarkable."

"Can I give you a tour, sir?"

Knight nodded. He looked to his right and caught sight of a doorway which opened to what was clearly a high-tech security room. There were monitors visible against one of the walls, as well as keyboards and fax machines set up on the counter. He pointed to the room. "Let's start there."

Foster walked them to the room. It was bigger than it had looked from the entry hall. If Knight didn't know better, he would think he had walked into NASA's Houston command center. Every wall was covered with some sort of electronic device, the soft hum from the computers reminding him of insects outside the summer house in Maine. "It's astounding, Foster. You did all this...in just three days?"

"I take none of the credit, sir. It was you who told me of this bunker that you and Emma had stumbled on years ago. And it was you who asked me to find good friends I could trust. And it was you who supplied the funds that allowed for those friends to bring in supplies and upgrade the technology to give you what you see here."

As if on cue, four men walked up. One was carrying a device that looked like a large cellphone.

Foster motioned to the man holding the device. "This is Patrick, sir."

Patrick was medium height with wireframe glasses and curly blond hair that looked as if it had been struck by lightning. Knight extended his hand. "Nice to meet you, Patrick."

Patrick bowed his head and said, "You too, sir."

Foster pointed to the man standing next to Patrick. "And this is Danny, sir."

Danny was tall and incredibly thin; he looked as if he would break with a simple nudge to the midsection. He had reddish-blonde hair to his shoulders. He stuck out his hand and smiled. "'Tis nice to finally meet ya, sir."

The heavy brogue left Knight to wonder if the man had recently emigrated. *Like maybe last week.* He reached out his hand. "Nice to meet you, too, Danny."

Next to him was a shorter man wearing a blue blazer and khakis. His hair was short and styled. He stuck out his hand. "I'm Kent. It's good to meet you, sir."

This man had no evidence of an Irish brogue; there was nothing Irish about him. Knight shook the man's hand and nodded. "You too, Kent."

Foster pointed to the last man, a big burly fellow with a thick white beard and a generous smile. "This is Santa."

The man held out his hand; Knight shook it and nodded. "Nice to meet you...Santa."

The man nodded, then quickly looked away. He seemed a bit more reserved than the others. Knight was curious what connected Foster to the four men. He would make a point of asking Foster about it later.

Foster turned to Knight. "These men are completely trustworthy, sir. I'd stake my life on it." He paused. "They've been waiting all their lives for this opportunity."

Knight frowned. "What opportunity?"

"To make a difference, sir."

Knight nodded; he understood. He, too, had waited a lifetime for the opportunity, though he had thought it would come about far differently. What had begun as a chance to save America from fading glory had now become an obligation to save it from the very man who had placed Knight in such a role.

He turned to his agent and shook his head. "This is utterly amazing, Foster."

Foster grinned proudly. "Think nothing of it, sir. We are honored to make it happen. Truth be told, I think the boys had quite a good time putting it together, sir."

He walked Knight back out to the great room and nodded proudly. "It's all yours, sir...a place to call home while you carry on with your role as Commander-in-Chief." He moved his arm in a sweeping motion as he said, "Welcome to Camp Katahdin."

CHAPTER 41

Tianjin, China

Henderson landed the Learjet on the Tianjin tarmac just after 8:00 a.m. Sunday, China Standard Time. He had lost an hour to refueling in Srinagar, India, and had then run into a front over Tibet, which had forced him to alter his course, adding another hour onto his travel time. The sun had just begun to rise over the Xishan mountains as he landed the plane. Had it not been for the uncertainty of his mission, Henderson might have enjoyed the glint of the sun against the reddish-brown peaks.

As he taxied across the empty tarmac, he did his best to make it look as if he had landed on that same tarmac a hundred times before. It helped that the Hendersons owned an investment firm in the area...this was just another business trip by a representative of its founder. He had posted a flight plan with the local government, but had yet to receive confirmation. He stopped the plane, thinking that his landing had gone unnoticed, until four soldiers with semi-automatic rifles appeared out of nowhere. Shouting in Chinese, they ordered him out of the plane. He put on his coat, then grabbed his briefcase – his grandfather's briefcase – and threw his backpack over his shoulder. He patted the bulge under his shirt and frowned. *Should I keep the gun?* He nodded. *Yes. I'm sure I'll need it.* In the meantime, he would simply pray that they didn't search him.

He stepped out of the cockpit and walked down a set of stairs that had unfolded upon landing. The soldiers were waiting for him. The air was bitter cold from the wind blowing in across the mountains. He popped his collar, but it was a meager shield against the wind...or the soldiers.

"Gaosu women ni di lunwen." *Show us your papers.*

Henderson pretended to not understand. One of the soldiers barked, "Papers!"

Henderson hadn't locked the briefcase since opening it at the castle, and he reached inside for the cover letter and passport that his dad had given him. The letter explained that he was Conrad Gibbons, and that he had come on a mission of mercy. It outlined Henderson Commodities' affiliation with a Chinese-based group, Kai Chek Investments. It detailed the historic relationship between the two companies, and the influx of cash to both entities that had come about as a result. At the bottom of the single-page letter was a notarized seal of the United States of America, along with the official seal of the People's Republic of China. It had been signed by both America's and China's Presidents. He handed the documents to one of the soldiers, confident that he would be let go. He was wrong.

"Ni weisheme zai zhell?" *Why are you here?*

Again, he pretended to not understand.

"Why you here?" the soldier said sternly.

"As the letter states, I have come to pick up friends of the Henderson family."

The other soldier frowned.

Henderson added quickly, "An employee, along with her daughter."

"Tamen zhu zai nall?" *Where do they stay?*

Henderson frowned and shook his head.

"Where they?"

"Um, outside Beijing. Near Fengsheng. The employee's mother is gravely ill. I need to get the woman and her little girl home before the woman's mother passes."

The guards stared at the documents, all the while exchanging heated comments. Henderson looked away, pretending to not understand. But he understood every word. One of the soldiers wanted to bring him before the Minister of Public Security as a possible spy. The other felt it was a bad idea, since the letter of introduction had been signed by both the U.S. and the Chinese Presidents. Henderson stared at the ground, hoping that they wouldn't search him and find the luger.

Finally, after arguing back and forth, the men took a step back, indicating that it was okay for him to go. One of the guards tossed the letter and the passport on the ground. "Zou bu duo yuan! Women jiang jixu guanzhu zai ni de feij," he shouted. *Don't go far...we will keep an eye on you and your plane.* Henderson frowned, again pretending that he didn't understand. The soldier said, "We watch you."

Henderson quickly picked up the letter and the passport, and stuffed them in the briefcase. His hope was that the soldiers would have little time to ponder his presence there, because he would find Lili and her caregiver and leave China within a few hours. Again, he would be wrong.

He shivered and buttoned his coat. As he walked away, he looked over his shoulder. The soldiers were staring at him. He picked up his pace. *Stay calm, keep your eyes on the road.* He flinched. *"...and whatever you do, Henderson, don't get caught."* The words came back to him like a gut punch. It had been lesson number one from the Morningstar school of How-To-Be-An-Assassin. And Henderson had learned it well. No one could dodge or evade better than he. More importantly, no one could hunt, hide, or kill like the well-trained assassin he thought he had left behind. He felt a surge of adrenalin...as if a switch had been flipped. His heart rate slowed, as did his breathing. He was back. Not Martin, not Matt, not even the soldier, James Calvin, whose face he had stolen by way of a revolutionary surgery. No, it was the Phoenix who had come out of nowhere, filling in holes of doubt with cold, calculating calm. He could feel the change in every part of his body; his muscles were taut, his eyes saw things others would miss, and his hands hung ready to strike a man dead with the slightest provocation. Uncertainty and compassion were gone, in their place a heartless detachment that would serve him well in the arena he was about to enter.

And he liked it. Far more than he expected, he *liked* the freedom of being unafraid. He could hear – no, it was more like he could *feel* – the hushed footsteps of the soldiers following him as he walked toward a small cargo terminal. Pretending to adjust his collar, he glanced over his shoulder and saw a soldier pull out a radio. He couldn't hear him; he didn't need to. The man was calling for other soldiers to track the Latvian businessman who had flown a Learjet onto a desolate tarmac in the early hours of Sunday. *Call in all the men you want, fellows. You'll never catch me.*

He reached the terminal and walked inside, glad for the warmth. It was packed at that hour, and he pushed his way through to a map of train routes that was hanging on the far wall. Within thirty seconds, he had memorized every route and every connection. Lili had said that she could see the Xishan Mountains and the Great Wall of China. That would put her northwest of Beijing.

Henderson walked to the front of the terminal. He exchanged euros for Yuan, then walked outside and fell in line to wait for a taxi. Though the sun was bright, the air was still bitterly cold. Within minutes, a blue cab with a yellow stripe pulled up; he slid in the back seat. In fluid Mandarin, he asked the driver to take him to the Lubeikou Train Station three miles away. He looked over his shoulder. He saw a black sedan and knew instantly; he was being followed. He had expected it. It took over fifteen minutes for the cab to maneuver the three miles through the busy traffic. They reached the station; the driver pulled to the curb. Henderson paid the fare and slid out of the taxi. He walked inside, his long strides meant to convey the confidence of a seasoned businessman. He looked around for a locker to stash his backpack. He found one outside a gift store, put in a few coins, then locked the backpack inside. He shoved the key in his pants pocket.

Still carrying the briefcase, he went into the gift shop and bought an insulated parka – a *waitao* – along with a thick hat and a pair of gloves. He put them on and, rather than walk out the front of the store, he found a back exit. When he was sure no one was watching, he slipped outside and sprinted to a clump of dense brush behind the station. It bordered a small forest. Staying low, he looked for a path. He found one twenty yards away: a narrow walking path which led to a river about a hundred feet from the station. He stole silently through the trees until he reached the river. He hugged the shore, staying low for about a mile, then left the trees and rounded back to the Nanyuan airport. He walked past the terminal to a train station a block away.

He checked his watch. *9:25.* China's day was well underway, evidenced by the number of passengers streaming into the train station. He stopped just shy of the station and watched them. A group of what he guessed were tourists neared the door. With his collar high and his head down, Henderson ran up and fell in with them as they walked inside. He stayed with them as they approached the ticket counter. One of them scowled at him, but said nothing as he continued to stand next to them. He bought a ticket for Yanwo. Two of the tourists broke away and walked to a gift shop. He went with them. He bought water and a sandwich, then followed them to where the others were sitting. He took a seat not far from them as he ate his food and waited for his train. It arrived three minutes later. He waited until the last minute, then left the group and boarded the train. He found a seat next to a woman and child, acting as if he belonged with them. Holding the briefcase in his lap, he nodded at the woman. She glared at him; he smiled. She continued to glare but made no effort to move.

Ten minutes later, the train stopped at Yanwo. He got off, went to the counter, and bought a ticket for Yanqing, which would take him northwest of Beijing and put him closer to the Xishan Mountains. That train was leaving in two minutes. Again, he found a locker. He locked the briefcase inside, put the key in his pants pocket along with the first key, then ran to the train and climbed aboard. He reached Yanqing at 10:23. He walked into the terminal, and, as he had done before, he snuck out a back door. But this time, he ran to the side of the building, where he would have a view of the front entrance. He waited to see if any soldiers had followed him. When he was confident they hadn't, he stole to the back of the station, where he again found a path through the trees. Staying low, he hiked north for about a mile. It was colder there; the wind swept through the mountains with little to block its path. He ignored it, as he had been trained to do by the Morningstar monster that had created him. *"Being cold is a state of mind, son."*

Henderson flinched. He thought back to the stanza from Lili's poem...

> *"I see the mountains of Xishan*
> *And as the leaves do take their fall*
> *I see the nearby Badaling*
> *And the magical Great Wall."*

He saw the mountains north of town, the bright sunlight creating shadows between the peaks. He walked toward them, slowing as the Great Wall came into view. He hiked a bit further and was able to see Badaling.

He was close. He looked around. Nothing. He hiked another half-mile and stopped. As the sunlight streamed over the mountains, it lit up the area below, and he was able to see the partial outline of a fairly large structure at the bottom of a vast ravine; it looked like an old warehouse. *That has to be it.*

He checked his watch: *Eleven a.m.* He rubbed his eyes. He hadn't slept in over twenty-four hours. He should be exhausted, but he wasn't. Or at least he told himself he wasn't; another trick taught to him by the madman from the Pentagon.

He stared at the building. Suddenly his heart ached. He had found her. Lili was in there. "I'm coming for you, Lili."

Those were his last words before he felt the gun at his temple.

PART II

"An invisible thread connects those who are destined to meet."

~ Chinese Proverb ~

SATURDAY, NOVEMBER 13TH, 2004

CHAPTER 42

Beijing, China

"Welcome to the world, you fool." The words of the headmaster had started echoing in his head several days ago, and now, no matter what Cobra did, he couldn't get the words to leave. He had tried everything; humming a tune, taunting an imaginary cellmate, anything to get rid of the incessant adage.

He didn't know which was worse; being forced to hear those words while imprisoned in a makeshift Chinese jail, or facing the fact that, for the second time in less than a month, he had failed to kill his target. Another voice – just as unwelcome – came into his head, the tenor deeper, the words far more condescending. *"Only the second time, you say? What about your prisoners at Dalgety Bay...you didn't do so well with them, now... did you?"*

"Shut up!" That voice had also been haunting him for the past several days, and between the two of them, they were starting to unnerve him. *If I didn't know better, I would think it was Justice.* But it didn't sound like him. Justice wasn't cruel. Very direct, but never cruel. Cobra sighed as he laid on his cot and stared at the stains on the ceiling. Whoever was taunting him, the words were taking their toll. They had made Cobra question himself. *I'm Cobra. I don't fail.*

He angled his head to look at the hallway, searching for a clock though he knew there wasn't one. *Don't the damned Chinese ever wonder what time it is?* He could hear rain on the metal roof, but he couldn't tell if it was day or night. There were no windows near his cell, and it was always dark in the prison. He had grown too weak to walk to the front of his cell in search of the sun or the moon, and was forced to mark time with nothing more than the guards' changing shadows as they paraded back and forth in front of his cell. Those shadows had become like town criers, announcing the end of each day as they grew tall and lean, declaring sunrise as they shrunk to nothing. He watched them and sighed. He could almost hear them say: *"Day ten will soon come to an end..."*

Cobra and Senator Sturgill landed in Beijing Sunday afternoon...three days before the hit. A uniformed soldier was waiting for them on the tarmac. He escorted them from the plane to a black sedan parked ten feet away. They said nothing as they drove through the city, using the time to learn all they could about the Ceremonial Hall, where they were to meet with Tai Chu after the National Heroes Day parade.

They were driven to a hotel and given separate rooms. Over the course of the next two days, they walked the city, continuing to focus on landmarks. On Thursday afternoon at 4:00, Cobra tapped on Sturgill's door. "Ready?"

Sturgill opened the door; he looked terrible. He was wearing a hotel robe, his eyes were red, his hair a mess.

Cobra sneered, "Second thoughts perhaps, Senator?"

Sturgill ignored him as he left the door open and walked back to his bed.

Cobra walked in and looked around. The room was a mess. Clearly Sturgill was dealing with something. "Are you going to be able to go through with this?"

The older man sighed, then got up from the bed and walked into the bathroom. Cobra could hear him showering.

On the trip from America, Sturgill had confided in Cobra that he thought the son of the military leader was his own son, Jamey, who had been kidnapped twenty-seven years ago. Cobra had been stunned...and amused. It might actually make his task easier. But he couldn't help but wonder how the oversized man with the ill-fitting suit would react when the young soldier was taken out right in front of him.

They left the hotel at five p.m. bringing their luggage with them; they wouldn't be back. They climbed into a town car sent over by the Minister of Defense. Sturgill was as nervous as a cat. They asked to be taken downtown to a café near the famous Tiananmen Square, "...so we can watch the parade." Leaving their bags in the car, they got a bite to eat at the café, keeping their dialog light. They felt certain that their conversations were being monitored.

The plan was simple: The parade was to pass through the square at six-thirty. Tai Chu would be with the other officers. Sturgill, as a representative of the United States, had made a request to speak with him afterward...in the name of international diplomacy. The request had been granted, greased along no doubt by Morningstar, who seemed to be able to strongarm well-connected leaders in every part of the world.

Once they were seated with the military leader, Tai Chu would probably ask Sturgill's bodyguard to leave. Sturgill would agree, as long as Tai Chu sent his men away, as well. "I have information that is intended for your ears only." Tai Chu would likely refuse, insisting he keep at least two of his guards in the room with him. Sturgill would agree, as long as his guard could stay, as well. Though they expected that Chu's guards would take Cobra's gun, Cobra had arranged to have two acetylcholine syringes sewn into the thick cording that edged the sleeves of his jacket. Once it was just the five of them, Tai Chu would offer tea. After the tea had been brought into the room, Sturgill would drop the bombshell that he was Tai Chu's father. The military leader would be overwhelmed by the news. He would likely deny it, but would be forced to look at the man sitting across from him and at least wonder if it was true. Sturgill would then stand and pace the room, and tell the story of the kidnapping so many years ago. Tai Chu would stare at the man who might be his father, and, when he and his guards were adequately distracted, Cobra would slip a bit of snake poison into the pot of tea. The poison, taken from the saliva of a Southeast Asian keelback, had been purchased early that morning from a dealer in a back alley in downtown Beijing. Cobra had told Sturgill that the poison was a sleeping potion. But it was far more powerful than a simple sleep aid. Absorbed through the intestinal lining, it would kill Tai Chu almost immediately.

Sturgill would sit back down and one of the guards would pour the tea. Then it would be a matter of waiting. Tai Chu would take a sip and, if, for some reason, the guards chose to not have tea, Cobra would tease away the lining of his sleeve and, without missing a beat, would stab each of them with the syringes. Either way, within minutes of their arrival at the Meeting Hall, Tai Chu and his guards would either be dead or incapacitated.

Sturgill, still thinking that Tai Chu had only been given a sleeping potion, would want to take him with them. That is when Cobra would tell him the truth. Sturgill would be devastated, but it wouldn't matter. Cobra would leave Jacob's note explaining the motivation for their actions on Tai Chu's desk. He would then drag Sturgill with him out the back door. He would tell Sturgill that they needed to split up, and would send him and their bags in the town car to the airport. Once Sturgill was on his way, Cobra would call the police and, pretending to be a Tai Chu guard, would tell them that Senator Sturgill from America had just poisoned the Military Minister's son and was on his way to the airport. He would be captured, and likely killed. In the meantime, Cobra would pull a soldier from the parade route, take him into a back alley, strangle him, and steal his uniform. He would then vanish into the crowd. It was flawless; any idiot could carry it out...

Cobra flinched. *So why the hell did it fail?* They had watched the parade in the Square, had waited for Tai Chu, and had walked to the Central Meeting Hall. They had been shown inside, Sturgill's Senate ID badge getting them past each security check point with little resistance. Sturgill had introduced Cobra as *'...my bodyguard, Frisk.'* Surprisingly, no one had challenged his presence. The guards had searched them and – as expected –had taken Cobra's gun, but they had missed the syringes. The guards had then led them through a series of corridors, finally reaching a room at the end of a long hallway. They had been shown inside and, within minutes, a young white man had walked into the room and had bowed his welcome.

That was when things had taken a turn for the worst. The resemblance between Sturgill and Tai Chu was hard to deny, and, before a single word had been spoken, Sturgill had fallen to his knees, overwhelmed. Cobra had been forced to run to his side, along with the two guards. They had lifted Sturgill to a chair, and Cobra had sat next to him, feigning attentiveness for his fallen charge. The stumble had definitely altered the plan, but Cobra had been quick on his feet. *"Tea please. Could we have some tea?"* One of the guards had run to get a pot of tea, while Cobra had tended to the pathetic senator. When the tea was brought in, Cobra had poured a cup for Sturgill, and had then snuck several drops of the poison into the pot. He had given Sturgill his tea, and, as Sturgill had regained his composure, Cobra had suggested that they all have tea. Sturgill had sat in his chair and had awkwardly stared at Tai Chu. After a minute or two, he had looked at Cobra and had shaken his head, whispering far too loudly, *"We can't do it, Viper."*

A guard had instantly pulled his semi-automatic to his shoulder. Tai Chu had said evenly, *"You can't do what, Senator?"* Sturgill had said nothing, and Cobra had jumped in with, *"He was about to tell you, sir, that he is your father."*

The man's jaw had dropped. He had stared first at Cobra, then at Sturgill. He had turned to a guard. *"Search them again."* The guard had done as instructed; that was when he found the syringes, along with the note in Cobra's pocket that stated that Tai Chu's death – on behalf of the U.S. government – was in retaliation for China's actions over the last decade. The guard had shown the note to Tai Chu, who had read it through. With his face beet red, he had sat silent for two very long minutes. He had slammed his fist on the desk and had said in Chinese, *"Get them out of here!"* He had shoved away the cup of tea, allowing it to spill on the floor. The guard had asked if he should kill them. Tai Chu had considered it. *"Not yet. Take them to the warehouse."*

The guard had aimed his rifle at Cobra's chest and had said, *"Ni xian. Gen wo lai."* You first. Come with me.

Cobra had said, *"Wait! It's true. Look at him."*

In spite of his anger, Tai Chu had looked at Sturgill. For a brief moment, it seemed as if he might soften. But then, like a tsunami in the South China Sea, he had roared, *"Take...them...away!"*

And that was when the strangest thing had happened. The normally quick Cobra had frozen; not out of fear or doubt, but out of physical weakness. He couldn't move quickly enough to challenge the command. No cry of retaliation, no kick to the man's groin. He had simply dropped his hands to his side in a moment of defeat unlike anything he had ever known. Both he and Sturgill had been grabbed from behind, cuffed, and brought to the prison, where they had been for the past ten days.

The place was a shithole; it smelled like old socks, and it was always dark, even in the daytime. There were hints of sunlight, but only for a few hours, then came the shadows...cellmates to keep Cobra company as he grew ever weaker. He wondered if maybe he had been poisoned. The last time he had felt this bad was when he had eaten fava beans and had discovered that he had a unique genetic disorder, G6PD deficiency. Could this be the same thing? *No.* His meals had consisted of rice, broth, and lettuce; nothing more. The water had seemed fine; no after-taste. And, though he and Sturgill had been separated, he had seen glimpses of the man as he had passed on his way to the shower. He seemed well enough. He wasn't sick, only broken. Cobra wondered if Tai Chu had even spoken to him. *I'll bet not.*

Truth be told, he didn't care. He knew only that he needed to get out of there. *Surely America will go to the mat for their missing senator.* He smirked. It wasn't like Sturgill was a great man or anything. As a matter of fact, he was one of the most spineless men Cobra had ever met. But he was a senator, and America would want him back, if for no other reason than to save face. Which meant that a manhunt was likely underway. Any minute now, armed soldiers would burst through the doors and slay the Chinese captors.

He shook his head and sighed. *It's more likely that they'll 'negotiate,' which means that I'll be here for quite a while.*

He would likely die there. He was sick and weak, and his ability to mount a fight was fading. As if in confirmation, a fierce spasm gripped his stomach and he writhed in pain. He crouched in a ball, crying for help. A guard walked over to the cell and looked in at him. He laughed. "Bi zui, ni zhege yuchun de shagua." *Shut up you stupid fool.*

As the rain pounded the roof, and the shadows grew even taller, Cobra lay on the cot in unrelenting pain. He was weak and his entire body felt like it was on fire. He was about to cry out again, when the voice returned, echoing the words of the headmaster. *"Welcome to the world, you fool."*

CHAPTER 43

Beijing, China

Henderson's back hurt. He had been beaten and kicked, and kicked some more since arriving at the jail cell of what looked like a converted warehouse. It had taken quite a bit out of him. Which surprised him. He should be tougher than that, hardened by years of torture and abuse.

Carrying the luger had been a mistake. Not only had they used it to beat him multiple times as they were transporting him to the prison, but it had given them an excuse to keep him there. *"No one carry gun in China!"* they had said repeatedly. But it wasn't like they needed an excuse. Though he had yet to see any of the other men who were being held there, he felt confident that most or all of them had done nothing to deserve such a fate.

He laid on a cot, his long legs falling over the edge, his solid frame barely able to fit on the narrow bed. He combed strands of stringy brown hair behind his left ear, his hand lingering as he brushed against the ear. The Russian surgeon who had done his face transplant had done well, but Henderson could still feel the scars across the back of that ear. It made him think of his donor, the man who had unwittingly given him his face; Corporal James Calvin, a hero of the Iraq war. Ever since the transplant, Henderson had been forced to see inside the man's head...to hear Calvin's thoughts, or view images of his life. And, though it was disconcerting, he had learned quite a bit from the man. Sometimes the lessons were practical...like when he had figured out through a Calvin memory that Maddi had been poisoned with arsenic. Or when Calvin's recollection of a childhood trauma had led him to Roger Clarkson in the catacombs beneath Paris. Other times the lessons were motivational; like when Calvin had inspired him to keep going in the midst of the fire at Dalgety Bay. As odd as it seemed, James Calvin had become a welcome interloper in Henderson's broken mind. He sighed as he tried to imagine what the man would tell him now.

He would tell you to escape.

He rubbed his unshaven chin and stared up at the ceiling. He was no longer wearing the beard he had put on as part of his disguise; it had come off after the second or third day. This beard was his own; faint, blondish-brown whiskers, that helped to hide his chin. Not that anyone noticed. The guards barely even looked at him...*even when they're kicking me in the ribs,* he thought, as he put a hand to his chest. His eyes were no longer green, either. He had removed the contact lenses soon after arrival. The only concern was his hair. Though he had no mirror to look at, he felt certain that his blond roots would soon begin to show. He couldn't afford to be recognized...not as the Phoenix, and certainly not as Martin Henderson. If China was to learn that they had the son of the renowned Walter Henderson in their midst, things would definitely change...and Henderson felt certain it wouldn't be for the better.

He was no longer wearing the clothes he had worn when he was captured. The soldiers had forced him to put on a smock that smelled like wet wool, and a pair of loose cotton pants. Luckily, he had had enough time to toss the locker keys – where he had hidden his backpack and briefcase – into a drainage ditch before the soldiers had made him strip out of his clothes. Though there was little inside either one that would interest the Chinese, Henderson didn't want them to have anything of his, and he certainly didn't want them to have access to the Henderson briefcase.

He turned onto his side and stared at the only window he could see... on the other side of a long hallway. He couldn't actually see outside – the window faced away from him – but occasionally he would get a sense of the sun or the moon as a random ray of light made its way through the glass. He had found that if he stood at the far end of the cell and pushed his face to the bars, he could see the branch of a tree outside the window. Several times a day, he would walk to the edge of his cell, push his face against the bars, and try to see the branch. On one occasion, a guard had smirked and had said in broken English, *"What you do?"* Henderson had said, *"I'm trying to see outside."* The guard had poked Henderson's ribcage with the butt of his rifle and had laughed. *"What you care is out there...you die in here anyhow."*

It was currently daytime – which he knew from the shadows on the walls – but the prison was still dark; it stayed dark. He could hear rain on what he guessed was a metal roof. The first time he had heard it, it had jolted him out of a restless sleep. It sounded like the rat-a-tat of gunfire. But by now, he had gotten used to it. Who knew it rained so much in China?

He continued to stare, his eyes drifting to the dark hallway beyond the window. It led to the shower where he was taken twice a week. That was all he had seen of the prison; his cell, the window, the hallway, and the shower.

He had barely been conscious when they had brought him to the jail two weeks ago. Beaten and thrown in the back of a van, he had been driven over winding roads for what had felt like hours. Sometime during the long ride, he had passed out. He had awakened in that lonely, eight-by-eight cell, certain that he was hundreds of miles from Beijing.

He sat up, hung his feet over the cot, and stretched his arms. He stood and walked to the edge of the cell. He pushed his face to the bars, craning his neck to look down the hall to the window. He could still hear the rain on the roof, and he stretched to try to see the branch of the tree. All he could see was the blur of rain against the glass. He smiled as he imagined puddles on the ground, or the magic of the mist as the rain faded and the sun fought to be seen. It was painful to envision such days; to wonder if he would ever see them again...if he would ever feel the reverence of dusk or the hope of dawn.

He sighed as he realized – with somewhat mixed feelings – that he would likely die there. Though he had been ready to die for months now, his death would end any chance he might have of saving Lili. The poor girl had gone missing nearly a year ago, and he had been told in January that she had died. The man behind it – Morningstar – had sent him a photo of the girl lying lifeless in the snow, along with a statement that said "Subject has been eliminated." To learn that she was, in fact, still alive, had given him new life. But now he was stuck in a desolate jail cell, miles from where he believed her to be, and lightyears away from helping her escape.

His only hope was that Walter might try to save her. He had seen Henderson's map; he should have some idea of where she was. Would he maybe send in a team of soldiers to free her? If not, then what about Dain Rozenblats, the man Henderson had hired soon after Lili had been kidnapped. Would he try to save her? Henderson had tried to call Rozenblats before he left for China, but the call had gone unanswered. Henderson hadn't left a message; now he wished he had. Then again, he wasn't even sure that Rozenblats was alive. He had tried to call the man several times since waking from his coma; none of the calls had been answered. He suspected that something bad had happened to him. *Just one more victim of this never-ending war.*

Henderson rubbed his eyes in disgust. He had put so many innocent people in harm's way; either by exposing them to danger, or by allowing them to be killed. But none had grieved him as much as Lili. He would have gladly given his life for hers, but there had never been the chance. And now, with his life rapidly slipping away in that bleak, soulless jail, his last chance to save her was gone.

Unless I can get of here, he thought, as he stared at the window he could barely see. He had tried to think of a way out of that hellhole from the minute he had awakened in his cell. He had continued to pretend that he didn't know Chinese; it had allowed him to get an idea of how many soldiers there were, and the orders they had been given. The most important order: *"Wǒmen xīwàng tā huózhe, dàn rúguǒ tā chángshì zuò rènhé shìqíng, qǐng háo bù yóuyù de bǎ tā dǎ dé luòhuāliúshuǐ." We want him alive, but if he tries anything, don't hesitate to beat the shit out of him.*

There were others in the prison; he had heard them. Voices that hummed in the middle of the night when everything else was quiet. On three occasions, he had walked to the front of the cell and had whispered 'hello' to a blind hallway, but each time he had been silenced by the butt of a rifle, held by a soldier who had seemingly come out of nowhere. He had had about twenty such assaults, usually from the same guard, and always to either his jaw or his ribcage. He winced as his hand went from his chest to his jaw, worried the blows might eventually undo the surgeon's efforts from eight months ago. He ran his fingers over his jawline and nodded. Still intact...for now.

He was surprised he wasn't dead. He had been beaten nearly to death, but always shy of the final blow. Why? Were they hoping to somehow use him? For negotiations, perhaps? A representative from Henderson Commodities, Inc. would certainly be a useful bargaining chip. But did anyone even know he was there? Had the Chinese government notified his family, or the Latvian embassy, perhaps? He frowned. *Of course they haven't.* Why would they? Why would they tell anyone that they had him. As a matter of fact, it was more likely they would deny he had ever landed at that airport outside Tianjin. They had done the same thing with American POWs after the Korean War. Deny that they were ever there, removing any need to explain what had happened to them. *So, why don't they just kill me?* He didn't know. The only thing he did know was that if he didn't get out of there soon, he would die.

From what he could determine, the facility's design was like an octopus; four hallways that extended like arms from a center circle. Though each of the hallways was filled with cells, there was no one near him. He had the entire hallway to himself. He had tried to count the guards as a truck came and let off new guards for the shift change. He had been unable to determine an exact number, but had learned their hours, their breaks, and their habits by listening to their comments back and forth. He guessed that there were close to twenty of them, and that they worked in twelve-hour shifts. A quarter of them covered the inside, another quarter covered the outside, which left time for the other half to sleep. It had been the same faces since he had arrived, which meant that it would be difficult to kill one of them and keep it from being noticed. Also, with men outside the facility, getting away would be a challenge. But he would try; he had to. *Otherwise, I'll die in this god-forsaken place.*

Though he couldn't see the exits from his cell, he had seen the guards wheel in food each morning and pick up empty boxes and dirty towels on their way out. He had originally thought he could maybe hide in one of the boxes as they were taken out of the facility, but had quickly let it go; the boxes weren't big enough to hide a grown man. Not only that; he was rarely let out of his cell. Only once every three days, a few hours after sunrise. That was when he was taken to the shower. He had tried to get a feel for the room during the four-minute shower, but there was little to see. It had no windows, and just one stall surrounded by three walls. The only light came from a bulb in the ceiling, which created more shadow than light, and was about fifteen feet above him. The walls – solid cement – were over twelve feet tall, which meant that he wasn't going to climb them, and the floor was tiled. Even if he could pull up the tiles and dig underneath, he wouldn't have time to create any sort of tunnel. Even so, he was convinced that the trip to the shower was his only chance to get away.

And it was Corporal James Calvin, the man who had given him his face, who had made him understand how. Just a few nights ago, while trying to sleep, he had seen a flash of red and blue lights, followed by an image of two men in the desert, hiding behind a Humvee. One had been injured; the other one – Calvin – was doing his best to fight off the enemy so he could get the soldier to safety. Explosions were coming from all directions; Calvin and his friend were trapped. Suddenly, Calvin spotted a drainage culvert not far away. Using scrub brush as cover, he grabbed his injured friend and, carrying the man on his back, crawled through the brush to the culvert. He laid his friend on the ground next to it and slid off the cover. He dropped down about five feet into an underground cave. He had no idea where it led; it didn't matter. He reached up, pulled his friend into the cave, and pulled the cover over top of them, just as a rocket was about to land on the injured soldier. They waited until they no longer heard the blasts, then Calvin reached up and pushed the cover aside. He raised up to make sure it was clear, then knelt down, and, with strength he didn't know he had, somehow lifted the soldier out of the cave. He climbed out himself and, with his friend on his back, trudged to the Humvee. Miraculously, the car was still operational, and he drove his friend to the base. As sunlight faded and they neared the base, the injured man looked at him and grinned. *"Thank God for Calvin's Culvert."*

That had been the end of it. The image had come in a flash, and, just as quickly, it was gone. That was how it was with the images. They would fill his head, then disappear, leaving him to wonder why they had come in the first place.

But the following day, two days ago, when the soldiers had led him to the shower, they had taken him a different way. Because of repairs to a leaky ceiling, instead of walking him down the main hallway, they had led him outside and into the shower through a back entrance. As they had come through the door, he had stumbled over what looked like the cover of a wide drain. *Calvin's Culvert!* he had thought. Though he had no idea where it led, one thing was certain; it led away from there. It was his only chance. Diplomacy – if it was even being attempted – would likely fail.

Fortunately, the same two guards took him to the shower every time. Over the past week, using stilted Chinese, he had begun to joke with them. Though they likely understood only half of the joke, they had started to laugh, which meant that they were letting down their guard. They still beat him whenever they got the chance, but the intensity had eased. If he could play on that lapse in intensity, he might be able to distract them, kill them with a chop to the windpipe, then remove the drain cover and sneak away. It was a suicide mission, but so was staying put. *I'll go tomorrow.*

The question he had yet to answer was what to do about the other prisoners. He couldn't take them with him. For one thing, he had no idea where they were being held. For another, it would make an impossible mission harder still. But he didn't see how he could leave them there to die. He felt certain that if the Chinese didn't kill them outright, the harsh conditions would take care of it soon enough.

I'll come back for them, he had decided. But he wasn't even sure they were real. Loneliness can do strange things to a man. Could it be that he had made up the hushed conversations or the frantic cries in the night, so desperate for companionship that he had conjured up broken men to keep him company in his own despair.

He shook his head. *I didn't imagine them, and I won't leave them here to die.* He sighed. *Maybe if I save at least one of them, it will make up for all the men I have killed.* He sighed. *I'd have to save every man in this damn prison to even get close.*

He sat his heavy frame on the cot, leaned back, and, using a shard of cement, made a notch in the wall. *Day 14.* All at once, a Pink Floyd song came into his head; a tune from his days at Harvard. He began humming the tune and tapping the beat against the side of the cot, "*...another brick in the wall.*" He kept it up, ignoring the glare of the guards, glad to hear something besides the sound of their pacing.

Suddenly, in the distance, he heard the taps being echoed. It was faint, and he thought his mind was playing tricks with him. He tapped again. The guards didn't seem to notice, and when Henderson heard more taps in reply, he nearly cried out with joy. Someone was communicating with him! *Does he know Morse code?*

His hands were shaking as he tapped in Morse code, "Who are you?"

He nearly fell off the cot when he heard the tapped reply. "My name is Lili."

CHAPTER 44

Beijing, China

Lili Platacis bit her lip as she tapped the bars, her tiny hands barely big enough – or strong enough – to make a sound. But it was clear the other prisoner had heard it. She had told him her name and waited, hoping he would tell her his. A new friend in a terrible place. She looked over her shoulder at Ching Lan; she was asleep. Lili didn't want to wake her; Ching Lan wasn't well. It was important that she sleep when she could.

Lili's ears perked up; she heard more tapping. She clung to the bars of the cell, her tiny knuckles turning white as she waited, finally stringing together four coded words. "I am Uncle Mart." Her eyes widened. She felt unsteady and found that her legs were unable to hold her. She fell to her knees, still clutching the bars. *My ears are playing tricks with me.* She tried to see him in her transcendent mind. There had been a time when that exchange alone would have been enough for her to get a clear picture of him, but all she could see now were flashing blue and red lights, and a man – a soldier – running across a desert with an injured man on his back. And neither one of those men was Uncle Mart. She could see the man who was doing the running. Not only did he look different than Uncle Mart, but he felt things differently, as well. *It is a trick of some kind.* Lili tapped back quickly, "How are you here?"

She waited, closing her eyes, trying desperately to see him.

The reply: "I came to find you."

She felt tears on her cheeks. She wiped them away. All she could think to tap was, "I miss you."

There was a long pause. She kept trying to see him. The soldier that had been running across the desert was gone. In his place was a woman with short brown hair running frantically through the streets of Beijing. The woman was in pain; Lili could feel it. The woman was looking for someone. Suddenly, Lili realized...*she is looking for me!* Could it be? Had the Special Lady heard her message? But the woman in her mind didn't look like the Special Lady. Was she wearing a disguise? It didn't matter; it was her...Lili knew it.

Lili was stunned. First Uncle Mart, and now the Special Lady?

She closed her eyes, wanting to see at least one of them. The woman was still there; she seemed to be lost. *Beijing is not a good city to be lost in,* Lili thought as she tightened her jaw. She did her best to send her a message. She had grown weak over the past several months, and weaker still over the last several days. But she forced herself to concentrate as she tried to come up with an image that might help the Special Lady find her. She looked out a narrow window at the mountains that were not too far away. If she could create in her mind her view of those mountains, the woman might be able to use that landmark to find her. *But will I be putting her in danger?* She frowned. *She is already in danger.*

Lili held her breath as she stared at the mountains and tried to draw them in her mind. She then tried to send the image to the Special Lady. She was having a hard time staying focused; she felt like she was about to pass out. She gave it one last try, then fell against the floor. She lay on the cold hard cement, exhausted.

Suddenly she opened her eyes. She heard more taps. She began to shake.

"I miss you, too. I'm getting us out of here. Be ready to go...tomorrow morning."

CHAPTER 45

London, England

Dr. James Samuels stretched his legs, his pants riding up as he sat back, rested his hands on his lap, and crossed his ankles. He looked around at his familiar office, glad to be back among the items that had given him such comfort over the years. The old phonograph that played the classical music that could eternally renew him, the antique clock that let out tired chimes as it marched through the hours of a day, the single window that looked out at a neighborhood rich with the well-earned scars of living and the pain of childhood's lost hopes. He combed his fingers through his gray beard and sighed. Yes, it was good to be back.

He looked down at the letter in front of him, a letter that had been received in his office ten days ago. He sighed as he thought of all that had gone into it. It was written by the hand of Mark Justice, but it was filled with the demons of Cobra and the heartache of a little boy. Samuels recognized the writing; he had seen it two weeks ago in a letter that Walter Henderson had received, also from Justice. The same flowery script, the same flowing hand. But this letter was far less direct. Though richly written and remarkably astute, it was vague and enigmatic, offering more questions than answers. It had included a poem, and the flow of the poem was eerily familiar. Cobra had written a technically similar poem as he had held seven victims at the Dalgety Bay schoolhouse back in March. And though

Samuels – who had been one of those victims – remembered little of Cobra's actual words, he did recall the depth of feeling – the depth of hate – conveyed in the killer's crafty prose.

Samuels had gotten a call about the letter ten days ago, on a Tuesday afternoon, while he had been convalescing at the Henderson estate. *"It's Betty, Doctor. I'm sorry to bother you, but you have received a letter that I think might interest you. The return address is the Honorable Mark Justice, Private Inquiry Agent, Belgrade Square, London."* She had then added breathlessly, *"That's him, isn't it, Doctor? The man you have spent so much time trying to find?"*

Betty had offered to open the letter and read it over the phone, but Samuels had warned against it, fearful it might contain a clue regarding Cobra's location. Samuels and Walter had agreed days before that they must protect Justice – and thereby Cobra – until Justice was able to undermine Cobra's efforts to escalate the Baltic war. Which meant that they must also protect his location. Samuels was unclear as to how Justice planned on stopping Cobra, but based on comments that Justice had made over the past couple of months, it would appear that he thought that Cobra had either weakened or was ill. Samuels' theory was that Justice hoped to take advantage of Cobra's compromised health to stop him, possibly forever.

Deciding that he must read the letter himself, Samuels had elected to return to London. He had been away for months; it was time to go home. So, with a mix of eagerness and regret, he had departed the Henderson castle, knowing he would miss not only the accommodations, but the impeccable grace of the Hendersons.

Concluding that travel by train would be less cumbersome due to the many flight restrictions imposed by the war, and needing to stop in Lithuania to gather his clothes and his books, he had departed from Riga, Latvia, last Wednesday afternoon, 24 hours after Betty's call. The journey had taken a full three days, and he had arrived in London late Saturday night. He had been too exhausted to go to the office, but had gone in first thing Sunday morning. He had walked into his humble second-story workplace, warmed by its familiarity, but overwhelmed when he saw four large piles of correspondence on his desk. He had walked to his chair and had let out a sigh as he had stared down at the stacks of mail. The letter from Justice had been placed in the middle of the four piles...*like a rose among the thorns.* He had pushed aside the mail, as if preparing his table for the gift he was about to receive.

Then, with shaking hands and a tentative heart, he had opened the letter...

"*My dear Dr. Samuels,*

I am writing you rather than calling, as I fear I am being spied upon. By whom, I cannot be sure. An overly-aggressive government? Or merely my own thoughts that derive from an entity within me that I loathe more and more each day. Sick in both spirit and body, I know now, more than ever, that entity – that man – must be stopped.

But even with this letter, I must be careful, though it is not only care that makes me cryptic. My recall of the events I'm about to share is a blur, the details racing across my mind not in sentences, but in scattered images. I'll do my best to convey them, but as I say, it is hazy in my mind, though I feel it deeply within my soul. Much like a dream, these are the happenings I feel beholden to share with you...

"*A cat sees all, but cannot speak*
As darkness soothes a sunlit sky
And tames the wasteland of the meek
Staring down the scoundrel eye.

"'*Twas months ago,' the cat would say*
If he could find a way to tell
What happened there at Blackburn Way
When heaven's gate was lost in hell

"*But instead he licks his fleece*
And hisses at a darkened alley
As two marked eyes within one face
Laugh boldly at a loner's folly

"But who's the victim, who's the prey?
Which one truly wields the knife?
'Tis he who steals one's life away?
Or she who has no use for life?

"The cat sits stonelike on a pillar
His soul decrying 'make him weak!'
As she defies a wanton killer
A cat sees all, but cannot speak."

Samuels had been stunned. *What is Justice trying to tell me?* he had wondered. He stared at it now, as he had done so many times over the past week, still baffled. Was it a warning? Did it pertain to the war? Or did it have to do with Cobra's presumed infirmity? If so, how? *What does Justice want me to see?*

Though Samuels had been tempted to schedule a patient or two to ease back into his workload, he had decided against it. Instead, he had informed Betty last Sunday morning that he would require another six weeks to get through his mail, and address the letter from Justice. *"We'll start fresh after the New Year,"* he had said, and had then set out to at least put a dent in over two months of unanswered mail.

By one p.m. he had gotten through what he could, and was eager to get to work on Justice's letter. He had started by taking each phrase of the poem and trying to decide if it was meant to be literal or figurative. Was there actually a cat? Had the cat witnessed something that Justice had somehow become privy to? Or had Justice become so attuned to his alter ego's thoughts that he had actually seen Cobra carrying out the deed? But what deed? What had Cobra done? And when had he done it? *""Twas months ago,' the cat would say—If he could find a way to tell—What happened there at Blackburn Way—When heaven's gate was lost in hell."*

Deciding that the reference to Blackburn Way would be a good place to begin, Samuels had gone to the local library and had looked up the street's name. He had learned that there were many Blackburn Ways scattered about, not only in England, but in different countries around the world. Knowing that Cobra rarely ventured far from the UK or Europe, he had refined his search, and had come up with 12 possible locations. Eight of them were in the UK. *I'll start close to home,* he had decided.

But he still hadn't determined what he was looking for. A cat? There were thousands of cats in England. A loner? That described hundreds of people, including himself. He was left with the hope that he would know it when he saw it.

He had left the library at seven p.m. Sunday night, and had come home to enjoy a quiet dinner, accompanied by smooth jazz and a glass or two of port.

Starting first thing Monday morning, he had taken the train west to Wales, and had then had a taxi drive him to a Blackburn Way on the outskirts of the town of Cardiff. It was little more than a dirt road, and the only house appeared to have been abandoned years ago. The journey had taken most of the day, and he had left there convinced that it was not the Blackburn Way that Justice had referenced in his poem.

He had returned home late Monday night, had rested as best he could, and had set out on Tuesday to do the same thing, this time traveling east to Dartford. Again, there had been nothing to suggest that he had found Justice's Blackburn Way, so he had come back home, and had repeated his efforts on Wednesday, Thursday, and Friday, traveling southeast to Hastings, south to Guildford, and southwest to Gosport. He had found nothing. There remained only four more Blackburn Ways in the entire UK, but, exhausted from so much time on the trains, he had elected to take a day off.

I'll get back to it tomorrow, he thought, as he stared down at the letter. He would devote today, Saturday, to analyzing the poem for clues he might have missed.

Though the sun had yet to rise, he grabbed a pen and paper, pulled a tray to his chair and, with the letter on the arm of the chair, he began to write down certain words from the poem. *"Cat, meek, scoundrel. Months ago. Blackburn Way. Dark alley, two marked eyes within one face, loner. Knife, killer, female victim."*

He got to the last stanza, suddenly mystified by the next-to-the-last line: *"As she defies a wanton killer."* His eyes widened. Had someone – a female loner with a cat, perhaps – survived a Cobra attack? If so, it would be the only woman to do so, as far as Samuels was aware. Even dear Cora, who had managed to leave a bloody clue before she died, had eventually succumbed to her wounds.

He reread the stanza, this time stopping at the line before. *"His soul decrying, 'make him weak!'"* Samuels frowned. *Make who weak?* His pulse quickened. *Cobra?* Could it be that whatever was happening to Cobra – whatever was making him frail or ill or compromised – had to do with this event? He sat back in his chair, stunned. If that was the case, then he was beginning to see what Justice was trying to tell him. *There is only one path for me to take,* he thought as he ran his hands through his sparse gray hair. *And I certainly can't wait until tomorrow to pursue it.*

He folded the letter and slid it in his pocket. He stood, put on his overcoat, and walked to the closet. He grabbed a prepacked travel bag with clothes for at least two days, and left the office. The remaining four Blackburn Ways were north of London. He would take the first train northwest and stop at Blackpool. If he didn't find what he was looking for there, he would continue east to Bradford, then to Leeds, and finally to York. He felt certain now that he knew what Justice was asking of him.

As he practically ran to Victoria Station, he nodded. *Justice wants me to find the woman who lived through a Cobra attack.* But why? How would it help him stop the escalation of war? He didn't know, but one thing was certain: Cobra's wellbeing – and perhaps the wellbeing of the entire world – lay with the woman who had somehow survived his attack.

CHAPTER 46

Uzava, Latvia

Morningstar closed his laptop and leaned back in the overstuffed chair that sat in front of a roaring fire in the bed and breakfast outside Uzava. He had been searching for updates…on Knight, on the war with Latvia, on the attempted murder of a Chinese leader's son. Though all three situations had resulted in chaos, which had been good for his cause, not one of those crises was going the way he had hoped.

One good thing had come from his efforts, however. Two nights ago, after Zebulun had so cleverly planted the seed, Morningstar had fielded a call from a Riga reporter wanting his thoughts on rumors that Latvia's Freedom Fighters may not be fully committed to the battle against Putin. The reporter had called him because of his close ties to the Hendersons, who – according to a well-publicized newspaper article – Morningstar had had dinner with just two weeks ago. The reporter had gone so far as to actually mention the Hendersons and a battalion they oversaw near Uzava. *"Is it possible that America has aligned itself with the wrong family on this one, sir?"*

Morningstar had seen it as an opportunity, not only to feign his respect for the Hendersons – which he had done effusively – but to lay down another marker for his wayward son, Joseph. He chuckled. *Wait until he reads my reply.*

As for his other son, Judah, the man was still missing. There hadn't even been as much as a sighting of Knight in over two weeks. *How could a U.S. President leave the White House so easily...and so effectively?* Morningstar wondered as he slid his laptop into his briefcase and locked it.

And the war in Latvia, according to a morning news release, had been slowed by 'diplomacy.' Latvia still hadn't declared war on Russia, and even Putin had been slow to act, continuing to deny he had played any role in the initial attack.

Regarding the assault on the Chinese warlord's son, which was supposed to have ended with that young man's death, along with the deaths of anyone who could link Morningstar to the mission, the assault had essentially not happened, at least according to the BBC. The Chinese were claiming to have no knowledge of any of it. *"Our records show that the senator returned to the United States eight days ago."*

The only good news regarding China was that yesterday afternoon, footage obtained by the CIA appeared to show that an attack of some kind had, in fact, taken place at the Central Meeting Hall on November 4th, just as Morningstar had planned. The report suggested that, as a result of the attack, a U.S. senator and his bodyguard were rumored to have been taken to a secret facility somewhere in China. Because of China's original statement, the U.S. State Department had immediately challenged China's version of events. The Chinese continued to deny the allegations, sticking to their story that Sturgill had left China on November 5th. Morningstar had gotten word of the CIA discovery from his boss, Alexander Daniels. The man had called, stunned. *"According to one of our spies, the missing senator, who claimed to be working on behalf of our government, tried to kill a Chinese military leader's son!"*

Morningstar had played dumb, not only about the man involved, but about the mission he was on. *"I don't know why Sturgill was over there, sir. And I certainly can't imagine why he'd try to kill a military leader's son and then try to hang it on our government."* He had added, *"But I will say, sir... he is a bit of a loose cannon."*

Daniels had told Morningstar to *"...get to the bottom of it, Edward...then clean up the damn mess!"*

As expected, the leak had made international news, which had created a strain between China and the U.S. Though that had been Morningstar's intent all along, he had hoped for something more than a strain; he had wanted a complete diplomatic breakdown. Not only that; he still had the problem that either Sturgill, Cobra, or both of them were alive, and therefore able, if pushed, to tell anyone who would listen about Morningstar's role in the attempted assassination.

So, he had gone through the motions of carrying out Daniels' wishes, going so far as to have his concubine, Janet, who worked at the State Department, urge her boss, the Deputy Secretary of State, to urge *her* boss, the Secretary, to issue a formal rebuke. He had then issued a statement on behalf of the Pentagon, calling on the Chinese to offer proof that Sturgill had left the country. *"If not, we will be forced to assume the worst."*

Needless to say, China had reacted in kind, insisting that it was the United States who should apologize for issuing false accusations, and for being unable to keep track of one of their own citizens – a senator, no less – traveling abroad.

The acting President, Bob Harrington, had fumbled the play entirely by gushing his apologies on behalf of the American people, *"...for possible errant behavior by a member of the United States Senate."* That had caused a firestorm, both at home and abroad, and the State Department had been forced to issue a statement of clarification. From Morningstar's point of view, the entire matter had become one of the biggest diplomatic screw-ups in American history.

He tapped his fingers on the chair. *What the hell happened over there?* His hope had been that once Cobra killed Tai Chu, the Chinese would kill Sturgill and Cobra, and then declare war on America. But instead, Morningstar had a mess to clean up. *And the idiots who know the truth are still alive!*

He stood and walked to the window, staring once again at the snow-covered path to the pond. He had been in Latvia for two weeks now, and it had only gotten colder and snowier; he could barely see the water's edge through the piles of snow. But the remoteness was growing on him. *A good place to raise a son.* Only it wouldn't be a bed and breakfast where Benjamin Morningstar would be raised; it would be a castle...an impenetrable fortress, with a staff to go with it. But he should have been in the castle by now, fielding Daniels' messages from inside the Henderson citadel, all while usurping Walter Henderson's role in the war against Russia. *So, why aren't I?* He frowned. *Because the Henderson staff refuses to take a hint.*

He hissed. *Coffee. I need coffee.* He yelled for his aide, Steve.

The young soldier ran into the sitting room. "Yes sir."

"Have the Klosky's bring me a cup of coffee."

"Yes sir."

Morningstar checked the time. Nine a.m. ...two a.m. in DC. He ran his hands through his thick black hair, noticing for the first time how much it had grown since his arrival in Latvia. *I wonder if they even have barbers in this godforsaken borough.* He cracked his knuckles as he turned and walked to the fireplace. He grabbed a log from a nearby stack, tossed it in the fire and, using a poker, shoved it in place. He breathed in, appreciating the scent of burning wood. He leaned against the mantel, watching as the flames rose higher. He needed to do something. Not only were Cobra and Sturgill missing, but Henderson, Hank, and Knight were missing, as well.

"And where the hell is Gad?" he said aloud as he smacked the mantel. He had been trying to get in touch with Gad for the past two weeks, to no avail. Which could only mean one thing: *Gad is dead.* It would explain why Knight hadn't returned to the White House. The plan to coerce Emma's compliance had clearly failed.

But who had killed him? Was it Knight? Or maybe one of his entourage? Morningstar hissed. *It had to be.* Regardless, the rest of them needed to die. Hank, Henderson, Sturgill, Cobra...even Knight. Every one of them had become a liability.

But of all of them, his biggest worry now was Sturgill. The senator knew far too much...about everything. And at this point, assuming he was still alive, he had nothing to lose. If Tai Chu was his son, it was clear the young man hadn't cared about the discovery of his biological father. Sturgill's marriage was a sham, and, in spite of his blathering each election about how much he loved the ole U.S. of A., Sturgill didn't give a damn about America. Morningstar sneered. Of all of them, Sturgill was most likely to talk. It was why Morningstar had wanted Cobra to kill him. The pitiful man wouldn't last more than two minutes under the fierce interrogation of a Chinese warlord.

He walked over to his chair and sat down. He stared at the chess board – the pieces all in place – as he tried to come up with a plan. He certainly couldn't fly to China and kill the man himself. Which meant that one of his sons would have to do it. He looked at each chess piece as he went through the list: Joseph (Henderson), Judah (Knight), Dan (Cobra), and Gad were either missing, in a Chinese jail, or dead. Issachar (Todd Jackson) was occupied, as was Zebulun, each one preparing for another vital mission. Levi was planting evidence and monitoring calls from the White House, and Reuben (Pocks) was on the hunt for Hank Clarkson. Simeon was on standby in case Pocks found him, as he and Naphtali continued to search for the missing warship. So, who was left? He shook his head and sighed. *No one.*

He sat back in the chair and crossed his legs. *I need to prioritize my sons' assignments.* Issachar and Zebulun couldn't be spared; their tasks were too important. As for Levi and Pocks, they would be useless for what was needed. Neither one had it in him to kill a man…not intentionally, anyway. That left Simeon or Naphtali, but it was vital that at least one of them keep looking for the Morning Star warship. He rubbed his forehead. He had already been willing to pull in Simeon to kill Hank once Pocks found the man. Could he maybe have him forego that task…at least for now? After all, whatever it was that had compelled Hank to abruptly end his plan to return home and extend his leave of absence, it almost assured that he wasn't a threat; at least not in the short term. *So…why don't I have Simeon kill Sturgill instead of Hank?*

He laughed as he thought of his colorful son, Simeon. No one could pull off a disguise like the cross-dressing former military man. Simeon's latest disguise – by far his best – had had him pretending to be a respected member of a secret organization known, ironically, as the Morning Star. The snooty group of men had been totally fooled by Simeon's impersonation of the fictional Johnny Canterbury. Membership in the group required proper lineage, so Morningstar – with Janet's help – had put together an ancestry that had allowed Simeon to enter the group as a British heir to one of the original founders. The role had been an important one, allowing Simeon, and thereby Morningstar, to gain access to the thoughts and actions not only of the entire group, but of two men in particular: Walter Henderson and Arthur Kauffold.

Simeon had pulled it off with ease, and had managed to become a trusted member of the organization. Morningstar laughed aloud. *Imagine what they'll do when they learn someday that a Son of Jacob had infiltrated their precious group.*

He stood and was about to walk into the kitchen to see where the Klosky's were with his coffee, when suddenly he stopped. "So, why don't I reprise the role!"

He began to pace in front of the fire as he formulated a plan. "Johnny Canterbury is from England, but has become good friends with his American overseers at the Pentagon. That much has already been established." He turned and walked the opposite direction. "What if the State Department – by way of Janet – was to reach out to Sir Arthur Kauffold to intercede in the situation in China? And what if the Secretary – by way of Janet – was to request that Kauffold take Canterbury with him. Why? Because Johnny, who is well-versed in China's language and culture as a part of his training, would be invaluable in the effort." He stopped and raised his hand. "If it was determined that the rumor was true – that a U.S. senator did, in fact, attack a Chinese military leader's son – and the Chinese have detained that senator and his bodyguard without notifying U.S. authorities, well, that would create an international crisis." He walked the other way, barely noticing as the hapless Mr. Klosky walked into the room and handed him a cup of coffee. The man left without a word, as Morningstar, with his hand still in the air, added, "...which would put China and the U.S. on the brink of war. Intervention isn't only expected, but required."

He stopped at the fire, took a sip of coffee, then rested the cup on the hearth. He stared down at the flames and nodded. It was perfect. His lovely Janet, acting on behalf of the Secretary of State, would reach out to Kauffold to request his help with the situation in China. He chuckled. *I could even convince that spineless Harrington to sign off on the request.* Once Kauffold agreed to intervene – which he would do because he was and always would be a diplomat – the State Department, through Janet, would arrange for Canterbury – Simeon – to accompany Kauffold to China. Morningstar frowned. He would need to have Harrington arrange a meeting between Kauffold and China's President. He nodded. *Easy enough...Harrington's a patsy.*

Meanwhile, Morningstar would have Levi plant photos that proved that Sturgill was being held in a Chinese prison, and would make sure those photos were picked up by Johannson, the trusted yet gullible Uzbekistan spy. Kauffold and Canterbury would use the photos to compel China's President to allow them to check on Sturgill and his bodyguard, Frisk (Cobra). Once they were taken to wherever the two men were being held,

Simeon would find an excuse to walk away from the group, and would then kill Sturgill and Dan. Morningstar would leave it up to Simeon as to whether he kept up his disguise with Kauffold, or killed him, too.

Morningstar ran back to his chair and grabbed his cellphone from his briefcase. As he scrolled to Simeon's number, he chuckled. "It's brilliant."

He dialed and, after two quick rings, he heard a somber, "Hello, Father."

Morningstar frowned. "Are you okay?"

He heard a sigh. "Yes. I'm just tired of looking for that blasted spaceship."

Morningstar laughed. "Well, good news...I have a mission for you."

"Does it get me out of here?"

"Yes, my son. You're going to China."

Another pause. "China?"

"Yes. Beijing, to be exact."

"Wonderful! I hear they have excellent night clubs. What will I be doing?"

"You're going to reprise your role as Johnny Canterbury, and you'll be representing America in a joint effort with the UK to find the missing senator who travelled to China two weeks ago and hasn't been heard from since."

A longer pause. "Why would I do that?"

Morningstar grinned. "Because, you know Chinese, you're close with Pentagon administrators, and you're friends with the former ambassador, Arthur Kauffold."

Morningstar heard a groan. "I wouldn't exactly call us friends."

Morningstar laughed. "It's good enough." He paused. "You'll be asked on behalf of the State Department to join your friend, Kauffold, in an attempt to broker a peaceful resolution."

"Does Kauffold know this?"

"No, Johnny, which is why you're going to give him a call the minute we hang up, and arrange to meet him in London...today...at noon."

There was a pause. "It's already eight a.m. here...seven a.m. in the UK. That's rather short notice, Father."

"Yes, Simeon, which means that you have a lot to do." He paused. "Do you have your Johnny Canterbury disguise with you?"

"I do."

"Good. Now get busy."

"But Father, what if Kauffold doesn't want to go to China?"

Morningstar grinned. "He'll go...once you tell him that it was agreed by his good friend, America's Secretary of State, and Britain's Prime Minister, that Sir Arthur Kauffold was the one man who could accomplish such a feat."

He heard a sigh. "This is terrible." A pause. "So...what am I supposed to do once I'm there?"

"I want you to find the missing senator – Charles Sturgill, in case you haven't been following the news – and I want you to kill him."

"Kill him?"

"Yes. And if you see that his bodyguard is still alive, kill him, too."

"His bodyguard?"

"Yes. You know him well. He's your brother, Dan."

Simeon whispered, "You want me to kill Cobra?"

Morningstar chuckled. "Yes. And then you'll get your ass out of there."

Silence. Then, "What about Kauffold?"

"Either take him with you, which means that you will keep up the disguise, or you can kill him." Morningstar paused. "Honestly, I don't care which."

"How will we gain access to the prisoners?"

"You'll insist on seeing for yourselves that Sturgill is still alive."

"But aren't the Chinese denying they have him?"

Morningstar sighed, irritated. "Yes, but you'll challenge them with photographs obtained from a Uzbekistan spy which will prove beyond a shadow of a doubt that he's there. I'll email them to you within the hour."

A pause. "Okay, but how do you expect me to kill Sturgill? I'm pretty sure I'll have Chinese guards watching my every move. And I'll have that blowhard Kauffold with me, too."

"Simeon, my boy, that I will leave to your capable hands."

Another pause. "I won't do it."

Morningstar's eyes narrowed. "I'm sorry, Simeon. It almost sounded as if you were refusing to follow through on an assignment." He paused. "I don't have to remind you what happened the last time someone failed to carry out an assignment, do I?" He paused, his anger rising. "As a matter of fact, Simeon, if you look at the missing finger on Naphtali's left hand, I'm sure you'll quickly be reminded."

He waited. Soon a frustrated Simeon said, "How soon do we leave?"

Morningstar chuckled. "You'll call Kauffold the minute we hang up. There's no time for me to schedule a military plane, but there's a direct flight to China leaving Heathrow at four p.m. I'll have Janet secure two first class tickets." He paused. "Simeon, this task must be completed within twenty-four hours. Understood?"

A pause, this one longer. Morningstar frowned. "I said, do you understand."

A solemn voice said, "Yes...certainly, Father. I'll get right on it."

CHAPTER 47

London, England

Roger Clarkson awoke from a restless sleep, his eyes burning from fatigue. He checked his watch. It was nine a.m. in London. He looked around the crowded bus terminal. He had received a tip from a contact in Wales that Cobra might have been spotted in Cornwall four days ago. He was waiting for the bus to Truro.

His stomach growled. He couldn't remember the last time he had eaten. He sat up on the plastic seat and grabbed the backpack that he had been using as a pillow. He reached inside and took out a granola bar and a bottle of juice. He ate the bar without tasting it, and swigged down the juice in two gulps. Without moving from his seat, he tossed the wrapper and the empty juice bottle in a nearby trashcan.

He looked up at the bus schedule. The bus to Truro was scheduled to leave in thirty minutes. The journey would take about eight hours, during which time Roger would once again try to sleep.

He had had little success with sleep, however. Whenever he closed his eyes, he would see Tonna's picture hanging on Cobra's wall, and would then imagine her body hanging from a tree, like the poor old woman outside Dalgety Bay, Scotland. He would immediately wake up, and would do whatever he could to stay awake. Yes, he was half psychotic from the lack of sleep, but he felt certain that if he saw one more image of Tonna hanging from a tree, it would send him over the edge.

So, he had stopped at a pharmacy on his way to the station, and had picked up an antihistamine, thinking he would drug himself once he was on the bus. He needed to sleep. And he needed to do it without those images pulling him awake.

Activity in the station had picked up quite a bit since he had walked in three hours ago. He was glad; he was more comfortable in a crowd. It was far easier to hide among a lot of people than it was when few were around. He no longer bothered with a disguise. At this point, he looked nothing like the man who had walked into Cobra's flat two weeks ago; that man had vanished. In both body and spirit, Roger Clarkson was gone.

It had been confirmed when he had caught a glimpse of himself in the mirror of the bus station bathroom earlier that morning. Even before he had entered Cobra's lair, he had let his hair grow, but now, two weeks later, the untamed curls made him look half-crazed. He hadn't shaved, either, and a tangled beard and mustache covered much of his face. Add in a pair of cheap sunglasses, and the disguise was complete.

He had spent most of the last two weeks trying to track Cobra's recent activities. A tip from a man in Hamburg, Germany, followed by another tip from a spy in France had offered some much-needed insight into the killer's mindset. For whatever reason, Cobra had changed his routine. Instead of killing every few weeks and leaving his calling card – a bloodless corpse with a bite mark on the forearm – he had apparently spent the last few months traveling Europe without a single murder in his wake. The change was intriguing, to say the least. *What are you up to, Cobra?*

The Hamburg tip had come from a Scotland Yard officer, though Roger hadn't spoken with Inspector Pritchard since the night he had entered Cobra's flat. He hadn't spoken to his boss, either. It wasn't unusual for Roger to go 'off the grid' for days or even weeks at a time; it was actually integral to his assignment. But he knew, sooner or later, he would need to check in, if only to continue to have the freedom to pursue Cobra on his own terms. And what were those terms? *Killing the man the minute I see his face.* Though many would applaud the outcome, they wouldn't applaud his methods. Roger no longer cared. *Cobra must die.*

The clue he was pursuing in Cornwall had come via an email message from his boss, Jack Miley. *Time to see if Miley's learned anything new,* Roger thought, as he reached in his bag for his laptop. He set it on the seat beside him, opened it, and connected it to his cellphone's hotspot. He was about to type in the first of three passwords to access the CIA website, when a quick ding told him that he had received an email. He clicked on the message; it took him to a blank page. He typed in a password. A paragraph of text appeared. Anyone who might read the text would see nothing more than an invitation to a soccer match in Wales. But within that text was a message, and Roger knew exactly who it was from.

Hobbs.

Hobbs – Roger had never learned the man's first name – was a former London spy who had played an early role in Roger's CIA training. Though the two men had gotten close during their time together, they hadn't spoken in months.

Until four days ago, when Roger had dropped in – unannounced – at Hobbs' flat on the East End. Hobbs had seen instantly that something was wrong.

"Ye don't look so good, spy boy."

Roger had frowned. *"My situation has changed."*

Hobbs had merely nodded, and had offered Roger a cup of tea. Roger had declined, and had looked Hobbs in the eye. *"I need your help."* Roger had then gone on to detail recent events, culminating with his discovery of the photo of Tonna hanging on Cobra's wall.

"Why've ye come to me, son?"

Roger had taken a deep breath and had sighed. *"Do I need to say it?"*

Hobbs had stared at him for a full thirty seconds, then had shaken his head. *"I don't guess ye do,"* he had said, adding, *"...let me look into it."*

And Roger knew that he would. More importantly, Roger knew that he would keep it under the radar. In spite of the fact that Hobbs had told him many times that he was *"...done with the spy business,"* Roger knew that what Hobbs was actually done with were the government agencies that had constrained him over the years.

Hobbs had spent nearly five decades spying for either the Allies after WWII, or for Great Britain during the Cold War. He was a treasure-trove of information. But an incident in 1989 had created doubt among a few of Hobbs' overseers. Hobbs had refused to elaborate, only to say that the experience had compelled him to 'retire.' He now spent the majority of his time with his homing pigeons. He had told Roger countless stories of the heroism of the clever birds. *"They've been known to fly five hundred miles into enemy territory just to get their message to their man."*

Roger had actually used the birds himself, to send messages to Tonna once he had recovered from his near-death experience in the Paris catacombs. Cobra's willingness to make Roger suffer had convinced him then that he would need to keep his ties to Tonna a secret. He flinched. *Clearly, I failed.*

He didn't want to even think what Cobra would be willing to do to Tonna to get back at him. *That man is a vile piece of filth,* Roger thought as he opened Hobbs' message. He was surprised to see that his hands were shaking.

He read through the message, reviewing in his mind the code the two men had used when they had exchanged messages in the past. The 'invitation' to the soccer match included a link that presumed to give details of the event. He clicked on the link; it pulled up another empty page. He typed in a password. After ten seconds, another blank page appeared. Then, slowly, words scrolled across the page. He looked closely; they would be gone in five seconds.

"Turn on BBC live feed."

That was it. Roger clicked to a BBC website and clicked on the live feed. A British reporter was standing outside London's Chinese embassy.

> "—footage is from America, taken two weeks ago, as U.S. Senator Charles Sturgill prepares to board a plane for China. Slated as a diplomatic visit to seek common ground in the West's approach to North Korea, the Senator – who was to return home within a few days – hasn't been seen since.
>
> "Though U.S. leaders caution against thinking the worst, that is exactly what is feared, at least by Sturgill's fellow senators. As one senator from North Dakota put it, "Chuck Sturgill went to China on a diplomatic mission, and has yet to return. I'd say we have a global incident on our hands. Our de facto President needs to do something about it.""

Roger continued to watch, but little more was said. He was about to turn it off, when an image on the screen caught his eye. He stared at it. It was a video showing Sturgill boarding the plane in DC. It was on a loop. Roger kept watching. But it wasn't Sturgill he was staring at. It was the man with him; the man who was acting as his bodyguard. Roger recognized him. Though he wasn't wearing his signature black cape, and his hair was short and blond, Roger had seen enough of the man to know exactly who it was. Roger's entire body tensed as he felt the hate surge through him.

Cobra.

It was confirmed when the bodyguard glanced at the camera. For a split second, the man offered a classic Cobra sneer. Hobbs must have seen it, as well.

Cobra is in China.

Roger clicked back to the email. He was about to send a reply, when the screen suddenly went black. In seconds, another message scrolled across the screen.

"A private plane will be waiting at Northolt. Ten a.m."

Roger shut off the laptop and slid it in his bag, allowing himself a quick smile as he thought, *Hobbs, you came through for me.*

He checked the time. Nine-ten. Northolt air force base was about forty minutes from London. He needed to hurry.

He pulled on his jacket, threw his backpack over his shoulder, and ran out the door. A taxi queue was less than a hundred yards away. He fell in line. After three minutes, a cab pulled up and he slid in back. "Uxbridge."

The driver nodded and pulled away.

The RAF Northolt airbase was only two nautical miles from Uxbridge. Roger would take a ferry once he got to Uxbridge, which was in the London Borough of Hillingdon. If the plane was waiting as Hobbs had said it would be, then Roger should leave London's airspace no later than 10:15. *Which means – if all goes well – I will be in China by tomorrow morning.*

CHAPTER 48

Somewhere in the Katahdin Mountains

Secret Service Agent Tom Cravens stared at the memo he had received from the FBI yesterday afternoon. "Jenny Clarkson, missing person. Status unchanged." He frowned as he stared at the two words that said so much. "Status unchanged." Jenny was still missing. *I guess it's better than finding her dead,* he thought with a sigh.

He had been forced to pull in the FBI after the DC police had failed to find her. Though Cravens had tried his best to make the FBI request seem routine, he knew that even by making it, he had put Hank, Maddi, and himself at risk. It couldn't be helped. Jenny was missing, and he had promised Hank that he would find her.

He laid the memo on the desk in the small but comfortable room he had been assigned in the mountain hide-away where the President had taken up residence. Not only was it unfathomable to think that such a situation existed, but it was even more unfathomable to think that he had now become a central part of the operation. His official role had begun two weeks ago, when he had been met in Bangor, Maine, just after midnight, by Agent Foster and another agent who had been introduced as Santa. The man was big and burly, and looked to be as strong as an ox. Cravens had been blindfolded and placed in the bed of a pickup truck. He had been driven for hours over winding roads to the base of a mountain. He had crawled out of the truck, relieved the journey was over, only to find that the hardest part was yet to come. Foster had handed him climbing gear, had pointed to the mountain, and had said, *"Ya ready?"* Cravens had offered a hesitant nod, more out of duty than confidence. He wasn't in the best shape, and it had only gotten worse since the plane crash. Santa had been forced to pretty much carry him up the side of the mountain. After about two hours, they had reached an enclosed area, and Foster had swept aside large limbs that had been placed in a row to cover a hidden door. He had plugged in a code, and when the door had opened, he had pulled Cravens inside, with Santa right behind him.

Cravens had been astounded. Never had he seen such a place. Tall, rock-covered walls, overhead lighting that adjusted for the time of day, and surveillance technology the likes of which he had never seen. Foster had given him a quick tour, bringing him up to speed on all that had happened to get them to that point. Cravens had been amazed to learn of Knight's escape from the White House; not only that he had gotten away with it, but that the Vice President, Bob Harrington, had been willing to serve as front man. *"Think about it, Cravens. All the glory, none of the work."*

Cravens had been shown to a room with a bed and a desk in the corner. *"Your bedroom and your office."* Cravens had set his duffel bag on the bed, had pulled out the baggies he had collected at the church, and had handed them to Foster. Foster had slid them in a briefcase, and had offered Cravens something to eat. Cravens had declined. *"But I don't suppose you'd have a beer?"* He had been stunned to learn that the facility had, in fact, been stocked with beer, wine, and whiskey. Foster had led him to a kitchen, and had handed him a cold bottle of domestic beer from a huge fridge. He had then proceeded to tell him about the kitchen. *"Though we don't have fresh vegetables or fruit, my friends have started growing carrots, beets, and onions in a room off to the side using artificial light...much like a greenhouse. And they've got two apple trees they're working on, as well. In the meantime, every few days Kent hikes down the mountain, then hitches a ride to Portland to pick up fresh food."*

Once Cravens had finished his beer, Foster had handed him a folder. *"These are your assignments."* Cravens had taken the folder, and had asked Foster if he was expected to stay there indefinitely. Foster's reply: *"You don't leave until we do."*

Foster had then outlined his assignments. Not only was he to try to learn more about Gad and his overseer, but he was also tasked with learning all he could about events from the last eight months that had brought the world to the brink of war. The murders in Ireland, Scotland, England, and France; the assassination of a U.S. President just months before his reelection; the threat against another U.S. President that had forced him to leave the White House; and Russia's attempt – out of the blue – to take Latvia. Added to that was a missing United States senator, who had flown to China two weeks ago. China had insisted that the senator had flown back to the States eight days ago, but there was no record of such a flight. *"The President is looking for something that ties it all together, Cravens."*

Cravens had spent each morning of the past two weeks either trying to address the President's request, or learning more about Gad. But hanging over him was the matter of Hank's missing ex-wife. So, about three days into his stay, Cravens had asked Foster if he could hike into town to address an ongoing concern he had been working on before coming to the hideaway. Reluctantly, Foster had allowed him to leave, but not until after dark. At six p.m. of his fourth night there, Cravens had hiked down the mountain, which had taken about an hour, then had walked about a mile before hitching a ride to Bangor, twenty miles away. He had purchased a trac phone and had called his contact from the DC police. The man had informed him that they had found nothing. *"No prints at the townhouse; no clues anywhere near that place."* That was when Cravens had decided to reach out to his friend at the FBI. He had used the same trac phone to make the call to his FBI friend, had sworn the man to secrecy, then had told him everything he knew about Jenny's disappearance. *"I can't stress this enough, Greg...no matter what you find, you talk only to me."* The agent had agreed and Cravens had destroyed the trac phone and had made his way back to the mountain. Santa had been waiting to help him make the climb up to the hideaway.

Once he was back inside, he had told Foster that he would need to continue such trips until his mission was complete. At first, Foster had refused, but Cravens had told him – truthfully – that a woman's life was at stake, and that he couldn't in good conscience just leave her to die. Foster had finally given in, allowing him to leave the facility every three to four days. On those days, Cravens would repeat the steps he had taken on that first trip down the mountain. He would purchase a trac phone and call his contact at the FBI. He would then destroy the phone and walk to a computer café, where he would print out a coded email from his FBI contact, which he would decode once he was back up the mountain. The only good thing that had come of it was that he had lost about ten pounds. He chuckled. *Betty would be proud.*

On one of the trips to town, he had called his boss, Sam Allen, on a phone that Foster had given him just for that purpose. *"I know Allen. If he hears from you, he won't be as inclined to try to find you."* His boss had asked far too many questions, not only about what he was up to, but about his mention of Emma Cannon after the incident at the church. Cravens had lied and had told him he had heard Emma's name from an FBI informant, but wasn't at liberty to reveal more. He had lied again, and had said he was in Florida, still carrying out *"...a mission for an American patriot."*

Though the Secret Service had some of the best technology available, Foster's friends seemed to have even better. Should Allen try to track Cravens – which Cravens felt certain he would – he would discover that Cravens was, in fact, calling from a deli in Key West. *"Fake GPS,"* one of Foster's friends had told him. *"We can ping a signal from your phone that will show that you're there, even when you're not."* Just to be sure, Foster had called on another friend – a retired agent – who lived in Key West, and had asked him to keep an eye on the deli. He was to let Foster know if any Secret Service agents came looking for Cravens. *"If so, could you maybe tell them you saw a man that fit his description twenty-four hours ago at the deli."* The former agent had agreed, but so far, had reported no sign of any government agents.

Cravens stared at the decoded FBI memo. "Jenny Clarkson, missing person. Status unchanged." He leaned back, his large frame stressing the chair as he ran a hand through thinning gray hair. *I'm too old for this.* The report had simply confirmed what his own eyes had already told him; Jenny Clarkson was missing, and everything suggested that she had been taken from Hank Clarkson's townhouse against her will.

Cravens stretched his arms and sighed. He folded the FBI memo and locked it in a drawer, then grabbed a DNA report labeled "Gad," which was sitting off to the side. Agent Foster had apparently flown Cravens' DNA evidence to a remote PO Box in Maryland ten days ago in the middle of the night. An hour later, another trusted agent – a friend that Foster had known for fifteen years – had driven to the PO Box, had picked up the evidence, and had spent the last week analyzing it in a DC lab. He had labeled the items, "John Doe, Michigan crime scene," and had shared the information with no one. He had gotten a DNA hit from the saliva for a man named Marcus King; a gang member from downtown DC who had been arrested four years ago, but had disappeared soon after, released to an unknown military man's recognizance. Who was the unknown military man, and why hadn't he needed to sign for the prisoner? Cravens had tried to find the guard who had overseen the transfer; the man had retired a year after the fact, and had died a year later. From what Cravens could tell, the guard had spoken to no one regarding the release. Cravens had then requested taped video surveillance from the jail, but held out little hope that he would get it; the facility was old and small, and had almost zero technology.

He set the document on the desk and sighed. *A military man – an overseer – who is so powerful that he comes and goes without having to account for his actions.*

He rubbed his eyes. He was tired. It was five-thirty in the morning, and he had been up since four, either reading summaries of Gad, or trying to piece together the events of the past eight months. He grabbed the folder that summarized the various upheavals around the globe and set it in front of him. Labeled only "surveillance," it contained reports of the events that had caused so much turmoil internationally. So far, he had found little to connect them. The earlier murders in the UK, Ireland, and France had been attributed to the assassin, Cobra, but there was a strong belief that he had been acting on behalf of someone else. *Who were you working for, Cobra?*

As for the later events, Cravens had found no tie whatsoever.

Foster had given him a new set of reports late last night, which Cravens had simply shoved into the folder before falling into bed. *Time to take a look,* he thought as he slowly opened the folder. The first report was a single-page outline of a series of email transmissions between two men. According to the report, the emails had been intercepted by a retired Secret Service agent, Scott Johnson, who at one time had been assigned to the former Vice President, James Conner. The exchange consisted of what appeared to be cooked up data that had been transmitted in such a way that it would be 'discovered' by an overseas analyst. *"A man named Jacob is talking to someone named Levi about planting evidence related to the Latvian war."*

Cravens had instantly thought of Gad in the church and his call to Judah. *"Jacob says that all will be forgiven."* As he stared at the emails, he considered the names. *Jacob and Gad, Jacob and Levi, Jacob and Judah.* He frowned. *Jacob and his sons...from the Bible?* He set the folder on the desk, then stood and walked to a makeshift library two doors down from his bedroom. He found a Bible and opened it to Genesis. Raised in St. Mary's Catholic School in Hoboken, New Jersey, Cravens had a decent grasp of the Old Testament. Starting at chapter 28, he did a quick read on Jacob and his sons. Could it be? An intriguing angle, but he found it hard to believe that someone would go to the trouble – or have the wherewithal – to pull together a family of soldiers for the purpose of disrupting the entire world. But he couldn't ignore the names, nor could he ignore the fact that every one of those men had been involved one way or another in events that had greatly affected America's foreign policy over the last eight months.

Carrying the Bible, he walked back to his bedroom. He laid the Bible on the corner of the desk, then sat and looked again at the folder. He reviewed what he knew of the four men, starting with Gad. The wiry young man had likely killed a driver at the Henderson estate in order to have access to the Hendersons. He had then been forewarned about a plane crash intended to kill a sitting U.S. Senator. Cravens had told no one of that fact. To do so would put the secret of Maddi's survival – and his and Hank's involvement in that secret – at risk. Two months later, Gad kidnapped a psychiatrist and used him to lure Henderson to Lithuania. He was also responsible for Michael Cannon's kidnapping a few days later. While pointing a gun to Cannon's temple, he had made a reference to the man's wife, Emma Melnikov Cannon, who Cravens soon learned was accused of being a spy. Which Cravens now felt to be highly improbable. Emma was far too kind and considerate to be a spy. Or if she was, she had totally duped him and everyone else on that mountain, including President Knight. He shook his head. Knight didn't appear to be a man who was easily duped.

As for Levi, whoever he was, he had allegedly planted false data to lure Latvia into a war. The amazing thing was that it had worked. Which suggested that Levi was not only technically savvy, but was very well-placed within America's government.

Then there was Judah, who had been addressed by Gad in a personal way...as if they knew one another. Gad had gone so far as to refer to himself as Judah's brother. Judah just happened to be the code name for the current U.S. President. A coincidence? Cravens had asked Knight about it; Knight had asked him to let it go.

Finally, was Jacob. Whoever he was, he seemed to have had a hand in all of it. Biblically, Jacob was the father of twelve sons. Did that mean that the Jacob referred to by Gad was overseeing a similar 'family' of twelve soldiers? If so, had they all carried out evil deeds at his request? Was he the mastermind behind the increased tensions around the globe? *Is Jacob the link that ties this whole damn thing together?*

Cravens leaned back and sighed. He had no proof of any of it. All he had was circumstantial evidence tying Gad and Judah to Jacob, and a printout – second-hand – from the former VP's Secret Service agent regarding emails between Levi and Jacob. He would need actual proof if he was to move forward with any accusations.

He was suddenly reminded of Henderson's request that he access a safe deposit box at a savings and loan in Boonsboro, Maryland. It had been for the same reason. *"You will need proof, Cravens, and the flash drive in that safe deposit box will have it."* Henderson had told Cravens that the flash drive alone wouldn't be enough, but that it would be needed if he was to bring down Gad's overseer. Cravens sighed. *Seems like Henderson and Knight might be looking for the same thing.*

He stared at the folder, unwilling to go to the next page. Not because he was exhausted – which he was – and not because he didn't want to get at the truth – which he did. What was bothering him was Knight's role in it all. His Secret Service code name was Judah. When Gad had called Knight from inside the church, he had dialed him directly. Who on earth had the ability to dial a U.S. President direct, except someone close to him? Cravens had told no one of his conversation with Knight that day; not even Foster. And he wouldn't until he had a better understanding of the role Knight had played. *But if Knight is part of it, why is he working so hard to expose it?*

He sighed and forced himself to turn to the next page. He read what appeared to be a summary of CIA surveillance. It confirmed that U.S. Senator Charles Sturgill had recently traveled to China with bodyguard Daniel Frisk. A photo of the two men boarding a plane was attached. The next page consisted of more surveillance. Though low on detail, it laid out a timeline that implied that Sturgill might have been involved in an effort to kill the son of one of China's military leaders. Even more shocking was that China was denying that it had happened.

He turned to the next page. It was a summary of another CIA surveillance video. It stated that two men had been spotted being dragged into an unmarked facility somewhere outside Beijing. The CIA had reason to think that the men were Sturgill and his bodyguard, Frisk. The report went on to say that there was evidence to suggest that Frisk had tried to poison China's military leader's son, Tai Chu. Apparently, a note found on Frisk stated that the assault had been sanctioned by the U.S. Government. China continued to deny the whole thing, insisting that Sturgill had left China eight days ago, and that neither he nor Frisk were being held in any sort of prison. Cravens shook his head. *Why deny such an awful series of events if they actually happened?*

He sat back and ran his hands through his hair. *I need a smoke,* he thought as he looked over at his jacket that was hanging on the back of a chair. His Marlboros were in one of the pockets. The President's secret hideaway had been designated as a no-smoking facility by its creators, insisting the fumes would ruin the clean air they had worked so hard to provide. Though Cravens knew he should just quit, he couldn't seem to do it, so Foster had come up with a plan that had him going to the 'courtyard' to light up when he could no longer resist the urge. *"But just a few puffs, Cravens, so you don't leave a signal."* The plan was for him to sneak out the only door, have a guard standing ready to open it when he was done, then stoop low behind a boulder and sneak four quick puffs. He didn't like it, but he had gotten used to it. He imagined his ex-wife, Betty wagging a finger. *"If you'd just quit the damn things it wouldn't be an issue, Tom."* He grinned as he stared at the jacket. "Someday, Betty. Someday."

He stood and stretched his arms. He checked the time. *Six a.m.* He looked at the closed curtains of a fake window, imagining the moon sinking in the canyon. It had been one of the hardest things to get used to; the fact that there were no windows anywhere in the mountain enclave... *no way for me to see the sun rise or the moon fade gently into dawn.*

He pulled his jacket from a chair, feeling for the bulge in the pocket, ever fearful that someone would decide that his habit was too great a risk. *Then what will I do?* Relieved that they were still there, he threw on the jacket and left the room. He saw Foster leaving the President's office. "Hey Foster, have you got a minute?"

"Sure. What do you need?"

Cravens motioned him to a private alcove. Keeping his voice low, he said, "Anything more about the senator who we think is being detained in China?"

Foster frowned. "Didn't you read my report from the CIA?"

Cravens nodded. "Yeah, but it makes no sense. Why would Sturgill – an uninspiring senator by all accounts – decide to take it upon himself to fly all the way to China to enact a destructive foreign policy that had been on no one's radar?"

Foster shook his head. "It's hard to say. Sturgill has always been kind of an odd duck. He lost his five-year-old son to Chinese kidnappers nearly thirty years ago. I wouldn't put it past him to harbor a grudge."

Cravens' eyes widened. "Geez, I didn't know that. I wouldn't put it past any man to harbor a grudge after such a thing. They never found his boy?"

Foster shook his head. "No. I think they eventually found his remains, but I'm not sure. I do know that they ended the search and declared the boy dead."

Cravens frowned. "That's terrible." He paused. "But if he tried to kill the military leader's son, then why doesn't China just tell us that and let us know that they're holding him. We would have little place to argue... assuming it's true."

Foster shook his head. "My guess? They're torturing him."

Cravens flinched, thinking back to the CIA report that suggested that Sturgill and his bodyguard had barely been able to walk. It made sense.

Foster added, "It leaves us without a play. If Sturgill did what the report suggests, then China would have every right to hold the two men. If he didn't, then we have a right to go in and get 'em, but we can't just send in a battalion of soldiers."

"Why not? If they're holding two Americans without cause?"

"What you're suggesting would provoke a war...another war." He sighed. "Knight needs to urge Harrington to keep the lines of communication open, while at the same time, beef up our presence in the region." He paused. "Not an easy task."

Cravens frowned. "I get that it's complicated, but it seems like a no-brainer to me. An *American senator* is being held prisoner by the Chinese, and they refuse to clarify why or where they're holding him."

Foster nodded. "Yes, but that same senator may have tried to kill a Chinese military leader's son. We have to figure out a way to get him out of there without pissing off a country that has an army almost as big as ours."

Cravens shook his head and sighed. "You're right...not an easy task."

Foster frowned. "There's even more to it than that. Senator Sturgill is the President's uncle, and he pretty much raised Knight after Knight's parents were killed in a car crash. The President wants to make sure that whatever we do, we don't jeopardize a chance to get Sturgill out of there alive."

Cravens let out a sigh. "Wow."

"Yep."

"Okay. But can you answer me one question?"

"I'll try."

Cravens frowned. "Who's our enemy? Who is it we're fighting here?"

Foster narrowed his eyes. "What do you mean?"

"Well, I've dug through the paperwork and I have yet to find a connection between the events that have brought about all this chaos." He paused. "But the President seems confident that such a connection exists. Why?"

Foster motioned him even deeper into the alcove. He whispered, "What I'm about to tell you can go no further. Understood?"

"Of course."

Still whispering, he said, "We think that a high-level U.S. government official is behind a lot of what's been going on."

Cravens widened his eyes. "High level? Who is it?"

"The main consensus: General Daniels' chief aide, Edward Morningstar."

Cravens stared at him, recalling the newspaper article he had read earlier that morning that had dared to question the Hendersons' support for Latvia's efforts against Russia. The article had quoted a high-ranking Pentagon aide who had stated unequivocally that the United States government had total faith in the Hendersons. He then recalled an article from two weeks ago, which had told of a visit between a man named Morningstar and the Hendersons. Apparently, he had spent the evening with them at their estate. "The guy who had dinner with the Hendersons in Latvia?"

Foster nodded. "Yes, he's Daniels' right-hand man, so we've had to tread carefully. We want to build a case against him, but until we have ironclad proof, we need to wait. Apparently, the general loves the man like a son. We'll have only one shot to convince him that Morningstar is anything other than the loyal aide who has been at his side for the past two-and-a-half decades."

Cravens frowned. "How do we do that?"

Foster hesitated. "It won't be easy. Not only does Daniels hold a deep affection for Morningstar; so does President Knight. Apparently, Morningstar was like a father to him after his parents were killed."

Cravens shifted awkwardly, again recalling Gad's comment for Judah to get back to the White House *"...and all will be forgiven."* He cleared his throat. "What do you think about the Biblical code names in those transcripts you gave me? You know...Jacob, Levi, Gad, Judah...and the repeated references to father and son?"

Foster shook his head. "It's pretty weird." He turned to leave, saying over his shoulder, "...especially since Knight's code name is Judah."

I couldn't have said it better. "So, is that just a coincidence?"

Foster stopped and turned. "I hope so." He walked back over to Cravens and whispered, "...because between you and me, I think Morningstar might be Jacob."

CHAPTER 49

Chesham, England

Jake Donovan walked down the impressive staircase of the Kauffold manor that sat just outside Chesham, England. He was still in awe of all that had happened in only two weeks. Twenty-four hours after Andrew had asked for his help to fly him out of the country, Donovan and Andrew had boarded a privately-owned Cessna at a small airport in Indiana, and Donovan himself had flown the Cessna to another small airport in Virginia. There they had waited a day-and-a-half for another private plane, this one a bit larger, and had used the time to pull together a new identity for Andrew. Once a new identity had been secured, Donovan had flown them across the ocean, and they had landed at a small airport outside Chesham on Wednesday, November 3rd. They had been picked up by Arthur Kauffold's personal chauffeur, who had been sent following a phone call Andrew had made to Kauffold just before they landed. He had taken them to the Kauffold estate, where they had been ever since.

The departure from the U.S. had been a bit more challenging than Donovan had anticipated. Something to do with increased tension between the U.S. and China. No one was allowed to come or go without a whole lot of scrutiny. So Donovan, whose credentials were impeccable, was forced to get Andrew similarly impeccable credentials. For that, he had needed help, and not all of it was legal. Using a recently-acquired resource, he was able to get Andrew a new identity, but was forced to make it as simple as possible, considering Andrew was a novice with disguises.

He had kept Andrew as his first name, knowing that Andrew would likely balk at answering to anything else. He had also stayed with Andrew's Midwest background; Andrew could talk convincingly about a home in the Midwest, he could not do the same about a home on the east or west coast, or anywhere else, for that matter. He had made only two changes to Andrew's appearance; his hair, which was now blonde, and his eye color, which was now blue. Ironically, Andrew now bore an uncanny resemblance to his sister, the senator who had died in a plane crash a few months ago.

Describing their travel to Chesham as a 'mission of diplomacy,' Donovan had used his Homeland Security credentials to say that he and Andrew – a fellow agent within the department – were visiting the former ambassador, Sir Arthur Kauffold, in an effort to cement global friendships at a time of increasing tension around the world. *"Members of the U.S. government have asked that we nurture ties to a strong ally,"* he had said in his request. The State Department had given their blessing, and within days of Donovan and Andrew's first meeting, they were at the Chesham estate.

But as hard as the whole 'mission of diplomacy' gig had been to sell, the actual purpose of the journey was even more unbelievable. By way of the listening device at the diner, Donovan had already figured out that Andrew's dead sister had had a child, a girl, who had been adopted years ago by the former ambassador. But during the layover in Virginia, Andrew had decided to tell Donovan everything he had learned. Apparently, the girl's name was Tonna, and Andrew's sister had only learned of her tie to Tonna within the past year or so. Andrew was pretty much consumed by the thought that, as he had put it, *"...a part of Maddi is out there somewhere."* Though his request to travel overseas had presented quite a challenge, Donovan understood why it was important to him. As a matter of fact, he understood it better than most.

But he hadn't forgotten about the tape recorder that Andrew had mentioned at their first meeting. *"Shouldn't we bring it with us?"* Donovan had asked. Andrew had shaken his head. *"No, it's best I keep it where it is for now."* Donovan had said, *"And where is that?"* Andrew had frowned. *"Somewhere safe."* Donovan had pushed the point. *"How about if you get it, let me listen to it, then hide it again. It might give me insight into this Jacob character."* Andrew had hesitated, then had shaken his head again. *"You can hear it when we get back to the States."*

But that, too, had been delayed. Their original intent had been to fly back to America after two or three days. But because of a recent threat against Tonna, Kauffold had begged for the two men to stay a bit longer, insisting that the more men that were there to look after her, the safer she would be. Kauffold already had his own security detail, and Scotland Yard had sent over four men after it was discovered that Tonna's photo was hanging on a serial killer's wall. In response, Arthur had hired two additional bodyguards to keep an eye on Tonna at all times. But even that hadn't been enough to reassure the old man, which is why Kauffold had more or less begged Andrew to stay. *"I don't know what I'd do without you, Andrew."* He had looked at Donovan and had added, *"...and you, too, Donovan. You are, after all, an actual Homeland Security agent."*

Donovan had merely smiled. *"My pleasure, Ambassador."* He had then called his boss to make sure that he was okay with Donovan's prolonged stay in the UK. The man had surprised Donovan, not only by approving the delay, but by seemingly being pleased with the change in plans. *"This could work out well for us."* And Donovan had to agree. Not only was the Chesham estate a remarkable place, and not only had Donovan and Andrew been treated like royalty, but it had been fascinating to view the developing international crises through the eyes of the ambassador. Donovan had always believed that the oceans that bordered America isolated the U.S., allowing it to detach itself from the problems of the world. Kauffold had argued that it wasn't that simple. *"It's not that America is isolationist, you have simply had the privilege of being far-removed from the realities of war."*

Andrew had jumped in, reminding Kauffold of World War II and the sacrifices made by so many Americans. The ambassador had nodded quickly. *"Yes, I would never want to discount such sacrifices, Andrew. And I will throw in the losses incurred by your valiant country in World War I, as well. America offered over four million soldiers to that brutal war. Sadly, over a hundred thousand of those brave souls lost their lives."* He had added, *"I'm simply saying that distance and two large oceans affect your country's stance on various events around the world. It is understandable. It takes you a bit longer to feel the need to get involved."*

Donovan smoothed down his shirt as he hurried down the stairs. He had slept late, and was hoping breakfast was still available. As he walked into the dining room, he was pleased to see that the kitchen staff had left out the most important items. *Eggs, bacon, toast...that's all I need.* He filled his plate and took a seat at the table.

"I was wondering if you were ever going to get up."

It was Andrew, who had just walked in from outside. The blond hair and blue eyes still caught Donovan by surprise, and, as Andrew took off his coat, Donovan looked at him and grinned. "You don't look too bad as a blond."

Andrew laughed as he hung his coat on a hanger by the door. "You think?"

Donovan motioned for Andrew to join him. "Absolutely. Have you eaten?"

Andrew nodded. "About three hours ago." He walked to a coffee pot. "But I'll have another cup of coffee." He poured a cup and carried it to the table. "By the way, Donovan, in case I haven't said it, I want to thank you for making this time with my niece possible." He sipped his coffee. "It has been good to get to know her."

Donovan nodded. "She actually resembles your sister quite a bit."

Andrew looked at him over the rim of his cup. "Did you know my sister?"

Donovan shook his head quickly. "No, I've just seen pictures."

Andrew nodded. "Though I've enjoyed my time here, I think it's time for us to go home, Donovan." He swallowed. "I really miss my family."

Donovan sipped his coffee. "I get it. I'm ready to go any time." He frowned. "But I think the ambassador will try to talk us out of it."

"He'll try to talk *you* out of it. It's you and that gun you carry that is making him feel like Tonna is safer with us here. I'm just along for the ride."

Donovan grinned. "Nonetheless, I agree. We need to go home. So far, it's been okay because of Kauffold's strong ties with so many American leaders. My boss has seen the value in that, but I think he's ready for me to get back to work."

Andrew nodded. "Before we go, there's something I'd like to do."

"What's that?" Donovan asked, his mouth full of bacon.

"I'd like to visit my grandparents' home in Darlington." He paused. "Actually, it's my home, I guess. They left it to me...me and Maddi." He looked away.

Donovan said quickly, "I get it. We can fly back to the U.S. after we make the trip." He sipped his coffee. "Today's Saturday. Maybe an overnight at the estate, then we leave for DC first thing Monday morning. Does that give you enough time?"

"I'll make it work. Tonna can go with us. After all, they were her great-grandparents. I think she'd enjoy visiting the estate as a future heir versus a guest."

Donovan nodded as he took a bite of eggs. "Just the three of us, then?"

Andrew frowned. "I would ask the ambassador, but I just ran into him as he was walking out the door. He's on his way to London."

Donovan wiped his mouth and shoved away his plate. "What's in London?"

"He's meeting...a friend there. Something about China."

"Did you say anything to him about us going to Darlington?"

"Yes. He didn't like it, but he accepted it...as long as you and the two body guards he hired go with us."

Donovan laughed. He checked his watch. "It's eleven o'clock. I'll pack a bag and meet you at the front door in twenty minutes."

"Great. I'll let Tonna know, and I'll say something to the bodyguards." Andrew stood and was about to leave the dining room, when he turned to Donovan and frowned. "I promised you that I'd let you listen to that tape, didn't I?"

Donovan's eyes widened. "Yes, you said I could hear it when we got back to the States."

Andrew walked to the door. "Well, I haven't forgotten."

Donovan nodded. "Good, Andrew. But don't worry too much about it." He grinned. "I'm a patient man."

Chapter 50

Somewhere in the Katahdin Mountains

Emma Cannon, formerly Emma Melnikov of the Russian Melnikov's from Lida, Belarus, was stretched out on the couch in a makeshift den in the hideout in the Katahdan Mountains. There was no fireplace due to the risk that smoke would give away their presence, but she had been allowed a couple of candles in metal holders, which she had placed side-by-side in the center of an old oak coffee table. She looked up from her novel and stared at the flames, shivering as she hugged her arms to her chest. *I wish you gave off some heat.*

Though there was a well-functioning furnace, the spacious enclave was drafty, especially the den, which was hidden toward the back of the compound. She was glad she had brought her long knitted scarf, which her mother, Dasha, had given her when Emma was only four. *"It was made in Belarus, dear Emma...so I know it will keep you warm."* She took the scarf from her shoulders as she combed black bangs from her forehead. Her mother had died from cancer one year to the day after giving Emma that scarf, leaving Emma with only her father, the scarf, and many words of wisdom.

Wearing a cashmere sweater and thick black tights, she draped the scarf over her long slender legs. Though it was still early morning, she had been unable to sleep, and had come to the den to seek solace in the writings of Edgar Allen Poe. She had chosen "The Telltale Heart," her favorite of all

Poe's works. He had a way of tapping into peoples' fears, shining a light on their greatest sins and the guilt brought about because of them. *Like leaving one's family without a proper goodbye.*

She closed the book, again fighting an unyielding sense of blame over how she had left things. It had been that way since they had run from the White House. The discovery of Michael in the hands of a kidnapper had only made it worse. Though she had been assured that he was now safe, her guilt was crushing her. She closed her eyes and held the book to her chest, wincing as she thought of all the pain she had caused.

"He'll corrupt you, you know."

Emma looked up to see Knight standing at the door. He was leaning against the frame, and Emma was immediately reminded of why she had chosen to leave her family in the first place. "Who will?"

"Poe."

She grinned. "Ah yes. Well, a little corruption is good from time to time."

He walked over and sat next to her, pulling her close, smelling her hair as he stroked it gently.

Emma's eyes filled with tears and she wiped them away, hoping he hadn't noticed. She swallowed as she thought, *I have to do this.* She sat back and looked him in the eye. "Can I talk to you for a minute, Romer?"

He frowned, shifting so that he was facing her. "Of course."

She grabbed his hand. "I—I need you to trust me...and I need you to help me with something."

His eyes flashed, the soft brown reflecting the manufactured light that was meant to simulate the first rays of morning. He swallowed. "I...I'll help you however I can."

"You might want to hear what I have to say before you agree to it, Romer."

Knight let out a sigh. He shook his head, then looked down. "It's been too much, hasn't it? You're regretting your decision." He looked at her, and she could see the sorrow in his eyes as he said, "You want to go home, don't you, Emma?"

Her eyes softened and she shook her head. "No. Not at all. If I were to die this very minute, I have no regrets...not about you and I, anyway." She leaned closer and grabbed his other hand. "I love you, Romer, and I know now that I always will."

He narrowed his eyes. "Then what is it?"

She took a deep breath and closed her eyes. *This is it.* She looked at Knight and frowned. "I need to talk to Michael. I need to explain to him why I left...and then I need to offer that very good man a proper goodbye."

CHAPTER 51

Chesham, England

Andrew ran upstairs to the bedroom where he had been staying the past ten days, surprised at how excited he was to see his grandparents' estate. *My estate,* he reminded himself. How strange to think that he now owned a castle in England. He had been eager to bring Tonna with him, but surprisingly, she had begged off. *"With Father away, someone needs to keep an eye on things here."* Andrew had been adamant. *"Come with us, Tonna. I hate to leave you here without either one of us to watch over you."* She had grinned. *"Though I appreciate you both, I have my father's security team, along with Scotland Yard's officers, and two private bodyguards who refuse to let me out of their sight. I'm safer here than anywhere else, Andrew."* It was hard to argue. And in that instant, she had reminded him more of Maddi than at any other time since he had met her. *Stubbornness must be genetic.*

But still he was worried for her. He had promised Kauffold he would keep an eye on her, so, at the last minute, he had asked Donovan to stay at the Kauffold estate. Donovan had agreed without hesitation. *"Whatever you need me to do, Andrew."*

Andrew had made a quick call to Kauffold, letting him know that he was still going to Darlington for the night, but that Tonna had elected not to go. Kauffold had been beside himself. Andrew had assured him that Donovan would look after her. And though Andrew felt confident with such an arrangement, for whatever reason, he sensed that Kauffold did not.

Tonna had told Andrew that she would use the time to dig deeper into the mysterious Jacob. There was no question that Tonna was well-suited for such a task. She had proven her skills with both technology and sleuthing when she had hacked multiple U.S. computer systems to determine that Maddi was her biological mother. Nonetheless, Andrew had felt it to be a bad idea. *"Snooping around like that will get you into trouble, Tonna."* She had assured him that she had perfected the art of cyberstalking. *"If the CIA and the Secret Service couldn't find me when I was digging into Maddi's life, I don't think this Jacob character will have any better luck."*

Andrew had to admit; it would be helpful to learn Jacob's identity. Andrew hadn't told Tonna of Todd Jackson's comment that Jacob might be tied in some way to Maddi's death. All he had told her was that a terrible man who had held a personal grudge against Maddi had made a reference to Jacob, and that whoever Jacob was, he was powerful, was somehow affiliated with the Pentagon, and had likely known Maddi personally. He hoped that those few details, along with the name Jacob, might lead her to his identity.

As Kauffold had been walking out the door of the estate, he had confided in Andrew that the 'old friend' he was meeting was Johnny Canterbury. Both Kauffold and Andrew had met Canterbury back in March when they had attended a meeting of a secret organization, The Morning Star. Established around sixty years ago, the group was committed to keeping secret the existence of a powerful warship that possessed technology beyond anything ever imagined. The meeting in March had been Andrew's and Canterbury's first time with the group, and Canterbury had tried to bond with him over that fact. Andrew hadn't been in the mood to bond with any of them, especially Canterbury. Something about him was off-putting. From what Andrew could tell, Kauffold had felt the same. As a matter of fact, Kauffold had made no secret of it during the meetings. But according to Kauffold, Canterbury's request had been uncharacteristically urgent. *"It concerns China, Andrew. Something about how he and I are the world's last best hope for peace."* He had chuckled. *"I can't very well ignore that, now can I?"*

No, I guess you can't, Andrew thought as he packed his bag. He was grateful – not for the first time – that it had been Maddi's destiny to deal with such concerns, not his.

He was disappointed that Tonna wasn't coming with him. He would have enjoyed her company. She reminded him of Maddi...easy to talk to, inquisitive, eager to listen, yet ready to offer her own point of view. He had gotten to know Tonna well in the ten days they had been there. Between long walks in the garden, and late nights with a bottle of Arthur's finest port, they had talked for hours about Maddi, his and Maddi's childhood growing up in Indiana, and Tonna's life as an aristocrat in England. It had been healing...for both of them.

Tonna had commented on Andrew's strong resemblance to Maddi, which he couldn't deny now that his hair was blonde and he was wearing the blue contacts. It had been Donovan's idea that he stay with the disguise while overseas. *"One never knows when we'll run into someone who might give a damn who you are, Andrew."* Andrew couldn't argue the point. No one knew better than he that the U.S. Pentagon had a very long reach.

At one point, Tonna had asked him about his current family, and he had choked up, realizing in that instant just how much he missed Adam and Amanda. Never had he gone so long without seeing or talking to them. *"You'll love Adam, Tonna. I'm sure he's going to be smart and kind...thanks to Amanda."*

She had laughed, and had then shaken her head. *"I'm so much older than he is. I'll seem more like an aunt than a cousin."*

He had nodded. *"I was older when I had him...and Maddi was so young when she had you."* He had quickly added, *"...and I can only imagine how hard it must have been for her to give up the baby that she had been carrying for nine months."*

Tonna had smiled and – with tears in her eyes – had said, *"Yes, at first I struggled with that. But then Father said the most wonderful thing. He said, 'It takes a remarkable woman – a selfless and a strong woman – to give away her child so that that child could have a better life.' I have thought of it that way ever since."*

It was then that the strangest thing happened. Andrew had pulled out the medallion his mother had left for him, prepared to share with Tonna the tragic story of Jeannie's despair over the loss of her husband – Tonna's grandfather – and her subsequent struggle with alcoholism. Tonna's eyes had lit up at the sight of the gold coin, and she had immediately run to her room. She had come back with a similar medallion, holding it out to Andrew as if it was the Holy Grail.

"Where did you get that?" he had asked.

"From Annabelle, my adoptive mother."

"Had she told you what it was?"

"No, only that I should hang onto it…that it might be important someday."

Which was more or less what Jeannie had told Andrew in her letter. Only according to Jeannie, the medallion had come from their grandfather, Harold. Tonna had said that she had tried to investigate the coin's history, but had come up empty. It wasn't listed in any registry, and she could find nothing about it on the internet. They had compared the two coins, stunned by their similarities, as well as their differences. Andrew hadn't given much thought to the letters on his coin, "NEATLAIDIBA," guessing the foreign word was inspirational, or that it identified some obscure person or town. On the other side of his coin was a faded image of a woman with wings; an angel, he had decided. He had more or less dismissed that, as well. But as he and Tonna had compared the two half-dollar-sized coins, for the first time he had noticed a faint "Partizans" etched just above the angel. Tonna's coin had the word "Mieru" carved over top of a different woman, also with wings. On the other side of her coin was written the word "PRETESTIBA."

"The all-capitalized word is Latvian," she had said, adding, *"It means resistance. But I can't find a meaning for the word 'Mieru' anywhere."*

Andrew had frowned. *"Latvian…interesting. What does Neatlaidiba mean?"*

Tonna had held up her hand. *"Give me a minute."* She had run out of the room and had come back quickly. *"Persistence. It means persistence in Latvian."*

Andrew had nodded. *"Resistance and persistence; good words for the '40's."*

He shoved a change of clothes into his overnight bag, and was about to zip it, when he pulled out the coin. He looked again at the woman with wings. He ran his thumb over the imprint, then shoved the coin in his pocket. It was intriguing that it had been Annabelle and Harold who had given them the coins. Though they had been friends, the coins would imply something stronger. Not necessarily romantic, but a tie to something far greater than simple friendship. Especially since both of them had insisted that the bearer of the coin *"…hold onto it as it might someday be important."*

He zipped his bag and sighed. *Maybe I'll find a clue at the castle.*

There were several things he hoped to find at the Darlington castle. First, was an answer to the question that had haunted him for the last thirty years. Why had his father left his advantaged life in Darlington to travel all the way to America to be a cop in a small Midwest town? Why would any man make such a choice?

He also hoped to learn what Jeannie might have meant in her final letter when she had referenced Maddi's locket and had said, *"...the locket holds the key."* He had searched Maddi's belongings, but had found no locket. *Maybe I'll find it at the castle.*

Lastly, he hoped to learn more about Maddi's time at the estate. She had been only fifteen years old at the time – and pregnant – likely feeling very alone in the world. And though it was that trip to their grandparents' castle that had transformed her into the amazing woman she had become, it had to have been quite an ordeal. Not only had she had a child while she was there...which she had more or less been forced to give up, but now he knew that just prior to coming, she had somehow been involved in the death of Evan Jackson. There was no question that she would have been struggling with the aftermath, regardless of her role.

Late last night, as he and Tonna had been sipping wine in the den, long after Arthur and Donovan had gone to bed, Tonna had asked Andrew about her biological father. *"I'm just so curious about him...what did he look like? What sort of work did he do in America?"* It had been the only time she had asked about him. Andrew had been hesitant to tell her much. *"Tonna, he wasn't a nice man."*

Tonna had sighed. *"Maddi told me the same thing."* She had frowned. *She said that his official cause of death was quite similar to her own father... that he had died from a robbery-gone-bad."*

Andrew had been at a loss for words. Had Maddi never told Tonna the truth about how Evan Jackson had died? Then again, how could she? She couldn't very well tell Tonna that Jackson had been killed...murdered, either by Maddi's mother – Tonna's grandmother – or by Maddi herself – Tonna's mom.

He had added, *"Did Maddi tell you anything else about him?"*

To which Tonna had replied, *"Only that he was a police officer...a rather corrupt police officer."*

Andrew had frowned, but had said nothing.

Tonna had narrowed her eyes. *"Can you maybe tell me a bit more about him? What he looked like? Or maybe something good about the man?"*

Andrew had let out a sigh. *"I didn't really know him, Tonna. I will tell you, however, that everything that happened to him was justified. Can we leave it at that?"*

She had agreed...reluctantly. But Andrew had seen a flash in her eyes, and he had known then that Tonna – like Maddi – wasn't only curious, but very determined.

As he threw his bag over his shoulder and walked out of the bedroom, he was suddenly uneasy. There was no doubt in his mind that, sooner or later, Tonna would learn the truth...not only about her father's despicable life, but also about his death.

CHAPTER 52

London, England

Arthur Kauffold leaned back in the sleek Rolls Royce as it barreled down the M1 highway on its way to London. The call from Johnny Canterbury had surprised him. Not only were members of the Morning Star supposed to keep their distance from one another, but the young man's intensity had seemed a bit uncharacteristic. *"You must join me, Ambassador. I feel we may be the last best hope for peace."* Kauffold could hardly turn down such a request, so here he was on an overcast Saturday morning heading to London to meet with Canterbury.

But why Canterbury? he kept asking himself. Yes, the man had been chosen to serve as liaison between the Pentagon and the UK, but that hardly seemed adequate to qualify him for a mission of such delicacy. The only thing Canterbury had offered as he had invited Kauffold to meet with him was that his fluency in Chinese, combined with his ties to the Pentagon, may prove to be a helpful combination. *Dear God, let's hope so,* Kauffold thought as he looked out at the darkening sky.

His other concern was that Johnny had told him to pack a bag. *"This may involve an overnight stay."* Kauffold didn't like to be away from his estate for more than a day, and he hardly thought that a visit with Johnny Canterbury should involve any sort of overnight endeavor. He had packed a bag, nonetheless, and he sighed as he looked over at the brown leather grip sitting next to him. He had brought a heavy winter coat, as well, in case negotiations forced him to venture into the night air.

He had to agree that some sort of intervention was needed on the world stage. Especially after Russia's antics. The world could hardly afford for a conflict between China and America to be added to the chaos. The recent intelligence suggesting that a U.S. senator had been sent to assassinate the son of a Chinese military leader seemed outrageous. A CIA claim that China was holding the man and his bodyguard prisoner in a secret prison seemed even more outrageous, and China's regime was becoming more indignant by the hour. The U.S. had been forced to issue a statement through the State Department pulling back on the claim, as well as denying government approval for any mission against China's military leaders. The back and forth had escalated over the past 24 hours, leaving the two nations about as far apart as they could be. *Which is where I come in,* thought Kauffold, though he hadn't served as a diplomat for nearly a decade. But he still knew what it took to bring leaders together.

And it didn't hurt that a representative from America's State Department had called him just minutes ago on the car phone in the back of his Rolls Royce. It had been patched through by way of the embassy. The representative, who said that she was calling on behalf of the Secretary herself, had passed on the Secretary's concerns regarding China. She had added that Kauffold's input would be immensely helpful. Kauffold had been touched by her confidence in him. He and the Secretary had met during the Earth Summit in Rio de Janeiro in June of 1992, when she, too, had been an ambassador. They had hit it off, and had made sure to stay in touch over the past twelve years. The representative had quoted the Secretary as saying, *"...Kauffold's brilliance with diplomacy is the one thing that might turn this debacle around."*

He chuckled. *How could I not at least look into the matter after such praise?*

He looked out at the sparse countryside and sighed. He had been good at his job, and had truly loved it. The thought that he might do it again – even remotely for just a few hours – was exhilarating. But why London? Why couldn't Johnny come to him in Chesham? Kauffold hated to leave Tonna...even for a short while. Especially when her safety was at risk. The Yard had refused to elaborate on who was after her, which had infuriated him. *"Not to worry, Ambassador...once we have the threat contained, we will tell you everything."* Kauffold bristled. *Like that is any comfort.*

To make matters worse, as Kauffold had been leaving the estate, Andrew had informed him that he was going to Darlington for the night. *I'd like to bring Tonna with me, so, of course, I'll bring Donovan, as well.* Though Kauffold had absolute faith in Andrew to keep Tonna safe, he didn't feel the same about Donovan. *There's just something not altogether genuine about that man.*

But then, just minutes ago, Andrew had called – also on the car phone because Kauffold refused to carry a cellphone – saying that Tonna had decided to stay home. Apparently, she had insisted that someone was needed to keep an eye on things while Kauffold was gone. *"That's preposterous, Andrew. There are plenty of aides to watch over the place."* Andrew had agreed, but had reminded Kauffold that Tonna was the genetic offspring of the very stubborn Maddi. Kauffold had had to laugh in spite of himself. Donovan had apparently agreed to stay behind. And though Kauffold couldn't say that he fully trusted the man, he did feel that Donovan wouldn't hurt Tonna...*would he?* Besides, Tonna would have Kauffold's security team and the men from the Yard. *That should surely be enough,* he thought as he sat back with a sigh.

He was surprised to find himself looking forward to seeing Canterbury. Though the young man was a bit over the top, he had energy and a sense of humor; two qualities Kauffold admired. He was curious how Canterbury had come to be involved in the negotiations. Though Johnny was quite personable, and apparently knew how to speak Chinese, he had seemed a bit naïve for such an endeavor. *I guess I'll find out soon enough.*

He arrived at the agreed-upon meeting place – an inn on the north side of London – just before noon. Known as the Copper Kettle, the exclusive inn was nestled in the Lake District of northern London. The remote location would give them privacy, as well as a first-rate cup of leek soup. Kauffold required the first; he relished the second.

His driver stopped the car, then stepped out and opened Kauffold's door. The former ambassador slid from the back, leaving his overcoat and his overnight bag on the seat. "Wait here, Conrad."

The man nodded, and Kauffold – smartly dressed in a charcoal suit with a black bowler hat – walked into the inn. He tugged at the lapels of his suitcoat, its broad cut only partially hiding his generous midsection, which had gotten even more generous since the suit had originally been fitted.

He was greeted by a smiling hostess, who escorted him toward where Johnny was sitting at a booth in the back. Kauffold noticed him right away. The young man was hard to miss. His long blonde hair was a bit flashy, but it was his demeanor that made him stand out in a crowd. He half-stood as he waved eagerly from the booth. His lean frame hadn't changed, and he was even wearing the same suit he had worn to that very first meeting of the Morning Star back in March.

Kauffold walked over and motioned for him to sit down. "You're supposed to keep a low profile, Canterbury!" he whispered sternly as he sat across from him.

Johnny grinned sheepishly. "Oh yes, I forgot."

Kauffold removed his hat, as he shook his head and sighed. "Have you ordered something to eat?"

Johnny nodded. "Yes, sir. I was starved. A bacon sandwich is on its way."

Kauffold waved for a waiter. "A cup of leek soup, please."

The waiter nodded and walked away. Kauffold looked at Johnny. "I'm surprised to say that it is actually good to see you. I hope all is well."

Johnny laughed. "Things are going quite well, thank you, sir."

"Glad to hear it. Now, let's cut to the chase. What is it you're proposing?"

Johnny pulled a rolled sheet of paper from his pocket, flattened it on the table, and, in a quiet voice, began reading.

> "The U.S. State Department requests that Johnny Canterbury, citizen of England, accompany Great Britain's former U.S. Ambassador, Sir Arthur Kauffold, to Beijing, China, to intercede regarding the possible rogue actions of Senator Charles Sturgill from Maine, and to investigate his disappearance."

The memo was signed by the Deputy Secretary of State, as well as the acting President, Robert Harrington III. It was stamped with the seal of the United States of America.

Kauffold's eyes widened. In a hushed whisper, he said, "I'm being asked to accompany you...to *China?*"

"Yes sir. How else are we to solve this mess?"

Kauffold's left eye was twitching. He leaned in. Still whispering, he said, "You didn't say anything about *going to China* in your phone call."

Johnny leaned in, as well. "I told you to pack a bag."

"Yes, and I thought that meant that we might deliberate – here in London –through the night perhaps, possibly accompanied by a representative from China."

Johnny grinned. "C'mon, Ambassador, it will be quite the adventure, yes?"

"No." Kauffold tugged at his mustache. Keeping his voice low, he added, "...assuming we get to China without incident, how do you propose we score a visit with the Chinese President?"

"It has already been taken care of. America's acting President, Harrington, has spoken with him. He has agreed to meet with us tomorrow morning."

Kauffold sat back, aghast. "Tomorrow morning? Why, that would mean that we need to leave...*for China*...in the next hour or two!"

Johnny nodded. "Yes, sir. We're booked on a flight out of Heathrow at four p.m. It will get us to China tomorrow morning around eight, their time."

Kauffold stared at Canterbury, dumbfounded. The waiter set his soup in front of him, but he wasn't sure he could eat. Then it occurred to him that he might not get a decent meal any time soon, so he picked up his spoon and dug in. Johnny's sandwich had come at the same time; he dug in, as well.

After several spoonful's, Kauffold looked at Johnny and frowned. "I don't want to go to China. I'm an old man, and China is a long plane ride away."

Johnny smiled soothingly. "I understand, but you were recommended by the Prime Minister himself." Johnny rubbed his chin. "How did he put it?" He lowered his voice dramatically, *"Why, Arthur Kauffold is the only man who can get it done."*

Kauffold stifled a grin. "The Prime Minister said that?"

Johnny nodded. "His exact words, according to my Pentagon friend."

Kauffold wiped his mouth with his napkin and sighed. "Fine. I'll do it... in the name of peace." He took a quick sip of water.

Johnny grabbed his water and held it in a salute. "For the sake of the world."

The two men clinked their glasses, but only Johnny was smiling. Kauffold didn't have a good feeling about the trip...not at all. He would need to call Tonna and let her know that he wouldn't be home for at least a couple of days.

He looked at Johnny and frowned. "If our flight is at four, we should probably get on our way." He reached for his wallet.

"It's on me, Ambassador." Johnny chuckled. "Actually, it's on the Pentagon." He pulled out his wallet and flashed a credit card. With a sly grin, he said, "Expense account for our journey."

Kauffold sighed and pushed back his chair. "A quick meeting tomorrow morning, then we'll be on our way home, right?"

Johnny nodded. "That's the plan." He smiled. "But I must let you know that I have been asked to look in on the prisoner...the senator, Charles Sturgill." Johnny shook his head and muttered, "Idiot." He gave a quick smile. "But I'm hoping that we can take care of that right after our meeting with China's President."

"And if we can't?"

"Well then, I guess we'll be forced to stay a bit longer, sir."

CHAPTER 53

Beijing, China

"Just a cup of coffee, please." Maddi gave a quick smile to a waitress, who, in spite of the language barrier, seemed to understand. Maddi had been in Beijing for nearly two weeks and she was exhausted. She hadn't heard from Lili since those first messages when she had said she needed help. *What if this is nothing but a silly goose chase? What if I was so desperate for a purpose to my life, that I imagined the girl's cry for help?* It was certainly plausible; Maddi had never felt so useless. And her search for Lili had turned up nothing. She had looked in so many places...in so many motels, hostels, and even in the orphanages that were prevalent throughout the city.

She pulled out her wallet. Only fifty euros left. She needed to find a place to stay and a way to live. Maddi needed a life. That was what she was supposed to have found back in Corsica. But she had given it up...*for this silly escapade that has done nothing but use up all the money I had.*

The waitress brought her coffee and she smiled her thanks. She picked up the cup and sipped the hot liquid which would likely cost her about twenty yuan; the equivalent of about a quarter of a euro. She grinned as she did the math. *I can have 199 more cups of coffee.*

She cupped her hands around the warm mug trying to think where she might sleep for the night. She had spent the last two nights in a nearby motel. But it had taken a lot of her cash. She couldn't afford another night there, and she certainly didn't want to sleep in any of the hostels she had seen in her quest to find Lili. *Maybe I'll just stay here for the night.*

She leaned back against the booth and closed her eyes, adjusting her bag under her head like a pillow. She was so tired. She had cat-napped for what seemed like most of her adult life, and it was starting to catch up with her. *What I wouldn't give for a real bed, with silk sheets and tons of blankets.*

Suddenly, out of nowhere, she saw a crystal-clear image. Richer than a dream and more vivid than a nightmare, she could see stark brown mountains, tall enough that they had snow on top, with narrow fir trees winding their way up the side in the shape of an "S."

Then, as quickly as it came, the image was gone. She opened her eyes and looked around, wondering if maybe she had dozed off after looking at the cover of a magazine or a newspaper. She saw nothing...no magazine or newspaper in sight. As a matter of fact, she had read neither in all the time she had been in China.

She stood and walked to the front of the diner, looking out a window for those same mountains, thinking maybe she had caught a glimpse of them when she had walked in. All she saw was a dark street with cars and lights and lots of people. She returned to her booth and picked up her coffee. The image had been so clear, so real. *Almost like a message,* came a thought from nowhere. She held the warm cup in both hands. As she was about to take a sip, it hit her. *Lili is trying to show me where she is.*

She set down her cup, put on a wool cape she had bought two days ago, and grabbed her carryon. She walked to the counter and pulled a euro from her wallet. As she handed it to the clerk, she spotted a box filled with ink pens. She picked up one of the pens. A bright pink flower was carved at the top, with writing underneath. It caught her eye. "What does this mean?" she asked as she pointed at the writing.

The woman smiled and bowed her head. "Lotus Flower. Important to China...to life. Symbol of honesty, purity." She handed Maddi her change.

Maddi pocketed the change. "May I?" she asked, as she again pointed to the pen. The girl nodded. Maddi slid the pen in her pocket. *Maybe it will bring me luck.*

She left the diner and turned right. Cold air had swept in from the north; she clung to the cape as she adjusted her carryon over her shoulder. She needed to find a picture of the mountains Lili had shown her. *I need a library.* She hurried down the street, scanning faces, looking for anyone who wasn't Asian. She ran straight into a Chinese woman carrying a bag of groceries. Several items fell to the ground.

"I am so sorry," Maddi said, as she helped the woman refill her bag.

"It is fine...but you must watch where you go."

She speaks English! "I...I wonder if you could direct me to a library."

The woman stuffed the last of her groceries into the bag. "That way," she said, and pointed toward downtown. "About two block. Tu Shu Guan."

Maddi thanked her and ran down the street, covering the two blocks in less than a minute. She looked everywhere. Just as she was about to cross the street to the next block, she saw it. A small, nondescript building, with the words "Tu Shu Guan" printed on the side, both in words and in Chinese symbols. Maddi ran inside.

A woman walked up to her and said "Wo men hen kuai jiu guan men le.".

Maddi frowned. "English?"

The woman flinched. "We close soon."

Maddi nodded. "I'll be quick." She smiled. "Map of Beijing mountains?"

The woman directed her to a row of books along one wall.

Maddi went to the row and searched the titles. She found a book with 'Beijing Topography' written in English on the spine. She opened it to a two-page map with different colors that represented different rises in the area comprising Beijing. Lili had given her two clues. The first was that she was near Beijing. The second – if Maddi was to believe the vision – was that she could see a mountain with a unique display of trees. From the map, it appeared her best bet for mountains was north of the city. For Lili to have such a detailed view, she would need to be close enough to see the fir trees. *But how do I find that exact spot?* There was no way she could cover the entire north end of Beijing on foot. *I'll need a cab.* She closed the book and pulled out her wallet. She frowned; only 49 euros. She shoved the wallet in her bag and left the library. She waved down a taxi, slid in back, and said, "Can you take me north?"

The man frowned.

"North of the city." Maddi started to pull out the ink pen to draw on her palm a map of where she wanted to go, when he waved his hand dismissively and eased into the flow of traffic. He made a few sharp turns, then pulled onto what looked like a highway. As they left the heart of the city, she began to see mountains silhouetted against the black sky. It helped that the moon was nearly full. Now all she needed was to find the mountain in her vision, with trees that covered it in the shape of an "S." When they had completely left the city behind, she asked the driver to drive back and forth so that she could look at each mountain. He scowled, but did as she asked.

"What you look for?" he asked after about fifteen minutes.

"I...I received a...photo...from a friend. It showed a mountain with a row of fir trees shaped like this," she made an S with her finger.

He nodded. "Ah yes. Yanqing District." He sped ahead. "It further west." He drove for about ten miles. The further they got from the city, the fewer cars they saw.

Maddi was looking out the window, when all at once, she yelled, "Stop!"

The driver slowed the taxi and pulled to the side of the road.

Maddi looked at the mountain. She was seeing almost the exact same image she had seen in her vision. She looked around for a house or a hotel. There was nothing. *Where are you, Lili...where were you looking from?* She was in the middle of nowhere. All she could see was a rundown shopping center, and remnants of an old train station that was clearly no longer in use. "Let me out here," she said.

The driver frowned. "Not good place."

She pulled out her wallet. "I'm...I'm sure I'll be fine."

She took out her last 49 euros and handed them to the driver. "I know it's not yuan, but it's all I've got."

He looked at her and frowned. He took the money and watched as she stepped out of the cab. She was about to walk away, when he yelled. "Wait." He got out of the car and handed her a one-hundred-yuan note. "Take. You might need."

She wanted to hug him, but instead, she took his hand and smiled. "Thank you." He gave a quick nod and hurried back to his cab. She stashed the money in her pocket, then stood there, unsure where to go or what to do. *Lili...whoever she is...is somewhere nearby, and she needs my help.*

She looked over her shoulder. The cab driver was still there. He was watching her. She gave him a quick wave, and yelled, "I'll be fine...I promise."

He shook his head, hesitated, then drove away.

Maddi was shivering and wrapped the cape so it covered the lower half of her face. She looked around. The cabby was right. It wasn't a good area. In spite of the moonlight, the road was dark and the area looked deserted. She pulled out the 100-yaun note and was about to stuff it in her wallet, when she realized that she had left the wallet and her travel bag in the cab. *My ID!* She was about to run after the driver, when all at once, she heard the sound of an engine. She darted behind a tree, waiting as it drew closer. She saw a military-type truck drive past and pull into a gate. It drove toward the old train station, then abruptly turned onto a dirt road. Staying low in the brush, she edged closer. Her legs were shaking. *I need to sit.* A newspaper was lying nearby; she grabbed it and laid it under her as she sat behind a thick oak tree.

She saw the truck go down a steep hill, then stop outside what looked like an old warehouse. She waited. Several men jumped from the back of the truck; they were dressed in uniform and were carrying rifles. *Soldiers.* She counted them. Ten in all. Half positioned themselves outside the warehouse, while the other half marched into the building. She then saw five soldiers come from inside and walk to the truck. They were joined by five soldiers outside the building. Now she understood. *Shift change.* Which meant that the building was some sort of military garrison. She tensed and slid lower in the brush. *And I'd bet my hundred-yuan bill that Lili is in there.*

CHAPTER 54

London, England

Kauffold scowled as he sat in the back of the Rolls Royce. Though Johnny had suggested that they ride together to the airport, Kauffold had insisted that he go alone. *"I have some rather delicate phone calls to make, Johnny."* He didn't actually have delicate phone calls to make, he just couldn't stomach the thought of spending the next 30-minutes with Johnny, especially when he was about to spend the next twenty-four hours with him.

Kauffold did need to make one phone call, however. He had to let Tonna know that he wouldn't be home for at least a couple of days. Andrew had indicated that he and Donovan were hoping to head back to America early Monday morning. Kauffold would do everything in his power to be home before they left.

He reached for his car phone to call Tonna, and was startled to hear it ring. Few people knew the number: only Tonna, his butler, the embassy, MI6, and Walter Henderson. Walter had been given the number due to the Morning Star; the MI6 administrator, Adam Percy, had been given the number due to their friendship.

There was no caller ID, so he answered with a stern, "Kauffold here."

"Ambassador, it's me, Percy."

Kauffold's eyes widened. He had reached out to Percy days ago regarding Walter's request for information related to a possible MI6 agent who went by the name Shaw. "Have you got news for me?"

"I do. But it wasn't easy. The guy isn't on any of the MI6 rolls; he is what is referred to as a lone operative."

"A lone operative?"

"Yes. He works off the grid."

"I see. And why is that?"

There was a pause. "He isn't necessarily on the...up and up."

Kauffold narrowed his eyes. "What type of work does he do?"

Another pause. "Tasks that we don't want MI6 to be associated with."

"I see. Can you tell me what the man has been up to? Or maybe where I might find him should I want to talk to him?"

Kauffold heard his friend clear his throat. "Here's the thing, Kauffold. Shaw hasn't been seen or heard from since August."

Kauffold sat back in the seat. "Oh my. I'm guessing that is unusual?"

He heard a sigh. "It most certainly is. Shaw is privy to information that could be damaging should it fall into the wrong hands. Because of that access, combined with his rather questionable history, he is expected to report in at least once a week."

"Oh dear. That definitely sounds like a problem." Kauffold frowned. "Thank you, Percy, for looking into this."

"My pleasure, Ambassador."

Kauffold ended the call. The information was disturbing, if for no other reason than the man – who Walter had implied might be a threat to the Morning Star – was now missing. He found Walter's number in the phone's contact list and dialed.

It was answered after only two rings. "This is Walter Henderson."

"Walter, it's me, Kauffold." He sighed. "I think we might have a problem."

CHAPTER 55

Somewhere in the Katahdan Mountains

Cravens had spent the last hour-and-a half pondering Foster's revelation about Morningstar. He had gone outside for a smoke – which was what he had been on his way to do when he had met Foster in the hall – and had then come back in and grabbed a cup of coffee from the make-shift kitchen. He had carried it to his bedroom, still stunned by Foster's proclamation. *"Between you and me, I think Morningstar might be Jacob."* If it was true; if a highly-positioned Pentagon aide was the mastermind behind not only all that was going on around the globe, but the plot against the President, then America – and the world – was in deep trouble. Especially since that same President felt compelled to protect him. It was actually an impossible situation, and Cravens knew, at some point, he would need to talk directly to Knight.

But that wasn't going to happen anytime soon; Knight was either holed up in his office trying to avert World War III, or he was at the far end of the hideaway where the makers had built a master suite of sorts, replete with a bedroom, a master bath and a den. The few times Cravens had seen him, the poor man looked exhausted.

Cravens was now on his second cup of coffee, and, after a deep sigh, felt ready to resume his review of the papers that Foster had delivered to his room the night before. He looked again at the first page, which involved email exchanges between a man named Levi and another man, Jacob. If what Foster had just told him was true, then that meant that the top aide to the top general of the United States military had *manufactured* a Russian assault on Latvia, an assault that was about to lead to an all-out war. Foster had said that he had urged Knight to have Harrington place a call to Latvia's military leaders to tell them to stand down, and let them know that Putin may not have initiated the attack, after all. Knight had decided against it, stating that it was too late. *"The conflict has progressed too far, Foster. Russia has already moved troops to the border. To stand down now would be like handing Latvia to Putin."* Knight had gone on to say that, regardless of whether taking Latvia had been Putin's original intent, to make it easy for him now seemed foolish. *"No, at this point it will take shrewd negotiating to stop what has already been put into motion."*

Cravens frowned and ran his hands through his hair. *Shrewd negotiating isn't the half of it...it'll take a damn miracle to stop this train.* He had finished the coffee and was contemplating a third cup. *I'll get through a few more of these first.* He thumbed through the next several pages, which he had already seen; summaries of the surveillance footage that showed Sturgill traveling to China, the accusation that he had tried to kill a Chinese military leader, and a description of two men being dragged into an unmarked facility near Beijing. *Now, on to the new stuff,* he thought with a sigh. He flipped to the next page. It was a grainy satellite photo that showed two men – Sturgill and Frisk? – standing against a cracked stone wall. He looked closer. As far as he was concerned, the two men could be anyone. He turned to the next page. Another grainy photo. He was able to see what looked like a carefully hidden fence; that was about it. A tag line read: "Chinese warehouse ten miles northwest of Beijing; possible prison." Though the U.S. had always suspected that such prisons existed, that satellite footage, dated just thirty-six hours ago, offered possible proof. But Cravens would need more than a grainy photograph of a fence to challenge the Chinese.

He reached for the next page. It was another photo. This one showed a truck stopped outside the fence. There was no writing on the truck; nothing to suggest its purpose. The next page was another photo of the same truck, now inside the fence line. Men – soldiers – could be seen in the process of jumping out of the back. Cravens' eyes narrowed. *Now we're getting somewhere.*

The next page was another photo, just as grainy. He laid it on the desk and grabbed a magnifying glass from his top drawer. He held it over the photo, and was able to see the vague outline of a building about a hundred yards behind what looked like the same truck. Though it was impossible to know for sure, it seemed likely that the soldiers were going to that building. Were they guarding it? *Also likely,* he thought. If it was a prison – which seemed like a safe bet considering the number of guards that had been assigned – then who was inside?

He looked closer at the building, using the magnifier to try to glean one or two meaningful details. He couldn't; the quality was too poor. He set the magnifying glass on the desk and flipped to the next page. It was a written summary documenting what appeared to be a shift-change at the very same facility. Every morning at eight a.m. China time, ten men were driven into the facility. They got off the truck, and then, a minute later, ten men climbed aboard. Two shifts of ten each, for a total of twenty soldiers who oversaw whatever was hidden inside that facility. A sizable force to guard what had been reported by China's map makers to be an empty warehouse. Cravens ran his hands through his hair. *What – or who – are you guarding, fellas?*

He turned to the next page. Another photo that showed soldiers in the process of getting on or off the truck. It was stamped for eight that same night. *No surprise.*

He stood and walked to the kitchen for another cup of coffee. As he filled his cup, he tried to think who or what might be hidden in the building north of Beijing. He added sugar, then walked back to his bedroom. When he walked in, he saw that several more pages of reports had been left for him on his desk. He sat down and grabbed the top sheet of paper. He looked at it and sighed. Another poor quality photograph. *Can't the CIA do any better than this?* He was about to lay it with the others when he stopped. There was a stamped insignia across the top, with a hand written name next to it. *"Uzbekistan. Timothy Johannson."* This photo hadn't come from the CIA; it had come out of Uzbekistan, likely picked up by an NSA reconnaissance agent doing routine surveillance. Date and time were stamped next to Johannson's name. *"Sat. Nov. 13th, 1:00 p.m., GMT + 5."* Cravens frowned. *One p.m. in Uzbekistan is four a.m. here...less than five hours ago.* He grabbed the magnifying glass and stared at the image. This time, he could make out five men; three of them were holding rifles. Using his desk phone, which had been hard-wired within the facility, he called the security room. "Patrick, if I give you a photo, can you work your magic so that I might be able to tell who the hell I'm looking at?"

"I can certainly try, Agent Cravens."

Cravens walked the document to the security room and handed it to Patrick.

The man took it and nodded. "I'll 'ave somethin' for ye soon, Agent."

Cravens nodded his thanks and walked back to his room. He sat and sipped his coffee as he grabbed the next document. Another blurry photo, this one from the Defense Intelligence Agency. Using the magnifier, he gave it a closer look. He was looking at three men. Details were vague, but he could see rifles in the hands of two of them. He looked at the third man. His eyes widened. He looked again. *No way.* He checked the time and date. *Thursday, November 11ᵗʰ, 11:05 a.m., China Standard Time.*

His hand was shaking so he set the coffee on his desk. He pulled out the next page from the stack of papers. It was the same image, only this time he could see details; the sun was shining directly on the prisoner's face. *How did this get missed?* He held the magnifying glass over the image. His heart began to pound. Though the man had different hair, he had the same eyes...the same face...the same body type. Cravens had spent 48 very intense hours with that man not too long ago; he would know him anywhere. He rubbed his eyes in disbelief. *Martin Henderson has been captured by the Chinese...and is being held inside what I'm now almost certain is a secret prison.*

CHAPTER 56

Latvia

Walter Henderson lowered the visor in his BMW as the sun broke free from the clouds. It was late in the day, and the glare made it almost impossible to see the highway. He shook his head and frowned. The phone call from Kauffold was troubling, to say the least. Not only had Walter already suspected that Shaw was questionable, but now the man who Cravens had unwittingly permitted to see secret drawings in his father's briefcase had gone missing. He frowned. *What do I do now?*

He would need to call a meeting of the Morning Star, that much was certain. But the timing couldn't be worse. Not only was he tied up with the war in Latvia, but his son had left for China two weeks ago to find the missing girl, Lili, and Walter had yet to hear from him. On top of it all, Morningstar had shown up – unannounced – at the Henderson castle every day for the past two weeks. At each visit he would request *'...another tour of your lovely estate, Walter,'* after which he would storm into the security room and insist on reviewing security protocols for various scenarios. *"I am here to help, Walter. Readiness is everything when it comes to fighting Putin."*

Whatever, Walter thought as he sped down the A11 highway. Though he wanted more than anything to tell the guy to go to hell, he couldn't. Morningstar was there on behalf of America's top military man, General Alexander Daniels. For now, Walter – and Dora – would simply have to put up with him.

I think she's gonna crack before I do, he thought with a chuckle. Dora hadn't liked or trusted Morningstar from the minute he walked through their door. And her call to Martin had only reinforced it. *"Why are we putting up with him, Walter?"* Though Walter was wondering the same thing, he had told her what he had been telling himself for the past two weeks. *"We must keep our friends close, our enemies closer."* Did he believe it? Not really, but he saw no way around it, at least for now.

He had been driving for nearly an hour and was eager to get back to the castle. He didn't like to leave Dora alone there, not with Morningstar popping in at odd hours throughout the day. But the meeting he had just attended was important, and couldn't be done over the phone. And though it had gone well, it hadn't gone as well as he had hoped.

He had met with the military leader of the Lithuanian army, a man by the name of Petrauskas, whom he knew from decades of their shared history fighting Russian insurgents. Though the man had only been Lithuania's military leader for less than a year, he had been serving in their army one way or another for the last twenty years. He knew what was at stake if Putin succeeded in taking Latvia.

Walter's journey had had a dual purpose. Not only did he want to reaffirm that the Lithuanian army would fight in lockstep with Latvian armed forces should the need arise, but he also wanted to learn if efforts were underway among Lithuania's civilian population to undermine that pledge. Based on recent newspaper articles, as well as Justice's comments to Samuels two months ago, there was cause for concern.

The military leader had started the meeting by commenting on a different newspaper article – from thirteen days ago – that had stated unambiguously that a representative from America's Pentagon, Edward Morningstar, had attended a dinner with the Hendersons, and was now working hand in hand with Walter Henderson to assure a victory in Latvia's fight against Russia. Walter had had to hide his disgust, as the Lithuanian leader expressed dismay and concern over the fact that America had asserted such a presence in the war, suggesting it would likely spur Putin to escalate.

Though Walter had seen the same article – the very morning after that dinner – and had felt the same as the Lithuanian leader, he couldn't very well say that, so he had merely nodded. *"I'm guessing that they've decided that a united front might deter Putin."* But Walter knew better; his Lithuanian friend was right. If anything, the article would inspire a response from Putin that no one welcomed.

Walter had wondered why the article had been written in the first place. America's military leaders had to know that it would provoke Putin. Had the generals approved it? *Not likely.* He had come up with only one logical explanation: the article had been written for Martin. Morningstar wanted to make sure that Martin was aware that he, Morningstar, had infiltrated the Henderson home. But why? What would he gain by taunting Martin with that fact? Whatever the answer, if Walter was right, then the two men were far more connected than Martin had been willing to admit.

Fortunately, the Lithuanian leader had assured Walter that, regardless of America's involvement, Lithuania was committed to stopping Putin, and Lithuania's army would be *"...a solid partner in our shared battle against Russia."* Walter had no choice but to take the man at his word. After all, it would be up to Petrauskas to oversee Lithuania's contribution to a war that was, thus far, confined to Latvia. But both men were well aware that if Latvia fell, Lithuania would be next on Putin's list.

Petrauskas had stopped short of committing troops, however, agreeing that he would consider it should Latvia's efforts begin to slow. Walter rubbed the back of his neck and frowned. *Will it be too little, too late?* He was reminded of the Greeks in the battle of Marathon in 490 BC. The Spartans, who had agreed to assist the Athenians in their fight against the Persians, had been celebrating the festival of Carneia when the battle had ensued. During the festival, all military conflict was forbidden, and the Spartans had refused to allow their army to leave. Though the Athenians managed to win that battle, it had nearly been lost, all because of the Spartans' refusal to join the fight. Would Lithuania's delay be more costly? He sighed. *I guess we'll find out.*

Walter had been working with the psychiatrist, Samuels, to try to gauge the pulse of Lithuania's citizens regarding a possible war with Russia. Samuels' research had had mixed results. For one thing, his efforts had been disrupted by his kidnapping. Nonetheless, he had managed to learn that there was, in fact, a sizeable minority who welcomed Russia's invasion of their country. Not only did many of them have family in the former Soviet Union, but they perceived Russia as a potentially powerful ally on the world stage. Walter had shared this information with Petrauskas, who had merely nodded. *"The important word there, Walter, is minority. Not enough to matter."* Again, Walter would be forced to take the man at his word.

Petrauskas had then added that an article written the day before had suggested that the same was true for Latvia's freedom fighters. *"If I'm not mistaken, Walter, your family was mentioned as a possible wild card, as well."*

Walter had been forced to hide his anger and defend his loyalty to Latvia.

While Walter had been meeting with Petrauskas, it was a safe bet that the psychiatrist, Samuels, who had returned to London ten days ago, had spent his day searching for Mark Justice. Justice had last been seen two weeks ago in Aberdeen, Scotland, the day before a coin show where he was to meet Walter. He hadn't made it to the show, but had had an actor from the show deliver a letter to Walter, which had reinforced Justice's claim that Cobra was somehow involved in escalating the Latvian war. Samuels' assertion that Justice might be trying to undermine Cobra's efforts, had led Samuels to conclude that it was now up to him and Walter to ensure the safety of Justice - hence Cobra – thereby giving Justice a chance to succeed. If nothing else, it had eased their consciences, as they finally had an excuse to protect the man.

But just three days later, Samuels had gotten a call from his secretary telling him that Justice had written *him* a letter, as well. Rather than have her read it over the phone, Samuels had elected to return home to London, so he could read the letter in the privacy of his office. He had left the Henderson estate twenty-four hours later, and had called Walter upon his arrival in London, to tell him what was in the letter. *"It's a bit convoluted, I'm afraid. A vague poem about a cat that can't speak, a loner, and a man with two unique eyes."* Samuels had told Walter that his plan was to start the next day to research clues in the letter. He had promised to get back to him with whatever he found. That had been over a week ago. Walter had heard nothing since.

He came to his exit and headed north. He tried to imagine what Justice might have meant by the cryptic phrases. The man with two unique eyes had to be Cobra, but what of the rest of it? He sighed. He would just have to wait to hear back from Samuels.

And the Morning Star meeting will have to wait, as well, he thought as he picked up speed. He couldn't very well leave Latvia to travel to a meeting somewhere in Europe until he was assured that Martin was okay and was on his way home.

He checked the time. It was four p.m. in Latvia, which meant that it was eleven p.m. in China. Was Martin asleep in some hotel? Had he found Lili? Was he on his way home? Walter had known when Martin left that his mission to save Lili wouldn't be easy, and that it was likely he wouldn't be in a position to call. But two weeks was quite a long time. *Where are you, Martin?*

His satellite phone rang. He answered with a quick, "Yes?"

"Uh, sir, it's Tom Cravens."

Walter's eyes widened. He hadn't talked to Cravens since they had said their goodbyes seventeen days ago; the day that Cravens had flown to America, and the day that Martin had taken a train to Lithuania, where he was then imprisoned outside Klaipeda. "It's good to hear your voice, Cravens. How are things in America?"

There was a pause. "Not good, sir." Another pause. "Is there any reason why your...um nephew...would be in China?"

Walter frowned. Cravens knew that Matt was Martin. Why not refer to him as such? *Because he's afraid someone might be listening.* He cleared his throat. "I trust that this will stay between you and I?"

"Absolutely, sir."

Walter frowned. "As a matter of fact, he is, Cravens. Why?"

Another pause. "Because I have just seen footage, sir, that suggests that... Matt, is being held in a secret Chinese prison."

CHAPTER 57

Uzava, Latvia

Morningstar poured himself a drink and carried it to his chair. Things were looking up. He had just received confirmation that Johnny Canterbury and Arthur Kauffold had checked in for their four-o'clock flight from Heathrow to Beijing, and that they were, in fact, scheduled to meet with the Chinese President tomorrow, Sunday, at nine a.m. ...which was three a.m. in Latvia. It was currently a few minutes after four in the afternoon. His plan was to be entrenched in the Henderson castle by the time Sturgill and Cobra were killed. *Which means that I have less than eleven hours to take over that damn castle.*

He was startled by the sound of his phone vibrating. He answered with a quick, "Yes?"

"Hey babe."

Morningstar felt his legs go weak. *Janet.* "What's up, baby?"

"You...now." She chuckled.

He couldn't help but laugh. "It's true." He crossed his legs. "I miss you."

"Which is why I'm calling. I'm coming to Latvia."

Morningstar's eyes widened. "You are?"

"Yes." She paused. "Due to the increased tension between China and the U.S., the Secretary of State has decided to join Kauffold and Canterbury in their meeting with the Chinese President. She left here two hours ago, and is expected to arrive there by around eight-thirty tomorrow morning, China Standard Time." There was a pause. "My understanding is that a meeting has been scheduled for nine."

The Secretary of State? He grinned. *My plan is being executed even better than expected.* "That's fantastic!"

She added, "Yes, but there's more, babe. She has decided to make a stop in Moscow, once she has completed her discussions with the Chinese."

He frowned. "Moscow? Won't that send the wrong message to the Latvians?"

"Yes. Which is why I've been asked to send another State Department representative to Latvia to reassure them that we aren't abandoning them."

I thought that was why I was here. He cleared his throat. "That's reassuring, Janet, but why are we kowtowing to Moscow in the first place?"

"Because the administration has decided that it's in America's best interest to do all that we can to avoid escalating the war with Russia... especially considering that we're on the brink of war with China."

Morningstar sneered. "The administration, huh." He narrowed his eyes. "Whatever."

She went on. "Apparently, there's a meeting taking place in Riga tomorrow morning to address concerns, not only about America's commitment to Latvia as they fight Putin, but about rumors suggesting a possible revolt from within." She paused. "Something about freedom militias and their lack of a commitment to the cause?"

Morningstar bristled. *Dammit!* Though he was thrilled that Zebulin's efforts to plant seeds of doubt about the motives of the Hendersons and their freedom fighters had clearly borne fruit, the last thing he needed was for the various fighting factions to sit at the very same table. He growled under his breath. *I'll deal with that later.*

Again, he cleared his throat. "So, tell me Janet, who are you sending to Latvia?"

"The Deputy Secretary. The good news is that she is four months pregnant, and she and I have bonded over that fact. So, I have offered to come with her to help with any clerical, logistic, or – God forbid – medical complications."

Morningstar shifted in his chair. The very thought of physically being with Janet had made him uncomfortable...in a good way. "How soon?"

"As I said, the meeting with China is taking place tomorrow at nine a.m., which is the middle of the night where you are, Babe. The Secretary insists that the Deputy Secretary arrive in Latvia before she leaves for Russia, which she hopes to do directly after the meeting." There was a pause. "Which means that, if everything goes as planned, I should have these long hungry legs wrapped around you by tomorrow's sunrise."

CHAPTER 58

Somewhere in the Katahdan Mountains

Cravens ran his hands through his hair. He wasn't sure what had made him call Walter, other than that he had gotten close to both him and Martin during his stay at their mansion in Latvia. *If it was my son, I would certainly want to know that the Chinese bastards were holding him prisoner.*

He had been careful to refer to Martin as Walter's nephew Matt out of an abundance of caution. One never knew who might be monitoring his – or Walter's – calls. But the conversation hadn't gone the way he had expected. Instead of simple outrage, followed by insistence that America's leaders look into it, Walter had decided to take matters into his own hands. Cravens shook his head and frowned. *Why would I think that this man of action would do anything less?*

He stared at his jacket on the back of the chair. How he longed for a smoke. But he had just had a cigarette – or at least four puffs – less than an hour ago. He was saved from the lure of his addiction by the ringing of the desk phone. "Cravens here."

"It's Patrick. I've reviewed the photo. The two men are most definitely the missing U.S. Senator, Sturgill, with a man who I'm guessing is his bodyguard."

Cravens' eyes widened. "You're certain?"

"As much as I can be. And I think the CIA must agree. I just learned that our Secretary of State and UK's former ambassador are going to China to confront them."

Cravens frowned. *Interesting.* "Do we know the bodyguard's name?"

"His passport lists him as Secret Service Agent Daniel Frisk. But we spoke to your boss, Sam Allen. He says there's no such person."

Cravens swallowed. "You spoke to my boss?"

"Well, not exactly. Foster reached out to him through Harrington." Another pause. "I have been assured that your name never came up, sir."

Cravens let out a sigh of a relief. "Good. Thank you, Patrick."

"Never a problem, Agent."

Cravens hung up the phone and frowned. *So, who is the guy that's pretending to be Sturgill's bodyguard?* If he wasn't Secret Service, then was it possible that he was somehow behind what happened in China, and that Sturgill might have been forced to do whatever he had done against his will?

Cravens leaned back and massaged his temples. It was certainly an angle they could pursue to calm the Chinese. *"It wasn't the senator who wanted the son of your military leader killed, it was the bodyguard with him who is to blame."* Regardless, they needed to do something soon. From what he could tell from the photo, it looked like Sturgill and the bodyguard weren't being treated well at all.

And now I know that Martin Henderson is in that prison, as well. What were the odds? And why had he been detained in the first place? Cravens had expected more information from his call to Walter. The last Cravens had heard, Martin had gone to Lithuania with every expectation that he would be detained, and possibly killed. What had changed? And how on earth had he ended up in China? All Walter had said was that Martin had flown over there to *'...save a friend.'*

Cravens sighed. It didn't really matter, because now he had a new problem. By telling Walter that his son was in a Chinese prison, he had unleashed a tempest...

"You're telling me, Cravens, that my nephew is a prisoner in China?"

"I believe that he is, sir. I don't know how long he's been there, but I'm almost certain that it was him that I saw."

"Are you in China?"

"No sir. I'm working from an undisclosed location. I saw him on a printout from a satellite feed."

"I see." Another pause, this one longer. "Matt flew to China two weeks ago."

Cravens frowned. "Can you tell me why he went there, sir?"

Again, a pause. "May I ask, Cravens, how it is that you're involved in this."

Cravens ran a hand through his hair. "Let's just say, sir, that I was in the wrong place at the wrong time."

"I see. Can I ask if you're currently working for the Secret Service?"

Cravens whispered, "No, but I assure you, I'm on the right side of things."

"I don't doubt it for a minute, Cravens." Another deep sigh. "Matt was looking for a friend of ours. We're almost certain she's being held against her will."

Cravens frowned. Walter had said 'she.' Who was he referring to? He cleared his throat. "I...I can't be sure it's your...nephew...sir, but it sure did look like him." He paused. "And now that you're telling me that he flew there two weeks ago, well—"

"What do you think we should do about it, Cravens?"

Cravens narrowed his eyes. There was an undercurrent of fear in Walter's voice that surprised him. He cleared his throat. "Well, sir, I know that diplomacy is being attempted on behalf of a senator who was recently taken prisoner."

"Sturgill, right?"

"Yes sir. I was just informed that our Secretary of State and the UK's former ambassador, Arthur Kauffold, have agreed to speak with the Chinese."

"Kauffold, eh...interesting." Walter seemed to have regained his sense of self-assuredness. "You're aware that I will now have to go to China...right Cravens?"

"I can certainly understand how you feel, sir, but—"

"I'll leave within the hour." Another pause. "I can only guess who you're working for. If there's any information you can give me regarding the location—"

Cravens had to catch his breath. "Sir, with all due respect—"

"Cravens, I think you know me well enough to know that I will do whatever it takes to get my – to get Matt – out of there." He added, "I know it's possible, if he's in that jail, that the Chinese may have already killed him, but I'm hoping they see him as a bargaining chip. He's of far greater value to them alive, wouldn't you agree?"

"Yes sir," Cravens said, but he didn't agree at all. He doubted they were interested in bargaining at this point.

Walter went on. "I intend on freeing him. If you can't give me details of his whereabouts, how about this: assuming I'm successful, I'll need a way out. There'll be no way for me to leave by a conventional route, especially once I break into their secret prison and remove one of the inmates."

"I agree. But sir, you are one man," one old man, he had wanted to say, but stopped himself, "...against an entire Chinese army."

"I'll take a couple of Latvian soldiers with me. The Hendersons have a small company in China with an office in Beijing. We'll go in as businessmen. It will give us an element of surprise." He paused. "We'll try to get Sturgill out of there, as well."

Cravens' eyes widened. "That might be my ticket to help you, sir. I could say that Latvia – in an effort to return a favor to America – has agreed to send in a covert team to try to free the senator, as well as any other Americans who might be there."

A pause. "Maybe say 'any other prisoners who might be there.'"

Cravens narrowed his eyes. Why? Was it because 'Matt' was wanted by the U.S., or was it because the woman he went to save wasn't American. "Yes, sir."

Walter said, "I'm guessing whoever you're working for has some authority?"

Cravens rubbed the back of his neck. "The highest there is, sir."

A pause. "We won't need anything other than a way out...maybe a Chinook helicopter on standby on a carrier in the South China Sea. I could call you when we're ready; they could fly in, pick us up, and get us out of there before the Chinese figure out what happened." He paused. "I know I'm asking a lot, Cravens."

That is the understatement of the year, Cravens thought as he took a deep breath and sighed. "Give me a minute, sir. I'll call you back."

Cravens held up the photo of Henderson and sighed. *What the hell am I doing?* Should he honor Walter's request? Or should he ignore it and let the chips fall where they may. He took another deep breath and sighed. *I need to talk to Knight.*

CHAPTER 59

Somewhere in the Katahdan Mountains

Jerome Knight was tired. He had known fatigue in his life, but nothing like what he felt now. Not only had he left the White House under a shroud of secrecy, but war was threatening around the globe. And as far as he could tell, much of it had been started by a man he had worshipped his entire adult life, Edward Morningstar.

But that wasn't all that was sapping his strength. Just hours ago, the woman he had loved for nearly just as long had insisted that she speak to her husband to explain to him why she had left him. Not only was it a security risk, but it was a relationship risk, as well. Who knew what might happen once she saw that man again.

Knight leaned back in his oversized chair and sighed. He had spent the last two weeks practically living in that makeshift Oval Office. He had spoken with Harrington more times than he could count, the two of them handling crisis after crisis. Knight had given the man strict instructions that whenever he needed to talk to Knight, he would unlock the phone in the bottom left drawer of the Resolute Desk, carry it into the secret room less than a hundred feet from the Oval Office, and call from there. Together they had addressed upheaval in America and around the world, and – so far – had handled it with surprising calm and efficiency.

But Emma's request had nearly done him in. Not only was it a threat to their relationship, but it would require some rather challenging logistics. For one thing, where would they meet? It couldn't be nearby; it would risk

315

revealing the hideaway. But it couldn't too far away, either, due to time constraints. The site would need to be secured, and both she and Michael would need to be taken there and returned to their respective locations with the utmost care. *Six agents at least,* he thought with a sigh.

He had told only Foster of her request, and had asked that he personally accompany her on the journey. Knight had shared his misgivings, but Foster had assured him that it was feasible. *"Patrick and Kent will prep the site. I've already got two trustworthy men keeping an eye on Cannon's house. They replaced Cravens' friend. They'll bring Michael. As for Emma, I'll bring Santa with me to take her to the site and ensure it stays secure. No new faces, sir. Just the same loyal men who have accompanied us this far."*

Knight had agreed, reluctantly, and the rendezvous had been scheduled for five p.m. Patrick and Kent had left immediately. Foster, Santa, and Emma were to leave at three. He frowned. *In half a day, I'll know if I'm to keep – or lose – Emma.*

But he couldn't dwell on it. He suddenly had a new crisis to address. For whatever reason, his uncle and adopted father, Senator Charles Sturgill from Maine, had flown to China ten days ago, had carried out some horrible deed, and had claimed that he had done it on behalf of America. Sturgill had told no one that he was going or why, but from what Knight had been able to piece together, he had tried to kill the son of a Chinese military leader. Harrington had called minutes ago, overwhelmed by the fallout as details began to leak to the Press. Knight had been forced to hold Harrington's hand as he walked him through a response to every possible scenario.

Maybe it's for the best, he thought, as he sat back with a sigh. The crisis had made it impossible for him to overthink the situation with Emma. He would just need to have faith not only in her love for him, but in her ability to find peace for herself.

He sighed as he stared at a memo he had just received from the CIA. It stated that two weeks ago Sturgill had traveled to China. Five days later he had tried to kill the son of a Chinese military leader. China had denied that the attack had happened, and had stuck to their story that Sturgill had left their airspace eight days ago. But as more details emerged, they had been forced to defend the claim that they were holding the senator in a secret prison. It had enraged them, to the point that they were on the verge of declaring war against America. Not only was Harrington distressed by the revelations, but so was Knight. Charles Sturgill, though distant and stern, had been a father to him for the past 24 years. Knight couldn't just leave him over there to die. But as much as he wanted to go in with guns blazing and bring the old man home, he couldn't, not as long as China continued to deny they had him. Such an act would surely lead to war. So, about three hours ago, he had told Harrington to send the Secretary of State to meet with China's President in a last ditch effort at diplomacy.

Harrington had said in his latest call that arrangements had been made, and the Secretary was on her way. He had added that the British, in a show of solidarity, had reached out to the State Department, and had offered their former ambassador, Arthur Kauffold, to assist with negotiations. Apparently, he and the Secretary were old friends. The two of them, along with another British citizen who Knight had never heard of, were scheduled to meet with China's President at nine tomorrow morning.

Knight had congratulated Harrington on his efforts. Then, just as Knight had been about to end the call, Harrington had dropped a bombshell. *"Um, sir, I thought I should let you know that I've also been advised to pressure Russia with nuclear war."*

Knight had nearly come out of his chair. *"What? Who on earth would advise such a thing."*

Harrington's answer: *"It was Daniels' aide...Edward Morningstar."*

And that was when Knight knew...*Morningstar is trying to force me to come back.* And Knight had to admit; it was a clever move. If Morningstar was willing to risk nuclear war to get Knight to return to the White House, then Knight had to at least consider going back. After all, holding Morningstar accountable for his crimes would mean little if the world was about to be obliterated by nukes. He had told Harrington to resist such pressure, reminding him that nuclear war shouldn't even be on the table.

Harrington had argued that Morningstar had likely only suggested it to use as a threat to make Putin come to his senses.

Knight's response. *"Trust me, Bob...the threat of nuclear war won't make Putin come to his senses...it will infuriate him, and he will retaliate in kind. You must avoid doing any such thing."*

Harrington had agreed. He had been about to end the call, when he had added, *"Wait, sir, I've just received a memo from the State Department. Apparently, the Secretary has decided to go to Russia once the meeting with the Chinese President has ended."*

Knight had frowned. *"Russia? I'm worried how that will play in Latvia, Bob."*

Harrington had sighed. *"It looks like they're sending the Dep—"* he had stopped midsentence. *"Um...I'll arrange for the Deputy Secretary of State to travel to Latvia at once to reassure them that America's priorities haven't changed."*

"Good idea, Harrington. You're doing great," Knight had said, though he doubted that Harrington had had a single thing to do with any of the decisions that had been made of late. It didn't matter. At least diplomacy was still on the table...for both wars.

Knight leaned back and sighed. The world felt like it was spinning out of control. Unease in America and the UK, war breaking out in the Baltics, and now the possibility of war with China. *On top of it all, the love of my life has insisted that she leave our safe refuge to speak to a man she has been married to for sixteen years.*

He heard a knock on the door, followed by the gruff voice of Tom Cravens. "Sir, it's Agent Cravens. May I talk to you for a minute?"

"Sure Agent. Come on in."

The burly Secret Service agent walked into the room and Knight pointed to a chair in front of the desk. "Have a seat."

The agent sighed as he sat his large frame in the chair. "I'm sorry to bother you, sir, but it's urgent."

"What do you need, Agent?"

"First of all, I have just confirmed – with CIA photos – that Senator Sturgill and his bodyguard are, in fact, being held in a Chinese prison north of Beijing."

Knight nodded. "I was just briefed on the same thing." He paused. "At least now we have physical evidence to challenge China's denials."

Cravens cleared his throat. "Here's the thing. There's another man being held in that prison sir." He paused. "His name is...Matt Henderson."

Knight stared at him. "Why would Matt Henderson be in a Chinese prison? The last I heard, the man was wanted here...in America. Homeland Security issued an APB on the man just under three weeks ago. I was told that he is somewhere in Latvia."

Cravens sighed. "Yes sir, all of that is true. But I saw him...just now...in a makeshift Chinese prison...on a CIA satellite feed from a few days ago."

"That's insane, Cravens."

Cravens nodded. "There's more, sir." He paused. "I've just been made aware that a group of men are about to go in and to try to free both Henderson and Sturgill."

Knight's eyes widened. "What? Who's going in?"

"Walter Henderson and a couple of his Latvian freedom fighters."

"Walter has to be over seventy years old!"

"Seventy-two to be exact, sir. But he's remarkably fit." He paused. "Anyway, he plans on leaving within the hour, which would have him in China by tomorrow morning. He has asked for nothing more than a bit of help to get out of there once he has freed the prisoners. Maybe a helicopter, a few soldiers...something like that."

Knight shook his head. "There's no way I can approve that, Cravens. We're already on the verge of war with China. A U.S. military chopper to aid in the rescue of prisoners that the Chinese are denying they have would most assuredly prompt a war. As for sending in a few soldiers, I can't send in even one soldier unless I'm willing to commit our entire force." He rubbed his forehead. "Our Secretary of State is on her way there now. Let's wait and see what she can do with a bit of diplomacy."

"With all due respect, sir, diplomacy isn't going to work here. If what has been reported is true, sir, then a U.S. senator – who has claimed to be acting on behalf of the United States – tried to kill the son of a Chinese military leader. There is no coming back from that, sir."

Knight frowned. The man was right. "What do you recommend, Cravens?"

"We send a Black Ops unit and a chopper to wait on standby on the USS George Washington. It's already stationed in the Yellow Sea. No new ships, nothing to suggest we're gearing up for war." He paused. "But we need to get them to the vessel as soon as we can, sir. As I said, Walter's leaving within the hour."

Knight frowned. It was too much...civilians sneaking into a foreign country to free prisoners being held in secret. *Like the Resistance in World War II.* Knight had only met Walter Henderson a couple of times at dinners at the White House, but he knew enough about him to know that he was used to getting his way. He was going after his nephew regardless of whether Knight agreed to help him get out of there.

Knight ran his hands through his hair. Walter Henderson was a patriot, and he had been a good friend to Jim Wilcox. Those reasons alone should be enough for Knight to help him. But there was no way that Knight could condone such a mission. "I can't do it, Cravens. I appreciate Henderson's desire to save his nephew, but—"

"Um, sir. There's something you need to know."

Knight narrowed his eyes. "What is it?"

Cravens shifted in his seat. "I'm sure that I'm not supposed to say anything, but I'm asking you to go to bat for this guy, so I think it's only fair that I tell you everything." He rubbed the back of his neck. "Matt isn't Walter's nephew, sir." He lowered his voice. "Matt is actually...Martin...the son that everyone thought was killed in that terrible hotel explosion in DC almost five years ago."

Knight stared at Cravens, doing his best to hide his shock. Matt Henderson was Martin, who had *survived* a terrible explosion...*at a DC hotel almost five years ago.* Could it be? His head was spinning as he suddenly recalled a conversation with Morningstar from years ago...a conversation that he had all but forgotten...

> *"Who is he, Father?"*
> *"It doesn't matter. Forget you saw him, son."*
> *"Why is he covered with scars?"*
> *Morningstar chuckled. "A mishap with a bomb at a DC hotel."*
> *"Is he...part of us, sir?"*
> *"Yes, my son, he is." Morningstar smiled. "He is perhaps the greatest of you all. His name is Joseph..."*

Knight was having a hard time catching his breath. *It can't be.* It must have been some other man who had survived a DC hotel fire. He thought back to what he knew about Joseph. Morningstar had said little about the man; only that he had come from wealth and power *"...and therefore*

understands what it means to hold sway over those who are less-advantaged."
Knight rubbed his temples, trying to imagine another explanation for what seemed like a monumental coincidence. There wasn't one. The man Walter was going to save – the man he had pretended was his nephew – was really Martin Henderson...*who just happens to be Morningstar's favored son!*

Knight's legs were shaking and he rubbed his thighs to try to calm them. Not only did he *want* to help Walter save his son, he *needed* to help him. Joseph was one of Morningstar's soldiers. But unlike the others, he had come from a home and a history not filled with betrayal and disappointment, but with hope. Like Knight, he had come from a family of heroes; men who knew the difference between right and wrong. *Yet, somehow, we both ended up working for a man who embodies none of it.*

"Sir?" Cravens narrowed his eyes.

Knight cleared his throat. "Walter plans on leaving in the next hour or so?"

"Yes sir."

Martin Henderson knows what I know...we've seen Morningstar for who he is. Is he as sickened by it as I am? Or, did he go to China to further the agenda of our deranged 'father'? It didn't matter. Either way, Knight needed to talk to him.

"And you say he has soldiers going with him?"

"Yes sir. A couple of freedom fighters from Latvia, sir."

Knight frowned. It wasn't like it would be a formal mission; neither the U.S. nor China would need to know, at least not until the men were safely away from there. But if it did come to light, then Harrington would need to have an explanation for why a helicopter from a U.S. carrier had assisted with the mission. He rubbed his chin, then nodded. He knew just the explanation.

"If I'm going to support this mission, then here is how it needs to go down." He leaned forward and put his hands on the desk. "I have a Black Ops unit with a Chinook that answers only to me." He paused. "Which means that even Harrington won't know what I'm about to condone. It stays between the two of us, got it?"

"Yes sir."

Knight frowned. "And if something goes wrong..."

Cravens nodded. "Yes sir...I understand."

"Okay. Tell Mr. Henderson that we'll help him, but under one condition."

"What is that, sir?"

Knight leaned forward. "The minute they're out of that prison and safely away from China, I need them brought straight to me. Is that understood?"

Cravens frowned. "Um...yes sir. But how will I do that? How do I get them here without compromising your location, sir?"

Knight stood from the desk and began pacing the room. He was thinking as he talked. "Once they clear Chinese airspace, have the team blindfold every one of them. Maybe even drug them so they sleep until they're safely within our camp."

Cravens tugged at his collar. "Okay. But if it comes to light, sir, that a renegade militia went to China to free secret prisoners and was aided in the effort by a helicopter and a team of soldiers from a U.S. military vessel, how do we defend it?"

Knight looked at Cravens. "Not really a team. Just two soldiers and someone to pilot the Chinook." He paused. "If we're forced to defend it, that's when I'll call Harrington. I won't tell him details, I'll just have him announce to the world that the mission to save the prisoners was conducted without America's knowledge. He'll add that once he learned that one of the prisoners was wanted in America, he felt that everyone on the helicopter had to be brought to DC for questioning. Does that work?"

Cravens sighed. "I think so, sir...as much as anything can, these days." He stood and nodded. "I'm sure Walter will be very appreciative, Mr. President."

Knight returned to his desk and stood with his hands on the back of his chair. "He's a good man. I'm glad to help him." He looked Cravens in the eye. "But I'm counting on you to get them here with no one – and I mean no one – knowing where they're going or why."

Cravens shifted awkwardly. "Yes sir." He hesitated. "Is that all, sir?"

Knight gave an almost imperceptible nod.

Cravens left the room, closing the door behind him.

Knight walked around his chair and sat down, oddly elated. Though the entire world was on the verge of war, and the love of his life was about to meet with a man she had been married to for over a decade-and-a-half,

Knight felt somehow invigorated. *Why?* he wondered as he stared at the documents on his desk. *Because for the first time in months – maybe even years – I am no longer alone in this fight.*

He had no idea what had happened to Martin Henderson that had made him one of Morningstar's men, and he had no idea how he had changed his appearance to become Matt. More importantly, he had no idea *why* the man had changed his appearance so dramatically. *Was it simply to rid himself of the scars? Or was it so he could escape our evil father?*

Knight sighed. It didn't matter. Either way, he had possibly found an ally...a good man who had lost his way...a decent man who had somehow become as deeply embedded in Morningstar's plot as Knight...*a moral man who – just maybe – has seen the light.*

Knight stood and rested his hands firmly on the desk. *I have found Joseph.*

CHAPTER 60

Beijing, China

Hank stared at his trac phone. *Don't do it, Hank.* It had been two weeks since he had called Cravens asking him to find his ex-wife Jenny. He had yet to hear any news from the man.

He ran a hand through his thick hair and sighed. He had been walking through downtown Beijing, no longer even sure why he was there or what he was looking for. He looked again at his phone, then stared up at the night sky. The stars were hidden, a sliver of moon was all he could see as it slid further and further behind thick dark clouds. Was it about to rain? *God, I hope not,* he thought as he shoved the phone in his pocket and resumed his walk.

He had called Cravens only once since that first call two weeks ago. He had been reluctant to make the call. Cravens had been adamant that they not talk on the phone. But Hank had been desperate. The call hadn't gone well...

> *"Cravens, it's me. Any luck?"*
> *There was a sigh. "Dammit, Hank, you shouldn't—"*
> *"I'm using a payphone. I just need to know what you've found."*
> *"Not much. I think she was at the townhouse a day or two before you called, but it looks like she left in a hurry."*

Hank frowned. 'Why?' he wondered. He took another deep breath, hesitant to ask the next question. "Was there any sign of foul play?"

Cravens said quickly, "No. It looks like she was interrupted in the middle of preparing a meal. I think she packed a bag; there was none of her stuff in the bathroom, and the bedroom dresser drawers were open and empty. Now I'm just trying to track where she went from there."

Hank sighed. "Okay. How will I know when you find her?"

Cravens cleared his throat. "Tell you what. Buy a new trac phone and text me the number ASAP. I'll call you the minute I get any news."

That had been a week ago. Hank had bought the new trac phone and had sent Cravens the number, but he still hadn't heard from him.

As for Maddi, Hank had been in Beijing a full two weeks but had seen no sign of her. He had described her – using her alias, Harriett Winthrop – to any public transit man or woman who would listen. He thought he had caught a break when a bus driver said he remembered a woman fitting her description getting off his bus in downtown Beijing. *"She help older woman who trip. Very pretty, very kind."* But that had been days ago, and the lead had gone nowhere. Hank had visited every downtown hostel, and had gone to nearly every hotel, hoping to catch Maddi checking in or out. And though his Homeland ID had worked well for him at the airport in Rome, he had decided against using it; he couldn't afford to draw attention to himself in China, especially with rumors surrounding a U.S. Senator who had vanished in Beijing, and whispers of war. He didn't want to be on anyone's radar, particularly the Chinese.

He had just left the Empark Prime Hotel in downtown Beijing, and was walking as fast as he could to nowhere in particular. The hotel had been a long shot. Though Maddi had started with a decent amount of cash, both from Angelo and from the money they had gotten in Hamburg, she had been in China for two full weeks. It was doubtful she had enough left to be spending it on a hotel, especially a halfway decent one in the heart of Beijing. But he didn't know where else to look. For whatever reason, Maddi had come all the way to China just to disappear. He frowned. Had that been her plan all along? He shook his head. There was no way.

Let it go, Hank.

But he couldn't. Either he needed to stay and look for Maddi, or he needed to go home and look for Jenny. *Which one will it be, Hank?* It was the same question he had asked himself years ago...only under far different circumstances.

His trac phone vibrated. "Yes?" he said eagerly. Only one man had that number.

"It's me...Cravens."

Hank held his breath. "Have you found her?"

"No. But I have news that you might find interesting."

"What?"

"Henderson's in China...Beijing."

Hank frowned. He hadn't told Cravens where he was.

Cravens added, "I know that you're there; or at least that you were two weeks ago. I was looking into this mess with Sturgill – the senator who flew to China and has caused so much trouble – and your name popped up on a plane manifest from Rome to China." He added, "Don't worry. I haven't told anyone." He paused. "But I have to think that Hanover is aware."

Hank sighed. "If he is, he hasn't called me. I'm still officially on a leave of absence."

"Yes...and the Director most certainly has his hands full."

Hank nodded. "That's true." He paused. "What is Henderson doing here?"

"According to his father, he's there to save a friend...a female friend."

Hank stiffened. *Maddi?* It couldn't be. Henderson – like the rest of the world – thought Maddi was dead.

Cravens went on. "I know what you're thinking. I'm pretty sure the woman isn't an American."

"So, who is it?"

"I don't know. But there's reason to believe that Henderson is now a prisoner somewhere near Beijing." He paused. "Walter Henderson is about to take a couple of Latvian soldiers and go in and save him, along with the woman and Sturgill." Another pause. "He has asked that we help him escape once he's completed the mission."

"Who's 'we?'"

"I…I can't say. But I was hoping that if you're still there, maybe you could help with logistics."

Hank didn't hesitate. "To hell with logistics. I'll help Walter free them."

There was a pause. "Hank, I'm pretty sure that would qualify as a suicide mission…if not for your life, then for your career."

Hank gripped the phone tighter. "Cravens, Henderson has risked his life to save so many people over the past year. Hell, he saved my life a time or two, and the life of my son." He shook his head. "That poor man has been through way too much."

There was a deep sigh. "I know…and I agree with you." A pause. "It's ten a.m. here…which means that it's ten p.m. there…right?"

"Eleven p.m. this time of year."

"Okay. My guess is that Walter will get to Beijing around five a.m. your time. He should get to the prison – an old warehouse, we think – at around ten. The warehouse is about ten miles northwest of Beijing, in a canyon near the base of the Xishan Mountains. It looks empty; it isn't."

"Got it. I'll be waiting." He paused. "And if you talk to Walter, give him this number and let him know that I'm ready to help."

"Will do, though I doubt I'll get a chance to talk to him before the mission is complete. All sides have agreed that radio silence is the best way to go."

"Understood. I'll talk to you soon." Hank ended the call and slid the phone in his pocket. He shivered and zipped his coat. The night air had turned colder. He looked up and down the street for a place to get warm. He saw what looked like an all-night diner and jogged toward it. He reached it and walked in. He found an out-of-the-way booth and sat down. He was tired and cold, and his heart was heavy. His world had gone crazy. Jenny was missing, Maddi had run off, Henderson was in a Chinese prison, and Walter was on his way to try to save him. *And now, I have agreed to help him and a couple of freedom fighters battle the Chinese Imperial Army.* He leaned back and sighed. *How do I get myself into these messes?*

A waitress came to take his order.

"Zhi shi ka fei." *Just coffee,* he said, his Mandarin weak, but getting better after two weeks in China. She nodded and walked away.

Though the entire situation was unsettling, Hank couldn't help but appreciate the irony. Here he was again, about to help Walter as he tried to save his son. But this time, instead of working on behalf of Homeland

Security, he was working on behalf of Tom Cravens and whoever he had aligned himself with. He sighed. Why had Henderson come to China in the first place? Cravens had said it was to save a woman who wasn't an American. *So, who the hell is it?* he wondered as he leaned against the back of the booth. *And why on earth did I jump in so quickly, thinking I could help?*

He sighed. He knew the answer. Not only was it his duty, but by some crazy quirk of fate, he was in China. Almost as if destiny had put him in that place to help Walter save his son. He had lost Maddi, he had lost Jenny. Truth be told, he had lost a good part of himself. He hadn't been home in months, and there was no one waiting for him should he return.

Though Cravens had promised to look for Jenny, it was clear he had a lot on his plate...like world peace and saving political prisoners. Hank knew that Cravens was doing all he could to find her; it just wasn't enough. *Which means that Jenny, who has been missing for over two weeks, will go on missing...unless I do something about it.* But there was nothing he could do. He was in China...about as far away from America as a person could be. He squeezed his temples in frustration. *I have to do something! I have to find someone to help me find Jenny. But who? Who can I trust?*

The waitress brought his coffee and, as he was taking a sip, his eyes widened. *I know just the man.* He opened his trac phone and dialed a number that he had been given – and had immediately memorized – eight months ago. It rang once, twice, three times. It went to voicemail. He said, "Roger, it's me. I need your help. Call me."

CHAPTER 61

Beijing, China

Maddi was freezing. The wind was sweeping down from the mountains, and she had only her brimmed hat and the wool cape to keep her warm. The bag with her clothes was gone, and so was her wallet with her ID. *What's it matter?* she thought. She had moved so far away from the Harriett Winthrop that Hank and Angelo had so painstakingly put together that it felt as if Harriett had died, too...just like Maddi. *I'll come up with a new identity...once I get Lili and her friend out of that warehouse.*

But how did she hope to do that? Not only did she have no ID, she had no resources of any kind. And she knew no one in China who could help her to free a child and her friend who were both likely weak, and maybe even ill from their lengthy stay in a Chinese prison. Maddi frowned. *The British Consulate. Once I'm sure Lili is inside that prison, I'll pretend I'm her aunt. I'll keep up my British accent, and say she was abducted several months ago from her home in Wales. I'll say that I'm Harriett Winthrop, that I was mugged and my ID was taken, but that I've come to try to save my niece. The few clues I was able to find have led me to that bleak prison.*

Maddi hugged her arms around her chest and nodded. Would it work? *It will have to.*

In spite of the cold air coming in off the mountains, Maddi had yet to move from her hiding place behind the tree. She didn't know how long she had been there, but guessed it had been at least a couple of hours. And during that time, she had watched the guards...their movements, their timing, the routes they took as they marched back and forth in front of the building. So far, they had taken no breaks. She watched as one of them moved behind a tree and relieved himself. She guessed that that was about as much of a break as he would get.

She felt certain that Lili was in that building. But to be sure, she periodically snuck a glance over her shoulder, reassured when she saw the exact same image – the mountains with the S-shaped fir trees – that had somehow entered her mind when she was in the diner. *I need to find a way inside.*

She wrapped the cape around her as she stared at the warehouse. Were only Lili and her friend in there? Or were there others? She guessed that there were. It seemed silly to have ten soldiers just to guard a little girl and her friend. But if others were in there, who were they? Political prisoners? Other girls like Lili who had been taken for god knows what reason, then abandoned? *There's only one way to find out.*

She watched the guard closest to her slip behind a tree. She quickly went from sitting to kneeling. Her legs were stiff; she rubbed them. She looked again at the guard. He was walking away from her. *Now, Maddi.* She took off her hat, set it on the newspaper she had been sitting on, and pulled up the cape's hood. Using the tree for support, she tried to stand. Her legs were shaking; they could barely hold her. She stretched each one as best she could behind the tree. When they felt stronger, she stooped low in the tall grass and crept slowly down the hill. The occasional leaf or stick crackled as she walked, forcing her to time her steps with the guard's. After about ten minutes she had reached the bottom. The grass wasn't as tall there; she fell to her knees. She watched the guard, estimating how far he went before he turned around. She nodded. Around forty feet. *Which means they're about eighty feet apart.*

She pulled the cape's hood low on her forehead, and raised the collar over her nose and mouth, leaving her face fully covered except for her eyes. She spotted a window about ten feet away; it was hidden behind a thick tree. She crawled toward it.

She stopped. The guard was coming back. She didn't move; she didn't even breathe. She waited. Once he made his turn, she would run to the window and hide behind the tree. She closed her eyes. *This is crazy. I'll likely be captured, or maybe even killed.* She shook her head dismissively. *What do I care...I'm dead anyway.*

The guard had reached the window. He turned and walked the other way. She looked up. A thick cloud was about to cover the moon. She waited. Within seconds, shadows darkened the ground. *Good...now go, Maddi.* She ran to the window and knelt behind the tree. She didn't move. She waited for the guard to reach the end of his route and turn around. She was trembling; she felt certain he could see her. She heard him marching toward her. He stopped. She held her breath. After a few seconds, she heard him turn and walk away. She exhaled as quietly as she could. She rose up and looked through the window. Wooden slats were covering the inside, but they were broken in several places, leaving gaps that allowed her to see into the building. She waited for her eyes to adjust. Suddenly she gasped. *Oh my god!*

She heard a noise. She dropped to her knees and pressed her face against the wall. She didn't breathe as she dared a glance over her shoulder. The guard was walking in her direction. She sunk even lower. He stopped. She waited. He hesitated, then walked away. She let out a sigh. On hands and knees, she crawled as fast as she could through the brush to the base of the hill. She caught her breath, then crawled up the hill to her hiding spot where she had left the newspaper. She pulled back her hood, put on her hat, and sat on the paper. She was shaking, but not from the cold.

In that brief glimpse inside the building, she had seen what were clearly prison cells. All were empty...but for one. Though it seemed farfetched, Maddi felt certain that she knew the man in the cell. He was a United States senator, Charles Sturgill from Maine. She had seen his picture in a Chinese newspaper a few days ago but had given it little thought, guessing he had come to China for some sort of fact-finding mission. *The man in that jail cell is Charles Sturgill...I'm sure of it. A bit thinner, perhaps, and his hair's a tangled mess, but it's him.* She frowned. How had he wound up in a secret prison outside Beijing? *It doesn't matter how he got there. I just need to let someone know that he's there.*

Holding onto the tree, she stood up slowly. She grabbed the newspaper she had been sitting on, folded it, and shoved it in a pocket of the cape. She wrapped herself in the cape, then snuck through the brush to the same dirt road where she had been dropped off. She would hitch a ride to downtown Beijing, then walk to the U.S. embassy. But she had to be careful. She couldn't risk being questioned or identified. It wasn't only her life that was at risk. Cravens and Hank could lose everything if the world ever learned what they had done. Which meant that she couldn't just waltz into the embassy and speak directly to an administrator, not even as Harriett Winthrop. The risk was too great that she might be found out. She could, however, deliver a written message to someone inside, and make them aware that an American senator was being held in a warehouse ten miles north of Beijing.

As she hiked down the road, she noted the landmarks she would share with the embassy so they would know exactly how to get to the warehouse. She still didn't know if Lili was in there. It seemed unlikely, considering that Sturgill – a political prisoner – was being held there. What would the Chinese want with a little girl? She trembled, imagining the worst, but then shook it off. *No, if they wanted to traffic her, they wouldn't keep her locked up in an old warehouse with political prisoners.*

But she couldn't seem to shake the sense that Lili was inside that warehouse. After all, Lili – or someone – had sent Maddi an image of the very same mountains that were outside that building. How could she do that if she wasn't in there? As the cold wind cut all the way to her bones, Maddi wrapped the cape tighter around her and picked up her pace, praying for a car or truck to come by soon.

CHAPTER 62

Somewhere in the Katahdan Mountains

Have faith in yourself, Jerome. Knight's father – his *real* father, the honorable Carlton Knight from the Fourth District – had said the expression many times when Knight was a boy, and he found himself seeking strength from those five words more and more every day.

He leaned back in his chair in the circular room that had been designed to represent the Oval Office in the Katahdan retreat. Foster's friends had gone so far as to hang reproductions of paintings of the Founding Fathers on the walls. As he looked up at the leader who inspired him most, George Washington, he sighed. *I'll bet you never imagined this scenario when you became the father of our country.*

He slid back the chair and stood, looking around at the remarkable room. Though not nearly as spacious as the real Oval, it was a close replica, and Knight found himself oddly comforted by the similarities to the White House. It surprised him. He had never felt comfortable in the White House. *I was an imposter.*

He paced the room, not bothering to stop at the makeshift window. There was nothing to see. The window – just like his role as President – was nothing but a fake. *I became President under false pretenses...to fulfill the prophecy of a terrible man.*

But he had to admit, the news about Martin Henderson had lightened his mood. Though tragic to think that another good man had been duped by Morningstar, there was comfort in knowing that Knight wasn't the only well-bred fool. What he had yet to learn was Henderson's role in Morningstar's 'family.' What had he done for him? More importantly, was he doing it still? Had he gone to China to carry out some horrible deed? If so, had he succeeded? And why had he been taken prisoner?

Yes, Henderson was a wanted man, but as far as Knight knew, it was only as Matt, and only in the U.S. for his role in January's bioterror attacks. Knight knew all there was to know about those attacks; he had been on the senate subcommittee that had investigated them. Back then, Matt Henderson wasn't on anyone's radar. And why would he be? The Hendersons were a remarkable family with an undeniable history of service. But a memo had come to light a few months ago that had implied that Matt Henderson had been an accomplice. According to the memo, he had been spotted at every one of the sites where the attacks had taken place. Knight had found it hard to believe, even before he knew that Matt was actually Martin. No member of the prestigious Henderson family would ever be involved in such a thing. Besides, it was the AWOL assassin Phoenix who had carried out those attacks. And from what the committee had been able to determine, Phoenix had acted alone. He looked at the painting of George Washington and sighed. *I guess I'll know soon enough.*

He had given Cravens the go-ahead to work with Foster to arrange for the helicopter and the extraction crew. It was a long shot and they all knew it. But they also knew that Walter Henderson was a determined man. Hell or high water, he was going in after his son. It was up to Knight to get him and the others out of there alive.

Should the mission fail, Knight had made it clear – through Cravens – that Walter would be on his own. *"Make sure he knows that this hasn't been sanctioned by either Harrington or the State Department. They know nothing about it."*

Knight shook his head, still stunned that Walter was breaking into a Chinese prison to save two, maybe three prisoners, with nothing more than a couple of freedom fighters. Like everything else that had happened of late, it was implausible.

He checked the time. Twelve-thirty p.m. The helicopter and the Special Ops team should be well on their way. Patrick and Kent should have completed their prep of the meeting site for Emma and Michael, and Foster was likely preparing for his role in the rendezvous. As for Emma,

Knight had left her in the bedroom to do whatever she needed to do to get ready. He sighed. *How does a woman prepare to say goodbye to a man that she's married to...and is still quite fond of?* He had no idea.

He walked back to the desk, thinking about how many days had passed since the two of them had left the White House and come to the mountain retreat. Fourteen. It had been a full fourteen days. He would sometimes wake in the middle of the night, overwhelmed by what he had done...what he had left behind. But then he would see Emma lying next to him, and would know that he had done the right thing.

How long would it be before he could return to the White House and follow through as America's Commander-in-Chief? He frowned. It was possible that he might never be able to go back. One thing was certain. He wouldn't go back until Morningstar had been exposed, and his entire operation had been taken down.

But it would be no easy task. Knight guessed that Morningstar had his tentacles in more than just the Pentagon. Probably in the State Department, and maybe even Homeland Security. He was tight with the Chairman of the Joint Chiefs, General Alexander Daniels. The man treated Morningstar like a son. It would take a considerable amount of evidence to convince Daniels and the leaders of those other departments that a man in Morningstar's position had gotten away with so much. For one thing, it would reveal a horrific lack of oversight and an unforgivable lapse in judgment on the part of his overseers. *No one will willingly admit to such a thing.*

He rubbed his forehead and sighed. *Which means that I will need irrefutable evidence.* He sat back in his chair, trying to imagine what that evidence might look like. Notes? Tape recordings? Videotapes?

There was a knock on the door. "Come in."

It was Foster. Seeing his smile was a comfort. *A reminder that there are still honorable men in this world.*

"Sir, if I may?"

Knight motioned him to the chair in front of his desk.

Foster sat and pulled out a sheet of paper. "Some updates, sir." He paused. "First, arrangements have been completed for the rendezvous with Emma and her—Michael. The site has been well-prepared, and I can guarantee her safety, Michael's safety, and the continued security of this location."

Knight flinched, but offered a quick nod. "Good work. Thank you, Foster."

"As for you, sir, there appears to be no one even close to figuring out where you are. I have a friend in the NSA who has told me in the strictest confidence that they have never been so blind with regard to your location."

Knight frowned. "Does this friend know your role in all of this?"

Foster shook his head. "Absolutely not, sir. He was confiding in me as a fellow government agent who he assumes is also looking for the missing President."

Knight nodded. "Go on."

"The helicopter and the Special Ops team left two hours ago, sir."

"Good. And no one is aware?"

"No, sir. At your command, I used the acting President's authority – without his knowledge – to send them north over Canada. They'll stop for fuel at a facility in Alaska, then in Guam, and then head west to China. I expect the journey to take about twelve hours, sir, which should have them in the Yellow Sea by noon, China time."

Knight considered it. Cravens had said that Walter was leaving "...*within the hour.*" That had been about three hours ago. Hopefully, the team would be there in time to help him. "Sounds good. Anything else, Foster?"

Foster nodded. "Regarding Russia, my contact in the White House has assured me that Harrington has made no comments regarding nuclear war, and that he has held to your plan for diplomacy. He has also made a call to Latvia's military leader, Jegors Ivanova, assuring him that America will stand behind them, regardless."

"Good."

"And our Secretary of State will be in China by tomorrow morning to meet with China's President. She plans on leaving that same day for Moscow."

"What does Latvia have to say about it?"

"They seem appeased by the fact that the Deputy Secretary is flying to Latvia." He paused. "The State Department has also asked for someone from the Henderson estate to talk to Latvia's military leaders to reassure them, not only about America's commitment to their efforts, but about the rumors of traitors among the various militia groups across the country."

Knight frowned. "Walter Henderson is unavailable. Who will talk to them?"

Foster nodded. "I believe that Dora Henderson will represent them, sir."

Knight's eyes widened. He nodded. He had never met Dora, but from all he had heard and read, she was remarkable in her own right, and would serve as an excellent ambassador. He looked at Foster. "I think you've got it all under control." He sat back and grinned. "Maybe I'm not needed after all."

Foster shook his head. "I can tell you for a fact, sir, that you are very much needed." He cleared his throat. "Which brings me to the next item."

"What is it, Foster?"

"There is someone not far from here who would like to speak with you."

Knight tensed. "I thought you said that no one knows where I am, Foster."

"It's the former Vice-President, sir. He's waiting at Millinocket, about 20 miles away. He has no idea you're here, sir. As a matter of fact, he thinks he was taken to that location because it is nowhere near you, sir." He paused. "But he wants very much to speak to you. He says it has to do with what his former Secret Service agent told me on the way to the mountain. He insists it's vital to the preservation of the country, and that he'll speak only to you." Foster paused. "If you should agree, I'll arrange for him to be blindfolded and flown by helicopter to a base in Michigan, where he will then be put on a private plane and flown to a small airfield outside Milwaukee. Still blindfolded, he will change planes and be flown to the base of this mountain. Different time zones, and a considerable amount of time in the air. He'll not even know what part of the country he's in. Once he reaches the base, my men will keep him blindfolded as they figure out a way to get him up the mountain."

Knight frowned. "You know, Foster, once we get him up here, he won't be able to leave...in spite of your precautions."

Foster nodded. "I anticipated as much, sir. I have told him that."

"What did he say?"

"His exact words were *If I have to die there to make things right, I will.*"

Knight nodded. That sounded like Conner.

Foster went on. "He also said this, sir. *I haven't necessarily always done the honorable thing, Foster. Perhaps it's time I start.*"

"Interesting. Does he plan on bringing anyone with him?"

Foster shook his head. "No, sir. He told his wife that he was needed in DC due to the crisis with the President."

Knight frowned. "He's willing to leave his wife…maybe forever?" It was well-known among Washington insiders that – though Conner hadn't always been faithful to his wife – he adored her above all else…even power.

Foster nodded. "Apparently so, sir."

Knight leaned back and sighed. "Okay, Foster. I'm guessing you'll use Patrick and Kent to transport the former Vice-President?"

"Yes sir. They have completed their task to secure the site for Emma and her—Michael. They got back a few minutes ago."

Knight took a deep breath, then nodded slowly. "Send them to get him, Foster. Let's see what the Vice-President – the *former* Vice-President – has to say."

CHAPTER 63

Beijing, China

Maddi trembled. She was so cold. It had taken hours to get from the warehouse to Beijing. She had been forced to walk several miles before a woman in a pickup truck stopped to give her a ride. She had gotten to Beijing's city center just as a clock had chimed one a.m. That had been about forty minutes ago. She was now standing outside the embassy, colder than she had ever been. But there was no time to dwell on it; she needed to get a message to those inside. She couldn't go in; she was supposedly dead. Though she looked far different from the woman she had been before the plane crash, she wasn't sure the changes were enough that no one would recognize her. After all, at least one or two of the people in that embassy had had dinner with her on more than one occasion. But who would she give the message to? She thought of the one woman that she knew for sure was still at the embassy. *Eileen Hopper, attaché for Ambassador Stevens. I'll write her a message she can't ignore.*

She would need a pen and paper. She checked her pockets. She smiled sadly as she pulled out the lotus flower pen from the diner. It was supposed to bring her luck. *Some luck,* she thought with a sigh. She was about to walk over to a trash can to find a scrap of paper, when she felt the newspaper in her other pocket. She pulled it out and was about to write on a corner of the page, when she realized that the paper was written in English. Beijing had only recently begun to allow foreign newspapers in their major cities. She checked the date. Friday, November 12th...*yesterday.*

How she longed for news. Though she was tempted to read it, now wasn't the time. She was about to start writing on the top corner, when she read the headline...

"Do Russian Insurgents have an Unexpected Ally in Latvia?"

She closed her eyes. *Latvia*. It made her think of Henderson. She tried to force him out of her mind. She failed, and soon found herself skimming the article.

"According to Latvia's military, there are factions among Latvia's longstanding support groups that may be trying to undermine Latvia's efforts to fight off Putin. Latvia's Minister of Defense, Jegors Ivanova, said just a day ago, 'There is evidence to suggest that freedom militias, particularly those from Latvia's west coast, are working diligently to undermine our efforts.'"

Maddi frowned. *Freedom militias from Latvia's west coast...it has to be the Hendersons. But working to undermine Latvia?* She shook her head. *There's no way.*

"There will be a meeting Sunday, November 14th, between Latvia's military leaders and representatives from freedom militias around the country to try to find common ground, and ensure a united front against Putin."

Maddi's eyes widened. *Sunday, November 14th...tomorrow.* She kept reading.

"Two weeks ago, the top aide to America's Chairman of the Joint Chiefs of Staff dined with Walter and Dora Henderson in their castle in Latvia. The aide, Edward Morningstar, was quoted as saying, 'In an effort to show support for our NATO ally, I've spent the evening with the respected Henderson family, who are leading a resistance effort within Latvia.'"

Maddi grabbed her chest. *Morningstar...at the Hendersons?* Why would Martin let Morningstar anywhere near the castle? She narrowed her eyes. *Because he isn't there to stop him.* It was the only thing that made sense. Which meant that, unless Henderson had shared with his parents his concerns about Morningstar, they would be left unaware. Reluctantly, she read the next paragraph.

> "Morningstar indicated that the dinner had been a delight, and that the Hendersons have expressed their willingness to include him in every strategic decision from this point forward, for the duration of the war."

Maddi bristled, recalling what she had come to realize about Morningstar just as her plane had been about to crash outside Liepaja. *Morningstar wants war, not peace.* Which meant that whatever he was doing at the Hendersons, it had nothing to do with peace. She couldn't help but wonder if maybe he had been the one to stir up doubt about Latvia's freedom militias. *I wouldn't put it past him.* If that was the case, then the meeting that was scheduled to take place tomorrow would be the last thing he would want. She frowned. *Which means he'll do whatever he can to stop it.*

She tightened her jaw and forced herself to finish the article.

> "Mr. Morningstar was recently asked to comment on questions surrounding the loyalty of the freedom militias, specifically those in the western part of the country, which are closely aligned with the Henderson's. His comment: "It is absurd. I can say with the utmost certainty that the Hendersons are as loyal to Latvia as the young lily is to springtime.""

Maddi dropped the paper as if it was poison. *Dear God,* she thought, as she recalled one of Henderson's journal entries, *"My overseer knows about Lili."* She had concluded that Morningstar had been Hendersons's overseer. Was it a coincidence that he had used Lili's name...*in an article that will be read around the world?*

She bent down and picked up the newspaper. *I have to let someone know...I have to let the Hendersons know that Morningstar isn't who they think he is, that he is likely trying to undermine Latvia's efforts against Putin, and that he's possibly willing to hurt Lili – who the Hendersons know well – to get what he wants.*

She took a deep breath, suddenly remembering why she had come to the embassy in the first place. *But first I need to let someone know about Sturgill.*

She found a blank corner of the page, and jotted a note about Sturgill's detention in a warehouse ten miles northwest of Beijing. She included the landmarks she had memorized, then tore off the note. She folded it and stood beside the embassy steps, waiting for someone who seemed at least somewhat approachable. She shook her head as a bitter cold breeze chilled her to her bones. *It's nearly two in the morning...why would anyone be walking into the embassy at this hour?*

After about ten minutes, an older woman, an Asian with a briefcase, walked briskly toward the steps. Maddi had never seen her before, which meant that the woman wasn't likely to recognize her. Maddi could only hope that she would be willing to take a note from a stranger.

She walked up to her and smiled. "Excuse me Ma'am."

The woman stopped and took a step back. She looked at Maddi over a pair of glasses, scrutinizing her with a careful eye. "Yes?" she said, in English.

"I...I need to get a message to someone in the embassy. I know this isn't the proper approach, but my...my life is in danger. Please, you must help me."

The woman narrowed her eyes. "Who are you? Why are you in danger?"

Maddi shook her head quickly. "I...I can't say. It would...put you at risk."

The woman frowned. Finally, she said, "What is the message?"

Maddi handed her the scrap of paper. "This note must get into the hands of Eileen Hopper, an attaché for Ambassador Stevens, I would greatly appreciate it."

The woman stared at her, then cautiously took the note from her hand. Maddi nodded. "Thank you so much."

The woman gave a subtle nod. With the note in her hand, she walked up the steps to the front door of the embassy. She was about to walk inside, when she stopped and looked over her shoulder. Maddi stood with her shoulders tall, suddenly aware of how desperately she missed her role on the world stage. The woman offered a weak smile, almost as if she knew, then turned and went inside. Maddi watched until she was no longer visible, ignoring a tear that had somehow found its way to her cheek. She wiped it away, then turned and walked toward town, praying that the note would find a proper recipient, and that someone at the embassy would look for America's missing senator.

CHAPTER 64

Darlington, England

Andrew looked around at the cozy, high-ceilinged study with its unparalleled view of the garden outside. His grandparents' estate grew more impressive with each visit. He felt comfortable there; almost as if he was coming home. He wished Tonna had come with him. He had tried one more time to get her to join him, but she had been adamant that she needed to stay in Chesham. She had promised to come next time he was in England. *"Bring Amanda and my wee cousin, Adam."*

Donovan, having agreed to stay back and keep an eye on her, had been thumbing through a magazine in the den when Andrew had left the manor. He had reassured Andrew that he had everything under control, and that Andrew should go and have a good time exploring *"...a creepy old castle in the middle of nowhere."* Andrew had laughed, curious how Donovan had known that the estate was, in fact, isolated and remote. He had brushed it off, deciding it had simply been a lucky guess.

He had reached the estate about two hours ago, and, as Donovan had pointed out, the old castle was most definitely in the middle of nowhere. Nestled among a thick grove of ancient firs, the enduring castle loomed large among the trees. His grandfather had told him that it had been there for nearly six centuries, and that it had come into Madison hands shortly after the Highland Clearances in the late seventeen-hundreds. *"My ancestors had wanted nothing to do with what the English general had done to those poor souls in the hills. The castle owner had bequeathed it to us, asking us to join with him to make sure that nothing like that ever happened again."*

And, as far as Andrew was aware; nothing had.

He had been greeted by the caretaker, Gilbert, whom he had met last year when he had made his annual pilgrimage to the estate. Andrew and Maddi had made a point of visiting the castle at least once a year to meet with the entire staff to ensure that all was well. Maddi would spend a good bit of time with each of them, while Andrew would meet with the financial advisors who had been looking after his grandparents' finances for the past forty years. Last year, he had brought Amanda there for their honeymoon. She had fallen in love with the place, and their goal was to bring Adam with them the next time they came.

Andrew had gotten to know Gilbert's grandfather during his first visit to the estate at the age of sixteen. Over the years, the two men had gotten close, and Andrew had been deeply grieved when the old man had died two years ago. Sadly, neither his son nor his daughter wanted to take over his tasks, but Gilbert and his wife had stepped in eagerly. And, from what Andrew could tell, they had done an excellent job. The castle itself was in good shape, and the grounds – including row after row of rose bushes – looked just as it had when Gilbert's grandfather had been alive. As Roger had looked at the young man, who couldn't be a day over twenty-five, he had seen the old caretaker in his eyes. *"You've done a wonderful job, Gilbert."*

"Thank you, sir." The man had given a quick bow and had slipped away.

There were four other staff: two maids, a butler, and a gardener, But in spite of their presence, the place had felt empty. Fortunately, Andrew had found an old turntable in the study, and had pulled a Frank Sinatra album from a collection inside a nearby chest. As the haunting words of "It Was a Very Good Year" had filled the room, he had felt the place come alive... as if the walls had relaxed and the curtains could breathe again.

He had turned up the volume so he could hear it throughout the castle, and had then begun his reacquaintance with the old mansion. He had gone first to the bedroom where he had stayed the first time he had come to that mansion, and every year since. It had amazed him how the room never changed...as if time itself stood still in that glorious castle in the middle of nowhere. The room looked much like he remembered, with tall ceilings and two large windows that let in the morning sun. He had been told during his first visit there that the room had had its share of colorful occupants. *"The Prince of Wales stayed here back in 1888 after an altercation with the Queen,"* his grandfather had told him with a wink. Andrew hadn't known if it was true, but he had explored every nook of that room in the off chance that he might find a royal keepsake. He had found nothing. Twenty-eight years later, he gave the room another look. Still nothing.

He had moved on to his father's old bedroom, which also looked the same, followed by the kitchen, where he had made himself a ham sandwich and had sat watching the birds outside tall French doors, as the sun had eased over the hillside to the west. By nightfall, he had ended where he was now, in the study, with scores of books lining one wall, an oversized fireplace lining another. He stood in the shadows, the fire's glow and an old floor lamp the only sources of light, casting eerie shadows on the walls and ceiling. He could practically see his grandfather at the hearth, and his grandmother in an old Georgian rocking chair, reading Tolstoy by the fire.

He liked the study. There was warmth there, and it wasn't only because of the fire that the caretaker had helped him build. He looked around, captivated – just as he had been at the age of sixteen – by a Roman era Lorica Segmentata, a full-plated suit of armor that stood in the far corner of the room. There were medals on one of the walls, along with black-and-white photos of his grandfather standing arm in arm, first with Dwight Eisenhower, then with Winston Churchill. Andrew hadn't had a full appreciation of those relationships when he had come to the estate as a younger man, but over the years he had acquired a newfound respect. It seemed that every time he came, he learned something new about his grandfather and his fascinating life.

Andrew walked up to a photo of his grandfather with Eisenhower. Both men were dressed in army fatigues; the date written underneath was June 5th, 1944. Andrew's eyes widened. He had never noticed it before, but that picture had been taken just a day before D-Day.

He walked over to the bookshelf and breathed in the scent of old books, their ancient pages bound tenuously to faded spines. There were row after row of classics, their edges dulled, the writing faded. Dickens, Longfellow, Doyle, Poe. He stopped when he came to an anthology of T.S. Eliot. He was about to reach for it, when his eye fell on the book next to it. Nothing was written on the oversized spine, and, in spite of being taller and wider than the anthology, the dark tome had been nudged in so tightly it was almost invisible as it hugged the edge of the bookcase. He teased it from the shelf and held it in his hands. Thick, full-grained black leather, it was surprisingly heavy, with no writing on the front or back. He opened it to the first page, surprised to see black and white photos. *A scrapbook.*

He carried it to a Chesterfield sofa, sat with it in his lap, and opened it, the feel of antiquity warming his soul. He thumbed through the first few pages; they were filled with photos of people he didn't know. But he was able to distinguish familiar characteristics...tall, dark-haired men with wide foreheads and strong jawlines, slender women with fair features and light eyes. He read the name under each photo, eager to find one he recognized. He flipped through more pages, and, as he turned to the last one, a batch of letters fell out of a folder and into his lap.

He set the scrapbook on the couch beside him and flipped through the letters. They were addressed to his grandmother, Gloria Madison, with a few being written to Gloria Douglas, her maiden name, he assumed. Every one of them had a date written on the back, as well as two small asterisks on the right bottom corner. He spread them out on a long, mahogany coffee table and placed them in order. There were a total of twenty letters, spanning the years from 1930 to the current year, 2004. The last three hadn't been opened, indicative of the fact that his grandmother had passed by the time they arrived. He frowned. *Who would've known to put these letters in the scrapbook?*

He shook his head and reached for the first envelope, dated 1930. He lifted the flap and pulled out the letter, surprised to see that it was written in a child's hand. He smiled. *A child wrote this to Grandmother, who was a child herself.* He was about to set the envelope on the table, when he felt something inside. He looked in and saw a gold chain hugging a corner. He turned it upside down and let the chain fall onto the table. Remarkably thin, it looked like it could break with the slightest stress. He set it next to the envelope, then laid the open letter in his lap. The words were in English, but accents and phrasing suggested that whoever wrote it was foreign...

"Dear Gloria,

"So glad we have become friends. I can't believe our birthdays are same day! Now that our fathers are friends, we can share what it is like to live someplace different than our homes. I hope you liked Lida. I want so badly to come to London. Father says it can happen, but not until our countries have signed papers. Not sure what that means; something about a League...I hope it happens soon. I give you this locket to show my friendship. I have put my grandparents' picture inside. Grandmother says the blue gem has special powers. I don't know if that is true, but I give it to you to use if it does.

"Your new friend,
Dasha Kosmodemyanskaya"

Andrew smiled as he tucked the letter inside the envelope. *Gloria had a pen pal.* He set the envelope on the table and reached for the gold chain. The little girl, Dasha, had mentioned a locket. He frowned, suddenly remembering what his mother had told Maddi in her letter. *"Hang onto the locket...the locket holds the key."*

So, where is it, he wondered, as he laid the bare chain on the arm of the couch. Had the locket once hung on the chain beside him? Was it the same locket that Jeannie had mentioned; the one she had told Maddi to hang onto?

He opened the next letter and read it through; it was more of the same. He read the third and fourth letters, all written by the same girl, Dasha Kosmodemyanskaya. He came to the fifth envelope and noticed that the writing had changed. No longer the oversized loops of a little girl, this letter had clearly been penned by an adult. He checked the date; the letter had been written in 1942. Andrew did the math. The girls would have been about twenty years old. In the letter, Dasha spoke of a new friend, Annabelle, whom she was eager for Gloria to meet. *"She thinks like we do, Gloria...she despises fascism and loves all things British. You'll be fast friends, I'm sure. Her father works at the embassy."*

He went to the sixth envelope, again checking the date. February 5th, 1944. He pulled out the letter and read it through, finally recognizing one of the names...

"Dear Gloria,

"I am so excited to share this news. I have met a man...a good man. He works at the embassy and he shares my thoughts...my hopes and dreams, and my fears of what Nazism means to the people I love. His name is Sergey. We have gone out several times. I feel things for him that I have never felt.

"Annabelle has met someone, as well. As you know, she has been working in London's U.S. Embassy, and there she has met a man with a kind face and a good heart. His name is Arthur Kauffold, and his family is close to the King. Can you imagine that? Being close to a King?

"I must go now. I am sending you a coin...a medallion. You must keep it. It is part of something big...bigger than anything we know. I can't speak of it in this letter. I will tell you more when I see you in the spring.

"Your friend,
Dasha"

Andrew's eyes widened. He pulled out the coin that his mother had given him – the very last thing that she would ever give him – the pendant that looked much like one that Tonna had been given by her adoptive mother...*Annabelle*. He rubbed his fingers over the coin and frowned. *What the hell have I stumbled onto?*

CHAPTER 65

Beijing, China

Maddi had left the embassy, had walked further into town, and had spent the last several minutes looking for a payphone. *I need to warn the Hendersons,* she thought as she rubbed her arms to try to warm them. It had gotten even colder, and it looked like it might rain. If she didn't find a place to get warm soon, she felt certain she would freeze to death. After another block, she found a phone booth and stepped inside, glad to be out of the cold. She reached absently in her pocket for change; all she had was the hundred yuan bill from the cab driver. She closed her eyes, fighting tears. She was losing her will to do any of it...save Sturgill, save Lili, alert the Hendersons to the Morningstar threat. She was cold and tired, and just wanted to find a place to lay down. Then she thought of the words from the newspaper. *"The Hendersons have expressed their willingness to include him in every strategic decision from this point forward, for the duration of the war."* She sighed. *You have to let them know who he really is, Maddi.*

She stepped out of the booth and ran to a nearby café. Her hand was shaking as she handed a boy behind the counter the hundred yuan bill. "Change, please."

He stared at her. A woman standing behind the boy said sternly, "Găibiàn!"

The young boy opened the register and handed Maddi a combination of bills and coins.

Maddi thanked him, then left the café and walked back to the payphone. She stepped in, lifted the receiver, put in coins, and pressed zero.

"Shì de?" *Yes?*

"Long...long distance call...to...to Latvia."

"Qǐngwèn hàomǎ?" *Number please.*

Maddi frowned. She had never known the number to the Henderson castle. *What now?* she thought, once again fighting despair. "I...I'm sorry. I'll call back."

Maddi leaned against the wall of the booth. Never had she felt so defeated. How could she find the number to the Henderson castle? Hank? She shook her head. He had been there, but had likely never called there. Her eyes widened. *Cravens! He was there in the spring after the attack on the security team. Surely, he would've been given the number.* She took a deep breath and sighed. *I can't call him, it would put him at risk.* Again, she was tempted to just let it go, but she thought of the words in the article that told of the 'strong ties' being cultivated between Morningstar and the Hendersons. She closed her eyes as she tried to recall Cravens' number. She had memorized it in case something ever happened to her phone. With a shaking hand, she picked up the receiver, put in more coins, and dialed a zero.

"Shì de?"

Maddi rattled off the number to Cravens' cellphone, suddenly doubtful that it had even survived the crash. She heard ringing, and found herself praying that it had.

Finally, after the fourth ring, she heard an impatient, "Cravens here."

Maddi felt tears come to her eyes. She whispered, "Oh my god, Cravens." She paused. "Please, don't ask any questions. I need to know the number to the Henderson castle. I promise I won't tell them who I am. It's a matter of life and death. Trust me, Cravens...please."

"Ma—Harriett, you shouldn't—"

"Please, Cravens. I wouldn't ask if it wasn't important."

There was a pause. "Are you okay?"

Maddi fought the urge to burst into tears. She was the furthest thing from okay. "I'm...I'm fine. How about you?"

She heard a sigh. "The world's gotten crazy."

"I know."

She heard another sigh, this one deeper. He rattled off a number, then whispered, "Where are you?"

Should she tell him? *No...it's best if no one knows where I am.* "I...I can't say, Cravens. I have to go." She ended the call before he could reply. She fell against the wall of the booth, and in spite of every effort to fight against it, she began to cry...slowly at first, then harder, until she could barely breathe. She missed Cravens. She missed her old life. *I'd rather be dead than live like this.*

Out of nowhere, she heard the weak voice of a little girl. "No! Don't think like that...please, Special Lady...never think such a thing."

Maddi's tearstained eyes widened. "Lili?" she said aloud as she looked around the booth. She said it again. "Lili...are you okay?"

"I...I am for now...but I need you. Please, be okay...I need you."

Maddi took a deep breath, smoothed down her cape, and wiped her eyes. That was it. She needed to pull herself together. *Lili needs me.*

She cleared her throat and picked up the receiver. The minute the operator asked who she was calling, she rattled off the number that Cravens had just given her.

She waited. After two rings, the call was answered with a crisp, "Henderson residence. May I help you?"

Maddi was shaking. "Dimitri?" she said, doing her best to disguise her voice.

There was a pause. "Who is calling?"

Maddi swallowed. "Is...is Matt there?" She stayed with the British accent she had used as Harriett Winthrop.

"Madam, I will need to know who you are before I can tell you anything."

Maddi gripped the phone tight. "I...I can't say. Just know, Dimitri, that I am a friend...a good friend. I need to talk to either Matt, Walter, or Dora."

"Madam, it is not customary—"

"Dimitri, please, just trust me...it is a matter of life and death."

There was another pause, this one longer. "Mrs. Henderson is here. Please wait, Madam."

Maddi closed her eyes. After a minute, she heard the familiar voice of Henderson's mother, and for about the fourth time in an hour she fought tears. Still trying to hide her voice and stay with the British accent, she said, "Dora, I am a friend of...Mar—Matt's. That is all I can say. But I need to tell you that Ed Morningstar is not who he claims to be," she took a deep breath, "...and I am almost certain that not only is Latvia at risk, but you and everyone in that castle is in imminent danger."

Chapter 66

Uzava, Latvia

Morningstar was irate. He had just received a call from Levi, telling him of an email he had intercepted a few minutes ago between the acting President, Bob Harrington, and the Chairman of the Joint Chiefs, Alexander Daniels. Apparently, someone from the Henderson castle had agreed to attend the bullshit meeting that was scheduled to take place tomorrow morning.

Not only did Morningstar not want a Henderson at the meeting; he didn't want the meeting to take place at all. It was too great a risk. It was quite possible that once the various entities talked to one another, they might conclude that the freedom militias were as loyal as ever, and that someone had worked hard to imply that they were not. More importantly, if a Henderson went to that meeting, and was to even suspect that things weren't as they seemed, the entire clan could become suspicious. Though Morningstar had given them no reason to doubt his intentions, it was possible they might 'circle the wagons,' and never allow him to step foot in the castle again.

Funny that Dora said nothing about it when I stopped by this afternoon, he thought with a sneer. Morningstar had gone to the castle just before dinner to check in on the motley crew. He had asked to speak to Walter, but had been told that he had left the estate. Morningstar had spoken with

Dora, who had been uncharacteristically standoffish. *No matter,* he thought with a wave of his hand. *She'll soon be marching to my orders.* He flinched. *But only if I can find a way to stop that blasted meeting.*

He cursed under his breath as he paced in front of the fire. He checked the time. Almost ten p.m. He had been in that living room for most of the day and night, and was beginning to think it was the room itself that was the problem. *Bad karma,* he thought as he looked around the small, stuffy room. Not only did he now have a Henderson attending a stupid meeting that would undermine all he had put in place over the last two weeks, but his lovely Janet was on her way to Latvia with nowhere decent to stay. According to Levi, two rooms had been reserved at Riga's Grand Hotel for the Deputy Secretary and Janet.

The Grand was certainly suitable, but he didn't want Janet to stay all the way in Riga. It was nearly three hours from his bed-and-breakfast, which would give him barely enough time to travel to the capital city, bed his paramour, and get back in time to taunt the Hendersons at their castle. He scowled. *If I had taken charge of that damn castle when I should have, the Deputy Secretary and Janet would be staying there.*

He had expected to be well-entrenched in the mansion by now. But infiltrating it had been more difficult than he had anticipated. The staff, as well as the soldiers on the security team, were fiercely loyal to the Hendersons. Their adoration was apparent in every word they spoke and every action they carried out on behalf of the family. It had annoyed him. And it hadn't taken long to see that it wasn't going to be easy to turn the help against their masters.

He had also expected to have undeniable confirmation that Martin wasn't anywhere at the estate. He had seen no sign of the fair-haired young man, but that didn't mean that the Hendersons weren't hiding him somewhere on the grounds. Then again, it would have been quite a challenge for them to have kept him hidden for the entire two weeks that Morningstar had stopped by, oftentimes unannounced.

And it made sense that he wasn't there. The man was, after all, wanted by the U.S. government. Not only for his actions regarding the January bioterror attacks, but for his escape from a U.S. military base in western Lithuania. Though many weren't aware of the second infraction, they were certainly aware of the first. Any agent worth his salt would begin the hunt for Matt at his uncle's estate. Which meant that, not only did Morningstar not yet have dominion over the castle, but he also had no idea where the betrayer, Joseph, had run off to. Morningstar needed to kill him before Cobra had a chance to tell the world of Cobra's ties to the Hendersons. Once that got out, Henderson would have no reason to not divulge all he knew...about Morningstar, about his family of sons, and about his role in every major upheaval around the globe. Yes, Henderson would be forced to reveal his own role in all of it, but once the world learned that Cobra was a Henderson, would the discovery that Martin had been an assassin for a corrupt government aide really matter all that much?

The same could be said for Sturgill and Cobra. They were loose cannons. And, like Henderson, they would soon have no reason to keep Morningstar's secrets.

He stopped in front of the fire and hissed at the flames. *The sooner every one of them dies, the better.* Fortunately, Johnny Canterbury and Arthur Kauffold were just hours from Beijing. If things went as planned, Simeon would soon take out Sturgill and Cobra, and at least those two would be out of the way by noon tomorrow, China time...which was six a.m. in Latvia. Janet was expected tomorrow morning – *"by sunrise"* – which meant that by eight a.m. at the latest – ten hours from now – two of his enemies would be dead, and his lover would be less than three hours away.

He bristled. *But she should be staying in my castle, dammit!* He had considered asking the Hendersons if they would host the Deputy Secretary, and had planned on bringing it up during his visit that afternoon. But Dora's aloofness had steered him from it. Then, once he had learned that Walter wasn't there, he knew for sure that he would make no such request. After all, one couldn't expect an American dignitary to stay at a home – even if it is a castle – when the head of the household was away. *A home isn't a home without a man to oversee its operations.*

He had drilled the head of security regarding Walter's absence. *"Had the trip been planned, Dimitri?"* The soldier had stammered, *"Uh...no sir."* That was about all he had been able to get out of the man. Though Dimitri had let it slip that Walter would be gone overnight, he had insisted he didn't know why or where he had gone.

Yeah, right.

But Walter's absence did present an interesting opportunity. With him gone, that left only Dora to oversee the castle and all its functions, at least until tomorrow. And though Dora was one of the more capable women he had ever met, she certainly wasn't Walter. He smiled. If ever there was a time to take over the castle, it was now.

But it wouldn't be easy. Dimitri and his team of loyal sycophants were quite formidable; there was no question that they would fight to the death to defend Dora and that castle. He smirked. *So...what if I could get Dora to leave.* He nodded. With Dora away, Morningstar could insist that whoever was running the castle in her absence make room for the Deputy Secretary of State and her entourage. He could then add that he, as a representative for the Joint Chiefs of Staff, should stay to provide the authority and respect of a military man. *Which would get me a foothold in the castle.* Then it would simply be a matter of devising a plausible reason to stay.

He leaned against the mantel and stared at the flames. *So...what could lure a woman like Dora away from her home?* He grabbed the poker and stabbed at the logs. The flames rose quickly and he was forced to take a step back. Suddenly, his eyes lit up. "The meeting!" From what Levi had said, it was scheduled for tomorrow at nine a.m. A Henderson had agreed to attend. Morningstar had assumed it would be Walter. But if neither he nor Martin was at the compound, that left only one Henderson.

He pulled out his cellphone and dialed the Henderson estate.

The call was answered with a crisp, "Henderson Residence. May I help you?"

"Dimitri, it's Morningstar. I've just been informed by the General that there is a meeting tomorrow in Riga. I'm assuming someone from your estate will be going?"

There was a pause. "Um...yes sir. Mrs. Henderson is planning to attend."

Morningstar smiled. "Excellent. I have high hopes for that meeting, Dimitri."

"Yes sir. We do, as well, sir."

Morningstar ended the call. Slowly, he began to chuckle. An idea had begun to form in his brain. *What if poor Dora was to have an accident on her way to the meeting? Or, better yet, what if she was murdered...viciously... and left by the side of the road?* Not only would she be out of the way, but the meeting would surely be cancelled, and the castle would fall into disarray. *Which would give me the perfect opportunity to swoop in and take over...not just for a night, but forever.* He laughed aloud. It was brilliant. With one simple murder, he will have solved all his problems.

He leaned the poker against the hearth and walked to the window. The plan was practically foolproof. The minute he was notified that Dora had been killed, he would send his condolences to the castle staff, and offer to stay there to bring some semblance of order in the absence of its caretakers. He would then arrange for the Deputy Secretary and Janet to be picked up in Riga and driven to the castle.

But what will I do when Walter returns? He sneered as he looked up at the night sky. It wouldn't matter. By then, Morningstar will have endeared himself to the staff, and will have cemented his role within those castle walls. *Poor Walter will return not only to find his wife dead, but his faithful staff committed fully to me.*

Again, he laughed. Everything was coming into focus. Within a mere day or two, it would be impossible to stop what he was putting in place. Yes, Sturgill and Dan had been taken by the Chinese and could spill their guts at any minute. Yes, somewhere out there was a recording that could tie Morningstar to the murder of a U.S. senator, as well as a video that did tie him to a bioterror attack. And yes, Judah was still missing, as were Hank and Henderson. But soon the matriarch of a respected American family – a family that was integral to the safety of an entire country – would be killed...*murdered*...on the side of the road. The entire world would come to a halt. At that point, no one would care what evidence or accusations a few desperate losers might have against Morningstar, the great man who had kindly taken on the duties of the illustrious castle in western Latvia.

He looked out at the snow, overcome as it reflected the silver-white glow of the moon. The night sky was infinite, countless stars serving as affirmation that, in spite of setbacks, he was on the right track. With tears in his eyes, he said aloud, "I hear you, God. You're pleased with me...and I can understand why. You want me to know that my power – *our* power – will soon be unchallenged by any man."

Suddenly, he flinched. *But what about a woman?*

Again, he thought of Janet, only this time not with fondness, but with fear. She had charmed him like no woman ever had, and, as a result, he had let her into his life, his plans, his inner circle. *But was I wise to do so?* After all, wasn't it in a woman's core to deceive, to take while pretending to give?

He was convinced that the female DNA was imprinted with protein sequences that led to treachery and betrayal. His eye twitched; he rubbed it. *I need a way to keep Janet from taking what is mine.*

He walked away from the window and again paced the den, surprised that Janet had gone so quickly from an ally to a foe. He stopped. "No, not a foe...an adversary. There is a difference. One is against all that I stand for. The other is simply a competitor." He thought of his son, his *real* son, Benjamin. Janet would soon give birth to that boy, which meant that it would be Janet who would hold legal dominion over the child. His eyes flashed. "The boy won't even bear my name!" He resumed his pacing. His son...his Benjamin was about to be born to Janet *Morgan.* The law would give Benjamin *her* last name.

He couldn't let it happen. But what could he do?

He picked up his pace. "Benjamin *must* be a Morningstar!" He nearly choked as he spit out the next sentence, "Dear god, I'll need to make that woman my...wife!"

He felt unsteady and stumbled to the chair. The very thought of it disgusted him. Marriage was what peasants did to make sense of their lives. A false contract masquerading as joy, while imprisoning the hearts and minds of weak, pathetic men.

Suddenly, he grinned. As objectionable as it seemed, there were gains to be achieved in such an arrangement. *If I wed the bitch, then it'll only make sense that she stay with me – in my castle – long after the Deputy Secretary returns to America."*

But it needed to happen soon...while she was still in Latvia. Which gave him less than twenty-four hours to pull together a wedding. He frowned. *I'll need a ring.* Janet wasn't expected to arrive in Riga until around seven a.m., which, if she came at once, would get her to the castle around 9:30. Perhaps he could go to Uzava first thing tomorrow morning and buy a ring before she arrived. He frowned. *Dammit! Tomorrow is Sunday...no jewelry store will be open in this godforsaken place.*

Suddenly his eyes lit up. He put his hand in his pocket and felt for the locket he had acquired just months ago...the locket that had been mailed to him by Gad soon after the 'tragic' plane crash that had ended the life of Cynthia Madison. *A bit unconventional perhaps,* he smiled, *...but poetically* *just.* He rubbed it between his fingers and chuckled, triumphant as he held up the locket and said aloud to no one, "I will marry that bitch with Madison's locket, and I'll do it in my own damn castle."

He sneered. *But first, I need to get Dora out of the way.* The question was, who should do it? Who was both capable and available to murder Dora tomorrow morning? Again, he laughed. *Nothing like a Russian to turn Latvia on its head.*

He pulled out his private cellphone and dialed.

The call was answered after one ring. "Yes, Father?"

"You did well, my son, with your disinformation campaign." He paused. "But now I have another task for you." Morningstar quickly laid out his plan. When he had finished, he made Zebulun say it back to him. "Perfect, my son. Now go, take care it."

CHAPTER 67

The Henderson Compound

Dora had spent most of the evening in the den. Though it wasn't typically where she spent her evenings, with both Walter and Martin gone, it was the place where she felt closest to them...the place where they spent a good deal of their time in the castle. She smiled as she sat back on the sofa and stared at the fire. She sipped a glass of wine, barely tasting it as she awaited word of her husband's success...or failure.

She flinched. *Failure isn't an option,* she thought as she heard a grandfather clock chime ten. But for the last hour, it wasn't Walter she was thinking about, or Martin, or even Lili...it was the caller who had given her the ominous – though unnecessary – warning regarding Morningstar. Dora had already figured out that he wasn't a nice man. But the caller had taken it a step further. She had insisted – with a tremor to her voice – that not only Latvia, but Dora and the castle were in imminent danger.

What could an aide - albeit to the Chairman of the Joint Chiefs - do to us, she wondered, as she took another sip of wine. *Nothing. I am safe...the castle is safe...and Latvia will be safe soon enough.*

Dora had taken the call without a second thought. Now that Walter was gone, she was the head of the castle, and would be responsible for all calls until his return. She had done it many times, and was not the least bit put out by a late night call. As a matter of fact, about thirty minutes ago, she had spoken to a representative for America's acting President, Bob Harrington. He had called to ask Walter to attend a meeting in Riga tomorrow morning. The meeting was intended to reassure Latvian leaders that, in spite of the Secretary of State's visit to Moscow tomorrow afternoon, America's commitment to Latvia was firm. The Deputy Secretary, who was to arrive in Riga just before the meeting, would be attending, as well, to convey a similar message.

Dora had informed the representative that Walter was away, but that she would be honored to attend on behalf of the Hendersons. *"I will make sure that they understand how deeply America is committed to the goal of a free and independent Latvia."*

She had already planned on going to the meeting so that she could reassure Latvia's leaders that the militias, particularly the Henderson Freedom Fighters, were as devoted to Latvia as they had ever been. It shouldn't be difficult. The Hendersons had a long, storied history of offering support and sacrifice for the cause of Latvian freedom.

The meeting was at nine a.m., which meant that she could leave no later than six if she wanted to arrive in time to visit with a few of the leaders she had met over the years. She was well aware that it was often during those brief chats over coffee and quiche when the real work got done.

She looked around the den. Though it was cozy and warm, she had to admit that being alone in the castle – with Morningstar just miles away – made her nervous. *Thank God Dimitri has agreed to stay through the night,* she thought as she walked to the window. She opened the curtain and stared out at the darkness. Lampposts lit up the front walkway, as well as the long drive. Here and there, she could see the shadowed outline of a guard posted either on a bulwark or behind a rock. She sensed that there were more guards than usual. *Good.* Suddenly, she closed the curtain. *What if he's watching?* she thought as she backed away. *Don't be silly,* she told herself. *Why would Morningstar watch when he can just come waltzing in whenever he wants.*

She thought again about the call from the mystery woman. There was no question it had unsettled her...for more than one reason. First of all, was the panic in the woman's voice. She was truly frightened. Whether for herself or the Hendersons, Dora couldn't say. But more than that had been the voice itself. Dora felt certain she had heard it before. And not only the voice, but the sentiment – the power – behind it.

Your imagination is running wild, she thought, as she picked up her glass and walked out of the den. She went down the hall to the security room and stuck her head in the door. "Dimitri, I'd like you to increase security for the next several days."

Dimitri nodded. "Already taken care of, Ma'am. Mr. Henderson asked that I do so upon his departure."

Dora smiled. "Thank you. And thank you again for staying on tonight."

"My pleasure, Ma'am."

She nodded. "I'm heading off to bed. Have a good evening, Dimitri."

"Yes Ma'am. And don't worry...I've got this place tucked in tight."

Again, she smiled. "I'm sure you do, Dimitri."

She turned right out of the security room, then turned left, and walked down a back hallway that would take her to the master bedroom. As she walked, she thought again about the call from the mysterious woman. It wasn't just her voice or her determination...it was the way that she had stumbled over the name Matt. As if she knew that he was actually Martin. But so few knew that truth, especially so few women. As a matter of fact, other than her, there had only been one other woman who had been aware of that fact.

She reached the bedroom, glad to see a fire burning in the hearth. A lamp had been left on by her bed, and a pitcher of water was sitting next to it on the nightstand. She slid into her nightgown, then brushed her teeth and washed her face, all the while thinking of the woman on the phone. She walked from the bathroom to the bed and filled a glass with water. She took a sip, trying to decide if she should turn off the lamp. After two more sips, she chose to keep it on. She pulled back a heavy quilt and sat on the bed, hoping that what Dimitri had said was true...that the place had been *'...tucked in tight.'*

She took a final sip of water, then slid under warm sheets and laid her head on the pillow. She closed her eyes and thought again of the phone call. *You're being silly, Dora.* But as she felt herself drift to sleep, all she kept thinking was...*Perhaps, but in spite of the British accent, that woman certainly sounded – and felt – like Maddi.*

CHAPTER 68

Somewhere in Maine

Emma clutched a gold medallion in her pocket. Given to her by her mother when Emma was five, she found that she often gained strength just from holding the coin in her hand. She kept it with her always – something her mother had asked her to do – and she would rub it when she felt nervous or afraid. *Like now,* she thought as she sat on a bench near a grove of tall Balsam Firs. Though she had lived with Michael Cannon for sixteen years and had given him a child, she was nervous to see him. She was sure he would be curious...and angry. *I'd be angry if I'd been kidnapped as a result of my wife's betrayal, then two weeks later some agent pulled me from my home and drove me to the mountains without telling me why.*

But it had been the only way. It was far more important to allow Michael to be angry than to reveal the secret of President Knight and his hideaway in the mountains. So, arrangements had been made and Michael had been 'kidnapped' once again. He was being brought to a small park near Maine's Kennebec River, hundreds of miles from the secret White House location. Emma had been flown to the site about an hour ago, and she looked for him now as she welcomed a gust of wind, the cool breeze a comfort after being stuck inside the mountain compound for two weeks.

Foster walked out to meet Michael and the agents as they approached. Emma spotted Michael immediately, recognizing the way he walked, and how he nervously ran his hand through his hair. She knew those things because she had lived with him for so long. They had been through life

364

together; heartache, birth, death, and had become close in that way that only a husband and wife can be. But they had never been close in the way they should have been...and that was what she was going to try to explain to him that day.

They reached the bench, and Foster and the other agents walked away. "We'll be just over here, Ma'am."

Michael looked at her and it made her want to cry. His face was pale and thin; his eyes red. But what was more apparent was that he was hurt... so deeply hurt. She stood and he leaned in and hugged her. "I'm so glad you're safe, Emma," he whispered. She felt his arms around her, and, for a brief moment, she was back in time...to when it was simple. Yes, her love for him had been far less than it should have been, but things with Michael had been easy...and safe. She could smell him; not the scent of passion, but of familiarity...comfortable, reassuring, easy. She missed it; she missed going to sleep at night knowing that everything was okay. *But I don't miss waking up at three a.m. longing for the only man I will ever truly love.*

He stepped back and looked at her. "So, tell me Emma...what's going on?"

She fought tears. "How—how are you, Michael?"

His eyes flashed. "I'm shitty, Emma. Okay? I'm shitty. Galina's shitty... we're shitty." He sighed and looked away.

"Michael, I—"

"Just tell me what the hell's going on. Just say it, dammit."

Just say it, Emma. "Michael, I needed to leave. I was unhappy. But it wasn't your fault. You're one of the finest men I have ever known. It was never your fault."

He glared at her. "So how long were you unhappy, Emma?"

For sixteen years. "The past year or so. There are things that you never knew about me, and, in the last year, they...re-emerged."

"Re-emerged? Is that what they call it now?"

Emma reached out her hand; he pushed it away. The air that had been a comfort only minutes ago now felt cold. She zipped her jacket. "Fine. I'm in love with another man. There, I said it. I did everything I could to fight it, Michael, but I couldn't seem to get him out of my head."

Michael was practically seething. "And *this man* comes equipped with bodyguards who carry weapons?"

Emma nodded. "Yes, he does."

"Who is it, Emma?"

Emma's eyes filled with tears. "You don't want to know this, Michael."

He tightened his jaw. "Why the hell wouldn't I want to know the name of the bastard who ruined our marriage?"

Emma shook her head. "Michael, I—"

"Tell me, dammit!"

She turned away, brushing her bangs from her forehead. She gripped the coin in her pocket. After a minute, she said evenly, "Jerome Knight."

There was silence. Michael's eyes widened. "Who?"

"The...the President of the United States...Jerome Knight."

She watched as the color drained from his face. His anger faded, replaced with something she couldn't recognize. *Shock? Skepticism?* He began to chuckle, and, though it was joyless, it was better than the scowl. "Of course."

"Michael, I am so sorry. I tried my hardest to ignore these feelings, but I couldn't. I was no good for myself, and I was no good for you. I needed to tell you that. I needed you to know that I respect you and that I tried my hardest, and I'm sorry." She looked down. "I'm so very sorry, Michael."

He shook his head. "So, when did you meet...*the President*, Emma?"

They had reached the hard part. She swallowed. "I...I knew him before he ever became the President, Michael...before he had become...anything"

He looked at her, tears in his eyes. "Before me then?"

She looked down, ashamed. "Yes, before you." She paused. "But it doesn't mean I didn't love you; I did. I still do. Just not in the right way. I know Galina will never forgive me, and I'm certain that you won't either. But I couldn't do it any longer, not even for the sake of doing the right thing." She looked at him pleadingly as she grabbed his arm. "To stay would've been dishonest, Michael. And though I know it was wrong to leave, I couldn't see how deceiving you could be right." She had begun to cry; she quickly wiped her eyes. "That's what I've been trying to figure out, Michael...how can living a lie be the right thing to do?"

Neither one said a word as they stood in the fading sunlight, her hand on his arm, the cold air making both of them shiver.

Finally, Michael looked at her, his dark eyes no longer the deep brown she recognized; now a subtle shade of gray...as if sadness had its own color. "I think I always knew. Not that you were in love with the President – I would never have guessed that one – but I always knew it just wasn't enough." He sighed. "We were an old married couple right from the start. It was good enough for me, but I understand that it wasn't enough for you. I'm just sorry I couldn't be who you needed me to be."

He looked down, but Emma made him look at her. "Don't you be sorry for a single thing, Michael Cannon. You were perfect. You were loving and kind, a wonderful husband, a wonderful father." She paused. "You were everything you needed to be. The only thing wrong with us happened before I ever met you. That isn't your fault. I value every minute we shared, every bit of our life together, and I don't regret a single day." She moved closer, cupping his cheek with her hand. "Do you understand what I'm saying, Michael? I don't regret it. The only thing I regret is that I'm hurting you...and Galina." Tears came again, coating her cheeks, blurring her vision of the man she had hurt so deeply. "I...am...so...sorry, Michael."

He looked past her to the mountains. Never had she seen such grief on a man's face. She would have done anything to keep him from it; anything but the one thing she couldn't do, which was pretend she loved him the way she knew she was supposed to. She had tried and she couldn't do it; her heart belonged to another man.

Michael looked at her, the gray-brown eyes filling with tears. "I know you are." He shook his head. "I can't tell you it's okay, because it isn't, but I'll do my best to understand. And I'll try to make Galina understand." More silence as he looked to the mountains. "Do you remember the time we came up here for a picnic?"

Emma nodded; she did remember. Galina had been only three, and Emma had encouraged the picnic to get them out of the small apartment where she was finding it harder and harder to breathe. She grinned. "Yes, and Galina ran off to the creek over there." She pointed.

He laughed. "And I was the one who had to go in after her."

Emma smiled sadly. "She called you her knight in shiny armor."

He sighed. "Some knight." He looked away and then turned back to look at her. "Did you know I was kidnapped?"

"Yes, I'm so sorry, Michael."

"And that the guy threatened my life?"

She shook her head, ashamed.

"There's a worldwide manhunt underway for your President, you know."

She nodded. "I know. And I hope you won't tell a soul that I'm with him. As crazy as it sounds, it truly would compromise national security."

He laughed outright. "Well, I certainly don't want to be responsible for that."

Emma had to laugh as well.

He suddenly frowned. "Is he safe? Are you safe?"

She nodded. "Yes, and he assures me that you and Galina are safe, as well. He hired men to—"

"I know. I've seen them. It's creepy, Emma."

She frowned. "I know. Again, I'm sorry."

He said nothing as he stared down at his shoes.

She went on. "We had to leave DC, but the President is very much involved in what is happening in this country...in this world. Please don't tell a soul, Michael."

He shook his head. "I won't." He sighed. "So, if you and your President come out of hiding, will you be at his side? Are you going to stay with him, Emma?"

She looked down. This was the hardest part. *You've come this far, Emma.* She looked at him, tightened her jaw, and nodded. "It's...it's what I'd like to do, Michael. But I don't want to embarrass you or make this any more difficult than it already is." She sighed. "How would you like me to handle it?"

He smiled; the first real smile she had seen on his face in quite a while, now that she thought about it. *Maybe he's been unhappy, too.*

He sighed. "I suppose if I'm going to lose you to another man, I could do worse than the President of the United States of America."

She offered a weak grin. "I won't make it a big deal. I'll stay out of the limelight when the President returns to the world stage."

He nodded. "I would appreciate that, Emma. At least in the beginning. Galina and I will be fine. It may take her a while to get used to things, but once she learns that it's the President who has broken up her happy home, that may help."

Though the words had been meant to inject humor, they hurt; they were words that marked the end. As she looked at the man she had built a life with and had then so quickly ended that life, she couldn't help but feel a crushing sense of guilt.

He must have sensed it and, like he had done throughout their marriage, he gave her a way out, a life raft in the middle of the storm. "Emma, I don't like your decision; I'd give anything to change your mind. But I can tell that it's not going to happen." He sighed. "I don't want to live that lie any more than you. I'll do my best with Galina. When she's ready, I'll have her get in touch. Is there a way to do that?"

Emma nodded. She and Knight had discussed it. He had had Foster buy her a burner phone, and he had told her she could give the number to Michael. "You can reach me at this number." She handed him a card. "I will answer...no matter what."

He turned to go. "Good luck, Emma." Suddenly he turned around and hugged her. She hugged him back, trying not to cry, but she couldn't stop herself. He patted her, comforting her the way he had always done. He had been her consoler; she had only brought him grief.

He stepped back and looked at her, his eyes deep brown once again, the gray vanishing as he blinked to keep from crying. "You made me happy, Emma, and it made me a better man. You gave me that and I thank you." He turned and walked away, and the agents moved closer. But she barely saw them. She was watching Michael; watching as her husband of sixteen years walked away. But he had been gracious, even kind. As much as she hated what she had done to him and Galina, it was he who would help her through it. Because of Michael, she could leave.

She watched until he disappeared into a black sedan, then she looked at the two agents standing next to her. She forced a smile as she wiped tears from her cheeks. "Shall we go back to the ranch, fellows?"

Foster grinned. "Yes Ma'am, we should. The President is worried, I'm sure."

Emma nodded. Yes, she knew 'the President' was worried. But he didn't have a thing to worry about, not from her anyway. *I'm yours forever, Romer. I always have been.*

CHAPTER 69

Somewhere in the Katahdin Mountains

Hurry home, Emma. Knight was pacing the office, eager to hear back from the woman who had insisted on speaking with her husband one last time. The thought that such a scenario even existed was troubling enough. Watching – *letting* – her go felt like utter foolishness. Once she saw Michael, would she decide to go back to that life, where walking out to get the newspaper didn't involve armed guards? Knight knew, once she was reunited with the man she had been married to for over a decade-and-a-half, she might choose to go home. Could he take it? *No.* He had gotten her back; if she left now, he wasn't sure he could survive it. But what could he do? He had to let her go. To keep her from it would be to treat her like a prisoner. Not only that; he needed her to be free of it...he needed Emma to have no regrets.

Fortunately, the distractions kept coming, not the least of which was that about six hours ago he had instructed Foster to send Patrick and Kent to pick up the former VP, James Conner, in Millinocket, Maine. The man claimed to have vital information that he would share only with Knight. He checked his watch. *Where the hell are they?* Though it would require a valiant effort to get the unhealthy Conner up the ridge, six hours seemed like plenty of time. *Did something go wrong?*

He didn't know what Conner was about to tell him, but he had a pretty good idea. Conner's former Secret Service agent had told Foster that he had intercepted an email exchange that he claimed implicated Morningstar

– Jacob – in an effort to use false data to start a war. They had apparently planted evidence to suggest that Putin was trying to take back Latvia. Knight's hope was that Conner would be able to give him something more concrete...something that would implicate Morningstar directly. *Something I can take to Daniels to convince him that his trusted aide is a traitor.*

He stopped at his desk, resting his hands on the back of the chair as he stared at a stack of papers. Most of them were memos from Harrington. *I should be working on those.* But he couldn't focus. Not only was Emma rendezvousing with her husband of sixteen years, and not only was the former VP expected at any minute to give him information about a traitor, but a respected civilian – *an old man* – was on his way to China to free at least two citizens from a secret military prison. Cravens was to notify Knight the minute he got word of their success...or their failure.

Knowing that one of the prisoners was Martin Henderson had made Walter's success with the mission that much more vital. Knight had put in place two requirements for the mission. The first was that the Special Ops soldiers would stay in the helicopter no matter what. *"They are not to engage with Chinese soldiers on the ground. Do you hear me, Cravens? We would never be able to come back from that."* As it stood now, U.S. soldiers were simply providing a way for an embattled American businessman to escape China as gunfire broke out in a Chinese province not far from Beijing. The second requirement was that Sturgill and the Hendersons be brought – blindfolded – directly to him at the Katahdan hideaway.

He walked to the far end of the room, once again wishing he had a window he could look through. It been weeks since he had seen the moon or the sun. *Probably the longest I've ever gone in my life...especially in these mountains.*

His cellphone vibrated. He answered quickly. "Yes?"

"He's here, sir."

Knight nodded. "Send him in."

Knight walked to his desk. There was a knock on the door. "Come in."

The former Vice-President, Jim Conner, walked into the room. Knight couldn't believe the change in the man. He looked terrible. His gray hair wasn't combed, his dark eyes were tired and red. He was wearing a parka, and Knight couldn't help but think of pictures he had seen of Alaskan

Eskimos. Knight offered to take the parka, and the older man slipped out of the coat, not taking his eyes off of the President. He handed him the coat, and said weakly, "Thank you, Mr. President."

Knight took the coat and laid it on a nearby sofa. "Sit down, Jim." He motioned Conner to a chair in front of the desk, while he took a seat behind it.

The man sat slowly, still staring at Knight. "Thank...thank you for seeing me, Mr. President." His eyes narrowed and he shifted in his seat. "This place...how...what the hell's going on, sir?"

"Tell me what you've come to tell me, Jim. Then I'll fill you in."

Conner combed through his hair and frowned. "Um...could I maybe have a drink of water...or something stronger?"

Knight nodded. "Certainly." He walked to a small bar and poured Conner a glass of Glenlivet Scotch. He walked it to him, then returned to his chair.

Conner drank it down in one gulp, and set the empty glass on the desk. He looked at Knight. "I'm sure you're familiar with Ed Morningstar from the Pentagon."

Knight tightened his jaw. "Yes, the chief aide to General Daniels."

"Yeah, for like twenty-five years or so." He cleared his throat. "Anyway, I think he might be involved in something...underhanded."

Knight forced a look of surprise. "Underhanded?"

Conner lifted his empty glass. Knight stood and carried it to the bar. He refilled it and handed it to Conner, who drank about half of it and wiped his mouth. He set the glass in front of him and stared into the honey-colored liquid as he said quietly, "I think he's trying to...undermine our country, sir."

Knight didn't move. "That's a bold claim, Jim."

Conner looked at him, his red eyes seeming even redder. "I know, sir, and I don't make it lightly."

Knight narrowed his eyes. "Your former Secret Service agent had pretty much said the same thing to Agent Foster."

"Yes. Johnson's a good guy. Loyal." He paused. "He intercepted an email exchange between a guy named Jacob and another guy named Levi."

Knight cleared his throat. "I was told that, as well. What else have you got for me?" He leaned forward. "I need something concrete, Conner. Something I can show to those who will undoubtedly come to

Morningstar's defense."

Conner rubbed his forehead. "I figured as much." He paused. "As far as the emails, I'm not sure that I can find you anything concrete. But from what Johnson was able to tell, the plan was to plant evidence to make Latvia think that Russia was about to attack them." He frowned. "If the guy on the other end of that email exchange is Morningstar – and I have good reason to think that he is—"

"Why, Conner? Why are you so willing to believe that a cryptic email between two guys named Levi and Jacob involves Morningstar?"

Conner finished off the whiskey, then put both hands on the desk. "I didn't believe it at first, but Johnson swears that when he traced it back, it led straight to Morningstar."

Knight frowned. His top-notch IT guys had been unable to make that connection. "How was Johnson able to link Morningstar to the emails?"

Conner shook his head. "I don't know, sir, but I do know that Johnson has spent the last six months tracking Morningstar...ever since the guy forced me out of the White House."

Knight sat back, unable to hide his surprise. This was new information. *Don't change the subject...just keep him talking.* Again, he cleared his throat. "And his tracking of Morningstar led him to believe that he's a traitor?"

Conner nodded. "Yes sir. He told me that he would stake his life on it."

Knight shook his head. "If what you're telling me is true – and we have zero proof from what I can see – it would implicate a high-ranking Pentagon aide in an attempt to pull Latvia...and potentially America...into a war with Russia."

"Yes sir. It's why I needed to talk to you, sir."

Knight frowned. "Just a minute ago, you said that Morningstar forced you to leave the White House. What did you mean?"

Conner nodded. "Exactly what I said, sir." He sighed. "It's a long story."

Knight leaned back in his chair and crossed his arms as he stared at the former Vice-President. "I've got nothing but time, Jim."

Conner looked at him, his eyes dark, determined. "Let's just say that the guy has something on me. Good enough?"

Knight frowned. "For now."

Conner nodded. "Thank you, sir." Again, he ran his hands through his hair. "There's something else you need to know about this guy...about Morningstar."

"Go on."

Conner hesitated. "He...hated...Cynthia Madison."

Knight narrowed his eyes. "Why?"

"Um, sir, we all did."

"Who's 'we all'?"

"The Bentley Group."

Knight sat up straight. "What the hell is the Bentley Group?"

Conner rubbed the back of his neck. "A...group...an organization of well-positioned men in DC. We met once a week to discuss...the status of America."

"The status of America?"

"Yes sir. You know...its strengths, its weaknesses." He cleared his throat. "Let me just say, sir, that every one of us love our country." His eye twitched and he rubbed it. "Everything we did we did to try to create a better America."

Knight frowned. He said evenly, "What did you do, Conner?"

The former VP rubbed his mouth. "We...sort of...started wars, sir. Minor scuffles. But only to wake up the country to the evil that's out there, sir, I swear it."

Knight couldn't hide his shock. "You started wars?"

Conner looked away. "Yes sir, and we may have profited a bit from the sale of weapons that were required to support those wars."

Knight had to fight not to reach across the desk and punch Conner in the face. He wanted to grab him by the throat and ask him what would compel powerful men – *like a Vice-President* – to start wars for profit. Instead, he said evenly, "Go on."

Conner loosened his collar. He used the back of his hand to wipe the sweat from his forehead. "Senator Madison knew something was up. She had begun a senate investigation." He looked at Knight. "She even pulled Morningstar before one of her subcommittees." He stifled a grin. "It pissed him off, for sure." He leaned back and sighed. "I think she was trying to do the right thing, but she was sure messing up our plans." He held out his hands, palms up. "She didn't understand us, sir. We truly were concerned about America's weakness on the world stage. What had Jimmy Carter called it?" He frowned. "Our *malaise*." He sighed. "Anyway, we were tired of spineless diplomacy; the refusal to use force against our enemies when it was necessary." He leaned forward. "And, you know, sir...sometimes, it is necessary."

Knight was having trouble catching his breath. But even though what Conner was telling him was shocking, Knight had heard it all before. Morningstar had uttered the same refrain time and time again. And, though Knight had believed it then, and even believed it still, he was beginning to see that Morningstar's solution was the equivalent of a worldwide holocaust.

Conner went on. "Madison wouldn't let it go. She kept holding hearings, and she had started to dig into Silverton. She devoted an entire hearing just to them."

Knight frowned. "Silverton...as in Silverton Industries? The arms manufacturer?"

"Yes sir. They worked with us...to supply arms for the...wars."

Knight was dumbfounded. He remembered that hearing. He had been on the committee at the time. It had been one of the few times he had gotten a phone call from Morningstar since becoming a U.S. Senator. *"Don't let that bitch steer your committee in the wrong direction, Judah. She's a weak-kneed pacifist. You hear me?"*

Conner continued. "Though she had no idea that the Bentley Group even existed, she was about to ruin everything. Thinking she was doing right, that woman was about to keep us from restoring America's greatness." He lowered his voice. "Morningstar would often say that he wanted her... out of the way."

Knight's hands had begun to shake; he gripped them in his lap. "Keep going."

Conner took a deep breath. "Morningstar was capable of a lot of things, sir. Things that weren't right." He paused. "But he didn't do any of it by himself. He had helpers." He added quickly, "Not us. We didn't condone murder."

"No, just war."

Conner rubbed the back of his neck. "Yeah." He looked at Knight. "I know I'll probably go to jail for some of the stuff I'm telling you. I don't want that, sir. But there's one thing I love more than my freedom, and it's this country. That's how all of us in the group felt. America is the greatest nation on earth, but it's fading, both in prosperity and in its power to bring about the positive changes needed to keep the world safe." He paused. "I really believe that, sir. Though we profited handily from what we were doing, I think every one of us was there to make America stronger."

Whatever. Knight frowned. "Get back to Senator Madison, Conner."

Conner shifted in his seat. "Sir, I don't know any other way to say it." He sighed. "It wouldn't surprise me, sir, if we were to learn that Morningstar had something to do with the plane crash that killed that poor woman."

Knight remembered the call he had taken from Hanover a few weeks ago. *"We have evidence to suggest that the plane crash that killed Cynthia Madison wasn't an accident."* He stared at Conner. "That's quite an accusation."

"I know, sir."

Both men were silent. Knight leaned back and looked at Conner. The former Vice-President had always been intimidating, but suddenly he looked small and weak; a far cry from the big man who had stood beside the even bigger Jim Wilcox. To think that Morningstar had been involved with a group that started wars for profit, and had possibly been behind the plane crash that had killed a U.S. Senator, lent further support to that the notion that it was Morningstar who had orchestrated the assassination of a great President. It was more than Knight could take. He was starting to feel sick.

He was about to excuse himself, when Conner said, "There's one more thing you need to know, sir."

Knight was afraid to ask. "What?"

"Do you remember the bioterror attacks?"

Knight swallowed back a sudden surge of bile. "Of course, I do."

Conner rubbed his hands on his pants. "Sir, I think he may have had something to do with that, as well."

Knight didn't believe it...he couldn't. Though it was clear now that the man had been involved in a number of dishonorable deeds, he had always gone after men – or women – who were his enemies. There was no way he would kill scores of innocent Americans just to advance an agenda. "Not possible. We found prints of a rogue assassin at each site of the poisonings."

"Yeah, well, that's another thing. That assassin, the Phoenix, he was Morningstar's dupe. Morningstar coerced him into doing some pretty awful things."

Knight frowned. "Phoenix worked for *Morningstar?*"

"Yes sir. He was his own special hit man."

"I was told he was CIA. That he had gone rogue, and that they were doing everything in their power to eliminate the man."

"That's what Morningstar wanted everyone to believe. The guy went missing about a year ago. We had him followed for a while, but we lost him after about a month or so. As far as I know, the Group didn't hear from him after that."

Knight frowned. "As far as you know? Aren't you part of the Group?"

Again, Conner's eye twitched; he rubbed it. "As I alluded to earlier, sir, Morningstar forced me out of the Vice-Presidency...and the group." He paused. "He threatened to reveal my ties to the Bentley Group if I didn't leave the Wilcox ticket. Morningstar *made* me leave...he blackmailed me in a way I couldn't get around."

Knight covered his mouth as he stood and bolted out of the room to the bathroom. He hung over the toilet, certain he was going to throw up. His stomach heaved, but nothing came up. After a few more times, he flushed the toilet and walked to the mirror, thinking back to the last time he had done that very same thing. It was in the warehouse in Falls Church, Virginia. And it was for the same reason. Only now, instead of *suspecting* that Morningstar – his mentor for the past quarter-century – might have had a hand in Knight's astounding ascendency to the White House, he now knew it for a fact. *It has been confirmed.* Knight's role as President had been planned from the start. His rise to prominence as a U.S. Senator, his sudden selection for VP when Conner 'mysteriously' stepped down, and his elevation to the highest post in the land by the death of a truly great man...*who just happened to be my friend.* Yes, now he knew: *Morningstar killed Wilcox.* It was doubtful he pulled the trigger, but there was no question that he killed him all the same. And now, on top of it all, not only had he had a hand in the murder of the remarkable Senator Madison, but he may have played a role in the worst bioterror attack on U.S. soil.

Knight splashed water on his face and stared in the mirror. He looked terrible. His eyes were bloodshot, and there were dark circles underneath. He was pale and his skin was blotchy-red, almost like he had been beaten up. He frowned. *I have been beaten up...by the truth.* He wiped his face with a paper towel. *Get back in there, Knight...hear the rest of it.*

He walked into the office and stopped at the doorway. Conner's head was bowed; he hadn't moved. Knight guessed that Conner had done his own share of heaving over the last several days.

Knight walked to his desk. Conner looked up. "You okay, sir?"

Knight nodded. "I'm fine. Something I ate. Tell me more about Phoenix."

Conner nodded. "Morningstar wouldn't tell us who he really was. From time to time he'd refer to him as Joseph. I'm guessing it must be the guy's real name."

Knight had been about to sit in his chair when he stopped halfway, one hand on the desk. He looked at Conner. "Did you say Joseph?"

"Yeah, he either called him Phoenix or Joseph. It confused us all."

Knight forced himself to keep his cool as he stood and walked to the bar. He leaned against it, certain he was about to pass out. His head was spinning, his vision blurred; he blinked to clear his head. It was too much. Not only was Morningstar a murdering psychopath, but if what Conner had just said was true, then Joseph – the man he had just learned was Martin Henderson – was also the Phoenix. *God no...it can't be.* The Hendersons – and the country – would be crushed by that truth. It had been bad enough when a Henderson nephew had been accused of merely collaborating on the Lassa fever attacks. To learn that the nephew was actually the son, and that he had *carried out* those attacks would be too much. The Phoenix had been accused of orchestrating a bioterror plot that had killed scores of innocent men, women, and children. Knight had begun to shake. Did that mean that *Martin Henderson* had killed all of those people...*for Morningstar?*

Knight combed back his hair as he paced the room. How could Henderson do such a thing? How could anyone do such a thing? He stopped at one of the fake windows and stared at the closed curtains. *Am I any different?* Knight, too, had done Morningstar's bidding, and, though he hadn't killed for him, he had done everything else the man had asked. He had violated his Oath of Office, he had disregarded the rights of Americans. He had even been about to declare Martial Law, simply because Morningstar told him to. He had turned a blind eye to murder and deceit, and he felt dead inside. *How many good men have lost their souls to Morningstar?*

He took a deep breath, then walked back to his desk. He stood with his hands on the back of his chair. He stared at the former Vice-President, who looked even worse than he had when he had walked into the room. "Here's the thing, Conner, it's your word against Morningstar's." He paused. "And I'm betting the others in your 'group' would be reluctant to vouch for your story."

Conner nodded. "I'm sure of it, sir." He sighed, rubbing his forehead with his sweaty, over-sized hand. "But I have proof, sir."

"Proof?"

"Well...maybe not proof, but something that is incredibly damning."

It was what Knight had been looking for...something to verify to General Daniels and others that Morningstar had done the unthinkable. "What have you got?"

"A letter, sir."

"A letter? From Morningstar?"

"No. But once you see it, you'll understand."

Knight frowned. *How can a letter prove anything?* "You have it with you?"

"No, sir, I hid it...in my house in Nantucket."

"Well, I'll need to see it, Jim. I'll send Foster to pick it up once he gets back." He paused. "It shouldn't be long." Knight closed his eyes, his thoughts suddenly turning to Emma. *It better not be long.* He took a deep breath. "You'll need to give your wife a call...to let her know he's coming."

Knight walked to the couch and grabbed Conner's coat. He handed it to him. "One of my men will meet you outside the door. He'll direct you to a room where you can stay, and he'll give you a phone to use to make the call. Call her now, Jim."

"Yes sir. Right away, sir." Conner stood and walked to the door.

As he was about to walk out, Knight said, "Hey Conner."

He looked over his shoulder. "Yes sir?"

"Be brief, and don't tell your wife where you are. Don't even suggest that you're with me." He paused. "And don't call anyone else. My men will be listening."

"I won't, Mr. President." Conner left the room.

Knight sat at his desk and put his head in his hands. How many were guilty? *And how deep does it go?* He had just learned that his mentor had likely killed an admired U.S. senator, and that he may have been responsible for the worst bioterror attack on American soil. His suspicions had also been confirmed that the man he had called father for most of his life was probably responsible for the assassination of a sitting U.S. President, and was doing his best to start a war with Russia. But the most shocking truth of all was that that same guy had somehow taken a good man from one of the finest families in America, and had turned him into a killer...an assassin who had killed scores of innocent Americans, as well as ten, maybe fifteen leaders from around the globe. How had it happened? How had Morningstar coerced not just one, but at least two honorable men to forego their principles, and commit crimes against the country they loved...*all while convincing them they were doing it on behalf of that very same country!*

He ran his hands through his hair and sighed. So, what now? He had to build a case against Morningstar and present it to the Department of Justice. But first, he would need to convince General Daniels that his beloved aide was a psychopath and a killer. But he couldn't base it solely on the word of a man who had just admitted that he had started wars for profit, even if that same man possessed some letter that he felt certain would serve as evidence. *And I definitely can't implicate another Henderson. Not without knowing more about how Martin Henderson was involved in all of this.*

Just hours ago, he had been heartened to learn that Martin wasn't only alive, but had become a soldier for the same man that Knight had revered for the past twenty-five years. He had thought that he had possibly found an ally. But if what Conner had just said was true, there was no way the two men could join forces. The man who had poisoned innocent American citizens with a Lassa fever virus could never be an ally. Knight would need to bring the man to justice. He would need to make him pay for what he had done.

He checked his watch. The Chinook helicopter with its Special Ops team was on its way to the Yellow Sea. Which meant that if all went well, within the next twenty-four hours, one of two things would be true. Either

Knight would have Martin Henderson sitting in front of him defending his ties to Morningstar and his role as the Phoenix...or Martin Henderson would be dead.

Knight nodded as he stared at Conner's empty glass of whiskey. *Either way, justice will be served.*

CHAPTER 70

Beijing, China

The military jet that Hobbs had somehow arranged for Roger landed at a small airport outside Beijing at four in the morning, China Standard Time. After taking the antihistamine he had bought in London, Roger had managed to sleep for a solid four hours without images of Tonna waking him, and he left the plane feeling somewhat renewed. He took a train to the Pinggu district and walked to a safehouse two miles from the station. Hobbs had sent the address in another cryptic email, along with a message to *"...watch your back, spy boy."* Though Roger appreciated the sentiment, his back was the last thing on his mind. All he could think about was killing Cobra.

The safehouse consisted of a single room at the top of a flight of stairs. It had a desk in one corner, a lamp on the desk, and a pad of paper and a pen. It was stocked with water, a few cans of beans, and granola bars. That was it. It was enough. Roger needed very little these days. He was fed by his hatred of Cobra.

There was a closet in the room, just big enough to hold a suit, a fedora on a top shelf, and a briefcase and a pair of dress shoes on the floor. Typical business attire. The clothes and shoes were the right size, which meant that Hobbs had had someone put them in there intentionally. *He wants me to appear as a businessman.*

He carried the items to a bathroom down the hall, and was surprised to see a razor and shaving cream on a counter by the sink. *Hobbs has thought of everything.* Roger shaved his scraggly beard and mustache, then washed up quickly, doing his best to tame his out-of-control hair. He put on the clothes, walked back to the saferoom, and shoved his old clothes into his backpack. He caught his reflection in the window and nodded. The suit had a nice cut to it. He felt like a new man.

But am I? he wondered as he slid his laptop and wallet into the briefcase. After all, this wasn't the first time that Roger had taken on the mantle of the avenger. He flinched, not wanting to think of where he might be if his father – and his father's friends – hadn't intervened when they had.

He had been only twenty-one at the time; a vulnerable time for many young men...especially if they were already nursing a healthy anger toward the world. The wrong crowd, misplaced emotions, and the next thing you know, you're participating in a lifestyle you never dreamed of. *Those days are behind you, Roger.* The deals, the drugs, the death of a friend. It had been only a few months of his life, but it had nearly destroyed him. It certainly wasn't a path that would have allowed him any sort of future. His attempts to right a wrong had nearly cost him his life.

He shook his head determinedly, not wanting to think of those dark, hate-filled days. But it had been harder to do of late. He felt the same anger, the same indignation, the same refusal to accept a world where the good were continually assaulted by the worst that mankind had to offer. Early on, that anger had aided him in his quest to hunt Cobra. Was it helping him still? *Of course it is,* he thought with a twist of his lip. *I'm better because of it.* But 'it' was no longer anger...it was hate. And it was consuming him.

He stood and put on his coat. *Get to work, Roger.* His first task was to meet up with a contact that Hobbs had given him; a man by the name of Hao Deng. Roger was to meet him in the CBD, Beijing's Central Business District.

Roger walked out of the safehouse at 4:44 in the morning. Dressed in the suit, and carrying the briefcase in one hand, the fedora in the other, he took a five o'clock train to the CBD. He set out walking toward an address in the Chaoyang district. Though it was still early and the sky was dark, the sidewalks were filled with businessmen. *That explains the suit and briefcase,* he thought as he stuffed his wild hair under the fedora. He reached the address, which was an upmarket high rise, and nodded. The sophisticated location likely allowed Deng to operate with less scrutiny than if he was lurking in some back alley.

Roger took an elevator to the fourth floor. He went to the last door in the hall, knocked twice, waited, then knocked four more times. The door was opened by a short man, about five-five, who wore his hair in tight black braids. He, too, was wearing a suit. Roger told him his name. The man said nothing, but waved for Roger to follow him through a reception area to a back office. He unlocked a safe and took out a SIG Sauer P229 pistol and a brown cloth satchel. He handed the items to Roger.

Roger frowned as he looked in the satchel and saw C4 explosives. "Why C4?"

The man, Deng, shrugged. "I no know...Hobbs say you need." He handed Roger a card with a phone number. "No use sat phone. They track you, they find me."

Roger nodded and tucked the card in his pocket. As a precaution, he locked the gun and satchel in the briefcase. Getting caught with either item would at the very least get him questioned and thrown in jail. He thanked the man and left the office.

He walked to the train, took it back to the Pinggu district, and walked the two miles to the safehouse. He spent the next hour on his laptop searching for video feed of Sturgill and his bodyguard. It was slow going. The Chinese placed strict controls over all information that went into or out of the country, which meant that Roger spent the first half-hour just finding a way around the firewall. Once he got past it, it took him another forty minutes to find anything on Sturgill or his bodyguard. Finally, just as the sun began to rise, Roger stumbled on video from a street cam that showed images of the two men sitting in a diner in downtown Beijing. The date: November 4th. From what Roger could tell, Sturgill and a disguised Cobra had spent much of the afternoon there. He continued to sift through video feed, soon spotting the hallmarks of a parade. He typed "parade, November 4th" in his search engine and quickly learned that the National Heroes Day Parade had gone through downtown Beijing between the hours of six and seven p.m. *That's got to be what they were waiting for.*

He read about the parade. It was exactly what it claimed to be; a parade for heroes. What sort of heroes? Proletariats? Artists? Government workers? Who had attended? Was it national, or merely a local celebration? He tried to find more about it, but could find nothing but what he had already read. *I'll ask Hao Deng.* He took Deng's card from his pocket. As he pulled his sat phone from his backpack, he remembered what Deng had told him. *"No sat phone. They track you, they find me."*

Fortunately, Roger had another phone he could use, a trac phone he had picked up soon after leaving Paris. Cobra had destroyed Roger's cellphone when he had left Roger to die in the cave beneath the city. Other than his father, Roger had told no one of the trac phone – not even Tonna – knowing that the minute someone called him, the connection alone could make them a target. The only reason he had told Hank was because Cobra was already aware that Hank was Roger's father.

He rummaged through his backpack for the trac phone. He was about to dial the Hobbs contact, when he saw that the phone's battery had died during the flight. He looked for an outlet. He found one behind the desk, but it needed an adapter. He opened the top drawer, pleased to see a universal adapter. He plugged it into the only outlet, then plugged his phone into the proper receptacle. He dialed Hao Deng.

The call was answered after the first ring. "Nǐhǎo?"

"It's spy boy."

"What you need?"

"There was a parade on November 4th. What can you tell me about it?"

"National Heroes Day. Honors heroes."

"I got that far. What sort of heroes?"

"From revolution."

"I see. Who attended? Was your President there?"

"No. He overseas. It mostly military. People's Liberation Army, People's Armed Police, Militia, CCP." There was a pause. "Mostly propaganda... for masses."

"Is it a national celebration? In other words, do people come to Beijing from out of town?"

"Yes."

"How about from around the world?"

There was a pause. "No...maybe visiting dignitary."

"Got it. Thanks."

Roger ended the call. As he set the phone on the desk, he noticed that the message light was blinking. He frowned. *Dad?* It had to be. He was the only one who knew the number. Roger shifted uneasily. He hadn't talked to his dad in months. Not since Paris, as a matter of fact. Should he listen to the message? *No...because then I'll feel compelled to call him back.*

He couldn't talk to Hank...not now. His father would sense the change in him, the overwhelming hatred that had taken hold of his heart. He would know how far Roger had fallen, how far he had drifted from the son Hank thought he knew...the son he thought he had saved six years ago. Not only would it devastate him, but it would cause him to worry about a past that he likely thought had been put to rest. Hank would know that the anger of those days had returned...and it would break his heart.

Roger stared at the phone. *I'll call him after I kill Cobra.*

He sat back in the chair and rubbed his eyes. Just thinking of his father had unsettled him and had weakened his resolve. *So, don't think of him. Don't think of any of them anymore...Hank, Jenny, Tonna. None of them... until Cobra is dead.*

He turned his focus to the parade. Deng had told him that it was mostly military. Had Sturgill planned his attack to coincide with the parade? Had he wanted to convey a message by choosing that particular event? Was he hoping to isolate the military leader's son at the one singular occasion meant to celebrate the man? If so, it suggested a great deal of forethought and planning. *Had Sturgill done all that by himself?* Roger shook his head. He doubted it. From what he had read about Sturgill, he wasn't smart, or wise, or even clever. He was seen as an unimaginative bottom feeder; just another DC lacky who did what he was told by the unelected bureaucrats in Washington, DC. Hardly the sort of man who would devise such a well-thought-out plan. But if Sturgill wasn't behind the plot, then who was? And how had Cobra gotten involved? Had Sturgill merely been a pathway for Cobra to gain access to the military leader's son? If that was the case, then it would suggest that Cobra had been sent to kill the man...that Cobra had been *hired* to carry out the assassination. Why? What would be gained from killing a military leader's son?

His laptop let out a beep; another message from Hobbs. He clicked a link within the email, waited, then typed in his password. A blank screen gave way to a grainy photograph of two men being dragged into a building. Sturgill and Cobra?

He enlarged the photo; it vanished from the screen. He could feel his chest tightening. He was about to send a request to Hobbs to resend the photo, when he received another alert. Again, he typed in his password, then waited for the five-second message.

"Satellite confirmation: subject is alive...with C.S., also alive. Coordinates: 40.1N x 116.2E"

Roger memorized the coordinates quickly, before the message left the screen. He typed them into a digitally secure locator on his laptop. A map appeared, with a circle on the site that matched the coordinates. It was about ten miles northwest of Beijing, at the foot of the Xishan Mountains. He measured the distance from his current location. *About forty minutes by train.*

He logged off the laptop, unplugged his trac phone, and slid both into his backpack. He was close; he could feel it. If all went well, Cobra would be dead by noon.

CHAPTER 71

Beijing, China

Hank stared at his cellphone for probably the hundredth time. *Where are you, Roger, and why aren't you calling me back?* Hank had called Roger over eight hours ago, thinking that Roger might be able to tap into his CIA resources to help Hank find Jenny. He hadn't been surprised that he had needed to leave a message; that was typical when Roger was in the field. What surprised him was that Roger hadn't returned the call. Granted, his job often put him in precarious positions; it was possible Roger wouldn't be able to call him back for days.

But still he worried. Was Roger in trouble? And not only from the criminals he had dedicated his life to pursue. Hank was worried about Roger's past...the events that had taken place six years ago that had nearly destroyed his son.

Hank blamed himself. The divorce had been tough on him. Roger had gotten in with the wrong crowd and, as a result, he had done things he wasn't proud of. But it was worse than that. He had begun to deal with troublemakers...mobsters from out of town. On a fateful night in late summer, as he and his friends had been partying with a couple of those thugs, a man had come out of nowhere and had shot not only the mobsters, but Roger's best friend. Roger had come unglued. His anger had consumed him and he had gone on a rampage of revenge. But he had picked the wrong men to wage war against. It was only with the intervention of well-placed operatives – friends of Maddi's – that Roger was kept safe, and was able to get away from them. No one knew of it; least of all the federal government. Roger would never have been permitted to be in the CIA if they had. Why? Because he had been unhinged for a full sixty days of his twenty-first year of life. The CIA couldn't put a man in the field who might come unglued at the first sign of injustice. And though Hank was convinced that Roger's hard-earned experience was what had made him so well-suited to take on Cobra, the people in DC would likely disagree.

Which was why not only could no one learn of it, but why, whenever Roger went dark, Hank would find himself wondering if he had returned to those dark days.

He thought back to the last time he had laid eyes on his son. It had been in Scotland, after the events at Dalgety Bay. Even then, it was only for a split second as he had watched Roger run up a hill in pursuit of Cobra. Prior to that had been when Roger had fought for his life in a hospital bed in Paris, after he had nearly died in the catacombs beneath the city. Cobra had, in fact, left Roger there to die, and if it hadn't been for Martin Henderson, he would have. Hank and Henderson had managed to find Roger, and Henderson had offered his life in exchange for Roger's. Cobra had taken him up on it, and had taken Henderson. He had left both Hank and Roger in the cave. Luckily, Henderson had managed to get a message to Maddi, who had brought help to the cave. They had gotten Roger to the hospital just in time, but he had spent the next several days hovering between life and death. Once he had come out of it, he had been more determined than ever to find Cobra. But a line had been crossed; Hank had seen it in Roger's eyes. Was it the same line that had been crossed six years ago? Hank was beginning to think so.

He ran his hand over his chin. There was nothing he could do about it. His only hope was that once Roger caught Cobra and turned him over to the authorities, he would let go of the hate and go back to who he had been. *But is that possible for any us,* Hank wondered as he leaned back in the booth. If Hank's own experience was any guide, then it wasn't. Every event, every trial, every disappointment changed a man forever. He sighed. *The challenge is to not let those changes destroy you.*

But Hank was still left with the dilemma of what to do about Jenny. If Roger wasn't available to help him find her, then he would need to rely on Cravens. But Cravens had turned it over to the FBI. *A premier organization,* he thought with a nod. But still, it didn't seem enough. Hank sighed. He would simply have to trust that they were doing all that could be done. In the meantime, there was nothing to do but wait.

Or, I can fly home and find her myself, he thought as he clenched his fists. It was what he should have done in the first place. But that option was off the table. He had just promised Cravens that he would help Walter free his son from a Chinese prison.

He shook his head as he looked around the diner. It was morning; he could see the sun rising through the window. He had been sitting in that same booth the entire night. He felt good there; less alone. There had been a shift change, but the waitresses had seemed to disregard the fact that he had more or less set up residence in the lonely booth in the back of the café. He had napped off and on, and at three a.m., had finally broken down and ordered a sandwich. It was the first thing he had eaten since the day before, as he was trying to save his cash in case he needed it for something important. *Like a quick plane ride out of here.* Fortunately, he still had some of the money that he and Maddi had gotten in Hamburg. He checked his wallet. *Two thousand yuan.* He sighed. Barely enough for a hotel, let alone a plane ticket.

And I'll need to buy a gun, as well. Hank would need a weapon if he was to help Walter battle the Chinese. But China's rules regarding guns were strict, to say the least. He would either need to steal a gun, or get one from Walter and his soldiers.

Cravens had told him that Walter should get to China by five a.m. or so, and to the jail no later than ten. He was flying in on a Henderson jet, and, according to Cravens, was bringing at least two soldiers. As for the exact site where Henderson was being held, all Cravens had given him was the general location. *"Ten miles northwest of Beijing, at the base of the Xishan Mountains. A warehouse in a valley."*

Through the course of the night, Hank had had plenty of time to ponder how Henderson had wound up in China. The most obvious answer – though he couldn't see how it would have happened – was that Maddi, who was also in China, had reached out to him; that she had called him in a moment of weakness and had set up a rendezvous. *But why China?* Then again; why not? China was about as far from the world that they had both been a part of as anyone could find. And there was no question that the love between them had often caused them to take risks they normally wouldn't take, and make decisions that seemed foolish and out of character.

But if that was the case, then where was Maddi? And how would she have gotten in touch with Henderson? He didn't have his old cellphone; Hank knew that much from his time with him in August. Which meant that Maddi would have had no way to call him directly. And she would have never risked calling the castle. As for Henderson, he couldn't have reached out to her. *She isn't even supposed to be alive!*

Hank had finally concluded that it was nothing more than a wild coincidence that both Maddi and Henderson were in China. He hoped that was the case. If not, then not only was the circle of those who knew that Maddi was alive growing ever wider, but if Maddi was with Henderson, then wasn't it possible – maybe even likely – that she had been imprisoned, as well? Was that why Hank had been unable to find her? Had he risked everything, including the love and safety of his ex-wife, simply so that Maddi could be taken prisoner – and possibly die – in a foreign jail? He frowned, disgusted by the whole thing. He didn't want to think about it.

He rubbed his eyes, then opened a map of the city that he had taken from a rack by the counter. He laid it on the table, reviewing again the area where Cravens had said the prison was located. He found the Xishan Mountains; the foothills started about ten miles northwest of Beijing. Walter was expected to be at the prison site no later than ten a.m. Hank checked the time. Seven-twenty. It would take him ten minutes to get a cab, another thirty or so to get to the base of the Xishan Mountains, then who knew how long to find the warehouse. *I need to get going.*

He laid thirty yuan on the table. He grabbed his bag – the same bag that had accompanied him through all of Europe and now China – and slid out of the booth. The mission was vague, to say the least. Who was he saving? Just Henderson, or Maddi, too? Did it matter? He sighed. *No, not really.* The only reason Hank's son was alive was because of sacrifices that had been made by Maddi and Martin Henderson. Which meant that Hank would do whatever he could to help Walter save his son.

CHAPTER 72

Beijing, China

Walter Henderson had arrived in his private jet on the tarmac of a small airport outside Beijing at four in the morning, CST. Though he had initially been challenged by two armed guards, he was able to quickly reassure them with a photo ID and a letter of introduction that identified him not only as a respected international businessman, but as a friend to the sitting Chinese President. He and two of his Latvian freedom fighters, who were also dressed in suits, had taken a cab to his downtown Beijing office. For all intents and purposes, they were there on routine business. After a friendly hello to a janitor who was cleaning the building, he and the two men had slipped into a storage closet, and had changed into black pants and black hooded sweatshirts. Wearing tinted glasses, they had snuck out a back window and had jogged to a downtown park. They had benefited from the early morning darkness, as well as dense foliage from age-old fir trees, which had hidden them most of the way as they had sprinted to the north end of town. Walter had then led them to a small depot, where they had hopped a freight train that had carried them to the base of the Xishan Mountains. A valley in those mountains was his only clue for where Martin might be.

They had reached the foothills about an hour ago, had climbed a rise, and had been camped out in the tall grass ever since. They were cold and eager for sunrise.

Though there might have been an advantage to attacking in the dark, they had yet to actually locate the prison. Sunrise would be essential, not only to finding it, but to determining its layout and the number of soldiers they were up against.

The only building he had spotted so far as he had looked through his high-powered binoculars had been an abandoned train station about a quarter mile to his right. He had seen a rusty gate next to it, which opened to an overgrown parking lot in front of the station. Though the clue he had picked up from Martin's notes had indicated that the prison was in a valley, Walter had kept his eyes focused on the old station, hoping against hope that Martin was inside. But after forty minutes with no activity anywhere near the place, it was now time to move his men to another hillside.

Then, about a minute ago, just as he had been about to give the order, he had spotted a truck passing through the gate. But instead of going to the parking lot, it had proceeded through the trees and down a hill along a barely-visible path.

He moved north along the hill, easing his way down, glad for a sudden ray of sunlight easing in over the mountains. His seventy-two-year-old joints ached, but still he kept going, never taking his eyes off the truck. He stopped about halfway down the hill, watching as the truck pulled up in front of an old building that was well-hidden amid tall trees. Soldiers jumped from the back. He counted ten in all, then watched as another ten came from either inside the building or its periphery. *Shift change.* Something – or someone – of high value was inside. Political prisoners? He frowned. *It has to be.*

He motioned for his two soldiers to follow him as he crept further down the hill. They stopped at a clump of trees about fifty yards from the bottom. The sun was brighter now, and though it offered a better view, it could easily expose them. Staying low behind the trees, he looked down at a side entrance of what appeared to be an old, single-story warehouse. The building was surrounded by a parking lot of cracked cement, overrun by the roots of ancient oak trees and dense brush.

All at once, he heard a rustling a few yards behind him. He pulled out his gun, lowered to his stomach, and motioned to his soldiers to do the same. He heard footsteps less than a yard away and tightened his finger on the trigger. He waited. He snuck a look over his shoulder. He didn't see anyone. He was about to order his soldiers to make a run up the hill, when he heard another rustle of grass, this time barely a foot away. He held his breath and readied his pistol to fire. He waited. He felt a hand on his shoulder and turned onto his back. Holding the pistol with both hands, he aimed it directly at the face of a white man with wild hair and a tangled beard.

"I thought that was you," the man whispered, in perfectly clear English.

Walter continued to hold the pistol in the man's face. He looked past the beard and the wild hair, and was stunned to see Hank Clarkson. Whispering as well, he said, "Hank, you look terrible."

Hank chuckled. "I am terrible."

"Where the hell have you been?"

"Well, as you might imagine, it's a long story. We don't have time now."

Walter stared at him. He looked different, and not only because of his tousled appearance. The last time Walter had seen Hank had been at the castle, when Walter had encouraged him to take a drive to clear his head. So much had happened since then, and he could only imagine what the man had been through. "Are you okay?"

"No, but I'm here, and I'm in good enough shape to help you." Hank knelt behind the trees and pointed at the warehouse. "So let's go in there and get your son."

CHAPTER 73

Darlington, England

Andrew Madison leaned back on the Chesterfield couch, stretching his long legs in front of him as he ran a hand through his thick brown hair. He shook his head as he saw how his jeans hung loosely on his lanky frame. The weight loss was a symptom...a symptom of a man who had been through too much.

He checked the time. *Twelve-thirty in the morning.* He had been in that den for nearly six hours, pausing only once to go to the bathroom and to make another sandwich. He was exhausted, but he couldn't stop reading the letters.

He had just finished letter number seventeen, and what he had read so far had stunned him. Spanning forty years, three women – his grandmother Gloria, her Belarus friend Dasha, and Kauffold's wife Annabelle – had experienced history, starting as pen pals at the age of eight, and winding up as resistance fighters in the second World War. Members of a group known as The Partisans, the three of them had formed a coalition within the group, replete with coins that had bound them in some special way that Andrew did not yet understand. The coins, like the one in his pocket, were a way of defining not only their friendship, but their commitment to one another, and to a cause that – as Dasha had put it time after time – *"...is bigger than us...bigger than anything that is happening...even bigger than the Nazis."*

After the tenth letter, he had decided to write down some of the more intriguing facts on a notepad he had found in a drawer. He had started with the women and their children. Though Tonna was adopted, she clearly belonged to Annabelle, and Dasha had had two daughters, Larissa and Emma. Andrew's grandmother, Gloria, had had a son, Stewart, who was Andrew's father. He was killed when Andrew was a boy, and Andrew guessed that that was how his mother Jeannie had ended up with the coin. There seemed a strong desire for the women to pass on the legacy to their female offspring, which made him wonder why it was Harold who had given the coin to Jeannie, and why he had instructed Jeannie to give it to Andrew *"...when he was ready."* Again, he pulled out the coin and ran his hand over the image of the angel. He shook his head and shoved the coin in his pocket.

Once he had documented the family trees, he had moved on to the women's journey through history: The Nazi takeover of Central Europe, the Soviet response, the alliance between Russia, the UK, and America, so much of that history embodied in the friendships of Dasha, Annabelle, and Gloria. In the letters, they spoke not only of events, but of how those events had impacted their world view. Over time, all three had become 'global thinkers,' no longer seeing the world through the eyes of just one country or one point of view. They had begun to appreciate a broader understanding; all nations unified in an effort to fight tyranny and make the world a better place.

The women had written in depth about many major historical events, and Andrew had found himself captivated; as if he was getting a birds-eye view of history. One of the more fascinating stories involved the friendship between his grandfather Harold and the future U.S. President, Dwight Eisenhower. Andrew had never understood why Harold had been with Eisenhower during the build-up to Operation Overlord, but he guessed he must have played some sort of role in the D-Day invasion. According to one of the letters, the two men had spent at least part of the night before D-Day playing rummy and drinking Scotch while waiting for the weather to clear. Andrew's grandfather had refused to say much about the War, and he had most certainly never mentioned that he had been close pals with Eisenhower.

Andrew had learned the depth of their alliance when he had been recruited to join the Morning Star organization back in March. Because of the friendship between the two men, Harold had reached out to Eisenhower in 1945, once he had become aware of the German warship, *Der Morgenstern,* and its powerful – and dangerous – technology. From there, the Morning Star organization was born.

Andrew leaned against the back of the couch and frowned. Secret alliances, clandestine coalitions...he was beginning to see that his legacy was far more colorful and far more significant than he had ever imagined. He felt a renewed sense of purpose; a sense of obligation. *But to what?* he wondered as he stared at the letters. That was the question...what was Andrew to do with his newfound ties to the past?

And those seventeen letters had made it all so real. It was as if he had been standing next to Eisenhower in the make-shift barracks at Southwick house on the southern coast of England as the allies had geared up for the Normandy Invasion. As if he had been camped with the soldiers, consumed by their intensity...and their fear, and annoyed right along with them as they had endured one more weather delay.

But the letters had relayed more than just the challenges of D-Day. They had also shed a light on the ugly world of Hitler's Germany. Though Andrew had read about the evils of the Third Reich many times over the years, never had it seemed so real as it did in Dasha's letters. Taken directly from comments by the few survivors she had met, her details of what had taken place in the concentration camps had left him physically ill. He was grateful when she got to the part where they were liberated. He rejoiced right along with her and the other two pen pals.

But the hell of Nazi Germany was only the beginning. Dasha had been in the thick of the atrocities committed by Josef Stalin, and, though Andrew had read about those events, as well, he had only understood them from the pages of a book. Dasha brought to life every horrific detail of every slaughter, every violation of the dignity of people she knew and loved. And it changed her. She began to see her life's purpose as making Russia not only safer and free, but a positive influence in a troubled world.

Sadly, Dasha's life was cut short. Her tragic death in 1972 from cancer, which played out on the pages of her letters, impacted Andrew as if he had known her. From what he could determine, her family, which had traveled from Belarus to Latvia in the early fifties, had then traveled to America in

1966 to obtain treatment for the cancer. They had been permitted to make the journey under the Geneva Convention, and it was there, soon after her arrival, that she had had her second child. She had died five years later. It grieved him that she hadn't been alive to see the thawing of relations between Russia and the West. But Gloria and Annabelle had celebrated it in several letters, written not only to mourn Dasha, but to honor her. In every letter, they mentioned the unique bond they shared, and the coins that were somehow instrumental in their relationship and their unified goal.

He leaned forward and stared at the letters that remained; the three letters that had never been opened, arriving after his grandmother had died. He was hesitant to open them; he wasn't sure why. All three were written in the current year, 2004, many years after the ones he had just finished. Dasha had died in 1972, Gloria had died about fourteen years later, and, from what Kauffold had told him, Annabelle had died in 1993, approximately seven years after Gloria's death.

So, who wrote these? he wondered as he reached for the first of the three remaining envelopes. And how had they ended up in the scrapbook with the others? Had the caretaker taken them from the mail and slid them in the scrapbook? How would he have known to do so? They were unopened, so he couldn't have known what was inside. Andrew noted that all of the letters – including these last three – had two small asterisks in the bottom right corner on the back. A code of some sort? It had to be. Had Gloria perhaps shared that code with the caretaker, who had then shared it with his grandson? Andrew frowned. *I'll ask him about it in the morning.*

The date written on the back of the first letter was February 3rd, 2004. He slid it from the envelope, noting that the handwriting was different from the prior letters.

> "Dear Gloria Madison,
>
> "You don't know me, but you knew my mother. I am the daughter of Dasha Melnikov...Dasha Kosmodemyanskaya. She may not have mentioned me; I think she was a bit protective of my gifts...maybe even worried for my safety because of them. Regardless, I know about you and Annabelle, and I know how much she valued your friendships. I also know that she shared with you at least a

few important truths about The Partisans. I would like to share a few more. Though the Nazis are long gone, The Partisans are not, and we have been fighting our own Russian government for over five decades. I'm uniquely qualified for this task. Not only did I inherit the spirit and strength of my mother, but, as I mentioned before, I have been blessed with rather unique gifts, one of which is an ability to recall every detail of every book I have ever read, every movie I have ever watched, and every newspaper I have ever laid eyes on. Both troubling and useful, I am doing my best to make it useful.

"Two years ago, I was asked to take on a project with the government in my adopted home of Latvia. Working undercover, I was to find Russian insurgents within my country, so that they could be stopped before they had a chance to gain a foothold. You may or may not be aware; they now have a foothold. I was to infiltrate their ranks, then use my gifts to stop them. I failed.

"Which is why I had to leave Latvia, and why it is now imperative that you guard your medallion with your life. I have learned only recently the significance of the coins. There are six of them, and, not only do they protect a secret and tell a vital story, but they also play a role in what I hope will be a solution. I have hidden mine in a secure place, with full knowledge that when the time comes, my daughter – who is also blessed with unique gifts – will be able to find it. She doesn't know I'm alive; she can't know. It would put her in danger. Though I have taken steps to keep her from being aware of me, she will be able to find the coin if prompted to do so. When it is time for you to pass down your coin to the next generation, please take care that whoever receives it is fully aware not only of its importance, but of its power.

"I hope to meet you someday,

"Sincerely,
Larissa Melnikov-Platacis"

Andrew sat back and sighed. For probably the twentieth time that night, he pulled the medallion from his pocket, the one his mother had left for him in a note placed unceremoniously on a table near the front door of her home in McCordsville, Indiana. Clearly, Jeannie had had no idea of the significance of the coin in his hand. If she had, she most certainly would have taken greater care to keep it safe.

He held it to the lamp. *Six of them? Mine, Tonna's, Larissa's...where are the other three?* He shook his head and once again shoved the coin in his pocket.

He opened the next letter. This one was shorter, suggesting that Larissa was either pressed for time, or was being surveilled, and therefore couldn't speak freely.

"Dear Gloria,

"I know this letter comes only days after the last, but I need help. Not for me. For the world. In my letter five days ago, I told you of a prophecy."

Andrew stopped. *"In my letter five days ago..."* He grabbed both of the opened envelopes and checked the dates. The first letter had been written in February of 2004; he noted that the postmark was from Istanbul. The letter he had just begun was dated September 30th, 2004, but it had been postmarked in Ulaangom, Mongolia. The third letter – the one he had yet to open – had been written in November, and had been postmarked from Novosibirsk, Russia. Clearly, Larissa had been on the move. Regardless, there was no letter that had been written five days before the one he was reading. He shook his head and frowned. *So, where is it?*

He read on...

"Since then, I have learned more. My efforts in Latvia have led me to Mongolia, and it is here where I have finally learned the truth. But because of it, I am now in hiding, afraid for my life. Nine days ago, there was an earthquake... in Kaliningrad. It was small, but its meaning is huge. And it is more important than ever that you understand the significance of the coins. Mama was forced to leave me when I was young, so I don't know how much she shared with you; I'll tell you what I know. She had another daughter, my sister Emma, who I'm guessing also has a coin. These coins not only tie us to the past, but are vital to the future. Their secret – their purpose – is far bigger than I had imagined...far bigger than anything this world could ever dream of.

"You need to find the coins, Gloria...all six of them. Find them and save the world. You cannot contact me, but I will do my best to keep in touch.

Larissa Melnikov-Platacis"

Andrew stared at the letter. *What the hell?* Larissa's ramblings were like something out of a Hollywood movie. *The poor girl must be deranged.* He laid the letter on the table with the others, then stared at them all as if they had suddenly been cursed. And in a way, they had. If any of what Larissa was suggesting was true, then the world was at risk...from something. She had mentioned an earthquake. Was that it? Another quake somewhere? *How can coins stop an earthquake?*

He ran his hands through his hair. He wanted to dismiss it; pretend that, whoever Larissa was, she was talking out of her head about things that weren't real. In Larissa's letter, she had said that her mother had gone to America, and had left her at home. How old had Larissa been at the time? Was she a mere child? Had she been left in Russia, or her adopted Latvia? Andrew shook his head. *She had to have been older,* he thought. He couldn't imagine a mother leaving behind a young child.

Did I maybe miss something in one of the letters from her mother? He leaned forward and rummaged through the letters until he found Dasha's letter that first showed a return address from America. The date was August, 1966. He opened it and read it quickly. He found what he was looking for in the second paragraph...

"My heart hurts at the thought of leaving my daughter behind, but it can't be helped. She is gifted...and I am ill. Not only would it devastate her to watch me endure this battle with cancer, but I fear that the world may not take kindly to her gifts. I know for a fact that she will soon be targeted because of them. As a result, I have left her in the care of a good and loving family...they live their lives behind tall gates; Larissa will be protected..."

He frowned. *A good and loving family that lives behind tall gates.* Who had raised the uniquely gifted Larissa? Were they aware of her gifts? Of her prophecy? Did they know of her fears of an apocalypse? *Do they think she's gifted...or crazy?*

He thought back to the Morning Star organization, and the airship of the same name. When he had been recruited to join the group, he had been asked to believe the unbelievable. The ship, *Der Morgenstern,* manufactured by the Nazis, was capable of destroying entire cities with a single strike. The technology was unlike anything that modern man had ever seen. Where had it come from? Who had supplied it with such advanced capabilities? A Nazi scientist? Or someone else...someone *gifted.*

Again, he pulled out the coin. Larissa had supposedly hidden her special coin somewhere in her adopted country of Latvia. How would he find it? She had said that her daughter could help, if prompted. *Who is her daughter?* Larissa had also said that her sister Emma might have one of the coins. *How do I find her sister?*

He looked back through his notes to the beginning; to the children of the three women. Annabelle had adopted Tonna in the early eighties, Gloria had had Stewart many years before that, and Dasha had had Larissa and Emma somewhere in-between. Dasha hadn't given Larissa's age at the time, but Emma had been born soon after Dasha had moved to America. *So, how old would that make you, Emma?*

He went through the timeline. The date of the first letter from America was August, 1966. Dasha had said that Emma had been born soon after Dasha had arrived there. He did the math. That would make Emma around 37 or 38 years old...a grown woman. *So where do you live, Emma?*

Again, he checked the return address of Dasha's first letter from America. *Mars Hill, Maine.* He doubted that there were many Melnikovs in Maine, though Emma might have moved to another state, or even out of the country. And by now, she had likely married and taken her husband's name.

He leaned back and sighed. He had reached a dead end. And the women who had started it all – Dasha, Annabelle, and Gloria – had died years ago. According to Larissa's letter, those three women had left behind six coins. Andrew had seen only two of them: his and Tonna's. That left four: Larissa's, Emma's, and two more.

He laid Dasha's letter on the table, and checked the date of Larissa's second letter. *September 30ᵗʰ...six weeks ago.* She had been desperate at the time. If any of what she had said was true, he needed to act quickly. *Maybe I'm already too late.*

There was still one unopened letter. He picked it up and stared at it, suddenly afraid to open it. He turned it over and checked the date on the back. November 1ˢᵗ, 2004. It had been written only two weeks ago. He stared at it a minute longer, then tossed it on the table.

He stood, walked to the fireplace, and leaned against the mantel. He shook his head as he looked into the flames. It was all too much. Mystical coins, daughters with special gifts, women with the power to save the world. He looked over his shoulder at the unopened letter that was lying on the coffee table. He knew he had to read it, but he couldn't seem to bring himself to do it. *Why? What am I afraid of?* Was he worried that the last letter might be even more ominous than the two that had come before it? He sighed. *Yes...but I'm even more afraid of what I'll need to do about it.*

CHAPTER 74

Beijing, China

Arthur Kauffold and Johnny Canterbury landed in Beijing's Capital Airport at 9:05 Sunday morning, the flight taking nearly an hour longer than expected. Kauffold, exhausted from the flight, wanted nothing more than a bath and a nap, but it wasn't to be. They had an appointment to keep, and they were already late.

They were met at the terminal by two Chinese officials, who, in reasonably clear English, informed them that they had been sent to escort the two men to "...a meeting with our Imperial leader." Kauffold was disappointed. He had hoped to meet first with China's Ambassador, and had even had Johnny try to arrange such a meeting through his contact at the Pentagon. Apparently, he had failed, as Kauffold and Johnny were taken directly to the office of the President. As they were about to step out of a black sedan, a car pulled up behind them, and Kauffold was stunned to see America's Secretary of State get out of the car. Though Kauffold had come mostly at her request, he had no idea that she would be joining them for the talks.

They exchanged quick hellos, then the three of them, along with a cadre of Secret Service agents, walked into the Presidential Palace. They were greeted by a team of soldiers who escorted them to the President's private office. The Secret Service agents were made to wait outside.

Kauffold, who had decided to refer to Johnny as a British/American liaison, handled the introductions. Though the President was cordial, the interplay among the leaders was strained, at best. Which wasn't surprising. As far as China's President was concerned, an American senator, working on behalf of his government, had tried to shoot the son of one of China's top military leaders. *I'd be a bit put off, too,* thought Kauffold as he stared across the table at the Chinese President.

Forty minutes later, they had failed to come to any sort of consensus. The U.S. Secretary had challenged the President of China on lying about the departure of Senator Sturgill from their country. The President had countered that he had only done so to buy time until he could learn more about the senator's motives.

"And have you, Mr. President? Have you come up with any reason whatsoever why the senator would have wanted to hurt the Military Minister's son?"

"If the note found in the bodyguard's pocket is to be believed, he was hoping to punish us for our treatment of the Uyghurs...which, of course, is not America's concern. I cannot allow such a thing to stand without a response, now can I?"

And that was the problem. Regardless of whatever diplomacy they might employ, the Chinese President was *obligated* to punish not only Sturgill, but America along with him. The four of them had ended the meeting with an agreement to talk again after lunch, giving each party a chance to speak to their respective advisors.

Just as they were about to leave the meeting, Johnny, who had sat silent throughout, suddenly blurted out, "Perhaps in the interim, we could look in on the Senator. I think it's only fitting that we lay eyes on the man to ensure that he's being treated properly."

The President was clearly indignant. "Of course he is being treated properly, though we would have been well within our rights to rough him up a bit."

Johnny shook his head. "I'm certain that before this negotiation can proceed further, we will be expected to have taken steps to verify that our senator is okay."

The President, though obviously irritated by the request, finally agreed, and plans were made for Kauffold, Johnny, and the Secretary of State to be taken to the prison. The President had stipulated that only two

American agents would be allowed to accompany them to the site. Though Kauffold had protested, the President had refused to budge, and the entourage, with just two of their agents, walked to their cars, ready to make the journey to the Chinese prison.

* * *

Roger, once again wearing his black sweatshirt, a coat, and a stocking cap, had been surveilling the warehouse for the past hour. The rectangular, single-story building sat at the base of a yellow-gray valley, surrounded by overgrown brush, thick oak trees, and cracked cement. Though he saw no signs of life, he felt certain that Cobra was inside. Why? Because Hobbs had said so. But even more than that; Roger could feel him...he could feel the brooding darkness inside that place.

He had chosen a spot on a hillside at the west end of the warehouse where the grass was tallest. Using binoculars, he was able to see trucks coming in and out of the parking lot. He had seen only one so far. It had delivered boxes of what he guessed was either bedding or dried food.

He shifted in the grass, grateful for the yellow fronds. They stood about three feet high, allowing him to kneel comfortably and study the building with little risk of being spotted. But his fur-lined jacket offered little protection against the wind, so, in spite of the stocking cap and thick leather gloves, he was chilled to the bone. He had done his best to ignore it, however, as he had surveilled the warehouse. After a full sweep, he had determined that there were five guards outside, and likely just as many inside. Though the best scenario would be for him to somehow get inside the warehouse and find and kill Cobra, he felt certain that he would be either detained or killed before he could get anywhere close to the man.

Why so many soldiers? he wondered as he watched a faceless man march resolutely back and forth along the west end of the building. Surely there wouldn't be ten guards for just two prisoners. Who else was in that broken-down building? *It doesn't matter,* he told himself for probably the tenth time. *Cobra is in there.*

But it hadn't changed the fact that there were ten soldiers to his one. He had finally concluded that his only option was to blow up the entire building. He took a quick look in the cloth satchel that was draped over his shoulder. Inside were six M112 demolition blocks. *"Enough C4 to take out a bridge or a large building,"* the man had told him. *Let's hope so,* Roger thought as he stared down at the warehouse.

After assessing the surveillance route taken by each of the guards, Roger had determined that he would have only a ten second window to place the explosives. He clenched his jaw. The task would require perfect timing; there could be no mistakes.

He shifted uneasily. Here he was, contemplating the blowing up of a building, with no proof that Cobra was even inside. He flinched, then nodded his head. *I trust Hobbs. If he says the killer is in that warehouse, then he is.* But wasn't destroying an entire building to kill one man extreme? Especially when it was almost a certainty that there were others inside? He tugged at the collar of his sweatshirt. There was no other way to go about it. He couldn't get inside, and Cobra needed to die. As a matter of fact, Roger had made a pact with himself that by the time the sun set over the Xishan Mountains, one of them – either Cobra or Roger – would be dead.

But what if the senator is one of those inside? he wondered as he continued to watch the guard. *Collateral damage,* he told himself, and was eventually able to push the concern from his mind. *Nothing else matters...Cobra needs to die.*

He had had only one moment when he had second-guessed himself. He had been watching a soldier marching along the west end of the building, and had seen him slip behind a tree to relieve himself. In that instant, he had seen the man not as a soldier, but as a human being. Roger didn't want to kill an innocent man who was simply carrying out his orders. But then he remembered Tonna's picture on Cobra's wall and he knew...*it doesn't matter who I kill...Cobra needs to die.* That applied to the Chinese soldiers, as well. *Soldiers die in war; it's what they do.* And there was no question in his mind; this was a war...against right and wrong, good and evil, heaven and hell. As far as Roger was concerned, killing Cobra was as vital as stamping out the evils of fascism or the horrors of the Holocaust.

He looked up, shielding his eyes from the bright sunlight spilling over the mountains. He had hoped the sun would warm the air. It hadn't, and he blew into his gloves to try to thaw his frozen fingers. Not only was the sun not warming the air, but the higher it got, the more it served as an unwanted spotlight. The good news was that dark clouds were gathering to the west. He would wait for them before he set the C4.

He had already chosen the sites. There were few windows in the warehouse, and they were spaced far apart. If he could get the C4 onto the frames of six of the windows that covered the majority of the building, the explosions would work together to destroy whatever was inside, and would have the added benefit of sending shards of glass in every direction. *Even if Cobra somehow survives the initial blast, he'll be taken out by a crystal javelin.*

Within minutes, the clouds eased in, snuffing out the sun as if daylight had somehow sprinted to dusk. The time had come. Staying low in the grass, he crept down the hill to its base. The grass wasn't as tall here, and he was forced to lay on his stomach as he surveyed the layout of the building. He was still facing the west end, but could now see around to the south side. He waited, mapping out the path he would take to place the C4. If he started where he was and went counter-clockwise, he would eventually wind up at the north end of the building, which would allow him to scale a hill similar to the one he had just come down. He could ignite the C4 from up there.

Roger rose to his knees and, moving with the utmost precision, timed his movements with those of the guard in front of him. When the guard walked away, Roger ran and hid between two thick oak trees about ten feet from the window. He waited, holding his breath as the guard turned, marched toward him, then turned again and marched away. Roger crept from the trees to an overgrown bush directly under the window. He knelt behind it and held his breath, waiting for the guard to make another pass. He looked up at the window. Though it had at one time been painted white, a century of dirt and decay had stained it to the point where it was leaden gray. The C4 paste would blend in well. Again, the guard marched toward him, then turned and walked away. As the soldier reached the furthest point from the window, Roger raised up and pressed the C4 onto the ledge, making sure to flatten the paste so it was flush with the sill. He fell to his knees just as the guard turned to walk back to the window. Roger waited, holding his breath. When the guard turned and walked away, Roger ran back to the oak trees, then fell to his knees and crawled to a clump of brush at the base of the hill. He snuck up the hill and, when he reached the peak, headed south until he was able to look down at the next window. Staying low in the grass, and using trees for cover, he crept down the hill to the warehouse and placed C4 on that windowsill, just as he had done with the first. He repeated the same steps, pasting C4 on the sills of three more windows on the south and east sides of the building.

He had one C4 explosive left. He crawled up the hill and rounded it until he was looking down at the northeast corner of the warehouse. Again, he crept down through the grass to the base of the hill. He was about to crawl to the window, when suddenly he stopped. He laid flat on the ground. He had spotted two soldiers guarding the front entrance of the warehouse, less than 50 feet away. He waited, holding his breath. Had they seen him? He didn't think so. *I need to get this done and get out of here!*

He raised up just enough to see the window. It was only about fifteen feet from where he was lying on the ground. A guard paraded toward it, then turned and marched away. With a close eye on the two guards by the door, Roger rose to his feet, and crept to a tree near the window. He knelt behind it and took out the C4. Just as he was about to reach up and paste it on the sill, he stopped. He had heard what sounded like a car door. He crouched lower behind the tree and waited.

* * *

It took twenty-five minutes to reach the prison, which, as far as Kauffold was concerned, looked like an old warehouse that should probably be condemned. The paint was chipped, and the few windows that were visible were hard to see through; he guessed they were shuttered from the inside. The place was depressing. He found himself regretting that he had let Johnny talk him into the trip. *I'm too old for this,* he thought as he looked over at Johnny, who simply raised his eyebrows and shrugged.

They stepped out of the car and Kauffold pulled on his heavy winter coat, glad he had thought to bring it. He had begun to shiver, not only from the ice-cold wind, unobstructed as it blew down from the mountains, but from the coldness of the rifle-wielding guards. The two agents that had been permitted to come with them stayed at their sides as the entourage walked toward a thick metal door.

Along with the two American agents, two Chinese guards had been assigned to accompany them into the warehouse. One of the guards nudged Kauffold with his rifle. Kauffold puffed out his chest and looked indignantly at the man. "I'll have you know that you are dealing with a representative of the Queen," he said with a clearing of his throat. He tugged at his jacket and took a hesitant step forward.

Canterbury chimed in. "Yes, and I represent both the Queen and the United States of America."

Kauffold rolled his eyes, then looked over his shoulder at the Secretary and gave her a weak smile. She nodded reassuringly. He took another step. *What have I gotten myself into?* he wondered as he walked into the musty building. Then he reminded himself, *I'm here to avert a world war.* But as he proceeded down a dark, moldy hallway, he wondered if there was more to this journey than just averting a war. As a matter of fact, the further he went, the more he felt certain that he would never walk out of there again.

* * *

Roger had heard voices. Some were speaking Chinese, but at least two of them were speaking English, both of them with thick British accents. He couldn't tell what they were saying. He moved a few inches closer. *Who are they?* he wondered. *Does it matter?* Whoever they were, they had spoken with authority, and they were now walking into that warehouse. Which meant that when Roger blew it up, he would be taking out at least two British agents or foreign diplomats. Could he live with it?

He closed his eyes, his thoughts turning again to his lovely Tonna. And, as all thoughts of Tonna had been for the past two days, that image was immediately followed by the image of her hanging from a tree. He clenched his jaw. *No…I won't be able to live with it, but I'll deal with my soul once I know that Tonna is safe.*

Chapter 75

Warehouse outside Beijing

Lili was cold; colder than she had ever been. Winter had come fast and furious to the Xishan Mountains. She had been at the prison for nearly nine months now, and was beginning to feel it deep inside, as if the cold outside the warehouse had passed through the walls and into her bones. It made her shiver all the time.

The shivering had worsened over the past few days, to the point where at times Lili was shaking so badly her teeth chattered. And always, her caregiver, Ching Lan, would hug her close and sing to her. Lili couldn't say why, but it helped, and, as she once again felt her teeth began to chatter, Ching pulled her next to her, wrapped her in the threadbare blanket, and sang. After she was finished, she whispered, "It will be okay, Lili. God is looking after us."

Lili wasn't sure about that; after all, a lot of good people had died on His watch. She wondered if all of those good people had gone to heaven, the way her Sunday school teacher had said they had. Was there even such a place? She wasn't sure, but one thing she did know...there was a Hell. She had seen it...on the train on the way to Tibet, and in that prison outside Beijing.

But she wasn't bitter. She had known much joy in her nearly ten years of life. Even if she was to die in that cold, heartless place, she could rest easy in the fact that her parents had been kind, Uncle Mart had been kind, and Danil and Anna, who had looked after her when everyone else was gone, had been kind. And now there was Ching Lan, the woman who had kept her safe and warm for nearly a year. *Perhaps this is how God works,* she thought. *He comes to us in the form of people who care for us when we need it most.* As she clung to Ching's warm thin body, she felt reassured that God was there, calming her from His place in that good woman's soul.

Perhaps the man in the prison would be kind, as well; the one who had spoken to her in Morse code. He had told her that he was Uncle Mart; she didn't believe it. Not only was it too good to be true, but it made no sense. Why would he be there? Had her letters actually reached the Henderson castle? She didn't think so. She had watched the soldiers throw them away. Besides, she felt certain that she would have sensed it if somehow one of those letters had made it into the hands of a Henderson.

And I would have sensed Uncle Mart coming for me...I'm sure of it.

She shook her head, reaffirming for probably the tenth time that the Morse code man wasn't Uncle Mart. She had decided that maybe he had *known* Uncle Mart, and it was simply a crazy turn of fate that he had wound up in the same prison where she was being held.

Whoever he was, he had said that he would get her out of there, and that it would happen that very morning. But when Lili had shared the news with Ching Lan, the woman had merely tightened her lips and narrowed her eyes. Lili guessed that Ching Lan didn't believe it. Ching Lan believed in very little anymore.

Lili looked up at her now and whispered, "If the man in this prison doesn't help us get out of here, then someone else will...won't they, Ching Lan?"

Ching Lan forced a smile – she did that a lot lately – and nodded reassuringly. "I'm sure they will, Lili." But she didn't believe that either; Lili could tell. Lili had forgiven the lie, however, because to say the truth *"...we will likely die in here..."* would be harsh, and Ching Lan was not a harsh woman. Ching Lan began to once again sing in Chinese the tune that Lili had heard many times since coming to China. "'Cause all I want is the moon upon a stick, just to see what if, just to see what is. The bird that's flown into my room..."

Lili closed her eyes, fighting tears, knowing that to cry was to give in. She often had to fight the tears that came whenever she felt the kindness of Ching's humanity.

Suddenly she sensed a change in the air. She looked up at Ching Lan; she had felt it too. The old woman frowned. "Shh," she whispered as she sat up on the cot. She used the wall to support her as she walked softly – like Chinese elders often do – to the front of the cell. She eased to her knees, put her ear to the bars, and listened. Lili waited. They both sensed it; something was about to happen. Was the Morse code man coming to save them...just as he had promised? It was too much to hope for, so Lili just closed her eyes and gripped the blanket tightly as she pulled it to her chest.

Suddenly, Lili looked up. She had heard what sounded like gunshots.

Ching looked over her shoulder, her eyes wide.

Lili's eyes widened, as well. "Yes, oh yes, Ching Lan...I think he's coming."

* * *

Henderson had carried Lili Platacis in his subconscious forever, it seemed. She had been the energy for everything that had happened, starting from the very minute Morningstar had learned of her existence and had used her against him, threatening to kill her if Henderson didn't do what he asked. And, though Henderson had gone along with it for years, he had finally had enough. That had been last November, when, as he had been about to kill Abdulkarim Al-Gharsi, he had seen Maddi sitting next to the man. Though Henderson had proceeded with the hit, he had seen the look – the devastation – in Maddi's eyes, and had known then that he could carry on no longer. So, he had left Morningstar. The man had told Henderson repeatedly that if he ever left him, then he – Morningstar – would kill Lili Platacis. Morningstar had convinced him that he had followed through with his promise, sending Henderson a photo of Lili lying lifeless in the snow. For ten long months, Henderson had been forced to live with the belief that his actions had ended the life of a remarkable little girl. To learn that she was still alive had been like a gift from God. But that gift had meant nothing once he was taken prisoner by the Chinese. He could not save Lili from her prison if he was in a prison hundreds of miles away. Finding out yesterday that she was in the very same prison had been the push he had needed to put his plan into action. As if God was giving him one more chance to get it right.

The guards had changed shifts a few hours ago. It would soon be time for his shower. He walked to the door of his cell and waited. A few minutes later, a guard walked up and unlocked his cell. A second guard stood back, his rifle raised as the first guard led Henderson out of the cell and down the hall to the shower. Henderson was calm; he had learned how to stay calm no matter what the situation. That hadn't come from Morningstar; that had come from his days as a Latvian freedom fighter.

They turned a corner; the first guard unlocked the door. He stepped back and shoved Henderson into the bathroom. Henderson took a step, then grabbed his chest. He fell to the floor, crying, "Help me...I think... I'm...having a heart attack."

The guard aimed his rifle at him and sneered. "Bi zui!" *Shut up!*

Henderson kept on. "I'm...I'm...dying, I say. I...need...help."

The guard took a step toward him and Henderson began to jerk his arms and legs, flailing in a fit of spasms. The guard raised his gun and glared, his nostrils flaring at the disruption so early in his shift. "Ting xialai!" *Stop it!* But Henderson kept on, holding his breath so his face would turn red and the veins would show in his neck. Suddenly he stopped. He lay perfectly still, continuing to hold his breath.

The guard leaned closer, watching for movement, putting a hesitant hand to Henderson's neck to feel for a pulse. In a split second, Henderson grabbed the hand and pulled the man's face to the cement floor with such force that the guard dropped his rifle and fell on top of Henderson, unconscious, if not dead. The second guard fired a shot, but it hit the guard that was on top of Henderson. Henderson grabbed the dead man's rifle, aimed it at the second guard, and pulled the trigger. The guard cried out as a bullet split his forehead, his cries echoing in the high-ceilinged walls of the shower. Henderson shoved the dead guard off of him and searched his pockets. He found a set of keys, along with a wallet with several hundred yuan and an ID. Though the ID looked nothing like him, it could maybe get him past a checkpoint if he made a few adjustments to his appearance.

He took a quick look at the culvert in the back of the bathroom, then ran to the door. He would grab Lili, bring her to the culvert, and they would escape. He would use the money and the ID to get help and come back for the others once Lili was safe.

Still holding the rifle, he snuck a look down the hall. There were two guards running toward the bathroom. He aimed the rifle and shot each one in the head. *Four down...one to go.* He ran down the hall and was about to turn the corner, when he pulled back. Two more soldiers were coming, their rifles raised. *Guards from outside.* Henderson fired; the two soldiers fired back as they fell to the floor, their shots ricocheting against the walls. A siren began to blare.

Two more guards came out of nowhere and fired at him. Henderson felt a pain in his arm, then another in his chest. He fell to his knees, firing back, ignoring the spray of bullets hitting the walls, the floor, the ceiling. Suddenly the shooting stopped. Both guards fell to the floor. Henderson waited. They didn't move. He ripped off his shirt and checked his wounds. From what he could tell, neither one had hit a major vessel. He ripped off the sleeve of his shirt and tied it above where his arm had been shot. He wrapped the remainder of the shirt around his chest to serve as a pressure dressing. Using the wall for support, he forced himself up, ignoring the pain as he stumbled down the hall to the first of the cells. A man was lying face-down on a cot. *Who is he? Should I take him with us?* What if he was a criminal, put inside that prison not for dissident behavior, but for breaking the law? *It doesn't matter...no one should have to stay in this hellhole.*

The siren continued to blare, and Henderson could hear soldiers' boots echoing in the hall. His breathing was labored as he pulled out the keys. He tried each one until he found the one that fit. As he was about to open the door, the prisoner raised up on his elbows and looked over his shoulder. He smiled. "Why, hello, Brother. Long time, no see."

* * *

Cobra stared at his half-brother, suddenly energized for the first time in days. The rounded jaw notwithstanding, Matt's lighter hair made him look more like the Martin he remembered from those few days in Baclayon when he had first laid eyes on him. "I see you're getting back to your roots, brother." He laughed at the joke, but then fell into a fit of coughing that forced him to lay back on the bed.

He covered his face with his hands. He knew he must look awful. Not only had he not combed his hair for weeks, but the dyed blonde had surely mixed with black roots by now. He put his hand to the sparse beard on his chin, then rubbed his eyes, which were no longer blue from contact lenses, but were now the mismatched gray for which he was known. The guards hadn't recognized him; would Martin? He looked at him and saw the look on his face. He grinned. *He knows who I am.* "Snake got your tongue, dear brother?"

Cobra tried to sit up, but fell back on the cot, too weak to even lean against the wall. He could tell that Henderson had seen his weakness and it made him angry. "Pull the trigger, asshole. You've killed others, why not me? An assassin brother killing an assassin brother." He sneered. "Rather poetic, I'd say."

Henderson said nothing. Cobra could see his finger twitching on the trigger. "You can't do it!" He coughed and laughed at the same time. "Perhaps now that you know that I saved your life, you feel it is only fair that you save mine." He sneered. "Or could it be that you are simply too weak to follow through."

Henderson narrowed his eyes. "I'm not the one lying half-dead on a cot."

If he could have, Cobra would have jumped up, run at the man, and choked him to death. But he could only lay there and wait. *For what...for my brother to shoot me?* He covered his face with a blanket, unwilling to watch as Martin ended his life.

* * *

Henderson couldn't move. In spite of the guards' footsteps getting closer, in spite of shouts and the occasional gunshot as soldiers searched the hallways for the defiant prisoner, he stood transfixed, his eyes locked on his half-brother. He hated him. He hated his weakness, his deceit...but most of all, he hated his eyes. *Henderson eyes.* He held the rifle steady, filled with revulsion as he realized that Cobra had become a mirror...*his* mirror. He hated Cobra because he hated himself. There was little that separated them...both had killed at the behest of others, and both had spent their lives – or at least the last several years – trying to erase who they were.

His hands began to shake; he squeezed the gun tighter. *Focus, Henderson.* His finger hung on the trigger; he couldn't seem to pull it. *Just shoot him!*

From nowhere, he heard a voice yelling down the hall. "Mar—Matt? What are you doing?"

He looked over his shoulder, shocked to see his father running toward him. *Why is he here? How is he here?* He looked in the cell. Cobra's face was covered, but Henderson could imagine the man's smirk...practically a summons for Henderson to go ahead and blow out his brains. And he wanted to. He wanted to kill the man who had killed so many, the man who had cruelly saved Henderson's life when he had wanted so badly to end it. *Why can't I shoot him?* Henderson had killed far better men than the one on the cot. He sighed and looked away. *Because it is the only thing that makes me not him.*

* * *

Walter and his small army, consisting of the two Latvian soldiers and Hank Clarkson, had been waiting near a side door of the warehouse, and had stormed in the minute they had heard the first shot. One of the soldiers had given Hank a handgun, which meant that there were four men with three rifles and a pistol, against a well-armed battalion of at least ten soldiers. *We can handle it,* Walter thought, though he knew it was almost a guarantee that more Chinese soldiers would be coming.

As he had burst into the warehouse, he had been stunned to see dead guards lining the hallways. He had tossed a rifle from one of the dead men to Hank, and had led his team further into the dark prison, even more stunned when he had seen his son – shirt off, chest bloodied – aiming a rifle, not at a Chinese guard, but at a prisoner.

He turned and stopped his team before they could see what was happening at the end of the hall. "We need to split up," he said as he sent Hank to check the hall to the right, and his Latvian soldiers to check the hall to the left. He then ran to his son and looked in the cell. A man was lying on a cot, his face covered with a blanket.

Suddenly, the prisoner lowered the blanket and grinned. "Hey pops."

Walter's jaw tightened. He turned away, ashamed to look at the eyes he had grown to hate. Somehow, that killer had come from him...from him and Nenita. His heart broke, not only for who Cobra was, but for Martin, who had never understood what a moment of weakness could do to a man. *Then again...maybe he does.*

Cobra sneered. "Glad to see me, Daddy?" He clasped his hands together and laughed. "Why...it's a family reunion!" The laugh turned into a fit of coughing.

Walter was tempted to shoot Cobra himself. He was distracted by the sound of footsteps in a hall not too far away. More guards were coming; reinforcements had been called in. They needed to get out of there. He was about to grab Martin by the arm, when he saw the blood-stained tourniquet. He frowned. "That looks bad, Mart."

"It's nothing."

It was far from nothing; Martin was pale and his entire body was shaking. He looked like he could drop at any minute...like the only thing keeping him upright was the hate in his eyes. The footsteps were getting closer. Walter put a hand on Martin's back and said, "Let's go, son. Someone else can deal with Cobra."

* * *

Henderson couldn't seem to get his feet to move. By some quirk of fate, not only was Cobra occupying a cell in the same prison where he, too, had been jailed, but his father had shown up out of nowhere and was trying to stop him from killing the man. Why was Walter there? *How* was he there? What on earth would compel a seventy-two-year-old man to infiltrate a Chinese prison? *Love...and a lot of courage.*

Henderson went to take a step, but his knees buckled and he grabbed his father by the arm. "Lili is...here...somewhere. We need to...to find her."

His father's eyes widened. "She's here? My god, son...where?"

"I don't know. We talked...yesterday...using Morse code. She didn't know how to tell me where she was. All she could say was that it was cold and damp."

"This whole place is cold and damp." Walter put his arm around Martin and helped him take a step. "I need to get you somewhere safe."

"No! I'm fine." Henderson was fighting the urge to pass out. "I'll...I'll take this hall, you take that one."

The footsteps had gotten louder. They could hear the guards yelling back and forth. Over Walter's protests, Henderson pulled away, and, using the wall for support, propelled himself down the hall. "We need to split up" he managed to say as he held his rifle ready to shoot. But he was having trouble seeing. He felt like at any minute he might pass out. *Keep it together, Henderson.*

He passed several fallen guards in the hallway; not one of them was moving. He kept going, and soon stumbled on one who was reaching for his rifle. Henderson was about to shoot him in the head, but at the last second, he merely kicked the gun away and knocked the soldier unconscious using the butt of his rifle.

He needed to find Lili. He tried to think from which direction he had heard the Morse code; it had sounded far away. His cell had been toward the front, which meant that Lili was likely toward the back. He reached the end of the hall, and, as he turned to go toward the back of the warehouse, he came face-to-face with a guard. He raised his rifle, but couldn't focus; it was as if he was looking down a tunnel. *I'm going to pass out.* He dropped the rifle and fell to his knees, prepared to die.

* * *

Simeon, Johnny Canterbury, had just followed the former ambassador and the Secretary of State through the front door of the warehouse, when the first shots were fired. Instantly, one of the American agents had grabbed the Secretary and had rushed her out the door, while the other had engaged in a gunfight with two Chinese soldiers and had been shot in the head. As he had fallen to the floor, Kauffold had run to him, and was now kneeling next to him trying to comfort the dying man.

In a split second, Simeon took out one of the Chinese guards with a kick to the groin, while downing the other one with an elbow jab to the throat. He bent down, grabbed a rifle from one of the fallen guards, then searched the man's pockets for a set of keys. He chuckled to himself. *Now's my chance to get Kauffold off my back.*

Pretending to be gallant, he grabbed Kauffold by the arm and dragged him away. "I need to get you somewhere safe, sir." Before the ambassador knew what was happening, Simeon had shoved him into an empty cell and was locking the door.

"What are you doing, Johnny? Let me out of here at once!"

"No. You're safer behind bars. No one will shoot you if you're in that cell."

Ignoring the ambassador's continued protests, Simeon ran down the hall. He would have only a minute or so to find Sturgill and Cobra, kill them, then get the hell out of there. As he rounded the corner, he was stunned to see someone he knew, or at least thought he knew. In spite of light brown hair, the man looked quite a bit like Martin Henderson. He was kneeling in front of a Chinese soldier, who was clearly about to shoot him. Acting on impulse, Simeon shot the soldier in the forehead. As the soldier fell to the floor, so did the man with brown hair. *Did I hit them both?* Simeon ran over and immediately kicked the fallen guard's gun away from him. He knelt beside the brown-haired man and nudged him. "Are you okay?" The man didn't move. Another guard rounded the corner; Simeon shot him in the head. He stared down at the brown-haired man, noting blond roots at his scalp. But the man's face, his jaw, was different, leading Simeon to conclude that he couldn't be Henderson. He checked for a pulse; it was weak, but steady. He nudged him again. "Hey, you okay?"

The man opened his eyes. Simeon sat back, speechless. He remembered those eyes. He had looked in those same eyes when he had pulled Martin Henderson from a hotel fire four years ago. In spite of the jawline, he knew...*it's him...it's Henderson.*

And he hated the man. Henderson had bested him more than once in the eyes of their father, Jacob. Had Henderson recognized him? Did he know that he was looking at Simeon? If so, he would surely tell the others. *I need to kill him.*

He looked down the hall. No one was coming. He aimed his rifle at the man's forehead. He couldn't seem to pull the trigger. Why? *Because Morningstar will kill me if I shoot this man.* Morningstar had made it clear on multiple occasions that he – Morningstar – needed to be the one to kill Martin Henderson.

He set down his rifle and continued to stare at Henderson. Years of being outdone by the man suddenly overwhelmed him, and – unable to stop himself – he wrapped his hands around the man's neck. *Goodbye, Henderson.* He squeezed as hard as he could, his hands shaking in his rage. "In the name of the Father, the son—"

All at once, Henderson reached up with his good arm and shoved Simeon's head hard against the wall. It was enough to allow Henderson to pull away. He was then able to use that same arm to grab his rifle and aim it at Simeon's forehead. "Here's how this is gonna go, Simeon," he said, as he coughed and rubbed his neck. "You're wearing a disguise. I don't know why and I don't care. But I'll keep your secret – and I won't kill you – if you help me get my people out of here alive."

CHAPTER 76

Warehouse outside Beijing

Though he knew it was insane, Roger had made up his mind to ignore the English-speaking voices he had heard in front of the warehouse. But just as he had been about to place the last of the C4 on the window sill, he had seen who one of those voices belonged to. *Arthur Kauffold...in China?*

With the transmitter in one hand, the C4 in the other, Roger had crept closer. He had seen the hefty man in a gray overcoat walk through the front door, and there had been no denying that it was him. Which meant that Roger had been faced with a dilemma. But he had had little time to dwell on it, as, out of nowhere, a burst of gunfire had erupted from inside the warehouse. He had panicked. Were the prisoners escaping? Was Cobra escaping?

He waited. The gunfire had intensified. He felt his entire body grow tense. *What's going on in there?* Was Cobra leading some sort of prison break and would soon shoot his way out, while Roger sat frozen with a block of C4 in his hand?

He clenched his jaw. Arthur Kauffold – Tonna's father by all accounts – was somewhere in that building. *I should go in and save him.* But it was quite possible that Cobra was about to escape. If Roger was going to kill him, now was the time.

He pulled out the ignitor and stared at it. There was no question that the blast from the C4 would kill Cobra, but it would also blow up Kauffold and whoever else was with him. He flinched. *I can't kill Tonna's father.*

Again, he thought of Tonna...his beautiful Tonna with a smile like nothing he had ever seen...the smile that had given Roger a reason to believe in happiness, to believe in hope. And again, the image changed, and he saw Tonna hanging from a tree, her blood spattering...drip, drip, drip on top of his head.

He narrowed his eyes. He had two choices. He could run into the building, drag Kauffold out of there, then let loose with the explosives, hoping and praying that Cobra hadn't had time to escape. Or he could trigger the switch right now and let every one of them die, including himself and Kauffold and any other diplomat who might be with him. But at least he would know that Cobra was dead, his ignoble reign of terror finally over. Any casualties would simply be part of a bigger war.

He took a deep breath, then nodded as he let it out slowly. He knew what he had to do. Cobra couldn't escape, he had to die. Nothing else mattered...not anymore.

And that was when the strangest thing happened. Just as Roger was about to place the last of the C4, an image flashed in his mind. But this time it wasn't Tonna. No, it was a child...a beautiful little girl. He didn't recognize her, but he could sense her goodness, and he heard her plea, *"Don't do it, Agent Clarkson. Please, don't do it."*

* * *

It had been nearly impossible for Walter to let Martin go back down that hallway on his own, but he knew that his son wouldn't leave until he found Lili. And Martin was right: they had a better chance of finding her if they split up. But there was no doubt about it, his son was struggling. They needed to find Lili and get the hell out of there.

Walter had run down a back hallway and had looked in every cell, surprised to see that every one of them was empty. He had run down another hall and had seen the same thing. He was now running back to where he and Martin had parted ways, hoping that Martin had had better luck.

He rounded the corner, and was stunned to see a man he recognized leaning awkwardly against the wall. "Johnny...Johnny Canterbury...is that you?"

Canterbury looked over at him. The man's forehead was bleeding, one of his eyes was starting to turn black and blue, and the collar of his shirt was torn. He wasn't holding a rifle or a pistol. Clearly, he had been in a scuffle, and, from the looks of it, he had lost. But something else seemed different about the man. His face and hair looked the same; he was even wearing the same suit he had worn when Walter had met him in the spring. But something about him no longer looked like the Johnny Canterbury that Walter remembered from their meeting eight months ago.

Johnny cleared his throat. "Um...yes, it's me." He pointed down the hall. "A man is hurt, Walter...around the corner. We were...uh...ambushed by the guards."

With his pistol raised, Walter rounded the corner, shocked to see Martin on his knees, rubbing his neck and coughing. Walter ran to him. "What happened?"

Henderson looked up at him with blank eyes. "Nothing. We need to find Lili."

Walter shook his head. "No, I need to get you out of here." Walter turned to Canterbury, who had run up behind him. "Help me get him up, Johnny."

"Sure thing, Walter."

The two men lifted Martin to standing, and, after a minute, Martin was able to stand on his own. Walter turned to Canterbury. "Walk him outside, Johnny...to the back of the building. God willing, there'll be a helicopter waiting for us."

Johnny was about to put Martin's arm over his shoulder, when Martin shoved him away. "I don't need his help." He took a few steps. "I'm going to find Lili."

Walter ran ahead and stopped in front of him. "You're in no condition to—"

Martin shoved past him. "I'm not leaving without her."

Walter frowned. Martin wasn't even carrying a rifle; he would be an easy target if he was to run into a Chinese soldier. "Fine. We'll all go...together."

Martin stumbled down the hall, pushing against the wall to stay upright. Walter and Johnny followed close behind, all three sliding into an empty jail cell whenever they heard the footsteps or the shouts of Chinese soldiers. They went down two more halls, looking in each cell for a little girl. In one of the cells they found an old man lying on a cot. He appeared to be oblivious to the sirens, the yelling of the guards, or the gunfire.

Walter yelled into the cell, "Who are you?" The man sat up and looked at him. Walter was shocked by what he saw. It was Senator Charles Sturgill, but the man looked nothing like the photos Walter had seen. His eyes were empty, his gray hair a mess, his chin covered with stubble. "It's Sturgill! We need to get him out of there."

Johnny pulled out a set of keys. "I'll get him out." He fumbled with the keys until he found one that fit, then opened the door. He ran in and helped the man sit up.

"Bring him with us, Johnny."

Sturgill raised a hand in the air. "I'm not leaving until I see my son!"

Walter had no idea what he was talking about, but now wasn't the time to argue. He leaned in and said, "I've got a chopper ready to take you to him, Senator."

The man stared at him. His mouth trembled as he said weakly, "You do?"

Walter nodded. "Yes, now let's go."

Sturgill tried to stand, his wild hair and even wilder eyes making him look half-crazed. He stared at Walter. "Why...you're Walter Henderson."

Walter nodded. "Yes. Now C'mon, Senator. We don't have much time."

The man took a step; his legs were wobbly. Johnny helped him out of the cell.

Walter said, "Take him out the back door, Johnny. We'll look for Lili."

Johnny nodded and walked Sturgill down the hall toward the back door.

Martin was leaning against the wall near Sturgill's cell. His eyes were closed, his face pale. Walter was glad to see Hank running toward him. "Hank, could you—"

Hank ran to Henderson's other side, and both men draped an arm over their shoulders. "We'll walk him to the back door, Hank. I'll come back for Lili."

Martin planted his feet. "No...there...isn't time. We...need to find...Lili."

Walter bristled, then nodded at Hank. Carrying Martin between them, they turned the corner and walked down a long, dark hallway toward a back section of the warehouse. It was quieter, more remote, and they soon came to an even narrower hall with empty drays lining the two sides. There was an oversized door at the end that looked like it had at one time been used for deliveries. A harsh breeze was coming in through a gap at the top of the door. Walter recalled Martin's comment *"...she said it was cold and damp."* They kept going. Several of the bays had been converted to cells, with metal bars nailed to the outside walls; every one of them was empty. They reached the end and still hadn't seen a prisoner. Walter was about to suggest they come back with reinforcements, when Henderson yelled, "There!"

Walter squinted in the dark and was barely able to see two tiny hands clinging to a set of bars in a free-standing cell in a back corner of the old loading dock.

They walked to the cell. Walter's heart ached as he saw Lili Platacis's blue eyes staring up at him from behind the bars. She was pale and way too thin, but there was no denying it was her.

She could barely talk "Hello...Mr. Henderson."

He smiled, choking up as he said, "Hello, Lili." He looked at Hank. "Johnny had the keys...we'll have to break down the door."

Henderson said weakly, "In my back pocket."

Walter reached in the pocket and pulled out a set of keys. He flipped through them, trying each one. "Got it!" he said, as he turned the key and opened the door.

Lili ran to Martin and hugged him. In his ear she whispered, "I knew you were alive!"

Walter grabbed Lili's hand. "We need to go!"

Lili said, "We have to get Ching Lan."

"Ching Lan?" Walter looked in the cell. He hadn't even noticed an older woman lying on the cot. The woman lifted her head, but said nothing.

Lili walked back into the cell and held out her hand. "Come, Ching Lan. We're leaving...just like you promised."

They heard a round of gunfire, followed by the sound of boots in a distant hallway. Walter looked at Hank. "Take Matt and Lili through that back door! Go!"

Lili hesitated. Walter said, "Go! I'll get your friend."

Lili grabbed Martin's hand, and she and Hank helped him down the hall to the door.

Walter went into the cell, his heart breaking as he looked into the tired but sharp eyes of an old Chinese woman. She was small in stature and remarkably thin. He said, "Ching Lan?" She nodded and he smiled. "I'm getting you out of here."

The woman gave a weak smile. Walter tried to help her stand. She was too weak. He was about to try to carry her, when the two Latvian freedom fighters came running down the hall. "Mr. Henderson, we need to get out of here...now!"

"Help me!"

One of the men ran into the cell and bent low so Ching Lan could put her arm around his neck. Walter grabbed her other side. The second soldier led the way as they walked her through the door and down the hall. Two Chinese guards came out of nowhere; the Latvian soldier shot each of the guards in the forehead.

They reached the back door. Hank was standing with Martin and Lili, who were leaning against the wall. It was hard to tell who was holding up who. Johnny was on the other side of the hallway, his hand on Sturgill's arm. Sturgill was leaning against the wall. His forehead was bleeding; he looked like he had taken a fall.

Walter looked at Johnny and frowned. "What happened to him?"

Johnny shrugged his shoulders. "He tripped."

Walter narrowed his eyes. He was about to say something, when he was distracted by what sounded like the engine of a plane...*or a helicopter?* "Open the door." Hank opened the door slightly. Walter looked out but saw nothing; no helicopter, no Special Ops soldiers ready to swoop in and save them. His heart sank.

Hank slammed the door shut as a barrage of bullets peppered the lot outside.

Walter tightened his jaw. *What now?* He was about to urge them all back to the front of the warehouse, when he heard the engine again, this time louder. "Open the door again!"

Hank opened it a few inches, and Walter leaned outside, this time looking further to the north. He rubbed his eyes, unwilling to believe what he was seeing. A Chinook helicopter was flying directly toward them. *Thank you, Cravens.*

He turned to Hank, "Do you think we can get to the chopper?"

Hank shook his head. "Too much gunfire." On cue, another barrage of bullets could be heard just outside the door. Again, Hank slammed it shut.

Walter ran back to the two guards the Latvian soldier had just killed. He grabbed their rifles, ran back, and tossed one of the rifles to Hank, which meant that Hank now had two rifles. Walter held onto the other one, giving him two, as well. "Johnny, Hank and I will cover you as you take Sturgill to the helicopter."

Johnny looked at him, his eyes wide. "Why me?"

Walter said firmly, "Because we're the ones with the guns. Now go!"

Johnny hissed, but then jerked Sturgill away from the wall. Keeping his own head down, he dragged the man with him as he ran out the door and half-carried Sturgill in the direction of the helicopter. Walter and Hank stepped just beyond the door, and, with four guns between them, fired nonstop into the trees and hillsides surrounding the parking lot. When Johnny had nearly reached the helicopter, Walter turned to the Latvian soldiers, who were holding Ching Lan. "Take her. Go. Now!"

The two soldiers carried Ching Lan between them as they ran to the chopper. Hank and Walter covered them. Two Special Ops soldiers were waiting at the door. Johnny managed to lift Sturgill enough for them to grab him by his arms and pull him into the helicopter. Johnny was able to climb in on his own.

The two Latvian soldiers reached the chopper soon after and lifted Ching Lan into the soldiers' waiting arms. Just as they let go of her, a cascade of bullets coming from the roof of the warehouse hit one of them in the back, the other in the head. Walter watched in horror as they fell back from the chopper and onto the ground.

He threw down one of his rifles. "Cover me!" he yelled as he ran into the firestorm. He fired to his right, then his left as he ran to the two fallen men. Over his shoulder, he could see Hank run into the parking lot. *What is he doing?* With one rifle aimed up at the roof, Hank used the other to spray bullets in a blind arc to his right and left. Walter frowned. *He's a sitting duck out there.* "Hank, go back to the doorway!" Hank didn't move. "Dammit Hank!" he yelled, then watched as at least four Chinese soldiers fell from the roof to the parking lot.

Walter fired his own rifle in an effort to cover Hank, then resumed his sprint to his fallen soldiers. He reached the first one, knelt beside him, and felt for a pulse. Nothing. He ran to the next man and did the same, then ran back to the warehouse.

Hank covered him until he was inside, then backed through the doorway and slammed shut the door.

Walter looked at the others and shook his head. "Both of the soldiers are dead. We need to get out of here. Hank, you take Lili. I'll help Matt."

Martin said evenly, "Give me a rifle."

Walter reached down and grabbed the rifle he had thrown down just minutes ago. He was about to hand it to his son, when he stopped. Martin's eyes were half-closed; he looked like he was about to pass out. "Matt, I—"

"Give me the gun."

Reluctantly, Walter handed him the gun.

Martin grabbed it with his good hand. With his jaw clenched, he said, "What about Cobra?"

Another salvo of gunfire outside the door made them all jump. Hank opened the door, fired a quick round into the parking lot, then shut it.

Walter narrowed his eyes. "Leave him."

Lili tugged at Walter's sleeve. "We can't leave him. He isn't well."

Both Walter and Martin looked down at her, stunned. "Do you know him?"

She nodded. "I've seen him...in my visions. He is hurting."

Martin frowned. "He is a terrible man, Lili."

She nodded. "Perhaps, but we can't just leave him."

"Sorry, Lili. We have to." Martin nodded at Hank, who opened the door partway.

Walter said, "Go, Hank. Take Lili. We'll be right behind you."

Hank dropped one of his rifles. He used that arm to lift Lili and hold her to his chest as he ran out the door and into the parking lot. Walter covered him, as Hank used the rifle he had kept to fire at the Chinese soldiers. He sprinted to the helicopter and handed Lili to a Special Ops soldier who was waiting at the door. He climbed in after her.

When Walter could see that both of them were safe, he turned to Martin. "You ready?" Martin nodded. Walter lifted Martin's injured arm over his shoulder. "Lean on me and use your good arm to fire."

Walter could feel Martin's weight against him; the man was barely able to stand on his own. Holding his rifle with one hand and Martin with the other, Walter led the way to the Chinook, as both he and Martin fired nonstop in an arc that covered the entire area. They reached the chopper just as a torrent of bullets sprayed the parking lot.

A Special Ops soldier was covering them from the doorway, while Hank and another soldier stood waiting to help Walter and Martin into the helicopter. Walter helped them get Martin inside, then climbed in after him.

As Hank fired a final spray of bullets into the lot, Walter yelled to the pilot, "Go!" The helicopter lifted in the air.

Suddenly, without warning, Lili leapt from the doorway down to the parking lot. Walter watched in horror as she landed on her knees, then jumped up and ran toward the prison. *Dear god!* he thought, as he immediately began to fire at Chinese soldiers surrounding the lot. "Lili, stop!" he cried, his heart breaking at her foolishness. But he was even more distraught when he saw Martin leap to the ground and run after her.

CHAPTER 77

Warehouse outside Beijing

Though it had stunned him, Roger had hesitated only seconds after hearing the warning from the little girl. *It's just guilt,* he had concluded, and had placed the last of the C4 on the window sill. The gunfight inside the building had moved to the back, but had shown no signs of easing. If he wanted to kill Cobra, he needed to hurry.

But then, just as he was about to push the ignitor switch, he heard something even more compelling. Amid all the gunfire and shouts from the soldiers, someone yelled the name Hank. Roger hesitated, but then quickly dismissed it. There was no way that Hank was in China, let alone in that building.

He held out the ignitor. *Here 'goes,* he thought, fully aware there wasn't time to scale the hill, and that he would die in the blast. It didn't matter. Cobra had to die.

But then he heard it again. Someone had definitely yelled the name Hank. He frowned. *It's gotta be a different Hank.*

But unable to shake it, he muttered a curse, then slid the ignitor in his pocket and reached for his gun. He crawled through thick brush toward the front door. The guards that had been guarding it were gone; no one was patrolling the front of the building. He would take a quick look inside, convince himself that whatever was going on in there had nothing to do with his dad, and then, since he was already inside, he would look for Kauffold. If he saw him, he would grab him. If he didn't, he would blow the place to smithereens.

He crept closer and hid behind a parked sedan less than two feet from the door. He raised his pistol and crept to the door. He opened it, stunned to see soldiers lying motionless on the floor. He knelt down, made sure each one was dead, then grabbed a rifle from the one who was closest. He slid his pistol in his pocket and listened. Though he could still hear gunfire toward the back, the front of the building was eerily quiet. He snuck down the hallway. Dead soldiers were everywhere. *What the hell happened?* He moved slowly, his breathing the only sound as he made a point of looking in every jail cell he passed. No one was in any of them. Where had they gone? Had they all escaped? He tensed. *Did Cobra escape?*

He came to the end of the hall and stopped. There was a hallway to the right, another to the left. He was about to go down the left hall, when he heard quick, quiet steps running to his right. He followed the sound. The steps stopped. With his rifle ready, he looked around the corner. He was shocked to see a little girl walking a man out of one of the cells. He shook his head. *You're seeing things, Roger.* He looked again. It wasn't just any girl, it was the same girl he had seen in his vision just minutes ago, the same girl who had asked him to not blow up the warehouse. But even more shocking was the man she was helping. *Cobra.* But the pathetic man leaning on the girl looked nothing like the killer that Roger had tracked for the past year. He was thin and sickly, his color pasty gray...*like he could die any minute.* Roger leveled his rifle; he had a clear shot. *I can finally end it here and now.*

He was about to pull the trigger, when Cobra spotted him, fell to his knees, and dragged the girl in front of him. Cobra started to laugh, but the laugh turned into a fit of coughing. When it had passed, he said, "Why, Agent Clarkson, how good of you to join us." He shook the child and grinned. "She's a sweet little thing, isn't she?"

Roger bristled as he stared at the little girl. "Let her go, Cobra." He moved closer, surprised that the child didn't seem frightened. He kept his rifle trained on Cobra, but did his best to give the girl a reassuring smile. "Who...who are you?"

She smiled in reply, and in her eyes he saw something remarkable. A kindness like nothing he had ever seen; a kindness he had all but forgotten. She said, "My...my name is Lili."

Roger nodded. "It's nice to meet you, Lili." He cleared his throat. Just seconds ago he had been willing to kill anyone and everyone in order to kill Cobra, but suddenly he felt shame that he had been about to kill that little girl. "Let her go, Cobra."

Cobra laughed, and again fell into a coughing fit. "Fat chance," he croaked.

Roger was about to shoot at Cobra's shoulder or maybe his kneecap, when the girl held up a tiny hand and said, "We need your help, Roger."

He stared at her. *How does she know my name?* He shook his head. "Lili, I can't help you if your goal is to help him. He is a terrible man."

Again, she smiled, and again, Roger felt helpless to do anything but smile back. She nodded. "You can do it, Roger. You can help me help him. And by doing so, you'll be helping yourself."

Roger stared at her. *Just shoot him, Roger!* But he couldn't. Though the girl, Lili, hadn't changed how he felt about Cobra, she had definitely challenged his commitment to what he had been about to do. For whatever reason, he felt unable to defy her.

He let out a deep sigh. Against every instinct within him, he lowered the rifle. He pulled out his pistol and, aiming it at Cobra, he moved closer. *I'll need handcuffs,* he thought as he reached down and grabbed Cobra by the arm. The man barely resisted. Roger turned to the little girl. "I'm going to search one of the guards for a pair of handcuffs, Lili. Can you come with me?" She nodded. He was about to drag Cobra down the hall, when he heard a familiar voice.

"Roger? Roger Clarkson...is that you? Dear god, son...get me out of here!"

Kauffold? Roger followed the sound. It had come from a nearby hall. Pushing Cobra ahead of him, his pistol trained on his back, he forced the killer to lead the way. They rounded a corner and Roger's jaw dropped. Arthur Kauffold was standing inside a jail cell clinging to the bars. Roger stared at the man. "What the—"

"Just get me out of here!"

"Yes...um, certainly, sir...give me a minute, sir."

Roger spotted a fallen guard further down the hall. Pushing Cobra in front of him, he walked up to the soldier and kicked him to make sure he was dead. The soldier didn't move. Roger shoved Cobra face-first against the wall and, with his pistol still aimed at Cobra's back, he knelt down and took handcuffs and a set of keys from the dead soldier's pockets. He stood, walked over to Cobra, and jerked the man's hands behind his back. Again, the man barely resisted. Roger slapped on the cuffs, then dragged him to Kauffold's cell, leaning him against the wall next to it, as he tried each of the keys.

He finally found the right one and the door opened.

Kauffold rushed into the hall. "Thank god you came along when you did, Roger."

"How did you get in there, Arthur?"

"It's a long story, son. I'll tell you later."

Roger slid the keys in his pocket. As he did so, his fingers brushed over the ignitor switch. He swallowed, again reminded of what he had been about to do. The guilt was overwhelming. *Don't think about it Roger...you need to find out if Hank is in here.* He took a deep breath and looked at Kauffold. "This is going to sound crazy, Arthur, but you didn't happen to see my father here, did you?"

Kauffold opened his mouth to answer, when a sudden blast of gunfire from the front of the warehouse caught them all by surprise.

"Follow me!" Roger yelled, as he grabbed Cobra by the arm and dragged him toward the back of the building. Kauffold and Lili were right behind them. He put the pistol in his pocket and raised his rifle, ready to fire at the first guard he saw. He came to a hallway with no windows, therefore no natural light. He could barely see and was forced to pat the wall with the tip of his rifle to guide him. He came to an intersection. As he rounded the corner, he was glad to see that the hall had a window which let in the sunlight. Not only could he once again see where he was going, but he was able to see a silhouetted image about twenty feet in front of him. The tall, shadowed man was looking away from him, firing a rifle out a barely-opened exit door. Luckily, Cobra's head was down and he was nearly unconscious. He hadn't noticed the man.

Roger readied his rifle and silently motioned for Kauffold and Lili to stay back. Staying in the shadows, and dragging Cobra with him, Roger took two steps forward.

Suddenly Cobra coughed. The man at the door turned and aimed his rifle at Roger. Roger stopped and held up his hand that was holding the rifle, making sure to keep a hold of Cobra with his other hand.

"Who's there?" The man at the door asked, his voice raspy and hoarse.

Roger stepped from the shadows into the light. "Roger Clarkson, CIA." He looked closer at the man, stunned to see a lighter-haired Matt Henderson.

Henderson didn't move. "You don't look like Roger."

Roger moved closer, dragging Cobra with him. "You don't look like Matt."

Henderson frowned. "I see you have a prisoner."

Roger nodded, and grabbed Cobra's arm even tighter.

"Ouch! Ease up, you bastard," Cobra said, but continued to stare at the floor.

Lili and Kauffold emerged from the shadows. Henderson dropped his rifle and ran to Lili. He swept her in his arms and hugged her. "Lili! Thank God you're safe. Why on earth did you run back into this hellhole?" He pointed at Cobra. "And why do you feel the need to save that man?"

A sudden salvo of gunfire was heard in a nearby hall. Roger yelled, "We have to get out of here!" He looked at Henderson. "Is there somewhere safe we can go?"

Henderson nodded. "Yes. There's a Chinook at the far end of the parking lot.

Roger's eyes widened. *Why is a helicopter in the parking lot?* He narrowed his eyes; it didn't matter. He suddenly had a way to follow through with his original plan.

He turned to Kauffold. "You and Henderson take Lili. I'll cover you."

Kauffold swallowed and looked at Henderson.

Henderson stared at Roger, his sharp eyes missing nothing. He said, "No Roger, Kauffold will take Lili. That way, you and I can both give them cover."

Kauffold looked at Roger, then at Henderson, then back at Roger, who gave him a reluctant nod. Without a word, Kauffold took Lili's hand. "Re... ready, Lili?"

"Yes, Mr. Kauffold."

Roger shoved Cobra to his knees. "Don't move or I'll shoot you." The killer didn't resist.

Roger walked over and stood next to Henderson, who had picked up his rifle and was holding it ready. Roger knelt in front of him, and Henderson opened the door. Both men began to fire. Henderson motioned to Kauffold. "Run!"

Kauffold didn't hesitate. Holding Lili's hand, he ran out the door and straight for the helicopter. Henderson fired in one direction while Roger fired in another. Roger was stunned to see a man that he was almost certain was Walter Henderson standing at the door of the helicopter. Kauffold lifted Lili into the man's waiting arms, and he carried her inside. Two Special Ops soldiers stepped to the doorway and helped Kauffold into the chopper. Once Roger saw that Kauffold was safely inside, he slid back into the warehouse. Henderson took a step back and slammed the door.

Roger grabbed Cobra by the arm, forced him up, and shoved him against the wall. Without looking at Henderson, Roger said, "You go next, Henderson. I'll cover you. I can bring Cobra once you're safely aboard."

Henderson shook his head. "No. That's not how this is gonna go, Roger."

Roger turned to Henderson, doing his best to hold back his anger. "He's my prisoner, now go, dammit."

Holding the rifle in his good hand, Henderson went to raise his injured arm to rest it on Roger's shoulder. He grimaced and let it fall to his side. "Listen, Roger. We don't have much time, but you need to hear this. I see the hate in your eyes, and I'm telling you, this asshole isn't worth it." Roger was about to say something. Henderson stopped him. "I recognize it...the hate. As a matter of fact, I have been completely destroyed by it. And I've allowed it to kill people I love." He swallowed. "Let it go, Roger. I'm telling you, let it go. I'll bring Cobra to the helicopter. You go on ahead."

Roger was seething. *I could kill the bastard right now. It's not like Henderson would tell anyone.*

"Don't do it, Roger. I hate him, too. But he isn't worth what it would do to me – what it would do to either one of us – to kill him."

Roger took a deep breath. There was only one man who could ever have the right to say such a thing to him. And it was the man who was looking at him now; the man who had risked his own life to save Roger, Hank, and countless others. Roger hesitated, then gave a subtle nod. "Okay. How about we both take him."

Henderson nodded. "Sounds good. Let's go."

Roger grabbed Cobra's arm with far more force than was needed and jerked him from the wall. Cobra could barely stand. Henderson took Cobra's other arm. They each held a rifle in their free hand. Henderson kicked open the door; the gunshots started immediately. Henderson sprayed an arc of bullets to his left, while Roger fired to his right, as the two of them dragged Cobra across the parking lot to the chopper. Walter was kneeling in the doorway, firing to help cover the three men. Another man came up behind Walter and started firing over his head. Roger looked at him, then looked again. He was seeing an exact replica of himself. Wild hair, the same eyes. *What the hell is my father doing here?* Clearly, the 'Hank' he had heard shouted earlier had been directed at his father. Like everything else that had happened in the last hour or so, there was no way it could be true, yet somehow it was.

They reached the doorway. Roger said, "Take Cobra and get into the chopper, Henderson. I'll cover you." Before Henderson could argue, Roger turned, faced the parking lot, and began firing, while one of the Special Ops soldiers covered him from the door. Walter and Hank helped Cobra, then Henderson into the chopper. Once they were safely inside, Hank knelt at the door and yelled, "Now Roger!"

Roger continued to fire as he stepped backward toward the door. He reached it and let Hank and Walter pull him inside, just as another barrage of bullets peppered the side of the chopper. He was only partway in when Walter yelled "Go!" to the man piloting the helicopter. As they lifted in the air, Hank and Walter pulled Roger the rest of the way. More Chinese guards had poured into the lot and were firing at them, but the helicopter had risen to the point that it was out of reach of their bullets.

Roger stood in the doorway and looked down at the warehouse. He had come so close to blowing up that entire building. And though he was alarmed at how easily he had nearly killed many decent men and a remarkable little girl, a part of him was furious that he hadn't followed through with it. *Cobra would be dead by now.*

He stepped back into the cabin. He felt the ignitor in his pocket. *I should blow up the place right now.* He flinched. He couldn't do it without revealing to the good people in that helicopter what he had so callously been willing to do. Besides, the only man he needed to kill was standing right beside him.

He walked up to Cobra, grabbed him by the arm, and dragged him to a spot a bit further from the door. Using the keys he had taken from the dead soldier, he undid the handcuffs, wrapped Cobra's wrists around a metal post, and clasped the cuffs.

Cobra looked up at him, his gray eyes even more empty than Roger remembered. The man sneered. "I...I like the mountain-man look, Roger. It becomes you." He then fell into a coughing fit that took his breath away.

Roger watched as Cobra stooped over and coughed deep from his chest. The man was clearly ill. From the looks of it, he might die soon without any help from Roger. Regardless, Roger had to fight not to shoot the man then and there. He thought of Henderson's warning and shook his head. *Henderson's wrong. Hate is hate, you can't really control it...and maybe you shouldn't try.* If Lili hadn't been watching from her seat across the cabin, he would have beaten the man to death. Instead, he just gave him a shove, then turned and walked over to where his father was sitting on a cargo trunk. He bent down and hugged the man. "You look terrible, Dad."

Hank laughed. "I could say the same for you." He added, "I tried to call you."

Roger said, "Was that you?" though he already knew that it was. "Sorry, Dad. I've been a bit busy."

"I can see that."

"Was it anything important?"

Hank started to say something, then stopped himself. "We'll talk later."

Roger nodded. Whatever it was, he was glad to put it off. He needed to keep his focus on Cobra...he needed to hold onto his hate. He said, "Once we land."

Hank nodded. "Once we land." He sighed. "Now, go have a seat, son."

Roger walked over and sat on a pile of rucksacks directly across from the man he had hunted for nearly a year...*the killer who is still alive.* He cursed under his breath as he leaned against the side of the helicopter. He combed his fingers through his hair and looked over at his father. The man was watching him. Had he seen what Henderson had seen? Did he, too, recognize the hate in Roger's eyes? He shook his head. *No way.* Hank wouldn't recognize hate...how could he recognize something that he wasn't capable of feeling.

Roger looked around the cabin. His eyes fell on Henderson, the man who had saved his life in Paris. He was sitting next to his father Walter, the man who, from what Roger could tell, had had the courage to bring a handful of men to take on an entire Chinese army. Roger had always respected the Hendersons; he respected them even more now. But

Henderson was wrong about hate. Sometimes it was the only thing that would allow a man to do what was necessary. *And because I eased back from that hate in a moment of weakness, I have failed.*

He looked to Walter's right, and caught the eye of the little girl. Who was she? It was obvious that she knew the Hendersons. How? And how had she seemingly spoken to Roger when she had been nowhere near him?

She smiled and he shifted awkwardly. That smile had a power all its own. How could she smile after all she had been through? She was thin and pale, but her spirit was clearly intact. A Chinese woman was sitting next to her and it was apparent that she and Lili were close. *Likely the reason that her spirit is intact.*

The U.S. senator, Sturgill, was seated on a blanket next to the Chinese woman. He was leaning against the wall, his eyes open but staring at nothing. Though Roger knew he should probably cuff him, too, it was clear that Sturgill didn't have it in him to be combative. And he certainly wasn't going anywhere. *He's already in chains...over something.*

Next to Sturgill, sat Kauffold. Roger suppressed a chuckle as he watched the former ambassador give a tongue-lashing to a man that Roger didn't recognize.

"Why on earth would you lock me in a cell, Johnny?"

"Like I told you, it was for your own good. I knew no one would bother you if you were inside that cell." Johnny paused. "And look at you...I was right, wasn't I?"

Roger had sympathy for the stranger; Roger had been on the receiving end of a tongue-lashing from Arthur Kauffold, as well, but in Roger's case it had centered around the fact that he had had the nerve to fall in love with Kauffold's daughter.

Again, Roger caught Hank's eye. Hank smiled; Roger did his best to smile back. A lot had happened and a lot had gone wrong. Two Latvian soldiers had died, and Cobra was still alive. But he had to admit, a lot had gone right. They had freed a U.S. Senator, as well as a little girl and her caregiver from a terrible ordeal. And they had saved Henderson, the man who had saved so many. Why had he been in the jail in the first place? Roger sighed. *I bet he wound up there after trying to save someone.*

He looked again at the little girl. The sunlight was streaming through a window of the helicopter and he was able to see her eyes. They were telling. Bold and blue, it was as if he was looking at a much older, much wiser girl.

He had to look at her tiny arms and legs to remind himself that she was merely a child. He was curious about her compassion for Cobra, a brutal killer who deserved no compassion at all. How did she know him? And why did she care about him? What had she seen? What did she know that Roger and the others did not?

He turned to Cobra, who was tugging at his chains, his mouth twisted in a perpetual sneer as his mismatched eyes flashed with hate. Roger could feel his own heart hardening. *I don't care what Henderson said, or what Lili saw or heard or felt. That man is rotten to the core...and I will kill him the minute I have the chance.*

* * *

Simeon sat there and took it as Kauffold berated him, all the while wanting nothing more than to choke the life out of the old man. But he couldn't. Not yet. His disguise was intact, and it would be to his benefit to keep it that way for as long as he could. But he had to admit, he was nervous. Martin Henderson had recognized him. He didn't know how; Simeon's hair was now blond, his eyes green from the contact lenses. It didn't matter; his cover as Johnny Canterbury, which had given him access to some very elite men, as well as a powerful warship, would soon be rendered useless. For whatever reason, Henderson had yet to tell anyone. Yes, he had promised to keep Simeon's secret if Simeon helped him get his friends out of that jail. Which is why Simeon had done it. But he knew, sooner or later, Henderson would give him up.

So, Simeon needed to either kill Henderson before he could talk, or he needed to come up with an escape plan. He looked around the cabin. There was no way he was going to be able to kill the man...not with Walter and the others sitting close by. Which meant that he had to escape. But the minute he did, his cover would be blown. Morningstar would be angry, not only that Simeon was no longer a part of the elite Morning Star organization, but that he had failed to kill either Cobra or Sturgill. As a matter of fact, it was possible that Morningstar might actually kill Simeon. Which meant that his escape wasn't just from the men in that helicopter.

He scanned the faces in the cabin, trying his hardest to avoid Henderson's glare. He looked again at the fat ambassador sitting next to him, and had to fight not to laugh. The old man was leaning against the wall, clearly spent. It was likely that he had never seen battle, or, if he had, it had been decades ago. Kauffold caught Johnny looking at him and narrowed his eyes. Simeon frowned. Had Henderson ratted him out, after all? Suddenly, Kauffold offered a snort, followed by the slightest hint of a grin. Simeon sighed, relieved. *Henderson hasn't told him...yet.*

The same was true of Walter. Though he had offered nothing close to a grin, his regard for Johnny was what it had always been...tolerant disregard. If Henderson had told Walter who Simeon really was, Simeon would be in handcuffs by now.

But it didn't matter. Simeon had failed his mission. Charles Sturgill, the man Morningstar had sent him to kill, was still alive, as was Cobra. *Jacob will destroy me long before these assholes have a chance.*

He looked at Cobra and Sturgill and frowned. Both of those men *looked* dead, at least on the inside. And it was more than just gaunt faces or wild hair. It was as if the air had been sucked out of them. Was it enough? Could he go back to Morningstar and tell him that the two men were dead in spirit, if not in the flesh? He smirked. *No.* As long as either one of them was alive, they were a threat...not only to Morningstar, but to Simeon. He had already failed to find the warship that Morningstar was so eager to possess. He narrowed his eyes. *I cannot fail another assignment.*

He stole a glance at Henderson. The man had his head down and his eyes closed. What was he waiting for? Why hadn't he told anyone that Johnny Canterbury was a fraud? Just to honor some stupid promise he had made? Simeon sneered. *Whatever the reason, the man's a fool for waiting. I will not only escape this metal heap, but I'll take out Cobra and Sturgill – and anyone else who gets in my way – in the process.*

CHAPTER 78

Beijing, China

Good versus evil…in a twelve-by-twelve cabin. Henderson looked up and rubbed his arm, which was now cleaned and dressed. His chest wound had been tended to, as well, and the IV in his arm was working miracles. They had been about to give him morphine for the pain, but he had pushed it away. *"I'll be fine,"* he had said, in a move the medics had likely seen as bravado. It wasn't bravado at all; it was the knowledge that his addiction to Dilaudid had been the start of a terrible ordeal that had ended with Lili nearly dead, and scores of others killed by his hand.

As he looked around at the faces in the small cabin, he was overcome. The most unusual collection of twelve people one might have ever imagined. As if a Marvel comic book had come to life – right versus wrong, good versus evil – the well-intentioned coming face-to-face with those whose hearts were filled with malice.

He did a mental checkoff for each one. Eight of the twelve were clearly the good guys; heroes who had gone out of their way to do the right thing. Topping that list was his father, Walter, who had risked his life – and international peace – to infiltrate a Chinese prison camp. He had lost two soldiers to the effort, and Henderson could see the toll it was taking on the man. Was it worth it? Was the loss of two brave freedom fighters worth the price of saving a man who had killed so many? Henderson didn't think so, and the guilt was eating him alive. But then he remembered…Lili had been saved, too. And, though it was hard to measure the value of one life against another, to think of Lili still able to offer her gifts to make the world better...well, that at least made the loss of the two men bearable.

Sitting next to Walter were two more heroes: Hank Clarkson and his son, Roger. They had apparently shown up unaware that the other was in China, but they had both been instrumental in not only saving Henderson's life, but in saving the lives of so many he cared about. It was like one lifelong give-and-take; the Hendersons saving the Clarksons one day, the Clarksons saving the Hendersons the next. He wasn't sure he could ever repay them...then again, they probably felt the same.

But he recognized something new in Roger...something he had seen in himself far too many times. The ability to hate...and to no longer care. It saddened him. Though he didn't know Roger well, he knew enough to know...the look didn't fit. *This man isn't a hater, and he isn't a killer.* But as Henderson watched the young Clarkson stare at Cobra, he knew all too well the hate that lived in Roger's heart. He could see it in his eyes, and could feel it oozing from Roger's pores like a fever.

But what could he do? There was nothing to say to Roger to make that hate go away. Much like a demon, it had found a home, and – like a demon – it would take nothing short of a spiritual awakening to cast it aside.

The fourth hero was Lili Platacis, who was looking at him now with a smile that warmed him. To see her alive after months of believing her dead felt like a miracle he didn't deserve. It only intensified his guilt. After all, it had been his choices – the actions he had taken as a desperate man – that had gotten her kidnapped in the first place. He could only hope that her journey hadn't been too painful. But he could tell by looking at her that it had. She was very thin, and her pale skin had gotten even paler. But her smile was intact, reassuring him that the slings and arrows of the underworld hadn't pierced her soul. He wished the same could be said of himself.

Lili's tight grasp of the hand of the Chinese woman sitting next to her told him all he needed to know about the goodness of that woman. *Hero number five,* he thought. She had clearly become important to Lili. Which meant – whoever she was – she was important to Henderson, as well.

Standing behind her were the Special Ops soldiers...two more heroes who had risked their lives to save a group of strangers they knew nothing about.

Last but not least of the 'good guys' was the UK's former Ambassador, Arthur Kauffold. How he had become a part of this team was hard to say, but it wasn't a complete surprise; he and Walter had been friends for a very long time. Watching their traded glances as the helicopter sped away from the warehouse spoke volumes. They had once again engaged in battle, and, thankfully, they had won.

Henderson hadn't seen Kauffold since the Queen's Ball, when he had enlisted the ambassador's help to figure out who had poisoned Maddi. Ironically, it had turned out to be the man sitting next to Kauffold, the blond-haired man with the green, lens-covered eyes. *Evil soul number one.* Though Henderson knew him as Simeon, more than once he had heard the man referred to as Johnny. Even worse, 'Johnny' and Kauffold were conversing as friends, or at least acquaintances. The imposter had even made a comment or two to Walter, who seemed to know him, as well. How had that come about? Though Henderson was eager to tell them the truth about Simeon, he first needed to know the role the man had played in their lives. He didn't want to disrupt a vital international relationship, and he certainly didn't want to risk a battle on a helicopter full of people. *Besides, I vowed to keep Simeon's secret if he helped me save these people's lives.* Did that matter? Was every promise worth keeping? He shook his head and sighed. He no longer knew the answer.

Across from Simeon sat Charles Sturgill, the senator who had unwittingly brought the world to the brink of war. *Evil soul number two.* Henderson had overheard Kauffold asking him point-blank why he had tried to kill the son of one of China's military leaders. *"Of all the foolhardy things a man could do, Senator!"* But Sturgill hadn't even responded. He had just looked at Kauffold with eyes that were beyond empty; they were cold...like death. As if his soul had been ripped out of him. Henderson knew a bit about that, and could only imagine what had happened to get him to that point. While the world would prosecute him for his crimes, Henderson knew: the sentence had already been imposed. Charles Sturgill was a broken man.

Sitting across from him, chained to a post near the door, was the third man in the quartet of evil. Cobra looked terrible...like he was about to die. And, though it would save the British taxpayers the trouble and expense of a trial, Henderson couldn't help but wonder what was ailing the man. Cobra's reptilian resilience was renowned. But looking at him now, resilience was not the word that came to mind. *More like defeat.*

Cobra caught him looking at him and he sneered. Henderson recalled a similar sneer...at the boarding school in Baclayon, where Henderson had gone as a college student on an outreach mission back in 1988. He had come across Cobra, a thirteen-year-old boy at the time, standing in the hall outside a classroom. Back then, his name had been Mark Villamor. Though Henderson had never met him, he had recognized him from a photo he had found in his father's desk drawer. *Mark Villamor...son of Nenita Villamor, my father's mistress.* He looked at his father. The man was watching him with narrowed eyes. Henderson looked away.

To think, that awful killer saved my life not so long ago. According to Walter, it was Cobra who had saved him when he had jumped out of his bedroom window with a noose around his neck. Why had he done it? Had it merely been an impulse? A quick reaction to keep a man from dying? Henderson shook his head. Cobra possessed no such impulse. If anything, Cobra's impulses were the opposite. More likely, it was a move of power. *I saved your son, Walter...now you owe me.*

Rounding out the quartet of evil was he himself, Martin Henderson. He had committed terrible acts during his time as the Phoenix. And, though he had spent the last year trying to make up for it, he knew he never could. No amount of good could erase the murders he had committed or the pain he had caused. Yes, his actions had been carried out under duress, but wouldn't a stronger man have been able to resist?

He looked at Lili. She was talking to Walter, the nine-year-old's animated gestures much the same as they had been when she was five. By some miracle, that little girl was alive...and not only on the outside. He could see it in her eyes; she remained hopeful and eager for life. He didn't share those sentiments; he had hurt too many, he had ruined far too many lives. On top of it all, he had lost the only woman he had ever loved. Yes, Henderson counted himself as one of the four evil men on that helicopter, but it was okay. He didn't matter anymore. It was enough that Lili was alive and well. It was enough that in the eternal battle between good and evil, this time, at least, good had won.

CHAPTER 79

Outside the Chinese prison

Maddi had awakened to the clap of rifles. Low on cash – she had used nearly all of it on a cab from Beijing – and unwilling to stay in a hostel, she had spent the night at a laundromat not far from the hill that overlooked the warehouse. Sopping wet, she had tossed her cape in a dryer, and had huddled close to the dryer for warmth. She had been the only one there, and had taken the opportunity to sleep. She had curled up in a chair, her head resting on her knees, and had been sleeping soundly when a barrage of gunfire had nearly caused her to fall off the chair.

She had grabbed her cape from the dryer, had thrown it around her, and had run to the door. She had looked outside, shocked at what she had seen. Pandemonium. Truckloads of soldiers speeding through the gate that led to the warehouse, their faces no longer jaded and empty, but filled with fire as they readied for battle.

Lili! Maddi had thought, and had run out the door and into the street. Luckily, the soldiers hadn't noticed her; they had been too focused on getting through the gate. She had slid behind a dumpster, had waited until the trucks were past, then had crept past the trees and through the tall grass to the top of the hill where she had hidden earlier. She had crouched behind the same tree, pulling the cape over her as she had stared down at the warehouse. She had knelt there for what had felt like hours, watching, stunned, as soldiers had run into the building amid increasing gunfire. She had been even more stunned to see a Chinook helicopter fly in and land in back of the facility. Soldiers from inside the chopper had fired at the Chinese guards, and she had watched as, one by one, they had fallen to the ground. Who was in the chopper? Had the embassy called in a team based solely on Maddi's pathetic, hand-scratched note?

She had been stunned to see several people – prisoners? – being hustled into the chopper. She had edged partway down the hill, hoping to make out Sturgill, or maybe a little girl, but had been too far away to see. Was Lili one of the freed prisoners? Had she been saved? *Maybe she'll send me a message to let me know.*

She watched a minute longer, tempted to run down the hill to the chopper, knowing that she would have no way out of China once it flew away. She had no money, no ID, no contacts. But as tempting as it was, she reminded herself that she was supposed to be dead. Besides, a mad dash down the hill and across the parking lot would likely get her killed, and would surely endanger those already on board.

Her heart broke as she watched the last of them climb into the helicopter. She felt a grief so deep it took her breath away. She shivered and quickly wrapped the cape around her. She stared at the chopper as it rose in the air, then grew smaller and smaller in the overcast sky. Tears stung her eyes; she wiped them away. Hopefully Lili, the girl who had come to her in heartfelt desperation, was safe and was on her way home.

More tears came; she ignored them as she tried to think of her next move. She had nothing; no money, no clothes other than those she was wearing, no place to stay. The only people she knew in China were diplomats; she certainly couldn't call on them. For all intents and purposes, Cynthia Madison was dead. Harriett Winthrop was dead, as well. This new woman, this nameless stranger, was completely on her own.

She was about to sneak to the road and hitch a ride back to town, when she heard the sound of tires on gravel. She sunk low in the grass and looked down at the warehouse. Two more trucks had pulled into the lot. Soldiers jumped out, but they didn't run inside. They fanned out around the warehouse. She saw two of them walking up the hill directly to where she was hiding. *I have to get out of here!* But she couldn't run; they were too close. She fell flat on the ground and pulled the cape over her head. She could hear footsteps; they were getting closer. She heard them stop. She stole a look from under the hood of her cape. They were less than ten feet away, but were walking in the opposite direction. After another ten seconds, she crawled to the top of the hill. She waited, then crept down the other side. She reached the base of the hill and spotted an oak tree about ten feet away in a clearing. She ran behind it, catching her breath as she stole a look up the hill. She could see the soldiers at the top. One of them saw her and raised his rifle. He fired and hit the tree. He fired again. *I need to find a place to hide!* She looked around. There was a cluster of trees about twenty feet away. *Go, Maddi!* Dodging bullets, she zigzagged to the trees and hid behind the thickest one. She looked up. The soldiers were running down the hill.

She grabbed the hems of her cape and her dress and sprinted from tree to tree, jumping fallen branches, skirting low-lying limbs. She waded across a narrow stream and, ignoring her wet feet, she stood on the bank and listened. She heard a rustle of leaves and ran as fast as she could in the opposite direction. She looked behind her, then looked back just seconds before she was about to run off the edge of a cliff. The only thing that saved her was a tree limb, which she now clung to for dear life as she stared into a deep ravine. She heard footsteps; the soldiers were getting closer. With the aid of the limb, she pulled herself back from the ledge. Her cape caught; she jerked it free and stared into the gorge. It was too steep to crawl down, let alone climb up the other side. The footsteps were getting closer. She had no choice; she would have to jump across.

The distance to the opposite ledge was about ten feet. She tightened her jaw as she backed up, took a deep breath, then ran as fast as she could to the edge. She leapt across the gorge, her legs flailing as she reached forward, ready to grab a branch or a rock. She landed at the crest of the ledge, grabbing a low hanging limb to keep from falling into the chasm. She landed hard, most of her weight falling on the ankle that had had surgery just months before. A sharp pain shot from the ankle into her leg. *Dammit!* Putting all her weight on her good leg, she used the limb to pull her the rest of the way, as she more or less hopped the distance to the ledge. She fell onto her knees and crawled to a grove of trees. The pain in her ankle was making her sick, but she forced herself to keep going. She spotted a group of low-lying limbs that formed a sort of tent, and crawled to them. She fell onto her back beneath the protective branches, wincing in pain and gasping for air. After a minute, she sat up and examined her injured leg. Though her ankle had begun to swell, she saw no deformity. She ran her hand over it. She didn't feel a break in the bones.

She looked around. The trees were sparse and too spread out; she couldn't stay there. She heard voices on the other side of the ravine. She waited. They were speaking Chinese; she couldn't understand them. Were they going to jump across? If not, did they know a way around? It was likely. *Which means I have to keep going.*

All at once, she heard a distant hum somewhere above her. She looked up through a break in the trees, her heart aching as she spotted the helicopter. She could barely see it. She laid on her back, watching until it was no longer visible. A rush of tears stung her eyes; she wiped them away. There was no time for tears; she needed to hide. *But how can I hide when I can't even walk?* The tears kept coming. She fought them as she lay stranded on her back. And that's when it hit her. For the first time in her life, she was helpless. She had no idea what to do or where to go. And this time, there was no one to save her. Hank was gone, Cravens was gone, Henderson was gone. All the men who had come to her rescue over the years were gone. She was completely and utterly alone. *I should just let the soldiers kill me,* she thought, as she wiped away more tears. *No, they might save me for later...and that would be worse.*

With great force of will, she pulled herself to standing. She leaned against the trunk of a tree as pain shot through the injured leg. She felt like she was going to pass out. *I can't do this,* she thought as she fought to stay conscious, *...I cannot take another step.* She closed her eyes and took a deep breath. *You have to, Maddi.*

She shifted all her weight to her good leg. She looked past the trees and was able to see a clearing. She clenched her jaw and, using a fallen limb as a cane, hopped slowly, painfully to the edge of the trees. Directly in front of her was a meadow with tall grass. Just beyond it was an immense forest. *I can hide there.*

She looked up at the sky. The sun was gone; clouds were moving in. All at once, she heard soldiers' boots somewhere behind her. *Go, Maddi!* She dropped to her knees and, breathing deep, forced herself to leave the safety of the trees. She crawled through the tall grass of the meadow, dragging her leg, fighting the urge to cry out in pain. The ground was uneven, and several times her injured ankle hit against the dirt. Each time, she had to stop, take a deep breath, and swallow, certain she was going to vomit from the pain. But still she kept going. She had nearly reached the edge of the forest when she felt the wind pick up. She looked up. She could see the tops of the trees swaying back and forth. Her heart sank. *It's about to storm.*

She moved even faster, ignoring the rough fronds of meadow grass as they cut across her face and scratched her eyes. She reached the first row of trees and crawled past them. She climbed over rocks and fallen limbs, pushing herself to go deeper and deeper into the forest. She kept going, her knees bruised, her hands bloody until she found a cluster of evergreens hidden deep among the trees. She crawled beneath a canopy of branches and fell onto her back on a soft bed of pine needles.

She breathed in, taking some comfort in the gentle scent of pine, suddenly mindful of better days so very long ago. The days when life was simple, when waiting for the rain was exciting and new. Again, she fought tears, closing her eyes tightly, focusing on the birds chirping nervously as they readied for the storm.

Her knees were bent; she needed to straighten them so she would be flat on the ground. She stretched out the good leg. Then, clenching her jaw and gripping her hands into fists, she extended her injured leg. The pain was unbearable. But she couldn't scream; she couldn't even groan. Her life depended on her silence. She lay shivering, the hood of the cape cushioning her head as she pulled the rest of the cape over her to cover what she could. Then, in the quiet stillness of the forest, she wept.

CHAPTER 80

Mount Katahdan, Maine

Knight sat back in his chair, startled as a clock somewhere in the mountain enclave began to chime. He counted the chimes, stunned when he realized it was eleven p.m. The last twenty-four hours had been challenging, to say the least. But even though the world was hovering on the brink of war, he found himself oddly renewed. Emma had come back to him. And for the first time since their reunion, he had seen nothing but love in her eyes. No regret, no fear, no anguish over decisions she had made, or the steps she would need to take to leave her old life behind.

She had gotten back to the hideaway sometime after nine p.m. the night before and had immediately come to the Oval Office. She had looked at him and, in that instance, he had known that no matter what happened... with him, with America, with the entire world, his love for Emma was perfect and whole. Emma had hugged him like he had never been hugged. *"How'd it go?"* he had asked awkwardly. She had kissed him, then had stepped back and nodded. *"It was good, Romer. He took it about as well as any man could."* He had sighed. *"No regrets?"* She had smiled. *"None."*

Knight had then lifted her in his arms and had carried her to the bedroom. They had spent the entire night together, fully aware that they may not have another chance any time soon. Not only because of the disasters that continued to require his attention, but because of the fact that either one of them could be killed at any time.

Over the last twenty-four hours, Knight had become acutely aware of the fact that Morningstar – who had tried to have Emma killed at least once already – no longer had a reason to keep either one of them alive. Knight had betrayed him; he had left the White House, he had left Morningstar...and he had made it clear he wasn't coming back. Which meant that Morningstar would soon try to have him killed. The man had a long reach and, in Knight's memory, he had never failed.

Which is why I have to take him down...soon.

Emma had fallen asleep in his arms and they had spent the night and much of today together. What was his hurry? If Walter Henderson had held true to his timeline, then he was only now completing his mission in China, which meant that he wouldn't get to the Katahdan hideaway for another twelve to fifteen hours. That was assuming that the Chinook helicopter with his Special Ops team had gotten there in time. As for the retrieval of the Vice-President's letter – the one that Conner had insisted would implicate Morningstar – that had also been delayed, as Knight had instructed Foster to take a round-about route to Nantucket. He was expected back by midnight.

But there were other challenges that required his attention, so, with much regret, Knight had pulled himself away from Emma at around four that afternoon. He had gone back to his office and had been there ever since.

He tapped his fingers on the desk, impatiently awaiting word, either from Cravens regarding Walter's mission in China, or from Foster regarding the letter that the Vice-President had sworn would indict Morningstar. He was about to reach for his phone to call Cravens, when he heard a knock on the door. "Come in."

It was Foster. He was carrying an envelope in his hand. He handed it to Knight. "The letter you asked me to get for you, sir."

Knight took the letter. "Thank you, Foster. Any trouble with Mrs. Conner?"

"No sir. Apparently, the former VP had told her that I would be coming to retrieve a letter that was vital to national security. She didn't seem to question it."

"Good."

Foster nodded. "As you requested, sir, I read it through, and I've jotted down a few notes to save you time." He handed him a folded sheet of paper.

Knight nodded. "Thank you, Foster. That will be all."

Foster left the room.

Knight sat down and opened the letter. He could see that it was written in Farsi – which he would normally be able to interpret – but it was a version that was no longer in use. He opened the page from Foster and laid it beside the letter. Thankfully, Foster had interpreted every word. The letter was addressed to a man named Fouad. Foster had apparently done some digging, and had learned that the man's full name was Fouad Al Rashid. He had written it on his cheat sheet, along with the fact that the man either was or had been the coordinator for a lab in Riyadh, Saudi Arabia.

Knight read Foster's full interpretation of the single page letter. He was stunned that a spy would put on paper what had been written in that note. The author, a woman by the name of Edi, had brazenly written that she was *"...involved with a powerful man from the Pentagon. He gives me information to help our cause...I give him sex."*

Was the powerful man from the Pentagon a reference to Morningstar? Knight ran his fingers through his hair. *Conner must think so.*

The woman had also written, *"Take what you need from the vault. You can start now."* She had signed the letter, followed by an identification number, then dated it. That was it.

According to Foster's note, the woman's full name was Edi Abu. and she was a UN diplomat who had gone missing in late January. Knight was already familiar with her. She had appeared before his senate subcommittee to discuss Middle East jihadists toward the end of last year. She was quite memorable. Young and beautiful, it wouldn't surprise Knight to learn that she had been a Morningstar lover.

Knight picked up the landline and dialed. "Yes, Patrick. Could you get me whatever you can find on a UN attaché by the name of Edi Abu." He paused. "She went missing back in January. I'm curious what's been done to find her."

Patrick agreed and Knight ended the call. He stared at the letter. It certainly wasn't the proof he was looking for. Edi had never referred to Morningstar by name; she had only alluded to a powerful man from the Pentagon. There were plenty of Pentagon employees who fit that description.

He shook his head. *I wonder if she's even alive.* Assuming the woman had been a Morningstar lover, it was no longer a reach to think that he might have gotten rid of her once she had fulfilled her purpose. But if she was alive, Knight needed to talk to her. If she would be willing to say under oath that Morningstar was the lover she had referenced in her letter, then Knight would at least have a witness to testify against him.

He read the letter again. He was curious about the lab coordinator, Fouad al Riyadh. He was also curious what cause Edi Abu may have been referring to.

Again, he reached for the landline.

"Yes sir?"

"Patrick, I also need you to investigate possible extremist activity in a lab in Riyadh, Saudi Arabia." Knight read off the specific address where the letter had been sent. "Look especially at the coordinator, Fouad al Riyadh." Knight checked the date of the letter. "He may not be there any longer, but he was there back in January."

He ended the call. His hope was that if Edi didn't have information to incriminate Morningstar, maybe Fouad would. It was a longshot. Not only that they would find Fouad, but that he would know anything about Edi's mystery lover. *Why did Conner think that this letter was proof?* He read it a fourth time and frowned, finally tossing it on the desk. *I'll just have to wait for Conner to fill me in tomorrow.*

At Knight's request, Conner had spent the day putting in writing what he had told Knight the night before. He had gone to bed about an hour ago. The two men had agreed to go over what he had written first thing tomorrow morning. He looked at the letter and frowned. *To hell with that.*

Again, he reached for the phone. "Kent, could you have someone wake the former Vice-President and bring him to my office at once?"

"Yes sir."

Knight hung up the phone and stared at the letter. He hoped that Connor could give him something more than what was in that letter. Otherwise, the former Vice-President had given up his livelihood – and his freedom – for nothing.

He stood and paced the room. *Maybe one of the Hendersons will have something concrete that will help me bring down Morningstar,* he thought as he awaited news from China. He was as nervous as a cat. Had Walter been successful? If so, who had he been able to save? Would Walter's son be among them? Would the Special Ops team succeed in getting them to the Katahdan hideaway without giving away its location? How would China handle the jail break? Was Harrison equipped to deal with it?

The questions were coming at him like daggers; he felt like he was smothering. He took off his jacket and unbuttoned the collar of his shirt. He walked the jacket to his chair. He was about to make another lap around the office, when his cellphone rang. "Yes, Foster?"

"Sir, Patrick has just intercepted an S.O.S. ...from overseas."

"An S.O.S? Is it from Walter Henderson?"

"No sir. It's from a woman, Larissa Platacis."

Knight frowned. "Is that a name I should know?"

"No sir, but I think what I have to share will interest you."

Knight rubbed his eyes and sighed. *Not another problem.* "Go ahead, Foster."

"Well, for starters, the woman's husband was a Latvian freedom fighter. His name was Albins Platacis. He died in battle nearly five years ago. "

"A Latvian freedom fighter. Was he a friend of the Hendersons?"

"I'm guessing that he was, sir."

"Okay. I'll ask them about her when – if – they get here."

"Yes sir, that is an excellent idea." There was an awkward pause.

"What is it, Foster? Is there more?"

"Um, yes sir. I think this woman, this Larissa, might be related to Emma."

Knight frowned. "Why would you think that, Foster? Emma told me that everyone in her family – which was from Belarus, by the way – is dead."

"Yes sir, but the S.O.S. is from a Larissa Melnikov Platacis."

Knight's eyes widened. "Melnikov?" He shook his head. "I see where you're going with this, but isn't Melnikov a common name in Russia?"

"Yes sir, it is. But the woman, Larissa, makes reference to a mother who died in America...in Maine...and a sister who lives there still." A pause. "It seemed like a lot of coincidences, sir."

Knight frowned. He had to agree. "I'll ask Emma about it tomorrow, Foster."

A pause. "Here's the thing, sir. From the sound of the letter, this woman, this Larissa, is in quite a bit of danger. She is convinced that her sister and her daughter are the only ones who can help." Another pause. "To be honest with you, sir, I don't think she has until tomorrow."

Chapter 81

Darlington, England

Andrew ran his hands through his hair. Still unwilling to read the last letter, he had paced the den for nearly an hour. He had then come back to the kitchen, this time for a bowl of soup. As he ate the soup and stared out at the darkness beyond the tall French doors, he found himself mystified, not only by the last two letters, but by the whole ordeal. Clearly, Larissa, whoever she was, was either overstating things or she was crazy. There was no way it could be as ominous as she had implied. *And there's no way the world can be saved by a bunch of stupid coins.*

He checked the time. It was well after four a.m. He had been up all night. He took a deep breath and sighed. *You need to finish this, Andrew.*

He stood and walked back to the den. As he stepped into the room, he was calmed by the wistful scent of burning wood. He stopped at the fire, stoked it a time or two, then returned to the Chesterfield sofa. He stared at the letters strewn across the top of the mahogany coffee table. They told a fascinating story that had somehow culminated in an apocalyptic prophecy. *And now, it's time to read the last one.*

He reached for the envelope, holding it carefully as he stared at what could only be described as the pen marks of an embattled soul. Again, he checked the date on the back. *"November 1st, 2004."* He frowned. *Just two weeks ago.* He pulled out the letter and saw the same desperate handwriting. He took a deep breath and read it through. His heart began to pound...

"Dear Gloria,

"I'm hiding in a cave outside Novosibirsk. The prophecy is happening. Whereas before I might have played it off as coincidence, I can no longer do so, certain I am seeing an aligning of events that have been foretold for centuries, even before the coming of Christ. I have learned that these prophecies have also been mentioned in the writings of the ancient Egyptians. Only days ago, another earthquake, another warning...this time in Japan.

"Time is limited; weeks, maybe months...but certainly not years. I'm certain now that not only do the coins reveal a truth, but they offer up an answer. All the coins must be joined together not only to understand, but to save us from the suffering that will soon come to pass. I'm in no position to do this, Gloria, which means that it is up to you to bring them all together. Two coins each...from my mother Dasha, from Annabelle, and from you. I'm hopeful that you have yours; I think my sister may have a coin, though I can't be sure. Mine is hidden in Latvia, and, though I've intentionally kept her out of my thoughts, Lili should be able to—"

That was it. A cryptic comment about someone named Lili, the words stopping midsentence as if Larissa had been interrupted.

Andrew saw that his hands were shaking; he dropped the letter in his lap and rubbed his thighs. What was she talking about...*and how on earth did she send this letter from a cave in Siberia when her life is clearly in jeopardy?* Had someone found the letter and sent it for her? He nodded. That had to be it.

He wanted to dismiss it; disregard the whole thing, but he couldn't. *I need to tell someone.* Who? Who would listen to such a story without thinking that Andrew had lost his mind? He thought again of the Morning Star, the ship that had confounded the few who knew of it. Not only was it a warship capable of mass destruction, but its features – which could only be described as supernatural – had inspired the formation of a group of men whose sole purpose was to protect the world from that very ship.

Andrew had been pulled into the group as part of a legacy... *similar to this one.* Only the legacy he was reading about now hadn't been meant for him; it had been meant for the daughters and granddaughters of Gloria, Annabelle, and Dasha. All three of those women were dead. Larissa seemed to be the only one alive who understood what was meant not only by the prophecy, but by the coins. But she was obviously in trouble. *And it is now up to me to somehow save her.*

And he would need help...not only to save her, but to explore crazy claims made by a woman who didn't seem crazy at all. And just like with the Morning Star, it would take someone open to such imaginings; someone who hadn't only witnessed the mystic power of the Morning Star, but who understood that there are things out there that can't be explained through our current prism of understanding.

Arthur Kauffold.

Not only did Kauffold appreciate truths that science can't explain, but it was possible – even likely – that Annabelle had confided in him about the prophecy, the coins, and the women who held them. Kauffold had said that he hoped to be back in Chesham soon. How soon? Andrew reread the letter. Larissa was stuck in a cave in Siberia, she was clearly frightened, and her letter had ended abruptly. She was in trouble. *I have to somehow find her...and get her out of there...soon.*

Andrew couldn't call Kauffold directly – the man didn't carry a cellphone – but he had told Andrew that he was meeting with Johnny Canterbury. Was he still with him? If so, Andrew could call Johnny. He had his number from their efforts to save Maddi and the others in Dalgety Bay...*but it's in my phone in South Carolina!*

He checked the time. *Four-thirty in the morning in Darlington...eleven-thirty at night in South Carolina.* Amanda was probably asleep, and Adam was asleep for sure. The cellphone was locked in Andrew's desk at the downtown clinic. Amanda wouldn't be going back there until Monday...*a full day-and-a-half from now!*

He stood and paced the den, trying to decide if he should call his wife and force her to wake their son and drive to the office. He looked again at the letters on the table. Less than two weeks ago, that poor woman, Larissa, was hiding in a cave, possibly freezing to death, clearly frightened for her life. And she was doing it all to guard a secret...a horrible, unimaginable secret. *I have to do something.*

He pulled out his phone and dialed. It took several rings, but then a sleepy voice said, "Andrew?"

Andrew swallowed. *I want to go home.* He cleared his throat. "Amanda, it is so good to hear your voice. I'm sorry to wake you."

"It's okay. Are you alright?"

Just swell. "I can't talk long. I need another number from my cellphone. I know it's at the office, and, as much as I hate to ask, I need you to get it... tonight."

There was a pause. "Okay...okay, I'll do it right away. I'll call you back as soon as I can." Another pause. "I miss you, Andrew. Adam misses you."

He closed his eyes. "I miss you too, babe." He ended the call. His hand was shaking as he slid the trac phone in his pocket. He rubbed his eyes and looked again at Larissa's letters. *I may be lonely, but Larissa is completely alone.*

He thought again about the letter that was missing; the letter that Larissa had referenced in her previous letter. Had it been lost...or had it been taken – confiscated – by someone who was about to hurt her?

He paced the room as he waited impatiently for his wife to call him with Johnny Canterbury's number. There was no question that Larissa was in danger, either from a faceless Apocalypse that she had vaguely described in her letters, or from some stranger who had seized her letter and would soon threaten her very life. Regardless, that poor woman – if she was still alive – was in trouble.

He walked back to the couch and stared down at the letters. What he was looking at was history...but it was more than that; it was the future. A future that a woman hiding in Novosibirsk, Russia seemed to be well aware of. *And it isn't good.*

He sat down with a sigh. He leaned against the back of the couch, kicked his feet on the table, and ran his hands through his hair. He frowned as he thought about the letter. It had ended abruptly, with the name of someone Andrew had never heard of. He watched the fire fade, waiting eagerly for Amanda's call. As his eyes grew heavy, he couldn't help but wonder...*who the hell is Lili?*

CHAPTER 82

Mount Katahdan, Maine

Emma opened her eyes and instantly felt for Romer next to her in the bed. It was empty, and she sighed. But she wasn't surprised. He was, after all, the President of the United States, even if he was in hiding. She rolled onto her side. *But I'd love – just one time – to go to bed with that man, and wake up with him next to me.*

She had gotten back to the mountain hideaway sometime after nine p.m. the night before, and had gone straight to the makeshift Oval Office, where she had guessed that Romer would be waiting for her. She hadn't been wrong. Not only had he been waiting, he had looked terrible. And, though she knew there was plenty on that poor man's mind, it was clear that her decision to meet with Michael had filled him with uncertainty. And it was understandable. Any man – even the most powerful man in the world – would find the situation worrisome.

So, she had immediately put his mind at ease. First with words, then with actions. They had made love like never before, because, for the first time in a very long time, Emma was free. Yes, there were formalities to tend to, and yes, the affair between her and the President would be hyped by a Press Corp eager for gossip, but those would be small obstacles. The greatest obstacle had now been dealt with; her marriage of sixteen years. As far as she was concerned, their most challenging problem had been put to rest.

But she would be wrong.

She was reaching for his pillow so she could smell him as she held it in her arms, when she heard a knock on the door. "Yes?"

Knight crept into the dark room. "I'm sorry to wake you, Emma." He walked over to the bed and switched on a lamp. He looked different; more serious. He sat next to her, and bent down and kissed her. He sat back with a sigh.

"What's wrong, Romer?"

As he looked at her, she saw a combination of adoration and concern. "I need to talk to you."

She sat up, ran her fingers through her tangled hair, and leaned against the headboard. "Go on."

He took another deep sigh. "I...I have something that I need to tell you."

She leaned forward and took his hand in hers. "I'm listening."

He smiled, and then he talked...nonstop...about them, about his time growing up in Maine, about his adopted father, Charles Sturgill, and about the terrible deeds of the terrible man, Edward Morningstar. And though he had shared some of it on their way to the mountain, this time there was more. Not only had Jerome been part of something truly awful, but he had learned within the last thirty-six hours that there was at least one other good man who had also been sucked into Morningstar's web. His name was Martin Henderson. Emma had read of the Hendersons in newspapers and magazines, but knew only that they were a highly respected American family. Which made Henderson's membership in Morningstar's terrible club just as shocking as Jerome's. But she was confused as to why Jerome had decided to share it with her.

"Why are you telling me this?"

He frowned. "Because that family...the Henderson family...not only has an estate in Boston, but they have a sizeable estate in Latvia."

Emma looked at him, puzzled. All she knew of Latvia were the stories her mother had told her when she was a little girl. Her family had emigrated from Belarus to Latvia before Emma was born. When they had moved to America, her sister had stayed in Latvia. Emma had learned nearly five years ago that the sister had died there, as well. There had been no burial or memorial service of any kind, however, so Emma hadn't made the trip overseas. She wasn't even sure she could find the former Soviet country on a map. "Go on."

He sighed. "Emma, just minutes ago, I was told of a letter – an S.O.S. – that was recovered quite by accident. It implies that something big is about to take place."

"What do you mean?" Emma brushed a strand of hair from her forehead. She was starting to feel concerned. "Just say what you're trying to say, Jerome."

He stared at her, his dark eyes even darker in the dim light of the bedroom. "I...I have reason to believe that you, Emma, might be essential to helping us find a woman who is somehow involved in a plot that threatens us...that threatens America...and maybe the entire world."

Emma sat back against the headboard and shook her head. "What are you talking about?"

Knight sighed. "Emma...I know you have a sister—"

"I *had* a sister, Jerome."

He nodded. "You never really said much about her."

"That's because I never knew her. She was much older than me, and lived thousands of miles away."

Knight frowned. "Why did she live so far away?"

Emma hesitated then let out a deep sigh. "Well, as you know, my parents moved to America before I was born so that Mama could be treated for cancer. Apparently, it was a rare type, and the U.S. offered more options than Latvia, especially back then." She paused. "I was born soon after, but I remember very little, except when Mama died." She looked away. "As for my sister, Mama said little about her, other than she was twelve years old when they moved to America." She looked at Knight. "My understanding is that she had stayed in Latvia with a nice family not far from where my parents had lived."

"Why would your parents leave their twelve-year-old daughter behind?"

"I'm not really sure. All Mama said was that my sister was happier there than she would've been in America." She hesitated. "But I think there was more to it."

"What do you mean?"

Emma sighed. "According to Mama, my sister was a bit...different."

"Different? In what way?"

Emma hesitated. "She was...special."

Knight narrowed his eyes. "Special?"

Emma shrugged. "Yes. Mama said that she was into magic, or psychic meditation, or something like that. Anyway, she was a bit odd, and I think Mama was worried that the Americans might make fun of her." She paused. "Mama said that there were people in Latvia who wanted to help her."

"Help her?"

"Yes. An institute of some kind that had reached out to my parents. The man in charge had told them that he had become aware of her...special abilities...and felt that those abilities were vital to humanity and should be cultivated."

Knight eyes widened. "I see."

Emma nodded. "Mama didn't like to talk about it. I could tell it hurt her deeply to leave her behind."

"How were you made aware of your sister's death?"

"Through a letter." Emma thought back to the single-page memo that had somehow wound up in her mailbox, like some meaningless advertisement. She had nearly thrown it away. "A telegram that said that they were sorry to inform me that my sister, Larissa Melnikov Platacis, passed away unexpectedly while working for the government."

Again, Knight's eyes widened. "Larissa Melnikov Platacis?"

"Yes."

"And it said that she was working for the government. Latvia's government?"

Emma tried to remember where the letter had come from. "Yes, I believe the telegram was from Riga."

"Were you able to confirm Larissa's death?"

Emma frowned. "No, not really. I guess I didn't feel a need to. I believed the telegram." She cleared her throat. "Like I said, I didn't even know my sister. My parents were both dead, and I had no one to call to learn more."

"Didn't she come to either of your parent's funerals?"

Emma shook her head. "No. Mama died first...from the cancer. Papa said the trip would be too much for Larissa, and that she was busy '...*saving the world*.'" As for Papa, I'm not even sure that Larissa was aware that he had died."

Knight stared at her. Finally, he said, "Emma. I was just made aware that your sister was married, and that she may have had a child."

Emma's eyes widened. "A child? I...dear God...I didn't know." She flinched. "How terrible to think that I have a brother-in-law and a niece or nephew out there whom I know nothing about."

Knight shook his head. "If my information is accurate, her husband, Albins Platacis, was killed in an uprising in Latvia about four years ago... in the spring of 2000."

Emma swallowed. "So that poor child is an orphan?"

Knight nodded. "I'm guessing so. My men have just started looking into it."

Emma frowned. "Dear god, Jerome, we need to find that child. With both Albins and Larissa gone, that makes me the child's only living relative."

Knight looked at her, his eyes suddenly hard to read. "Not quite, Emma."

She narrowed her eyes. "What are you trying to say, Jerome?"

Knight took a deep breath and let it out slowly. "Emma, what if I was to tell you that your sister might still be alive."

Emma shook her head. "You would be mistaken, Jerome. She died five years ago. I received the official telegram saying that it was so."

He sighed. "I know. But governments sometimes lie." He moved closer. "Emma, Larissa isn't dead...or at least she wasn't as recently as several weeks ago."

Emma stared at him. "So...why would the Latvian authorities send me a telegram saying that she was?"

"To give her cover."

Emma's eyes flashed. "Cover? For what? Unless that cover was essential for the very survival of the planet, I can't think of any *cover* that justifies forcing a family – she had a child for Christ's sake – to falsely mourn their loved one."

Knight nodded. "I'm not sure about the survival of the planet, Emma, but I do think that the preservation of a free Latvia was likely at stake." He reached for her hand and offered a weak smile. "Emma, it would appear that your sister was – is – quite possibly a hero."

Emma stared at him, unsure what to think...what to feel. She had begun to shake. He squeezed her hand and pushed a strand of hair from her forehead. "Emma, I'm going to need your help." He hesitated. "Not only is Larissa alive, but we think that she's hiding...somewhere in Mongolia. She has been sending messages by way of a courier to a contact in Latvia." He cleared his throat. "Earlier tonight, that courier was found shot dead in a safehouse outside Istanbul."

Emma shook her head. It was too much. Her sister Larissa not dead, but alive, sending messages to a Latvian operative by way of a courier in Istanbul? *There is no way.* It was like something out of a spy novel.

Knight went on. "It's how we intercepted the letter."

"What letter?"

"The letter she wrote...to a woman named Gloria."

Emma wanted to ask, *Who's Gloria?* but she couldn't seem to find her voice.

He brushed his fingers tenderly over her hand. "It was hidden in a secret pocket in the dead courier's jacket, undelivered." He paused. "Apparently, Larissa had been writing this woman in secret." Another pause. "Emma, do you know a woman by the name of Gloria Madison?"

Emma shook her head. She said weakly, "I'm...I'm sorry, Jerome, I don't."

"It's okay, Emma. I know this is a lot." He hesitated. "Have you ever heard of a group known as The Partisans?"

Emma's eyes widened. She had heard of them. Her mother, Dasha, had told her stories about her adventures as a member of the group prior to coming to America. But Dasha had died when Emma was five, so the stories had been simple...mostly just the adventures of a young woman in Soviet Russia during World War II. "I recognize that name, but I...I can't say I know much about them, why?"

Knight took her other hand and turned her to face him. "Emma, your sister's letter to Gloria wasn't good. She was frightened...and she mentioned your name."

Emma sat back, stunned. "My name? Why?"

He hesitated. "Because she said that whatever horror is about to befall this world, you are one of only a few who can stop it. You...and someone by the name of Lili."

CHAPTER 83

Beijing, China

Lili Platacis brushed her stringy, overgrown bangs from her eyes and looked at Uncle Mart. She smiled. Never in her wildest dreams had she imagined she would see him again...not in this lifetime, anyway. They had had little chance to talk, however. Mart was hurt, he was weak, and the noise from the helicopter was loud. Lili was weak, as well, and most of the last hour had been devoted to getting everyone some much-needed medical care. When the medic had gotten to her, he had used terms like dehydration and malnutrition, and – though Lili appreciated the IV and the medicine they were putting in her arm – she knew that what she really needed were the comforts of home.

And, though home no longer included her mama, Larissa, or her papa, Albins, she was nonetheless eager to see the two people who had more or less adopted her: Danil Latkovskis and his sister, Anna. She had all but given up on the notion that she would ever see them again. To hug Uncle Dan and catch a glimpse of Anna's shy smile...it would feel like a miracle. *And I'll get to see the cats!*

She looked around the cabin. She knew only a few of the faces. Walter, Uncle Mart, and, of course, Ching Lan. The others were strangers, though she got the sense that she knew at least a few of them on a different level. She found herself especially curious about the man near the door; the gaunt, blond-and-black-haired man with eyes that left her cold. Though he was clearly a bad man, there was something that drew her to him. She tried not to look at him, but she couldn't help herself.

The two had communicated over the past ten days. She hadn't understood it at first; she hadn't known who he was or where he was being held. All she had known was that he was close by, he was ill, and he was haunted. But somehow, his thoughts had become readable, and – like often happened when Lili was able to see inside someone's mind – she felt pity for the man. It wasn't that she hadn't heard the evil thoughts that hummed inside him like locusts, or felt the anger that oozed from his skin like the blood-tinged sweat of Judas. She was just able to see something else; something valid. She would never tell anyone; it was clear that – whoever he was – no one on that helicopter had high regard for him. Especially Uncle Mart; she sensed that he hated him most of all. But she found the man intriguing, and, in spite of the evil in his soul, she had picked up on the heartache of a wounded child. It made her heart hurt. She, too, had been wounded.

But there had been more that had taken place in their silent conversations. The man they called Cobra was complicated. She sensed several people inside the one, and she was having trouble sorting them out. There was the little boy, with whom she had bonded to some degree, and there was the man himself, with whom she had done her best to not get too close. Then there was a far more dignified man who seemed to have rules for Cobra that Cobra refused to follow. He had been the first person she had met, and Cobra's reaction to him had amused her. But there was another presence inside Cobra. A dark ball of nothing that seemed to be taking over and making him weak. Though Lili was afraid of it, she was curious, and eager to learn more. But the one she was most eager to know better was the shy, frightened little boy.

The man, Cobra, looked at her. Though she wanted to turn away, she couldn't. She crossed her arms over her chest, more scared than she had ever been. Then, he smiled. A real smile...from somewhere deep in his soul. *It's the little boy,* she thought. She closed her eyes, trying to see him...trying to see the little boy. She couldn't. It was like he was buried too deep.

She finally gave up and leaned against Ching Lan. She looked again at Uncle Mart. He was watching her and she grinned. He grinned back and her heart felt like it was going to burst. *He's alive...and he's here...with me.*

Suddenly, she felt her breaths quicken and her heart start to race. She was seeing a new image...behind her eyes. She closed them, and could see someone...a woman that she recognized. She winced and, without thinking, grabbed her ankle as she felt the woman writhe in pain. She tried to see where the woman was...why she was hurting; she couldn't. All she could see were trees, and the vague image of a Chinese shrine known as the Temple of Heaven.

She leaned over and tugged on Uncle Mart's sleeve.

"What is it, Lili?"

"We need to go back."

"Where?"

"To the mountains near the prison."

"Why?"

"She's there."

"Who's there?"

"The Special Lady."

"Who...is the...special lady, Lili?" Mart was weak; he was struggling to talk.

"Don't you remember? The lady you were going to bring back from America. You were to bring her to Latvia so you could take care of me...both of you, together."

She was stunned to see Mart's eyes fill with tears. He leaned closer and said, "Lili, that lady – that special lady – was...killed...in a plane crash two months ago."

Lili shook her head. "No...no, she wasn't. I have been trying to tell you that. And I tell you now, I can see her...in a forest...beyond a meadow...near a deep ravine...past a hill. You can see the Temple of Heaven from the top of the hill. She's there, she's hiding, and she's crying...alone."

CHAPTER 84

Beijing, China

The Temple of Heaven? Henderson shook his head. *Lili's delusional. She's dehydrated and not thinking straight.* He tightened his jaw. He had to force himself to not be angry with her. He swallowed; he was having trouble catching his breath. It felt as if Maddi had died all over again. Clearly, whatever Lili was seeing wasn't real, and though he wanted to believe her – she did, after all, have unique gifts – he knew it wasn't true. "The Special Lady is dead, Lili!" he whispered, a bit louder than he had intended.

But Lili held her ground. "No, she's not. I'm telling you...I asked her to come to help us, and she did!"

Henderson frowned. "How did you ask her to come help you?"

"Like I always do."

"But you never even knew her."

Lili frowned. "I know...but it was as if I did...as if she had suddenly found a place in my memory...as if she had been there for quite some time."

Out of nowhere, Ching Lan, who had yet to say a single word, said softly, "An invisible thread connects those who are destined to meet."

Henderson stared at Ching Lan, then at Lili. Though he knew he shouldn't indulge the sudden hope that was welling up inside him, and though he knew that he was about to revive a grief that had taken him months to bury, he leaned over to his father and told him what Lili had said.

Walter looked at him, clearly stunned, then shook his head firmly. "No. Absolutely not."

Henderson stared at Walter. Then, in spite of his father's objection, Henderson yelled up to the pilot, "We need to turn around and go back to the warehouse."

The pilot shook his head and said over his shoulder, "We can't."

"What do you mean, we can't? We have to. We think we may have left someone behind."

"No. I have strict orders."

Walter turned and looked at the pilot. "From who?"

"I can't say."

"What do you mean, 'you can't say'?"

The pilot hesitated. "The man who sent us...he insists that we bring you to him straightaway, sir."

Walter frowned. "And where is he?"

The pilot shifted awkwardly in his seat. "I'm sorry, Mr. Henderson, but I'm not at liberty to say."

Walter stared at him, but said nothing. He turned to Henderson. "Mar—Matt, we can't go back; the pilot has made that rather clear. Besides, it isn't safe."

Henderson shook his head. He spoke in a whisper, his raspy voice barely audible. "You know Lili's powers, Da—Walter. If she says that someone is back there, then someone is back there. We can't in good conscience leave them there; not after the hostility we've stirred up by our escape."

Henderson wasn't sure what it was that compelled his father to give in; maybe it was a need to let Henderson have a moment's hope. Whatever the reason, Walter raised his hand and said to those in the cabin, "We have become aware of a possible survivor who might be stranded near the warehouse."

Kauffold was the first to speak. "A survivor? That's preposterous." He narrowed his eyes. "You're not suggesting that we go back for him, are you?"

Walter nodded. "I am...and it's a woman."

Hank's eyes widened. "A woman? What woman?"

Henderson was about to speak, but Walter beat him to it. "Likely a prisoner that escaped in the chaos. Regardless, she may be stranded somewhere in the mountains."

Hank narrowed his eyes, but said nothing. Roger was focused on Cobra, who had his head down and was ignoring the entire conversation. Sturgill, too, didn't seem to care. As for Simeon – the mysterious 'Johnny' – he refused to look at Henderson, but glared at Walter with poorly masked scorn. "Not a good plan, Walter. It's way too dangerous."

Henderson wanted to choke him. Instead, he cleared his throat and said to everyone in the cabin, "I know this is a lot to take in, but you must believe us...if Lili says there is somewhere back there, then I'm telling you... there is."

Walter added, "...and we can't very well leave someone – a woman – back there to die at the hand of the Chinese."

"Let's take a vote." It was Kauffold.

Henderson nodded. "Fair enough. All in favor."

One by one, the hands went up: First Hank, then Lili, then Walter. Finally, Kauffold raised a reluctant hand in the air. At the last minute, Ching Lan raised a weak hand, as well.

Henderson let out a sigh of relief. "With me, that makes six. Against?"

Only Simeon raised his hand. Both Kauffold and Walter glared at him; he quickly lowered it.

Walter turned to the pilot. "I understand your orders, soldier. But it will only take about an hour to go back, and about forty-five minutes to do a search. Less than two hours...to maybe save someone's life." He bristled. "And then you can take us wherever the hell you need to take us."

The pilot said nothing. After several seconds, he cursed under his breath and turned the helicopter around.

But in spite of Walter's assurance that it would be a "quick search," everyone on that helicopter knew that it wouldn't be...not at all. They were returning to enemy territory after having fired at – and killed – Chinese soldiers. The Chinese would be waiting for them. It was quite possible that the decision they had just made would get every one of them killed.

After some discussion, the decision was made to land the helicopter a couple of miles from the warehouse, and send just one of them to search for the possible survivor. The helicopter would fly north and find a place to refuel, then come back in forty-five minutes.

Henderson volunteered. "I'm the one who brought it up. I'll be the one to go."

Hank stood and looked around the cabin. "Nonsense. You've been injured, Henderson; you're not well." He paused. "But I am totally fine. I'll go."

Roger stood and said, "No, Dad, this is exactly the sort of thing that I've been trained to do. I'll go."

Hank shook his head and motioned toward Cobra, who was still staring at the ground. "No, you have a prisoner to watch." He held up his hand. "I'm going."

Henderson was about to challenge him again, when Walter looked at Hank and frowned. "Are you sure about this, Hank?"

Hank nodded. "Let me do this, Walter."

Walter stared at him, then nodded his head slowly. He turned to the others. "Hank is a trained agent from America's Department of Homeland Security. He is qualified, and if he wants to do this, then he should be the one to go."

An hour later, they swooped in low between two mountains of the Xishan range. The pilot set down in a field about three miles from the warehouse. Hank moved to the door and grabbed one of the rifles that had been taken from the Chinese soldiers. He turned, gave a quick nod to Roger, then jumped to the ground.

The helicopter began to lift in the air. Suddenly, before anyone could stop him, Henderson yanked out his IV, slapped on a bandage, and ran to the door. He grabbed a rifle and jumped out, landing hard on the ground. The jolt shot pain up his legs and into his battered body. Though he wanted to cry out, he didn't, merely grimacing as he tried to stand on shaking legs.

Hank ran over to him and reached out his hand. "You're an idiot, Henderson. You can barely walk."

Henderson grabbed Hank's outstretched hand, swallowing back the pain as he regained his balance. "I'm fine, Hank. I've had two IV boluses; I feel better than I've felt in weeks." He hiked the rifle over his shoulder and nudged Hank. "Let's go."

He looked back. Thick clouds were coming in over the mountains as the helicopter lifted in the air. His father was standing in the doorway, the look on his face saying everything there was to say. Yes, the mission was dangerous, and yes, Henderson wasn't as healthy as he should be for such an undertaking. But there had been no other option. If what Lili had said was true, then Maddi was lying helpless somewhere near that warehouse.

It made no sense; none whatsoever. Even if Maddi was somehow miraculously alive, there would be no way and no reason for her to be in China...let alone near the warehouse. But Lili had unique gifts – no one knew that better than Henderson – and he had learned over the years that she was never wrong. *I need to see this through.*

He gave a quick wave to Walter; it was possibly the last time that they would see one another. Walter offered an almost imperceptible nod as the helicopter flew off into the gathering clouds.

CHAPTER 85

On the road to Riga, Latvia

"Cry 'havoc!' and let slip the dogs of war." Dora sipped her coffee as she recalled the quote from Shakespeare's "Julius Caesar." Mark Antony had spoken the command soon after the assassination of Caesar in the Curia of Pompey. *Why is that on my mind?* she wondered as she sat back on the plush seats of the BMW. She shook her head and sighed. *The remnants of a sleepless night.*

Her favorite chauffeur, Kyle, was driving them down highway A1 in the darkness of early dawn. He, like so many others at the castle, felt like a beacon of strength. She found herself seeking those who had been with her for some time...the men and women who felt as connected to the castle as she did. Kyle was a bit older than the other drivers, which was also a comfort. He had lived through a war or two.

She could see a lighter sky off to the east. Dawn would be breaking soon. Dora didn't mind getting up and about before the sun rose; as a matter of fact, she looked forward to the chance to greet the sunrise. For as long as she could remember, the rising of the sun felt like a promise; an assurance that hope was alive and options were favorable for the day ahead.

Hopefully, that promise will hold true for this day, as well, she thought as she took another sip of coffee. The meeting she was being driven to was vital...not only for the future of Latvia, but possibly for the future of the world. Dora wasn't prone to hyperbole, but she felt, in this instance, the statement was accurate. There was no doubt in her mind that if Latvia fell to Putin, the world would not be far behind.

She crossed her legs, pulling her skirt over her knees as she adjusted her Chanel coat over her long, lean frame. She hadn't been sure what to wear. Should she look businesslike, in an effort to reinforce the seriousness of the Henderson commitment to Latvia? Or should she play to her more feminine side, thereby making sure to pull in the men who chose to view themselves as saviors of the weaker sex? She chuckled as she thought of how many tools women truly had in their arsenal...tools only made possible by the foolish misconceptions of men.

She reviewed in her mind the main points she hoped to convey. The first was that the Henderson soldiers – commonly referred to as Latvian Freedom Fighters – were as committed to Latvian independence as they had ever been. The notion that they were somehow *not* as committed mystified Dora. It was absurd on the face of it, which made her wonder if perhaps the confusion had been intentional. Regardless, she would do all that she could to dispel any doubts.

Her next task would be to help America reinforce their pledge to the fight against Russia. That seed of doubt had been planted by the Secretary of State herself, when she had insisted on flying to Moscow the minute she left Beijing. Though Dora could appreciate the worthiness of seeking peace from all sides, the Secretary's decision had interjected a level of mistrust in a situation that required everything but.

But Dora felt confident that she could smooth over that uncertainty, as well. Though she was rarely the family member tasked with such negotiations, she had done enough of them that she had acquired the skill set required. It didn't hurt that she had come from a notable Scottish family with ties to old world nobility. Even before she was a Henderson, she had been expected to know how to act.

She set the coffee in a holder by the door, reached for her briefcase, and pulled out two pages of notes that she had jotted down at four in the morning. As a rule, Dora never slept well, but she had slept particularly badly last night, a combination of anxiety over the fate of today's meeting, combined with unease over the phone call she had taken just before going to bed.

The caller – a woman with a subtle British accent – had warned Dora that she and every other member of the castle were in imminent danger from Edward Morningstar. For the most part, Dora had managed to dismiss the warning. For one thing, Dora was no stranger to Morningstar, and for another, she was guarded by a top-rate security team. But there was one aspect of the call that she couldn't seem to dismiss; an unnerving sense that she knew the woman. But even now, she felt that it couldn't be. *Perhaps it isn't that I knew her, but that she reminded me of someone.* Dora frowned. The caller had reminded her of Maddi.

Maddi is dead. No one knew that better than Dora. She had watched the news of Maddi's death destroy her son, and unsettle an entire nation. *Maybe the caller was a relative of Maddi's...maybe she was Maddi's sister.* She frowned. *Did Maddi even have a sister? And if she did, why would she be British?* Dora thought back to the obituary from Maddi's Memorial service. Maddi had been survived by her only sibling, her brother Andrew. Dora took a deep breath and sighed. *Let it go, Dora. It wasn't Maddi's sister, and it wasn't Maddi. Maddi is dead.*

She laid her sheet of notes on her lap and leaned back against the leather seat. The call from the British woman wasn't the only call she had taken that had left her uneasy. She pulled a scrap of paper from her coat pocket and stared at her hastily written note. A man had called on her private cellphone just as she was leaving the castle. Though she was curious how he had gotten her number, she hadn't had a chance to ask, as the call had been brief. *"Give the following name and number to your husband."* He had recited a name and a number, then had ended the call.

Dora was eager to talk to Walter. Not only to tell him about the call, but to learn if his mission had been a success. She slid the note in her pocket and checked her watch. *Seven in the morning in Latvia...one in the afternoon in China.* She had expected to hear from him by now. He had told her that his plan was to have Martin, and, with any luck, Lili out of China by one p.m. at the latest, China time. Which meant that – if all had gone well – he was concluding the mission at that very minute.

She felt a sudden chill and wrapped her coat around her. *Failure isn't an option,* she thought, as she grabbed her coffee from the holder and took another sip. How many times had she buried or nearly buried her only son? She was beginning to lose count. One thing she knew for certain: she couldn't do it again.

Don't think about it, Dora. Work on your meeting prep. She stared down at her notes, but she didn't really see them. Her thoughts continued to drift. She was about to open her briefcase and put the notes away, when she saw flashing lights on the road ahead.

"What's happening, Kyle?"

Her driver shook his head and pulled to the side of the road. Over his shoulder, he said, "I'm not sure, Ma'am. I see only the one car with flashing lights." He leaned forward, his eyes glued to whatever was happening in front of them. "Wait. Someone is walking toward us."

Dora edged forward on the seat and looked out the front window of the car. The sun had begun to rise, and hints of sunlight were sneaking through the trees on her left. The flashes of light shone on the man as he approached. Short, bearded, and carrying a rifle, he wore a military uniform, though it wasn't the uniform normally worn by Latvia's state police or the Latvian military.

She felt herself grow tense. She felt a sudden sense of peril...a stillness in the air, an uneasiness even more pervasive than that which she had tried to ignore for the past ten hours. As she saw the soldier aim his rifle directly at the car, she was reminded of Mark Antony's fiery edict, *"Cry 'havoc!' and let slip the dogs of war."*

CHAPTER 86

Beijing, China

Lili had described, in detail, the location where "the Special Lady" was supposedly hiding. *"In a forest...beyond a meadow...near a deep ravine...past a hill. You can see the Temple of Heaven from the top of the hill."*

Henderson had shared those details with Hank, who had led the way to a thick grove of trees at the base of the mountains. The sun had begun to fade behind darkening clouds as they reached the first rise. Hank had more or less taken charge of the mission; Henderson had let him. Though Henderson felt better than he had in weeks, he certainly wasn't well. The plan was for Hank to take the hill from the south, while Henderson kept watch at the base, hidden by the trees, his rifle ready in case the Chinese soldiers attacked.

As Hank hiked up the mountain, Henderson found a sheltered spot behind two tall oak trees. He settled onto a large rock as he watched Hank disappear over the rise. He waited, just as they had planned, his rifle ready, but his frustration growing the longer he sat there. As the minutes ticked by, he couldn't help but think that he was wasting his time just sitting on that rock. A gust of wind made him shiver, and he shoved his hands in his pockets.

Finally, when he could stand it no longer, he stood, threw the rifle's strap over his shoulder, and started up the hill. *I'll be able to spot the Chinese just as easily from up there.*

Using trees for cover and also for support, he trudged up the hill. He was weak, but he felt energized, not only from the IV's, but from hope. And, though he knew he shouldn't indulge it, he couldn't stop himself. After all, to his knowledge, Lili had never been wrong. Nonetheless, with every step, he reminded himself that Maddi was dead. *She's gone, Henderson. Everyone who investigated that crash confirmed it. The country mourned her...hell, the entire world mourned her.*

A sudden rush of wind swept thick gray storm clouds over what little sun remained, darkening the sky as if it was dusk. Henderson was glad for it; they would be harder to spot. What they were doing – what he had insisted they do – had made a target of them both. It occurred to him that he had once again put an innocent person in harm's way. He looked at the sky as if challenging the sun: *Don't you dare light this day and take away what little protection we have.*

The wind picked up; he zipped his coat and hiked his collar. He kept to the tree line as he tackled the hill, knowing that he was a dead man if he was spotted. The trees were becoming sparser the higher he went; it was getting harder to find cover. The few trees he could find were close to the edge, which meant that to hide behind them required him to hover at the edge of ever-deeper ravines. Worst of all, he had no idea what – or who – he was looking for. He had the landmarks that Lili had given him, but that was all. As for Maddi, there was no logical reason why she would be anywhere near those mountains. Maybe Lili had seen someone else; someone she had thought was Maddi. Even then, whoever it was had likely left the area by now to find a better hiding place...or she was dead.

But still he marched on, and, after another twenty minutes or so, he had reached the top. He could see the prison warehouse down below on the other side of the mountain. There were soldiers everywhere. They covered the entire south side of the range. Henderson looked for Hank. He didn't see him. He looked for the Temple of Heaven. He didn't see it. He kept going.

He climbed down the hill and followed a path to the next rise. The trees were getting sparser, but the grass was getting taller; he was able to kneel low enough to stay hidden. But it was hard to move when he was so low to the ground, especially after all he had been through. He had hardly eaten, had hardly slept, and had been beaten by the guards. His legs were weak, his breathing labored, but still he kept going. Drops of rain began to fall, but he pushed on, needing to prove to himself that it wasn't Maddi who Lili had seen. After another fifteen minutes or so, he came to the top of the rise and looked for the Temple of Heaven. He couldn't see it. His heart began to ache. *Lili must have imagined it. She saw the Temple somewhere else, and got it mixed up with the image of the woman.* But still he kept looking; he had made up his mind that he would check every inch of that range before giving up. Only then would he be willing to go back and tell Lili she was wrong.

Then he saw it; far off in the distance, nearly hidden by the clouds, a classic spiral that circled the Temple of Heaven. His heart swelled with hope. Lili had surely seen something – *someone* – on one of those hills.

He ran down the back side of the hill to a grove of trees, the effort easier now that he was no longer climbing. He hiked through the grove of trees, then sprinted ahead, but was forced to come to a halt just as he was about to fall headlong into a ravine. He took a step back and looked down. The gorge was deep; too deep to climb down and then up the other side. He guessed that it was at least ten feet across.

He frowned. *I'll have to jump.* He backed up several yards, and – with every ounce of strength he had left – he sprinted to the edge of the ravine and jumped, grasping for a tree limb as he landed just shy of the other side. He clung to the limb with his uninjured arm, and, using his spent legs and his one good arm, he clawed his way up to the ledge. Once he reached it, he fell to the ground, exhausted. He heard a rustle in the trees to his left, followed by the sound of male voices speaking Chinese.

Move, Henderson! He rose to his knees and crawled to a clump of trees. He crept in among them, hidden by their low-lying branches, and laid flat on his back. He did his best to stay quiet as he tried to recover. His legs were burning; he was having trouble catching his breath. He listened for the soldiers; he heard nothing. After another minute or so, his breathing had returned to normal and he was able to rise to his knees. He crawled to a tree and used it to try to stand; his legs wouldn't hold him and he fell back onto his knees. He tightened his jaw. *Come on, Henderson...someone out there needs you.* He looked around for something to use as a cane. He spotted a tree limb a few feet away. He crawled to it, picked it up, and crawled back to the tree. Using the trunk of the tree and the cane for support, he was able to stand. He took a deep breath and tried to walk. Slowly, awkwardly he stumbled from tree to tree. All the while, he kept his eyes peeled for a woman in distress.

The rain was falling harder, but still he kept going until he reached the last few trees. He still hadn't seen her; he hadn't seen anyone. *Where are you, Maddi...or whoever the hell I'm looking for?* Should he go on? *What choice do I have,* he thought as a crash of thunder was quickly followed by a lightning flash that lit up the sky. He leaned against an old oak tree, and looked out at a meadow of tall grass. He could see a thick forest beyond. He thought of Lili's clue. *"In a forest...beyond a meadow."*

Still using the cane, he stepped into the meadow, irrationally hopeful amid the pouring rain. He actually welcomed it, not caring in the least that he was on a mission that would likely get him killed. Half-blinded by the rain, he trudged through the mud and tall grass of the meadow. It was as if nothing else mattered; as if he was getting one last chance to make peace with what had happened to the woman he loved.

He pushed on against the fronds of grass, relieved when he reached the edge of the forest. He hiked past the outer row of trees, not caring about the pain in his legs or the threat of the Chinese. He no longer cared about anything other than putting to rest his misguided hope. And it was misguided; he knew it now. No one could survive the travails that he had just endured. But it didn't matter; he had to see it through.

He kept going, his chest burning, his legs on fire. But it was getting harder to push himself; harder to come to grips with the fact that he was likely chasing a fantasy. Finally, as his last bit of hope was fading away, he raised his cane in the air and yelled defiantly, "I either find you alive...or I bury you...at least in my mind."

He stopped. He had heard a sound.

The snapping of a limb, was followed by a weak, "Please, don't bury me."

Your mind is playing tricks with you, Henderson. He couldn't move. He was afraid to breathe; afraid that, like waking from a dream, whatever he had heard would disappear...*and my hope of finding Maddi along with it.*

He waited.

"Henderson..."

Though his legs could barely hold him, he tossed away the cane and stumbled toward the sound. He tripped over a tree limb and fell face-first into a row of thistles. He got up and kept running, wiping blood from his forehead as it fell into his eyes.

"Over here."

He ran faster, certain he was imagining it, but no longer caring. *I'd rather imagine the lie than live another minute with the truth.* He was surprised to feel tears on his face; the first time he had cried more than a drop or two since the explosion that had changed his life so many years ago. He didn't bother wiping them away, content to let them mix with the blood and the rain. Maddi was dead, but these few moments of imagining her alive had been the happiest he had known in months. He didn't want it to end, so he kept running, letting himself believe in the sound of her voice. "Maddi... where are you? I'm coming...where are you?"

"Here...under the fir trees."

Her voice was weak, but it was the same voice, Maddi's voice, and he dug his feet into the mud and plowed through thick brush toward a cluster of fir trees not far ahead. Another bolt of lightning lit up the sky. He looked for her; he couldn't see her.

He kept going, his legs so weak he didn't think he could take another step. It was getting harder to breathe, and his heart was pounding. Just as he was about to collapse, he saw what looked like the ruffled edge of a dress. His heart sank; he knew it now...whoever was lying in a bed of pine needles wasn't Maddi. *Maddi doesn't wear ruffled dresses.* It didn't matter. He ran to the ruffles, slowed by fallen limbs scattered in his path. He climbed over them, then tripped on a tangled vine and fell to his knees. He crawled on his hands and knees toward the ruffled dress. He didn't know if he could go much further. He was so weak. *I will go on...or I will die.*

Then he saw her. Sprawled on the ground beneath low-lying limbs, one leg pitched awkwardly in front of her, a woman lay there – not the woman he remembered – but a woman, nonetheless. She was wearing a black cape that was clinging to her body from the rain. She was terribly thin and her hair was short and brown, not long and blonde. The breath left his lungs as he realized; whoever it was that Lili had seen, it wasn't Maddi. He closed his eyes, the grief almost more than he could bear. He let out a sigh as he thought, *It doesn't matter...you need to help this poor woman, Henderson.*

The air had turned colder and the rain felt like bullets against his skin. He grabbed onto the limb of a tree and pulled himself forward. He crawled under several more limbs to where she was laying. "I'm coming, Ma'am. Hang on...I'm coming."

"You...have got to be...the slowest man...I have ever known."

The voice was weak. But then he heard her laugh. He stopped. *I'd know that laugh anywhere.* He took a deep breath, then rose to his feet. With strength he didn't have, he pushed himself forward, past the trees, stumbling the last few steps to where she lay. He fell beside her with his eyes closed, afraid to look at her and see that she wasn't Maddi. *Just let me have one more minute to pretend.*

He felt her touch his cheek. His entire body trembled. Still, he wouldn't open his eyes. The tears continued to fall. He could feel her wiping them away.

"Henderson," she whispered, "...it's me."

He opened his eyes and looked at her. He didn't see the brown hair or the gaunt cheeks. What he saw were the eyes he had never forgotten, the smile that had kept him alive through fires and beatings and despair. He wasn't sure how it could be, but Maddi – his Maddi – was lying next to him. *I've died...and this is heaven.*

She, too, had begun to cry. "Henderson, it's me...it's Maddi."

He put a hand to her face. The rain had eased, but droplets were streaming down her cheeks; he wiped them away. "How...how can it be?" he asked.

She moved closer. "It...it was all we knew to do, Henderson."

He frowned. *All who knew to do?*

She said, "I'll explain later." She leaned closer and kissed him, first on the cheek, then on the forehead, then on every part of his face.

He laughed, then pulled her to him and kissed her so hard he was afraid he might hurt her. He couldn't help it. She hugged him, and he held her tight. The tears wouldn't stop. He whispered, "Am I dreaming? Have I... died?"

She chuckled. "No. But we'll both die if we stay here much longer."

CHAPTER 87

Beijing, China

Cobra felt sick. Not only because he had been fighting something for months, but because he had been taken from the hellhole that was the Chinese prison and placed in an even worse hellhole, forced to stare at the one man he hated most in the world, his father, Walter Henderson. He was fighting hard not to vomit.

But his anger was eased by the little girl sitting next to Walter. She was looking at him...staring at him with eyes that were far too wise for a child. He sneered at her, but she didn't react. *Now that's interesting.*

He tugged on his chains; a pair of iron cuffs that were holding him to a metal post not far from the door of the helicopter. They were tight on his wrists and he was about to complain, but held his tongue. He was weak, and would save his words for when he needed them.

The Chinese woman sitting next to the girl had begun to stare at him. She, too, had wise eyes, but she was more obvious with her disdain. *You don't know me, bitch.* He smirked and she looked away. He laughed and looked once again at Walter.

The man had yet to look at him. As a matter of fact, Walter had made every effort to *not* look at him. It amused him. "What's the matter, Walter? Do I resemble you too greatly?"

Walter didn't react. No one else seemed to notice the comment, as they were deeply engrossed in the foolish yet brave departure of Walter's beloved 'nephew.' *False heroics,* Cobra thought with a sneer. After all, it was clear that the man cared little for his own life. Cobra was about to repeat his comment to Walter, this time louder, when he caught the eye of Roger Clarkson, the CIA agent who had shot him not once, but twice, on two separate occasions. The agent hadn't taken his eyes off of Cobra since they had boarded the helicopter. Cobra knew exactly what he was thinking. *He'd like to kill me...but he can't. Not here, anyway.* He blew Roger a kiss; the CIA agent didn't react.

Cobra sighed and leaned against the wall. He needed to come up with a way to get out of there. Otherwise, he would be taken to London, interrogated by Scotland Yard's pompous Inspector Pritchard, and thrown into a jail cell, where he would most certainly die. And though he wasn't afraid to die, he had not yet completed his final mission. *I don't die until they do...Walter, Martin, and Dora.*

All of a sudden, he felt a twinge in his temple. He couldn't call it pain; it was more like a tickle. His chained hands couldn't reach it, so he rubbed his head against a coat that was hanging on a hook by the door. Was it Justice coming back for another go at ruining his life?

The feeling was intensifying. He closed his eyes. Suddenly he could see her, the little girl across from him in the helicopter. Only somehow, she was sitting next to him. And they weren't in the helicopter, they were at the boarding school...

> *"My name is Lili. What's yours?"*
> *Ten-year-old Mark Villamor looked at the girl and grinned. No one had ever been nice to him at the school, except for his teacher, Mrs. Reginald.*
> *"My...my name is Mark."*
> *She smiled; his heart ached. "What's that in your hand?"*
> *Mark looked down at the gold peso given to him by his mother. "Just an old coin."*
> *"Do you like coins?"*
> *He nodded, then held it out for her to see. "It's from the 1800's...somewhere in Spain, I think."*
> *She took it and suddenly her eyes lit up. "This is helpful, you know."*
> *He frowned. "What do you mean?"*
> *"The fact that you know about coins."*

"How is that helpful?"

She tilted her head and laughed. "I'm not really sure."

She handed back the coin and he slid it in his pocket.

"Why are you here?" she asked. She was referring to the sitting area outside the headmaster's office. Mark had spent many afternoons there...waiting to see the man who would abuse him, in his efforts to – as he had put it – beat the evil out of him.

Mark looked at the girl, and, with as much control as he could muster, he said, "I'm here...to see the headmaster."

"What for?"

"I've...been...bad."

The girl's eyes widened. "You don't seem bad. What did you do?"

He couldn't tell her. He couldn't tell her that he had reacted to praise from his teacher with the wrong part of his body. "I'm...I'm not sure."

She laughed. It made him happy. She said, "You surely have to know why you've been bad."

From nowhere, anger coursed through him, and he turned to her and snarled, "I don't know, alright? Why don't you just let it go."

She sat back and crossed her arms, not the slightest bit ruffled. "I won't let it go...there's more to this than you know, and I'm going to look into getting you out of here..."

Cobra opened his eyes. He looked at her...at Lili. She was smiling at him. She knew exactly what had happened. Somehow...some way...that little girl had gotten inside his head. *And she is going to help me escape.*

CHAPTER 88

Beijing, China

Lili found herself conflicted. Or, perhaps it was the man himself that was causing her confusion...with his many wide-ranging personalities. She had known him only as Justice when they had first met. They hadn't actually met; Lili had sensed the man's presence just before she had learned of the little boy. It had started with an image...a vague, white cloud of a man who had appeared out of nowhere with a look and feel of desperation that Lili had found impossible to ignore. Who was this man that had been clinging to life, not as a prisoner in a Chinese warehouse, but as a different sort of prisoner, behind bars that Lili couldn't see?

She had replied to his presence guardedly, knowing that, though his goodness was apparent, there was more to him that required caution. But it hadn't taken long for her to appreciate the remarkable man who referred to himself as Mark Justice.

"I grew up far from London," he had told her. *"I actually don't remember my early years. There is little that I recall, I'm afraid."*

Lili had frowned. *"Is there a time you do remember...besides now?"*

The image had become a bit clearer, and, as the man had used a hand to brush back his long blond hair, she had been reminded of someone. He had nodded with a heartfelt smile. *"I remember time at Manchester College."* He had frowned. *"Though, even there, I only remember bits and pieces."* His face had lit up. *"But there had been a woman…a young girl who had turned my head and eventually consumed me with her magic."* He had laughed. *"Not real magic; the magic of love."*

At the mention of love, Lili had hugged her chest, the feeling of warmth so welcome in the cold confines of the prison. *"Please, tell me more about her."*

The image had become even clearer, and his smile had been comforting. *"Her name was Margaret…Margaret McLain."*

"A lovely name."

"For a lovely woman," the man had said with the nod of one who is sure. *"She and I met,"* he had paused; it was as if he was struggling to remember even that most important of events, *"…in the library, I do believe."*

"So, you were studying?"

The man had laughed. *"Or pretending to."* He had paused. *"I bought her a coffee, she helped me with Proust."*

"I like Proust."

The man had nodded. *"So did she."* He had smiled sadly. *"Anyway, we spent most of that semester together."*

"What happened to her?"

The man had frowned. Lili had been able to see the pain in his eyes more clearly than she could see his cheeks or his chin. He had shaken his head and, when he had looked at Lili, she had felt her own soul take a hit. *"I…I don't know. She just…disappeared."*

Lili had nodded sadly. *"I've learned that people often disappear,"* she had paused, *"…but it doesn't mean they're gone."*

The man had looked at her with a puzzled, yet hopeful nod. *"Perhaps."*

Then she had thought of her papa, Albins, with his long blonde hair and blue eyes. Justice reminded her of him. But it was more than just their looks…it was a sense of goodness, of nobility that surpassed even the nobility of a soldier's heart. Lili had felt it in Justice's words, in his heartbreak. Her own heart had felt wounded as she had asked, *"What is the next thing you can remember?"*

He had rubbed his temples as if in pain. *"It is difficult."* Then, suddenly, his eyes had lit up, their blue glistening even in the haze of a poorly-wrought image. *"I remember…I was talking to a real estate agent about a property in downtown London."* He had smiled proudly. *"I was starting my own business, you see."*

"What is your business?"

He had tugged at the lapels of his white suitcoat proudly. *"I am a private investigator."*

Lili had nodded, impressed.

"I quickly made a name for myself. Soon, even the Yard was asking for my help."

Lili's eyes had widened. *"Scotland Yard?"*

"One and the same."

She had smiled. *"That is impressive."*

"Yes," he had said with a sigh, *"...and I am eager to get back to work."*

"How did you end up in your current predicament?"

"I suppose it depends which 'predicament' you're referring to."

Lili had laughed in spite of herself. *"This awful prison, silly."*

He had smiled and it had warmed her. *"I'm not really in prison here,"* he had spread his arms, *"...nearly as much as I am in prison here,"* he had pointed to his head.

She had frowned. *"You're in prison inside your head?"*

He had nodded. *"Actually, inside* his *head."*

Lili's eyes had narrowed. *"I don't understand."*

He had sighed. *"I would prefer not to talk about it. But I will tell you this. You have freed me...at least for these few minutes...and I am grateful."* His image had begun to fade. *"Should I never see you again, I am better for having met you."*

She had reached for him but had felt nothing but air. It was as if her papa Albins was leaving her all over again. *"Please...don't go!"* she had cried, a sense of helplessness suddenly overwhelming her. *"I...I sense that you are kind...and troubled. Can I help you? Please, let me help you!"*

He had faded almost completely. *"You already have, my dear."*

"What...what is your name?" she had asked quickly.

A whisper in the air had said, *"Justice. Mark Justice."*

Then, he was gone. Lili's heart had ached. But she had felt him many times after that conversation, though never as clearly as that first time, and never in a way that allowed them to speak. But he was there...somewhere nearby, and it brought her comfort. She knew – even in the midst of that dreadful prison – there was a good man nearby...there was Justice.

And, though she still didn't understand how Justice lived inside Cobra, the very fact that he did was reassuring. It meant that even a man as awful as Cobra had goodness inside him.

It was soon after that that she became aware of the little boy. And, though she knew little about who he was or how he, too, lived in Cobra's head, his presence added yet another layer to Cobra. How could so many good people live inside such a bad man? She hadn't answered the question by the time she laid eyes on Cobra. And she had yet to address the need she felt to help him escape. Was it merely because of her attachment to those who dwelled inside him...to Justice and the little boy? Or was there something more that was pushing her to free a terrible man from his chains?

She looked across the cabin at Cobra, his dark eyes and even darker soul chilling her to the bone. She leaned against the wall. She couldn't do it; she couldn't turn such a man loose on the world. She closed her eyes, and was suddenly able to see Justice, his features vague except for his kind blue eyes...*like Albins'.*

Suddenly, her own eyes flew open. She understood it now. *Justice is vital; he's essential!* For what? She didn't know, but she could feel it...as if an important truth had pierced her skin, shoved aside the fear in her heart, and landed in her soul.

She looked again at the man they called Cobra, trying her hardest to reconcile the two men...or, better yet, the three of them: Cobra, Justice, and the little boy. She didn't understand it, and was afraid that she might never, but one thing was clear: Justice was significant...*and he is needed.*

Which meant that Lili had a decision to make.

CHAPTER 89

Beijing, China

Cobra tugged at his chains. They were tight and they hurt. The helicopter had been flying for quite some time now. They had failed to find a place to refuel, and were on their way back to pick up Henderson and Clarkson. *I need to figure out how to get out of this heap before we get there!* He looked up and caught the little girl staring at him. She was frowning; it looked as if she was concentrating on something.

He had watched her off and on for the last fifteen minutes. And he could see her little mind working. It amused him; a troubled mind always amused him. Her face had reflected everything from joy to sorrow to anger to fear, and he couldn't help but wonder what the poor girl was so torn about. He chuckled. *Perhaps, since she seems able to get inside my head, I need to give her something worthwhile to think about.*

He was about to fill her mind with images from some of his finer work, when he felt a loosening of his chains. They didn't come off...they were just looser. He looked at her and narrowed his eyes.

She smiled. His eyes widened. *That little girl is going to set me free!*

He looked around. Everyone was distracted. Except for Roger...Roger hadn't taken his eyes off of Cobra. But everyone else was either worrying about the two buffoons who had left the helicopter to save some imaginary waif, or were deep in thought about something in their own pathetic lives. He tugged at the chains. Though looser, they were still too tight for him to slide out of. He needed to somehow tell the girl to finish the job. But even more important; he needed to come up with a way to distract Roger. Because even if he did manage to get out of those chains, he couldn't escape the helicopter with Roger watching his every move. He chuckled. *I know how to get him off his game.*

He looked at Roger, cleared his throat, and grinned. "How's Tonna?" he said, raising his voice to be heard above the roar of the engines. "I hear she's pretty good...when she's lying on her back."

Roger jumped from his seat and lunged at him. Cobra turned his head, but not before Roger punched him hard in the jaw.

"Roger!" It was Walter. "Stop! We need him alive."

Roger stood over him, his fist raised, his stare alone fiercer than anything Cobra had ever seen. *I do believe the boy hates me.* Finally, with considerable restraint, Roger lowered his fist and walked back to his seat. But the hate in his eyes hadn't eased. It was as palpable as that punch to Cobra's jaw. He chuckled. *I've gotten under the poor boy's skin.*

Cobra looked at Lili. She had looked away, probably troubled by the assault on her new friend. *I need to get her to focus...not on me, but on the little boy, Mark. She likes Mark.*

He took a deep breath and once again did something that he had spent the last six years trying *not* to do...he conjured up the boy, Mark Villamor. He had to be careful. He had expended quite a bit of energy to get that boy to leave him alone. Who knew what would happen if he continued to give the boy time in his mind. *I'll allow him only one minute to appeal to his new best friend.*

He closed his eyes, and with a great deal of dread, once again recalled his days outside the headmaster's office. He would make sure to stop before he got to the part where he walked through the black oak door; otherwise he would lose his edge.

Trying his hardest to pick up where he had left off, he pulled up images of the young Mark Villamor sitting on one of several wooden chairs, his gym-shoed feet swinging back and forth as he held his hands over his pants where his offending organ had betrayed him. Then, he waited.

Soon he saw her...the little girl, sitting next to him just like before, her thin little legs dangling like his as she asked him again what he had done. Offering his kindest smile, he looked at her and said, *"It was a misunderstanding...that's all. You said you would get me out of here. Can you really do that?"*

"I loosened the chains...isn't it enough?"

He sighed and shook his head. *"I'm afraid not."*

She narrowed her eyes and sighed. *"Before I go any further, I need to talk to the man who wears the white suit."*

Cobra bristled. *"Are you referring to Justice?"*

"Yes, that's his name. May I speak with him?"

Cobra sneered. *"He's worthless. You don't need to speak with him."*

She shook her head. *"But I do."*

Cobra cleared his throat. Trying his hardest to maintain his tie to the boy Mark, he said, *"Why do you need to speak to Justice?"*

She frowned. *"He's important; he is needed. There is a task that he must take care of...a task that only he can do."*

Cobra narrowed his eyes. *"Fine. I'll get him, but you will need to completely remove these chains."*

He saw the girl shake her head. *"I'm afraid to. The man, Cobra, will do horrible things if he is set free."*

Forcing young Mark's response, he said *"Perhaps, but the only way to free Justice is to free Cobra."*

There was a long pause. Cobra felt like he was losing her. She looked at him and he could see the struggle in her eyes. *I need to convince her that this is a good idea.* Should he dig deep and try to find Justice? *Talk about letting the genie out of the bottle.* But if he didn't do something, he would be sent to jail to die.

He took a deep breath, closed his eyes, and did his best to muster the alter ego he hated almost as much as Walter Henderson. It didn't take long...as if the man had been waiting in the wings. But he felt Justice before he saw him...his condescension heavy and thick as it tamped down Cobra's creative ingenuity. Without giving him a chance to speak, Cobra said to him in his mind, *"You need to give this little girl a reason to let me go. She thinks you're important and she wants to set you free."*

Justice smiled. Cobra wanted to vomit.

The infuriating alter ego nodded smugly. *"Let me handle it."*

Justice waited for an image of the girl to appear. He combed back his hair and adjusted his glasses. *"It is so good to see you again, Lili."*

Her eyes it up. *"I'm so glad we have another chance to talk, Mr. Justice."*

Justice nodded. *"I've been told that you need to speak to me. May I ask why?"*

She frowned. *"Actually, I'm not completely sure. All I know is that you have an important role to play."*

"In what?"

"I've tried to see it...but I can't."

"Fascinating." He rubbed his chin. *"But the truth of the matter is...I can't be free unless Cobra is free."* He paused. *"However, I can promise you that I will keep him from...doing what he does."*

"How will you do that?"

Justice narrowed his eyes. *"By offering my life as a guarantee."*

Lili's eyes widened. *"That's quite an offer."*

Justice nodded. *"Yes, and I don't make it lightly. I have known for some time now that I am inextricably tied to this dreadful man. I have come to see it as a responsibility...my purpose in life, if you will."* He paused. *"Check with me in this remarkable way that you have, once a week...maybe even once a day. If you find me, then I've upheld the promise."*

"And if I don't find you?"

"Then I'm dead," he paused, *"...which means, of course, that Cobra is dead, as well."*

The little girl's eyes widened even further. Cobra forced his own ego back in charge, grinning as he thought, *Good work, Justice...I didn't know you had it in you.*

He waited, watching Lili as she thought it through. She rubbed her chin and wrinkled her brow. It was quite adorable, actually. *Come on, Lili...you can do it.*

He waited. He could only assume that she was digging deep for the concentration that was required to perform such a feat. *I do believe that she is going to do it!* He looked around the cabin. Everyone was distracted... except for Roger. The persistent CIA agent had still not taken his eyes off of Cobra. Suddenly, out of nowhere, Cobra felt the pressure on his wrists ease. First the left, then the right, the cuffs loosened completely. But he couldn't draw attention to it; he couldn't let anyone – especially Roger – know that he was free. He angled his wrists so that the loosened cuffs didn't fall off. He looked at Roger to see if he had noticed; he hadn't, and continued to glare at Cobra from across the cabin.

Cobra merely laughed, causing the man's jaw to tighten. *I should ask him if he knows Tonna like I'm about to.* But he couldn't even muster the words; he was too tired. So instead, he simply leaned against the wall of the helicopter. He would need to save his strength for his grand escape.

But how would he get out of there? Even if he managed to somehow leave the helicopter without being stopped, he was miles from the ground. And he certainly couldn't wait for them to land. They were going back to the warehouse; even if he did find some way to get past the do-gooders on that chopper, he was weak. The Chinese guards would capture him in no time. But there was no way he could stay on that helicopter.

He felt it lowering as they neared the mountains. He needed to hurry. He looked around the cabin. He spotted a fire extinguisher hanging from the wall, a gurney next to it, and a first aid kit sitting on top of the gurney. Then he saw it...what looked like a parachute dangling within three feet of him. *That will work,* he thought with a grin. But first he would need a distraction.

* * *

Arthur Kauffold was feeling every one of his seventy-five years. He hadn't been in battle since his twenties, and the muscles in his arms and legs kept reminding him of it. His nerves were reminding him of it, as well.

But there had been little time to dwell on it. Walter's nephew had brazenly put every one of them at risk based on nothing more than the whims of a little girl. Kauffold had never met Lili, but it was clear that she was important to the Hendersons. It was also clear that, for whatever reason, they took whatever she said to heart. He could only hope that this diversion into enemy territory was worth it. He sighed. *I guess we'll find out soon enough.*

The good news was that Walter had spoken to a friend of his at the State Department, and – revealing nothing of his own involvement – had learned that the Secretary of State had been driven away from the prison soon after the shooting began. She hadn't been injured, and was now in intense negotiations with China in an attempt to avoid an all-out war. She had quite a challenge on her hands: not only had a U.S. senator tried to kill the son of one of their top military men, but a battalion of soldiers – all of whom spoke perfectly clear English – had attacked one of their secret prisons and had killed several of their guards. Though the secretary would swear the prison break wasn't a U.S. operation, Kauffold felt certain that the Chinese President would disagree. *What other country would have the nerve to undertake such an act?*

He heard someone's cellphone vibrate and he bristled. *The cursed things never stop buzzing,* he thought.

Johnny Canterbury reached in his pocket and pulled out his phone. "Yes?" He looked at Kauffold and frowned. "Why, yes, he's right here." He turned to Kauffold. "It's Andrew Madison. He says he needs to talk to you."

Kauffold frowned. "So why did he call you?"

"Because the last he knew, you refused to carry a cellphone."

Kauffold sighed. "How does he have your number?"

"Dalgety Bay." Johnny nodded. "We needed to stay in touch." He smirked. "I'm sure you're aware that it was I who saved everyone's arses in that debacle."

Kauffold rolled his eyes and grabbed the phone. He held it to his ear. "Andrew?"

"Hey Kauffold. Are you on your way home?"

"Yes, more or less. But there has been a bit of a...um...situation here, and I won't be there for another day or two, at least."

"Well, I need to ask you something and it won't wait." There was a pause. "Do you know someone with the last name Melnikov?"

Kauffold frowned. *Where have I heard that name?* "I can't place it, but it's ringing a bell. Why do you ask?"

"How about the last name Platacis?"

Kauffold's eyes widened. He looked at the little girl, Lili. He could have sworn that Walter had introduced her as Lili Platacis. He leaned forward and said to her, "I'm sorry, dear child, but would you be good enough to tell me your last name?"

She smiled and it melted his heart. "Platacis. It comes from ancient Latvia, and it means warrior," she said proudly.

Kauffold nodded and said into the phone. "I have just met a lovely little girl with that last name. Why do you ask?"

"Oh my god, Arthur. Is her name Lili?"

"Why, yes, it is. Do you know her?"

"Ask her if she has ever heard of Larissa Platacis."

Kauffold looked at Lili and smiled. "My friend wonders if you know anyone with the name Larissa Platacis."

Walter's head jerked around. He stared at Kauffold as Lili's eyes grew wide and filled with tears. Her lower lip began to quiver. "She...she was my Mama."

Kauffold frowned. "You said she *was* your mama?"

Lili nodded. "Yes. She...she died...five years ago."

Kauffold cleared his throat. "Um, Andrew, Larissa is the little girl's mother...but she's...um...deceased. Apparently, she died five years ago."

There was a pause. "She's not dead, Arthur. But she's in danger, and she needs our help."

* * *

I do believe a Higher Power is watching over me! Cobra chuckled. Whatever the fat ambassador had been told on the phone had created quite a stir in the cabin. Fortunately, it had happened after the little girl had already undone his chains. First she had cried, and then her eyes had lit up and her entire countenance had changed. Cobra found himself feeling oddly happy for her. *Get over that now, Cobra!*

He looked around. Wonder of all wonders, even Roger had joined in whatever discussion the Ambassador's call had brought about. *No time like the present, Cobra.*

In one quick move, he pulled his hands out of the chains, reached for the parachute bag, and sprung to the open doorway. Holding tightly to the bag, he flung himself out of the helicopter. As he fell toward the ground, he did his best to hold onto the bag. Rain pelted his face as he felt everywhere for the release. He couldn't find it. He was falling fast. He would hit the ground too hard if he didn't do something quickly. His fingers brushed over a lever. He grabbed it and pulled. The chute opened, jerking him to the point where he was nearly forced to let go of the bag. But he managed to hang on and he coasted the rest of the way to the ground.

He hit the ground hard, falling forward onto his face and hands. He looked up at the helicopter, surprised to see Roger standing in the doorway with a bag on his back, about to jump. *Dammit...he's coming after me.* There was another man standing behind Roger, and it looked like he, too, was preparing to jump. *Are two of them coming?* He sneered. *It takes a village.*

He was completely entangled in the chute, and, as he wriggled his way out, he saw blood coming from both of his palms. He wiped his forehead with his sleeve and saw that it, too, was covered in blood. He felt like he was about to pass out, so he stood there for a few seconds, hands on his knees, breathing slowly until he felt that he could run without fainting. Though the rain was cold, it was a comfort. He turned his face to the sky and laughed. He had done it. He had escaped a helicopter where his fiercest enemies wanted him dead.

Only a cobra could evade such predators.

He needed to go. Roger and whoever was coming with him wouldn't be far behind. He gathered up the parachute and flung it into the trees, doing his best to cover it with brush and tree limbs. *Mustn't make it too easy for them.*

But he was struggling. Not only did he feel weak, but he was battered and bleeding and was fighting just to stay conscious. Again, he put his hands on his knees and sucked in air. *You have to go, Cobra...now!*

He took a final deep breath, then forced himself to jog toward the thicker part of the forest. He had nothing – no ID, no money – but it didn't matter. He was free. *I'm sure I'll come up with something,* he thought, and started to laugh. The laugh made him cough and he grabbed his chest in pain.

He kept running, every part of him either throbbing with pain or slowed by his weakness. But as he struggled over fallen limbs and slogged through shallow creeks, he couldn't help but smile. *You won't catch me, Roger...nobody will catch me. I now have a helper...a magical little girl...and her name is Lili.*

CHAPTER 90

Beijing, China

Henderson laid on the ground, eyes closed, reluctant to move. The rain, though ice-cold, felt good somehow...as if it was washing away all that had happened; the hotel explosion that had left him broken, the addiction to Dilaudid that had turned him into a Morningstar pawn, the murder of good men just to appease the madman, the kidnapping of Lili because Henderson had been too weak to stand up to him, and, finally, Henderson's attempt to kill himself because of the death of the woman who was lying next to him. That ice-cold rain was washing all of it away.

He needed to get up, but he couldn't seem to move. Those few moments beside Maddi had been the most calming he had ever known. He felt certain that the minute he opened his eyes, his past would come back at him like a wrecking ball, and Maddi would disappear. But real or not, she was right. If they didn't get out of there, they would be taken by the Chinese. They had heard muffled exchanges somewhere in the trees, and it was clear from the voices that they were getting closer. He and Maddi had to go. He turned to look at her. *God, she's beautiful.*

He gave her one last hug, then sat up and again noticed her leg stretched awkwardly in front of her. "You're hurt."

"Just my ankle."

He looked at the swollen ankle, heartbroken when he saw the jagged, healing scar just below it. He touched it gently and frowned. "What happened?"

She shook her head. "It's a long story."

"Can you put weight on it?"

She shook her head. "I don't think so."

He nodded. *I can do this.* Hopefully those few minutes of lying beside Maddi had allowed him to regain his strength. He grabbed the limb of a tree and pulled himself to standing. He gave himself a second to regain his balance. He stretched his legs, then took a deep breath and bent down. He put his good arm under Maddi's back, his injured arm under her legs. Though that arm had taken a bullet just hours ago, it was as if it had never happened; as if he had already recovered. He lifted her, noting that she was far lighter than the last time he had done that. His heart ached as he imagined all she had been through. She clung to his neck as he plotted a path to evade the soldiers. The voices had come from deep in the trees. He would go back the way he had come, though he had no idea how he would get her across the ravine.

Suddenly, he heard shouts back and forth; the soldiers had gotten even closer. With Maddi in his arms, he ran through the trees to the edge of the forest, then ran headlong into the meadow. He pushed his way through the tall grass to the smaller grove of trees, and hiked past them to the ravine. He stopped at the ledge and stared down. He couldn't jump it; not with Maddi in his arms. He heard more shouts, this time followed by gunshots; the soldiers were right behind them. He looked up at the sky. The rain had stopped and the clouds had started to fade. He could see the subtle glow of the sun as it faded to the west; he ran in that direction. He hiked down a steep incline, half running, half falling, finally losing his balance about twenty feet from the bottom of the hill. He stumbled and fell, but managed to keep hold of Maddi.

"Are you okay?" he asked, as he held her tightly to his chest.

She looked up at him and nodded. "I'm...I'm fine. Don't worry about me."

He kissed her. "It's all I do...it is all I have ever done." He stood with her in his arms and continued the rest of the way down the hill, zigzagging through the trees and leaping over fallen branches as if he had the strength of twenty men.

He heard a voice at the base of the mountain. He looked down. It was Hank.

"Run!"

He ran even faster, jumping the last six feet to the bottom. He landed hard and nearly fell, but was able to keep his balance as he held Maddi tight to his chest. He followed Hank through a maze of trees that took them around the base of the mountain, running as fast as he could toward the field where the helicopter would hopefully be waiting.

They heard more gunshots; they ran harder. But Henderson found himself oblivious to it all. Somehow – through some strange miracle that he didn't understand and most definitely didn't deserve – Maddi was in his arms. He looked again at her face. In spite of the pouring rain and the obvious pain from her injured ankle, in spite of the fact that she hadn't eaten and had clearly been on the run for months, she was smiling. His heart felt like it might explode. As he jumped over rocks and branches and ran through the tall grass, he took a moment to offer a silent prayer of thanks. Somehow...by some amazing miracle...his Maddi was alive.

EPILOGUE

Anatolij Arpa scowled as he heard the barkeep yell last call. He downed the last of his beer and cried, "Cits!" *Another!* The barkeep glared at him, but reluctantly brought him a glass of Aldaris Lager. Anatolij nodded his thanks, nearly falling off his stool as he reached for the glass. He grabbed the counter to steady himself, laughing as he chugged the beer. Though it was two a.m. on a Sunday – well, actually, a Monday – he wasn't ready to go home. Not yet, anyway...maybe not ever. Inese, his wife of four years, had left him, and had taken their two-year-old daughter Aina with her. He had pleaded with her to stay, but she had merely laughed. Then, with Aina in one hand, her suitcase in the other, she had stormed out of the small house at the end of the alley where they had lived since they were married.

That had been five days ago. Anatolij had left the house soon after, and hadn't been back since. And he hadn't been to work, either. As a matter of fact, Anatolij hadn't done a damn thing since Inese had walked out that door.

Could he blame her? *Sure, I can,* he thought. But he knew he had never been what one might call attentive, or even kind. And it had only gotten worse over the last few months. Ever since that fateful night when he had stepped out of the bar – the same Liepaja bar that he was in right now – and had seen a plane crashing headlong into the ground. Though he had run to help, it had been clear almost immediately that there was nothing he could do. No one could have survived such a crash.

But it wasn't only the thought that no one could have survived that had made him turn around before he had reached the site...it was fear; stone cold fear. Flames were spewing from shattered debris, and, though he had thought at the time that he might have heard one or two weak cries, he had decided that he had imagined it.

But now he knew...he hadn't.

He bristled as he stared at the empty glass in front of him. His father wouldn't have run away. Good ole Drosmis Arpa would have gone in and pulled any number of poor wretches from that fiery wreckage. The gruff, oversized brute would have run headfirst into those flames, fearless in the face of danger. But not Anatolij. He was weak and spineless; nothing but a coward. That was what his father had always told him. And his refusal to run to help those in that crash had proved it, once and for all.

His agony had only deepened when, days later, he had learned that someone *had* survived the crash...just one man. Anatolij's soul had been crushed. If one man survived, did that mean that there had been others clinging to life, just waiting for his help? *Could I have maybe saved another one of them?* he had asked himself, over and over again. *Is there someone who is now dead, that would've been alive but for me?*

Inese had told him that he was being silly; that he hadn't been the one to cause that plane to crash. *"And it would have been reckless for you to run into the flames, Anatolij."* But for whatever reason, her comforting words hadn't been enough. As a matter of fact, as he thought of it now, Inese's words had never been enough.

He patted his shirt pocket and frowned. There was something else that was haunting him from that ill-fated night...a small booklet he had found not far from the wreckage. About the size of a paperback, it had been evident from the very first page that the man who had penned it had been a tortured, tormented soul. A miserable man who, for whatever reason, had done awful things, only to ask for forgiveness over and over, not from his God, but from a woman named Maddi. It had led Anatolij to wonder, *Who is this Maddi that can make a killer cry?*

The diary had been written in English. Anatolij knew little English, and had had a hard time reading it. At first, he had been glad. It wasn't right for him to read it. Though whoever had written it was likely dead, Anatolij was convinced that he would be cast into Hell if he violated the sacred trust of a man's private thoughts. *'Tis none of my business what a dead man holds deep in his heart,* he had thought, resisting the urge to translate any part of it for well over a month. But as his guilt over his reluctance to try to save those passengers deepened, he found himself seeking solace. *Perhaps I will find it in that booklet...in the words of one of the men who died.*

So, finally, two months later, on a cold October morning, he had decided not to go to work, and instead go to the local library to find a book to help him translate the diary. But translating English to Latvian was an arduous process, and it had taken him days to get through just the first few pages. And what he had read had stunned him. It had started with simple pleas for forgiveness, but as he had gone further, he had realized that he was reading the confessions of a killer, a true hitman from what he could determine. But not just any hitman. The names in that diary – the victims of this man's kills – weren't just targets that had been selected randomly, or wealthy tycoons that had been extorted and then killed for their money. No, the victims of this man's handiwork were well-placed, powerful leaders...from around the world.

Anatolij's first inclination had been to turn the diary over to the authorities. After all, the crimes in that book were some of the worst kind... brutal assassinations that had destroyed monarchies, and had changed the course of history.

But then he had reconsidered. Why? He wasn't sure. Perhaps out of respect for a man who had died so unceremoniously. Or, more likely, Anatolij had begun to realize that if he played his cards right, he might be able to profit from his find.

To his credit, he had fought the temptation for another month. But it was during that time that he began to pull away from his wife, his family, his work...from everything. All he could think of was the diary, and how to use it to his advantage. But the very thought of it sickened him, and he had continued to resist the urge.

Until Inese left him. After that, everything changed. He had spent every night since in that dark, dingy bar, looking at the sad faces of the men he now mirrored. And, after nearly a week of long, lonely nights, he had had an epiphany. *What does it matter?* Why worry about his soul or morality or doing the right thing, when his wife – and his life – had done nothing but betray him.

From that moment on, his view toward the diary changed. Not only did he no longer care if he was betraying a man's privacy, he would make it his mission to find a way to profit from the diary. Dark secrets were contained in that booklet, which meant that he, Anatolij Arpa, suddenly had power over someone. The question was who. The killer had claimed no allegiance to any agency or government; he had claimed full responsibility for every kill. It had surprised Anatolij. *An honorable assassin,* he had thought the first time he had actually read the diary all the way through. But buried deep within was a theme: yes, the author of that diary had done terrible deeds, but there had been a reason for it...a dark, unholy reason. And from what Anatolij could tell, there was one man, one overseer, that had been responsible.

"Jacob," Anatolij said aloud as he stared into his empty glass. He had no idea who Jacob was, but whoever he was, he was powerful...so powerful that he had somehow made a decent man do terrible things. It wasn't until the end of the diary that the assassin had revealed any details about Jacob. Not so much how he looked or where he lived, but the realm within which he moved. His influence with power brokers from around the globe. If Anatolij could learn more about that world, he might be able to find the man, Jacob. But Anatolij was just a poor factory worker from Liepaja; he wasn't familiar with any of the names or the places.

Ironically, just two weeks ago, he had met a man who was knowledgeable of such things...or at least he claimed to be. The old man had been at the same bar that Anatolij was at now. The guy had been nursing a beer, along with a deep-seated hatred over injuries sustained from a bombing eight months earlier. The explosion had left him crippled, leaving the old man to walk with a cane. From what he had been willing to share, the incident had taken place somewhere in France.

"So what on earth brought you to Liepaja?" Anatolij had asked him.

The man had claimed that he had come there to, as he had put it, *"... find the bastard who spearheaded the whole goddamned thing."* He had refused to say more, other than *"...that man will regret the day he challenged me."*

One night when the man was especially drunk, he had bragged that he had once worked directly under a powerful German leader. *"I rubbed elbows with every big shot on this whole goddamned planet; presidents, kings... even a high priestess."*

Anatolij doubted it was true, though the man did wear an impressive German medal. He had pinned the medal to a cheap reefer jacket he had purchased at some goodwill store in downtown Liepaja, and made sure to point to it whenever he had had more than a glass or two of beer.

The man had told Anatolij that he was staying at a nearby inn, until – as he had put it – *"I figure out where that asshole lives."* The two men had bonded over their anger regarding the wrongs that had been done to them, and, a week ago, the man had asked Anatolij to come by for a visit. *"The Liepaja Inn,"* he had told him. *"Stop by anytime. I have more stories to tell."* Anatolij had promised he would, but had yet to do so. Why? He wasn't sure. Maybe because he wasn't looking forward to hearing stories from a bitter, washed up German.

He pulled out his wallet and laid twenty euros on the counter. It was time to leave, but Anatolij wasn't sure where to go. He couldn't go home; he could never go home again. There was no way he would be able to set foot in the house that had been dishonored by his faithless wife. He would simply have to go back to the same place he had gone the last five nights; a cheap hotel a block away. He was about to shove his wallet in his pocket when he checked his cash. Only twenty euros left...hardly enough for a meal, let alone a hotel.

He pulled on his coat, grabbed his scarf, and walked outside into the bitter cold. He spat on the sidewalk as he wrapped the scarf around his neck. Life hadn't been good to him; that much was sure. His wife had left him, he had been fired from his job, and he was broke with no place to stay. He needed money. Again, he patted the pocket with the booklet. He hissed. *I'll bet this Jacob fellow would pay a whole lotta cash for this diary.* If only Anatolij could find him.

He thought again of the German's offer for Anatolij to stop by. His eyes widened. *It would be a place for me to stay, at least for a night or two...and it would give me a chance to pick the man's brain about people and places I know nothing about.* Maybe Anatolij could use that information to learn more about the mysterious Jacob. It couldn't hurt to at least ask the man a few questions.

He chuckled as he shuffled down the street. Perhaps his new friend Adolf – the once-powerful German – could help him after all.

The End

ABOUT THE AUTHOR

Dr. Jill Vosler is a family physician whose medical studies took her abroad to the University of Edinburgh in Scotland and on to extensive travel throughout the UK and Europe. Her love for these places has flavored her novels, along with the many years spent as a deputy coroner under the guidance of her father, who was the county coroner well into his eighties. She has a keen interest in geopolitics and a passion for music, but most enjoys traveling the world with family and friends.

NewAtlantianLibrary.com or
AbsolutelyAmazingEbooks.com
or AA-eBooks.com

Thank you for reading. Please review this book. Reviews help others find Absolutely Amazing eBooks and inspire us to keep providing these marvelous tales.

If you would like to be put on our email list to receive updates on new releases, contests, and promotions, please go to AbsolutelyAmazingEbooks.com and sign up.

For sales, editorial information, subsidiary rights information
or a catalog, please write or phone or e-mail

AbsolutelyAmazingEbooks
Manhanset House
Shelter Island Hts., New York 11965, US
Tel: 212-427-7139
www.AbsolutelyAmazingEbooks.com
bricktower@aol.com
www.IngramContent.com